Mika in Real Life

ALSO BY EMIKO JEAN

Tokyo Ever After

Empress of All Seasons

We'll Never Be Apart

Mika in Real Life

A Novel

Emiko Jean

HARPER LARGE PRINT

An Imprint of HarperCollinsPublishers

MIKA IN REAL LIFE. Copyright © 2022 by Emiko Jean and Alloy Entertainment, LLC. All rights reserved. Printed in the United States of America. No part of this book may be used or reproduced in any manner whatsoever without written permission except in the case of brief quotations embodied in critical articles and reviews. For information, address HarperCollins Publishers, 195 Broadway, New York, NY 10007.

HarperCollins books may be purchased for educational, business, or sales promotional use. For information, please e-mail the Special Markets Department at SPsales@harpercollins.com.

FIRST HARPER LARGE PRINT EDITION

ISBN: 978-0-06-324206-7

Library of Congress Cataloging-in-Publication Data is available upon request.

22 23 24 25 26   LSC   10 9 8 7 6 5 4 3 2 1

To Yumi and Kenzo
for inspiring me to write this

Mika in Real Life

Dear Penny,

It rained the day you were born. Outside the maternity ward, the sky was the color of liquid ash, and there was a sign that read: BIRTHDAYS ARE OUR SPECIALTY. I focused on it as I labored, as the nurses and doctor clamored around me. *You're nearly there*, a nurse exclaimed.

I trembled and bore down, wanting it to be over. A scream tore from my mouth. I pushed. The doctor pulled. And there you were. <u>There. You. Were.</u> Held aloft in a blistering cone of light.

Terrible silence ensued, one agonizing second stretching into eternity. As if you were deciding how your entrance into the world should be. Finally, you wailed, so high-pitched and piercing even the doctor commented on it. *This one has a lot to say already*, she said. Secretly, I was pleased by the fury in your voice. This boded well for you, I believed. You would not be easily silenced.

The doctor cut the cord, and I reached for you. For a moment, I forgot you were not mine to keep. She placed you in my arms. I marveled at your tiny hands, your sable hair, your bow-shaped mouth, your nose that resembled a bull's when your nostrils flared. My body had a purpose, and it was you. In the span of a single breath, I was unmade and made again.

What followed was a blur of stitches, fresh bed linens, and binge eating. Hana was there. Had been there since the beginning. A nurse had taken one look at Hana and me, at our nineteen-year-old faces, at how terrifyingly young we were, and clucked her tongue. *Babies having babies*, she'd said. It was easy to translate her meaning—dumb girls, irresponsible girls, *those girls*. She saw Hana treating the room service menu like her own personal vending machine, saw her pilfering kidney-shaped dishes, saw her lining her pockets with pads. But she didn't see Hana helping me shower after I'd grown dizzy trying to stand. Didn't see me weeping in the bathroom, mumbling *I'm sorry* over and over as Hana soaped circles on my body, cleaned under my arms, and gently between my legs. And she didn't see the way Hana smiled in response like it was no big deal.

Mrs. Pearson, my adoption agent, came around the time when my hair was still drying. She produced some paperwork from her bag. It had been prefilled. All I had to do was sign. Bells chimed, echoing down the hospital corridor. A song called "Breath of Life" that played every time a baby was born. Right as I reached for the pen, Hana squeezed my hand. *Are you sure?* she asked.

All I could do was nod. Breathe. Turning the pages, I scribbled my name. I ignored the tiny noises you made in your sleep. Ignored how the whole room smelled like antiseptic. Paid all my attention to the neon pink arrow marking where my final signature should go. Above it was a warning in bold letters. **"Upon surrender, the original birth certificate will be sealed, and a new birth certificate will be issued"**—one with your adoptive parents' names.

I signed, erasing myself from your life. It was done. Then I held you one last time. Unwrapping your swaddle, I kissed each of your ten fingers, your two cheeks, your one little nose. Finally, I pressed my palm to your chest. You were warm, and I felt you brand me. *I'm sorry*, I whispered, apologizing for what I wanted but could not keep. I held you close a minute longer. Then I let you go. I let Mrs. Pearson carry you away.

I couldn't watch. Instead, I bowed my head and clung to the memory of the first time I saw you on an ultrasound—potbellied, hand waving around, umbilical cord floating—a little diver. I saw myself then as one of those calves that circle in shallow water and keep beaching themselves, failing over and over again. I didn't want you to swim in vain. I wanted you to find open water, to dive deep—your life to be a single, straight, perfect line.

The door closed, and I remember the quiet snick, the sound of you slipping away from me. When you were gone, the hospital room felt so empty; I thought I might die from loneliness. Someone else would watch you sleep. Someone else would touch your chest and make sure you were breathing. I cried with such wild abandon Hana thought I'd torn my stitches.

That's it. That's all. All these moments live in me still. You live in me still. Half of my breaths, a quarter of each heartbeat, are yours. I guess that is what happens when you have children—they take a piece of you.

I didn't think about the future that day. I didn't think about the Calvins, your new mother and father, how white they were. Who would teach you to be a yellow body in America? I didn't think about what I might tell you if you came to me and asked "Why, who are you, who am I?" Of course, I dreamed I might be a part of your life, but in the same way someone wishes upon a star or buys lottery tickets. I never believed it actually might happen. And I never believed we would be back in the same hospital—you sixteen years old, me thirty-five—or that *you'd* be in the bed this time, and I would be apologizing anew.

I'm sorry, Penny. I messed up. I hurt you.

I can't promise I will never hurt you again. The truth is, there isn't much I can promise you. *Still, still.* What little I have is yours. No matter what happens. If you forgive me or not. I want you to know I will always be around. Like any parent, I will be here, waiting for my child to come home.

Mika

Seven months earlier . . .

Chapter One

*F*ired.

Mika blinked. "I'm sorry, what?" she asked Greg, in his shoebox of an office. In fact, it wasn't really an office. It was a cubicle carved out of the large copy room at Kennedy, Smith & McDougal Law. But Greg wielded the tiny space like a corner office on the thirtieth floor. He'd even decorated it—a bonsai tree in the corner of his desk, a cheap samurai sword tacked crookedly to the wall. Greg was white and a self-described Japanophile. On more than one occasion, he'd tried to converse with Mika in Japanese, and she'd demurred—she was fluent, she just wasn't fluent for him. So yeah, that guy.

Greg leaned back in his chair. "This shouldn't come as a surprise," he said, steepling his fingers together and placing them under his hairless chin. "I'm sure you've heard the rumors."

Mika nodded vacantly. A senior partner, a rainmaker, had recently departed for another firm. Profit shares were down. She opened her hands. "But I make twenty dollars an hour." A pittance compared to the other salaried employees. Did the powers that be think laying off a copy assistant would make a dent in their financial woes?

Greg waved a hand. "I get it," he said. "But you know how these things go, last in the pecking order . . ." He trailed off.

"Please." She hated begging, especially to Greg. "I need this job." She liked it at Kennedy, Smith & McDougal. The work was easy. The pay was good. Enough for her to make rent and utilities every month with a little left over to buy groceries, mostly of the soft cheese variety. Plus, the building was located near the museum. She went there on her lunch break, letting her food digest while gazing at Monets and strolling through the antiquities section, her soul at rest. "What about Stephanie?" She'd been hired after Mika.

"Stephanie has more paralegal experience than you. The decision came down to who was a better asset for the company. Look, I'm sure you'll find something else. Unfortunately, you won't qualify for severance since you've been here for less than a year, but I'll give you a great recommendation." Greg started to stand. End of discussion.

"I'll take a pay cut," Mika blurted. Her gaze landed on the floor, near where her pride was. She couldn't handle it. Tears threatened to spill. Thirty-five and fired from another job. Again.

Greg shook his head. "I'm sorry, Mika. It's no use. Today is your last day."

• • •

The faint scent of stale popcorn. The emotionally healing candles on clearance. What was it about this particular store that sucked Mika in? She stood in the home section, examining a pillow embroidered with the saying MONEY CAN BUY A HOUSE, BUT NOT A HOME. On the phone, Hana laughed. "So, let me get this straight. He asked you out at the same time he was firing you?"

"Directly after," Mika corrected. Greg had escorted her to her desk, watched while she packed up her stuff, and *then* asked if she'd like to see a movie later or maybe attend the Cherry Blossom Festival at the university next weekend. The angry humiliation ran deep.

Hana snorted another laugh.

Mika's mouth quirked into a smile. "Please don't. I'm in a very vulnerable place right now."

"You're in a Target," Hana pointed out.

Mika tilted her head, contemplating the pillow. It was designed by a couple who had become filthy rich making new houses look old. It was all about the shiplap. The pillow could be hers for $29.99. "I never thought I'd be laid off *and* sexually harassed all in the same day. It's a new first." Mika bypassed the pillow and went on to the wine section. Her pocketbook was lighter, but a five-dollar bottle of wine was a necessity.

Hana made a sympathetic noise. "It could be worse. Remember the time you were fired from that donut shop for keeping a box of maple bars in the freezer and eating them between filling orders?"

"That was in college." Mika tucked the phone between her ear and shoulder. Finished choosing wine, she was in the food aisle now, filling her basket with Cheez-Its. Class all the way.

"Or that nanny job for showing the kids *The Shining*?"

"They said they wanted a ghost story," she defended.

"How about when you wrote X-rated *Predator* fan fiction, then left it open on your work computer?"

Confusion rippled across her face. "That never happened." Hana laughed again. Mika rubbed her forehead, feeling as if she'd fallen from an unlucky tree, hitting every branch on the way down, then landing in a pit of snakes and bears. "What am I going to do?"

"I don't know. But you're in good company. I found out this morning Pearl Jam chose Garrett for their summer tour." Hana was an ASL interpreter for bands, and Garrett, having recently crossed over from the Christian alt-rock circuit, had edged into Hana's territory. "I'm probably going to have to do a bunch of Earth, Wind & Fire gigs now. Fucking Garrett. Come home. We'll eat and drink our feelings together."

"Will do." Mika hung up and dropped her phone in her purse. A minute passed. Mika wandered. Her phone rang. Might be Hana again. Or her mother—Hiromi had already left a message that morning. *I just stopped by the church and met the new congregant. His name is Hayato, and he works for Nike. I gave him your number.*

Her phone rang again. Sometimes Hiromi called two, three times in a row, inducing panic. Last time Mika answered breathless, reaching for her keys, ready to head to the hospital. *What's the matter?*

Hiromi replied, *Nothing. Why do you sound so winded? I wanted to tell you Fred Meyer is having a sale on chicken . . .*

Mika listened, temper rising. *You can't call so many times. I thought something was wrong,* she said.

To which Hiromi scoffed, *I'm sorry I'm not more dead for you.* The ringing continued. Mika fished the phone from her purse and peered at the screen. A blocked number.

Curious, she swiped to answer. "Hello?" she said, brows knitting together. *Shit,* she thought too late. It could be the new congregant, Hayato. Quickly, she cycled through possible excuses. *My phone is dying. I'm dying.*

"Oh, wow! You picked up! I wasn't sure if you would!" a hyper-positive young voice said. The connection became muffled, as though a hand had been placed over the phone's speaker. "She picked up. What do I do?" the voice said to someone in the background.

"Hello?" Mika spoke louder.

"Sorry, my friend Sophie is here. You know, for moral support? Is this Mika Suzuki?"

"It is." Mika set the basket down at her feet. "Who is this?"

"This is Penny. Penelope Calvin. I think I'm your daughter."

• • •

Mika managed to keep a hold on the phone even as her limbs went completely slack. Even as the blood raced in her veins and her vision blurred, then tunneled. Even as she hurdled back in time, back to the hospital, to Penny as a newborn. The day returned in heart-stopping flashes. Holding Penny in the crook of her arm. Kissing her brow. Slicking her hair away to place a thin blue-and-pink-striped cap on her head. All so unbearable and beautiful.

"Are you still there?" Penny asked. "Is this the right Mika Suzuki? I paid for one of those online search finder thingies. I used my dad's credit card for a free trial. He'll kill me if he finds out! But no worries, I'll cancel before they charge."

Silence then. Penny was waiting for Mika to say something. She closed her eyes, opened them. "That's very clever," she murmured, trembling. Sit. She needed to sit down. She stumbled back into a plastic outdoor chair, gripping the armrest to regain her balance, her knuckles turning white. How had she wound up in the garden section?

"I know, right? My dad always says: 'If only you'd use your powers for good!'" Penny lowered her voice an octave, impersonating her father. Mika almost smiled. *Almost.* "So, is this the right Mika Suzuki? There aren't very many in Oregon. The only other two candidates were older. I mean, I guess they could be my bio mom. There was, like, that lady who gave birth to twins at the age of fifty? But I was pretty sure it was you . . . Are you there?"

Mika was sweating, the phone slippery against her ear. She breathed in and out. In and out. "I'm here."

"And are you Mika Suzuki? Did you give a baby up for adoption sixteen years ago?"

A throb settled in her temples. "I am. I did," Mika said, her throat dry. Secretly, she'd dreamed of this moment. The day she might hear her daughter's voice. *Talk to her.* Sometimes the fantasy bordered on delusional. Over the years, she thought she'd seen Penny a couple of times. Which was ridiculous. She knew Penny lived in the Midwest. But then she'd spot a dark-headed little girl with blunt bangs, and Mika's body would swell with certainty. She'd feel an invisible tug. *That's my daughter,* she'd think, only to deflate when the girl turned around, and the nose was wrong, or the eyes were green, not a deep brown. Not Penny. *An imposter.*

Mika released the lawn chair from her death grip, her legs wobbly as she stood. She began to wander the aisles. She needed to move. It helped to ground her, to keep her in the present. Helped to exorcise the storm of emotions brewing.

"This is awesome!" Penny squealed.

"I can't believe you found me," Mika said, still just so stunned. She passed a display of purple-bottled magnesium tablets.

"It wasn't hard. Your name is super unique and cool. I wish I had a Japanese name," sighed Penny wistfully.

"Oh." Mika frowned, not knowing what to say. She'd chosen Penny's name. Had made a big deal about it, insisted it be part of the legal agreement. *You can have my daughter, but you cannot have her name.* While Mrs. Pearson had tried hard to make the adoption feel less transactional, certain parts couldn't be helped. There were lawyers. Negotiations. Ironclad paperwork that leaned slightly in the adoptive family's favor. But the name . . . the name was Mika's. At first, she'd considered Holly—a plant that blooms in winter. It was traditional in Japan to select a moniker based on your hopes for the child. Mika's name in kanji translated to "beautiful fragrance." It told Mika much about her value to her mother. As an accessory. As something meant to attract. She didn't want that for her child. So ultimately, Mika settled on Penelope, meaning "weaver," from Homer's *Odyssey.* It was a strong, resilient, and aspirational name; it fit the life Mika wanted for her daughter. The person she thought she might be. The family she might belong to.

She had also hoped a more American-sounding name would ease Penny's way in life. Mika had years of mispronunciations and misspellings under her belt. She'd been called Mickey more times than she could count. She'd wanted Penny to blend in. But it didn't seem the right time to say all this. Instead, she said, "I was sorry to hear about your mom." When Mrs. Pearson had informed Mika five years ago that Caroline Calvin had cancer and was dying, she'd begged to be put in touch with Penny, swore she could feel her daughter's grief pressing against her skin like a hot iron.

She needs me, Mika had said.

I'll try, Mrs. Pearson had replied. Then Thomas Calvin denied the request. *I'm sorry, Mika,* Mrs. Pearson said, *Caroline doesn't have much time. Cancer. Stage four. Very sudden. He wants it to be the three of them these last few days.*

"Yeah." Penny's voice dimmed. "That was a bad time. We just came up on the fifth anniversary. I kind of can't believe it's been so long."

Quiet fell on the line again. Mika kept walking. Destination unknown. Her entire body was in an uproar. She passed the aisle of pregnancy tests. Nearly seventeen years ago, she'd picked through Hana's car to find enough money to buy a test at the dollar store, then peed on the stick in the bathroom of a grocery store nearby. She'd barely wiped when the two pink lines appeared, when her world fell apart.

Mika realized she'd gone silent for too long. "She wrote me letters, your mom, and sent me packages with pictures of you, drawings you made. She had nice handwriting," she blurted. Mika didn't know much about the couple who adopted Penny. She'd chosen them from dozens of scrapbook family profiles. She used to stare at the photographs of Penny's future parents. At Thomas, a copyright attorney, pictured in college on his rowing team. She would focus on his hands wrapped around the oars, at the scowly dent between his green eyes. *He is strong*, Mika remembered thinking. He'd stand up for Penny. Then she'd peer at Caroline, also in college wearing a sweatshirt with Greek letters, her smile wide. It was easy to imagine her smiling the same way at Penny, saying wonderful things like *I'm proud of you. I'm so happy you're mine. I'd run blind through the dark for you.*

"She did have nice handwriting. It was perfect," Penny said warmly. It didn't surprise Mika. Caroline seemed perfect in all aspects of her life. "Mine is so sloppy. I always wondered if that was something genetic?"

Mika didn't think it was. But she longed for a connection to Penny, any way to bind them together. "My handwriting is terrible too."

"It is?" A note of hope in Penny's voice.

Mika slowed. Calmed a little. "I like to think of it as my own font. It'd be called 'too much coffee and donuts.'"

Penny laughed. It was a pleasant sound, full-bodied and earnest. *Her daughter.* "Or 'clean up your mess.'"

Finally, Mika paused in the detergent aisle. No one was in it. She leaned back, inhaled the scent of clean laundry. She'd thought in time the memory of Penny, what happened before, might fade, but it only grew sharper against the blurred, less important memories of her recent past. Graduating college, her first paying job, even some of the pregnancy—the ever-ticking clock had worn smooth all those rough edges. But Penny, the baby, *Mika's baby*, had stayed, a hand cast in concrete. She wished she knew then what she knew now. That every day she would wake and think of Penny. Of how old she was. What she might be wearing. Whom she might be smiling at. That her love would be teeth and nails, unwilling to let go.

"Are you okay?" A mother with two kids rounded the corner.

Mika jolted upright. "Fine. I'm fine." One of the

children had chocolate all over his face. He licked a slow circle around his lips. The mom waited until Mika got moving before moving on herself.

"Is someone else with you?" Penny asked.

"No. I'm shopping. I'm in a Target," Mika said before she could think better of it. She wanted to punch herself in the face. *Hard.* What would Penny think? A grown woman in a Target on a Wednesday afternoon. Would she wonder why Mika wasn't at work?

Penny swore. "I'm sorry. I should've asked if now was a good time to talk. I should let you go."

Mika didn't like the sound of that. The threat of this tiny tenuous string being cut again. Could Penny feel it too? This flow of bliss-like energy between them. "No. It's okay."

"I should go anyway. My dad will be home soon."

No. Keep talking. I'd listen to you read War and Peace. She stifled the sudden urge to cry. "Of course. It was nice speaking with you." Mika stepped out of the store. The sky was gray—end of winter in Portland. A couple of crows picked at trash in the parking lot. She blinked and, on the inside of her eyelids, saw another set of crows. From a long time ago, fighting over a discarded watermelon container. She pushed the memory away. "If you ever need anything. If I can ever do anything . . ."

"Actually." Penny exhaled audibly. "I'd like to keep talking. I'd like to call you again. Maybe even Skype? It would be nice to see each other face-to-face."

"Oh," Mika said, too stunned to breathe, too flustered with disbelief. Penny wanted her. Penny wanted *her*. And Mika was pierced with such an acute longing she feared she might crumble. So she spoke on impulse, on raging desire, and answered, "Yes, of course. I'd like that."

Chapter Two

Mika drove home in a fugue state. She didn't remember placing her key in the ignition, starting the car, leaving the lot, the streetlights, blinkers, turns, or parking along the curb. Once there, she sat in the driver's seat, engine off. Rain spattered the windshield. "Penny," she whispered into the quiet. Saying her daughter's name felt like a prayer, like a secret, like a bell ringing, calling her home to dinner. "Penny, Penny, Penny," she said over and over again. Her mouth lifted at the corners into a full smile as she stepped from her car.

Weeds and various thorny plants peeked through a chipped and peeling white fence. The walkway was narrowly visible. The house was a cottage. One of its shutters hung on its side, a single nail holding it in place. *Eyesore* was a generous term. Mika unlocked the door and pushed . . . only . . . something blocked it. After much grunting, she tumbled through, shoving boxes out of the way.

Irritation chipped away at joy. "Wow. Did you wake up this morning and say: 'Today's the day I'm going to take this hoarding shit to the next level and barricade myself until they find my skeleton twenty years from now'?" Mika huffed out to Hana.

Hana kept her eyes trained on the television, a half-eaten cake in her lap. "So weird. That's exactly what I said to myself. You're late." Hana shoveled a bite of cake into her mouth. "I started without you. Also, I've been brainstorming. I think we should get a dog and teach it that 'shit' means 'Garrett.' Like, instead of saying 'take a shit,' we say 'take a Garrett.' Then I'll film it and send it to him." She glanced up. "Where's the wine?"

"No dog. No film. No sending to Garrett. And I forgot the wine." Mika skirted around unopened boxes and dead plants, then pushed a stack of magazines off a chair to sit in it. For a while, Hana had kept her compulsive collecting habits under control. She'd bought the house with her girlfriend, Nicole. They'd been happy, filling it with garage sale and flea market finds.

They'd even adopted a puppy. Then Nicole cheated. Hana got the house. Nicole got their golden retriever. Mika, fresh off a breakup from Leif and short on cash, had offered to move in with Hana. Together, they'd drowned their broken hearts in wine and expensive takeout and agreed their friendship was much better than that with either of their previous lovers. They understood each other more. Mika didn't mind that Hana treated online shopping like her patriotic duty. Hana didn't mind Mika's lousy track record of employment. Nobody was perfect. Embracing each other's faults was the bedrock upon which their friendship was built.

So, it didn't faze Mika seeing Hana on the couch, bitching about a coworker and watching . . . "*Monster*? Are you seriously watching *Monster*? A movie about serial-killing lesbians?" Mika found the remote between cans of Red Bull and Mountain Dew. She clicked off the television.

"Hey," Hana said.

"There's a lot to unpack here." Mika used her hand to circle the room, encompassing the whole hoarding, cake-eating, *Monster*-watching situation in general. "And I don't have the time. I need to tell you something."

Hana sat up and put the cake down. "I'm intrigued."

There was a tiny bit of frosting on her cropped roller derby T-shirt.

"Penny called."

"Ha!" Hana barked out a laugh. Then at Mika's face, she said, "Holy shit. You're serious."

Mika could only nod. Her stomach flipped, thinking about it. *She has new-baby smell*, Hana had purred in the hospital as she held newborn Penny, rubbing her cheek against hers.

Hana sat back. "Whoa. Heavy."

"You're telling me." Mika opened her mouth, but her phone beeped—an incoming text. *Penny again?*

"Is it her?" Hana leaned forward, reading Mika's mind.

Mika glanced down. "No, it's Charlie." She checked the message. "She's thinking of buying Tuan"—Charlie's husband—"a life-size Lego portrait."

Hana rolled her eyes. "Ignore her. How'd Penny find you?" Hana reached for a wooden box on the coffee table and flipped it open. Inside was a tiny plastic baggie full of weed and some papers. She set to rolling a joint between her long fingers.

Mika shrugged. "It's the internet, Penny explained, you can find anyone these days." But then again . . . how had Penny found her? Mika had chosen a closed adoption: her identity was kept private, and she received annual updates in exchange. Any more would have been too painful. She'd opted for scraps knowing she'd gorge herself otherwise. She guessed it didn't matter whether Thomas Calvin told Penny Mika's name or if Penny had stumbled upon the information snooping through her parents' things. What mattered was the here and now. That Penny had called Mika. That Penny wanted to know Mika.

"True." Hana licked the paper and sealed the joint. Out of anyone, Mika's best friend would know how easy it was to find people online. A few years ago, she had tracked down her former elementary school teacher—the one who had called the color of her skin "half-and-half," like coffee creamer. Hana was part Black, a quarter Vietnamese, and a quarter white—Hungarian and Irish. She trolled the woman into quitting social media.

Hana lit the joint, took a drag, and offered it to Mika. "What's she like?"

Mika pinched the joint between her fingers and eyed the ceiling. There was a crack running through it that trailed down, splitting the wall. She was pretty sure they had foundation troubles. "I don't know. The conversation was short. She's young, hopeful, positive." *A force of nature.* "She used her dad's credit card to sign up for a free trial to find people." Mika aimed a lopsided smile at Hana and put the joint to her lips. "She was going to cancel it before he found out." Mika passed the joint back to Hana.

"Reminds me of us." Hana smiled and took a drag. "So," she said, exhaling, "what did she want?"

Mika chewed her bottom lip. Her bedroom door was open. The bed was a rumpled mess, the comforter pushed down to the end. No point in making it if she was going to slip back between the sheets a few hours later. On the floor was her favorite T-shirt featuring a Gudetama—a cartoon by the makers of Hello Kitty. What looked like a yellow blob was a lazy egg. "She wants to get to know me." Her wheels started to turn. She took greater stock of her surroundings, her life, herself, and instantly regretted it.

What could she offer Penny? What had she accomplished? Her love life was anemic. A handful of boyfriends, one serious relationship with Leif that ended in a garbage fire. And her work life just as thin. A series of unfulfilling jobs. All of them placeholders. She had thought of herself as a stone skipping over murky water. Time passing without consequence, without thinking, staying the same, getting farther and farther from the shore. But a pebble never reaches the other side. Eventually, it sinks. *When did I sink?* Mika's stomach bottomed out. "I said we could talk again, but now . . . I don't know." She felt as inadequate as that day in the hospital.

"Elaborate." Hana stamped out the joint.

Mika tore her gaze from the house and focused on her lap. What were the stakes of connecting with Penny? "She might hate me. I might hate her," Mika thought out loud. Although Mika couldn't see herself ever hating Penny. Penny could murder someone, and Mika would bring her a shovel to bury the body. She'd always give Penny the benefit of the doubt. *Believe her.* "I'm sure she has questions. Lots of questions. She seems . . . persistent. She might want to know about her biological father. She wishes she had a Japanese name."

Hana inhaled. She scooted down the couch, closer to Mika. "No doubt she's curious. We all want to know where we come from. But she's not entitled to that information until you're ready."

Under penalty of law, Mika had signed a form attesting she did not know anything about her baby's biological father, such as his age or location, or that he had a birthmark shaped like the state of Maine on his chest. "What if she's angry with me?" she asked in a slight voice.

Hana inhaled. "Can I give you some unsolicited advice?"

"Never stopped you before."

"When Nicole cheated, Charlie sat me down and said: 'There is strength in leaving and strength in staying.'" Hana flicked some ash from her knee. "I'm pretty sure she got it from one of those self-help gurus."

Mika frowned. "I'm not following."

"What I mean is there would have been strength in you keeping Penny, but there was also strength in relinquishing her. And if Penny is as smart as she seems to be, she won't care what you've done; she'll care about who you are."

"And who am I?" Mika asked it like a dare. She thought about her unimpressive life résumé. Unemployment enthusiast. Weed smoker. Biological mom.

Hana ticked off a list on her fingers. "First thing, you're loyal. Second thing, you're compassionate. Third thing, you have a beautiful heart. Fourth thing, you are an amazing artist who knows all sorts of things about art, especially really uninteresting things like which caves have paintings of cavemen dongs. Fifth thing—"

"That's good." Mika held up her hands, cutting Hana off. "I'm not exactly emotionally prepared for this." Hana knew how messy this could get. Each year around Penny's birthday, a package arrived. Mika would read the letter from Caroline or Thomas, stare at the photographs of Penny with her happy family, rub her thumbs over Penny's crayon drawings, then spread it all around her in a suffocating hug. Mika would stay in bed all day. Hana would stay too. She would crawl in behind Mika, wordlessly wrap her arms around her in a mourning cocoon. Together they cried. Mika for Penny. And Hana for Mika.

"Are we ever prepared? That's the whole point of emotions. The least you expect them, the more intense they are. That's the beauty of feeling."

"That's dumb." Mika lay her head back against the chair. The whole situation was overwhelming in every way. But Hana was there. Had always been there. "Love your face," she said to her best friend. The three words had been their mantra since meeting as freshmen at the same alternative high school, the kind of place where students are put when folks don't expect too much of them. Mika had taken one look at Hana and sensed a kindred spirit. Both of them, wayward branches growing from their family trees.

"Love your face too."

Mika felt around the cushion for her phone. Right

before hanging up, Penny had given Mika her number. Now, she messaged her. Excited to video chat. What time works for you?

There, done. She placed her phone away from herself. Drummed her fingers against her thighs. *It will be okay.* She flashed again to the hospital. To seeing Penny for the first time cradled in the doctor's hands. Yes, it would be okay. How could it not? Penny and Mika had been a love story from the beginning.

Chapter Three

A week later, Mika attended church. With her parents. Squished into the corner of the pew, Mika snuck a glance at her mother. Hiromi Suzuki stared straight ahead. Her black button eyes focused on the pulpit. Her face was small with delicate features and a mouth that frowned more than it smiled. At home, she had a closet full of velour tracksuits. Today, she wore eggplant. It complemented her short dark hair permed into half-domes to curl away from her head, like the queen of England's. Next to Hiromi, Mika's father, Shige, snoozed.

The sermon continued, something about friendship, and Mika reached for her phone, popping open her Instagram profile. It featured exactly five photos. Her toes in the sand from a trip she took to Puerto

Rico with Leif, right before they broke up. Another of her and Leif on the same trip dressed up for the evening. Hana's backyard after she'd first moved in—they'd strung fairy lights all around and drunk margaritas with top-shelf tequila. A bridesmaid photo from Charlie's wedding. And a photograph of a beet and goat cheese salad. That was all. Penny had liked all of them. They'd scheduled a call for tomorrow, their first Skype meeting. She clicked out of her profile and onto the magnifying glass—the explore tab.

Her screen populated with posts, the algorithm producing content for her based on previous clicks and searches. There were a lot of women with symmetrical faces who matched the perfect beige houses they lived in. An ad to celebrate a new federal holiday by purchasing commemorative toilet paper. A celebrity whom Hiromi loved because she didn't have a nanny. How impressive.

In the search line, she entered the word *adoption.* The screen repopulated. Mostly with adoptive moms describing their journey. *He's finally home. Mateo (we've been calling him Matty!) is six weeks old and has never been held. To reacclimate him, I've been wearing him in the Ring Sling (not a paid sponsorship) as much as possible. My back is tired, and I'm* tired in general—*Mateo has been waking up every two hours. Any other mamas out there feeling a little overwhelmed today?* People had commented with: *You can do this! You got it! Try this smoothie recipe for an extra energy boost.* Mika frowned at the twist in her gut. Nobody said *It's okay to stop. It's okay to admit you can't. This is beyond you.* There was so much emphasis placed on women doing everything on their own. To keep going even if they were tired, poor, hanging on by a thread. She peered at the picture again of the woman holding her newly adopted son. Smiling like a hero. Is this what Thomas and Caroline thought, that they'd rescued Penny?

A hand snaked behind Mika's arm and pinched the thin-skinned underside. "Pay attention," said her mother in the same tone she used when sending Mika to her room in elementary school.

"Ow," Mika hissed, rubbing her arm and glaring at her mother. *And this was better here than visiting them at home.*

At the thought of her childhood house, Mika's anxiety stretched and prepared for a sprint. The house itself wasn't particularly intimidating. A 1970s bungalow with all its original charm—puke green shag carpet, yellow globe lights, and paneled den. On the outside, it was similar to all the other homes on the block, the architecture unremarkable—definitely not worthy of any art history textbook. But on the inside, there were all the classical Japanese touches: soy sauce packets and plastic silverware shoved into drawers, slippers neatly aligned by the front door, a drying line in the backyard, a sprinkle of pistachio shells her dad liked to eat while watching NHK or Japanese baseball, the Hanshin Tigers, his favorite team.

Despite the clutter, the incense smell, and the dated décor, the drive for perfection persisted within its walls. It was in the dusty kimono Mika refused to wear after she quit odori. In the empty frames where Mika's Ivy League degree and wedding photos should have gone. In the pots and pans Mika had never learned to cook with.

By the fifth month of Mika's pregnancy, she had started to show. She couldn't hide it any longer, didn't want to. She and Hiromi were cleaning the lime-green-tiled kitchen when Mika blurted out the truth. *I'm pregnant.* Mika's father was watching television in the next room. All the doors in the hallway were neatly closed—you only saw what Hiromi wanted you to see. Hiromi stopped wiping down the counters. For one single moment, she stayed still. Unable to comprehend this new reality. *Did you hear me? I said I'm pregnant.* Against the inside of Mika's belly, Penny moved—a gentle flutter like wings. The quickening, the ob-gyn at the free health clinic on campus had told her.

Hiromi blinked once. Straightened. *Who's the father?* she asked coolly.

The house smelled of sukiyaki—boiled beef and vegetable in mirin, soy sauce, and sugar. They always ate the traditional hotpot meal when the weather turned cold. That night, snow was forecast. *It's a girl,* Mika said.

Hiromi wrung out the sponge in the sink. *Girls are difficult.* "You are difficult," Hiromi meant. Someone laughed on the television.

I'm giving her up for adoption. The statement was spontaneous. Mika hadn't decided anything. She was still processing the pregnancy, a pendulum swinging between disbelief and stark fear. What had she been expecting her mother to say? Too late, Mika realized she wanted Hiromi to tell her to keep the baby. To promise to help raise the bundle of cells. But Mika should have known. Hiromi's support always came at a high price, and Mika had never quite figured out how to afford it. Still, Mika couldn't help coming to her mother, offering her broken need on a platter, hoping for more, for better, for her mother to change—to heal Mika. The word *adoption* was mentioned as a kind of dare.

Hiromi turned on the faucet to flush food scraps down the drain. Hot water scalded her hands red, and steam dampened the hollow of her throat. *That's probably best. What do you know about raising a baby?* Another way in which she'd failed her mother. Hiromi had tried to teach Mika how to be a good housewife, how to cook, how to host and be a house-keeper. All in preparation for the day she'd have her own partner and child. But Hiromi had never taught Mika about birth control or sex or love or what to do if you found yourself suddenly pregnant. Because that was an undesirable outcome. And you did not talk of that which you did not want to happen.

In the kitchen, Mika was stunned for a moment. Disappointment suffocated her like a clot of over-cooked rice in her throat. *That's it? That's all you want to say to me?*

Hiromi's eyes snapped to Mika's, then roved over Mika's stomach. Her expression the same as when Mika came home with secondhand clothing from a thrift store in high school. That had been the style then—ripped jeans, flannels, crop tees. *What will the ladies at church think?* Hiromi had said, focusing on Mika's bare midriff.

What else do you want me to say? I'll tell your father about it. "It." That's how Hiromi referred to Penny. She turned away from Mika, her fingers curled in. *Do you want leftovers to take back to the dorm?*

Mika cupped her belly. *No. No, thanks.*

She didn't see her parents until after Penny was born, after she'd flunked part of her freshman and sophomore years. *It* became an unspeakable thing, contained behind one of the closed doors in Hiromi's home.

Now, Mika settled back in the pew. Outside the stained-glass windows, a rainbow and BLM flag flapped in the wind—Hiromi and Shige tolerated the church's progressive views and attended services every Sunday. Mika wasn't even sure they believed in a Christian God. Statues of the Buddha and little altars, butsudan, covered their home. They came to drink ocha, to mingle with the ninety-nine percent Japanese congregation, and to find Mika dates.

"We're looking for someone to maintain our social media accounts," Pastor Barbara announced from the pulpit. "Keep them updated with all the goings-on." White but fluent in Japanese, Pastor Barbara was a stout woman with a gentle voice. She liked to hold both your hands while she spoke to you. Behind her was a specially commissioned Asian Jesus—the woodworker used only fallen logs found on non-tribal land and plastic pieces harvested from the floating garbage patch in the Pacific Ocean.

Really Mika's mother should be the one applauded for sustainable living. The woman had been using the same sour cream container as Tupperware for the last twenty years. She also reused wrapping paper like it was her job. Five birthdays in a row, Mika's present was wrapped in the same My Little Pony paper. Hiromi's parents had been World War II survivors in Japan, had grown up in a time when fruit was a memory, their lives shaped by war and famine. They'd taught Hiromi to save every scrap of paper, to stir-fry field grasses, to take soil blackened from bombs and make it rich again.

"We're also looking for volunteers for the annual bazaar for food prep," Pastor Barbara went on. "But what we really need are taiko players or dancers for the exhibit portion. If you've got a special talent, now is the time to let it shine!" Once a year, in the spring, the church held a fundraiser. Tents went up in the parking lot. Chicken was marinated in tubs of teriyaki sauce. Soba noodles sizzled in woks. They sold Japanese street food outside. Inside, handicrafts were displayed on tables—crocheted potholders, kokeshi dolls, yosegi. In the evening, congregants danced and played music in a showcase.

Another pinch from her mother. "You should do that. Help with the food or dance in the showcase." Hiromi elbowed Shige, waking him with a start. "Remember how Mika danced?" Before Shige swept her off her feet, before becoming a wife, Mika's mother had trained as a maiko, a geisha apprentice. And when they moved to the States, Hiromi tracked down a sensei to teach Mika. If Hiromi couldn't be a maiko, Mika would be a dancer. Hiromi wanted a foil. Mika wanted to be free.

He nodded dazedly. "Yes, yes, of course."

Mika scooted away until she was pressed against the end of the pew. She didn't say anything. The refusal was in the set line of her mouth. Mika would dance again the same day Hiromi used a microwave. Which would be never.

"All those lessons. What a waste." Hiromi clucked her tongue. School. Chores. Dance. Once upon a time, Mika's world had been a tiny matchstick model built in the center of her mother's palm.

After the service, Mika drifted to the refreshments table. She piled a plate high with dorayaki, tiny squares of chiffon, and matcha cake . . . all while balancing a cup of tea in one hand. Her temples throbbed. The official line was a headache, not a hangover from box wine the night before.

Mika stuffed a sweet-potato cake in her mouth. "Dad, what have you been up to lately?"

Shige turned to her. "I watched a documentary about the United States Postal System."

"Oh, yeah?" Mika feigned interest. Her mom scanned the room, bowing her head at a friend, then kept going, clearly on the hunt for someone else.

Her father sipped his tea, served by Mika's mother. No longer a maiko, Hiromi was a sengyō shufu now, a professional housewife. This was her ikigai, her motivation to live, to entertain, and to care. Mika couldn't remember a meal or snack her father had ever prepared for himself. "Did you know you can send birds through the mail?" Shige smiled, and it was disarmingly charming. When Mika was growing up, he had been kind to her but stayed out of the parenting. Mika understood. Hiromi Suzuki was a force Shige elected not to reckon with. Unfortunately, that left Mika alone to weather her mother's storms. Riding around in their Ford Taurus station wagon, Mika used to write "Help, I've been kidnapped" in the condensation on the window in hopes someone would pull them over.

Mika smiled too, bolstered by his good humor. Her

mother was momentarily distracted by Mrs. Ito showing off pictures of her trip to Japan. Hiromi and Mrs.
Ito were best friends and mortal enemies. They had re-
duced mothering to a competitive sport. Correction, a
war. With judgment the preferred weapon of torture.
Anyway, now was the perfect time. She had her father's
attention and didn't have her mother's. "Otōsan . . ."
Mika started. "I've recently had a little setback."

Shige's face crinkled. "Not again."

Mika had never been good at saving. She lived her
life impulsively, check to check. Operating on the
motto "You can't take it with you." Funds became
short rather quickly. Within days, her circumstances
teetered on dire. Rent was due. Utilities too. Plan A,
getting another job ASAP, hadn't panned out. Plan B,
not eating, lasted all of four hours. Now, it was time
for plan C, asking her parents for money, and Mika
had to say, it fucking sucked. Mika licked her lips and
plowed on. "I'm applying for new jobs like crazy. I'm
sure I'll have something lined up in no time. I just
need a little help to get me through the rest of this
month. I'm sorry," she said. It was a global apology—
for all her deficits, for asking for money in a public
place. She couldn't bear to visit them and ask at home.

"What's this?" Hiromi swept over, finished with
Mrs. Ito.

For a moment, her father said nothing. He cast his gaze around, making sure they wouldn't be overheard. "Mi-chan has asked for money," he said, voice lowered, nearly inaudible.

Hiromi's face cooled. Mika knew that expressionless look; it was all in the eyes. It cut through her—that concealed disappointment. But also fear. *Who is this woman-child I've raised? So ignorant. So disconnected from her past, how can she have a future? I have so many regrets.* Shamed and feeling small, Mika peered down at her plate.

"How much do you need?" Shige asked.

Mika rubbed her thumbs against her plate. "A couple thousand. I'll pay you back."

Hiromi waved it off. "Yes. That is what you always say."

Mika kept quiet. She swore she'd never ask her parents for money again. How many times had she broken that promise to herself?

Hiromi's gaze lit on someone. "Put your plate down," she commanded, scowling at the amount of food on Mika's plate. Mrs. Ito often commented what a good eater Mika was. "I see the new congregant." She took in Mika's outfit—pants and a blouse with a button missing, the last clean clothing items in her closet. "This is what you're wearing?"

Mika frowned. "I don't want to meet anyone." When Mika broke up with Leif, Hiromi had said, *How will you survive?* "And what about the loan—"

"Shush," Hiromi said. "Everyone will see you disagreeing with me. You will meet this person." Hiromi's eyes flickered. "And your father will write you a check." Mika was waiting for this part, to feel the tug of the strings to which the money was attached.

Dating someone her mother approved of was about as appealing as a full body cavity search. "Kaasan—"

"Listen to your mother. Show us you are willing to change," her father said. When choosing sides, Shige always picked his wife's. "You must begin taking your life more seriously, which includes searching for the right partner."

Mika swallowed and set her plate down. "Fine."

Hiromi smiled like a cat and ushered Mika to the new congregant. He was talking to the pastor. "Mika-san," the pastor said, taking both of Mika's hands. Her smile was warm. "How are you?"

"I've come to introduce Mika to our new member." Hiromi smiled sweetly. She squeezed Mika's arm like she'd just encountered good fortune.

"Oh, of course!" the pastor said, letting go of Mika's hands. "This is Hayato Nakaya. He just transferred from Nike Japan to our fair city."

Hayato bowed. "How do you do?" He was lean and taller than Mika, which wasn't saying much. Mika was five-two on a good day. He had a nice smile, she supposed.

"Pastor, I need to speak with you about the bazaar," Hiromi said gravely. "Esther Watanabe wants to use her tempura recipe again. I wonder if we might persuade her in a different direction."

"Sure, sure." The pastor nodded, and they stepped away, leaving Mika alone with Hayato.

"Well, this is uncomfortable," Hayato said in perfect English.

"Did you grow up in Japan?" Mika asked to be polite.

"No, in California. LA." He rocked back on his heels. "My mother is first-generation Japanese American. How about you?"

"Mine too. I was born in Daito, just outside of Osaka." Mika had only impressions of her home in Japan. The sloping roof with curling tiles. The plastic sheeting around the porch. The muddy backyard bordering a sweet potato farm. The tansu chest left by a previous owner, which her mother loved but was too expensive to transport to the United States. "We moved when I was six."

She remembered the day they arrived in the States.

Their little family of three rumpled and irritable from flying near fifteen hours. What day was it? What time? You couldn't tell in the windowless customs corridor. Fans blew, and the air was stale with travelers' breath. A man in a blue uniform behind plexiglass examined their passports while Shige spoke of his job, how they'd arranged his work visa, even an apartment. Hiromi stared at the agent as if down the barrel of a gun. And Mika slipped away. She remembered the steps. One. Two. Three. Like walking a tightrope until she came to a wall and looked up.

To an oil portrait of Louis Armstrong.

It was as if a door in the sky had opened, and Mika was peeking into another world. She had to swallow back the tears. Something inside of her stirred to life. *A miracle*, Mika remembered thinking as she traced the brushstrokes with her eyes. *It's a miracle*. That was the day her world collapsed and reinflated. Roads were lines to draw. Trees were colors to be filled in. The sun was light to be used. Endless possibilities. Much like Mika's love for Penny, her love for painting was instinctual, prelingual. Mika ceased being a person—she was the stroke of a brush, a bottle of paint, a blank canvas waiting.

"Thought so. I'm familiar with the whole forcing two singles together in the hopes of producing Japanese love spawns," said Hayato, pulling Mika from the past.

Mika forced a smile. "I know my mom gave you my phone number the other day. But I'm not really looking to date anyone right now. No offense."

"None taken. In fact, I am only interested in dating men." Hayato pointed at himself with two thumbs. "Super gay."

Mika's smile was genuine now. "Well, then."

"Well, then," Hayato said back warmly.

They chatted for a while. Agreeing to meet up sometime. Maybe Mika would invite him to Charlie's housewarming party in a few weeks. After church, her father wrote a check in the parking lot.

"If you go out with him," Hiromi said, meaning Hayato, "wear a dress. Maybe some perfume. Nothing too heavy."

"He's not interested," Mika said, plucking the check from Shige's fingers.

"What do you mean he's not interested? What did you do?" Hiromi's voice grew shrill—the sound of seagulls fighting over a rotten fish.

Mika stiffened. "I didn't *do* anything."

"You have to make him interested," Hiromi insisted.

"No means no," Mika answered firmly.

"Eh." Shige rubbed his brow. "Can you two go five minutes without fighting? You're like two flames, always burning everything down around you."

Mika's jaw tensed, but she stayed silent. She folded up the check and stuffed it in her pocket, squeezing out a quiet thanks before walking away.

Chapter Four

A video call.

It didn't hit Mika until a few minutes before she was supposed to dial Penny's number that she would see her daughter live for the first time in sixteen years. Of course, she'd seen pictures enclosed in the letters from Caroline once a year. But they'd been static pieces. Moments frozen in time, trapped in thick amber. Mika couldn't observe Penny's facial tics. The way her hands moved when she was excited or sad or scared. Or hear the sound of her voice when she spoke, how the inflection changed. The most alive she'd ever seen Penny was as a baby.

She sat at the eat-in dining table in the kitchen. Hana had cleared out after helping Mika. Mika flicked on the camera and studied herself. Her sweater had a small hole in the sleeve. Hana had chosen it, picking through Mika's clothes, searching for a piece that didn't offend her. "This will have to do," she'd said, pinching the navy cable-knit number between her fingers and handing it off to Mika.

Then she'd left Mika alone with the screen, her heart beating fast and her palms slick with sweat. One minute to go. They'd scheduled the call for four p.m., seven p.m. Penny's time. Mika typed in her login information and dialed Penny's number. It rang once. And there she was. *There she was*—Mika's daughter. Mika wondered at her cheekbones, at her bullish nose, at her shiny hair. *I made her.* The feeling similar to when Mika gave birth and held Penny for the first time. A sense of awe and fascination. A piece of Mika's soul recognizing itself.

Mika smiled at Penny as if she were an old friend. "Hi."

"Wow!" Penny's own smile was wide and open, every single tooth on display. Mika had smiled like that before. When she was sixteen. When you had the world at your fingertips. When you held the balance of time in your own two hands. It was a special feeling—having nothing to lose. "You look so young," said Penny.

"Yeah, well, you know, Asian don't raisin."

Penny laughed. "It's so weird, but all I can think right now is: 'She has my face, she has my face!'"

Mika smiled brighter. They both grew quiet. It was near dark where Penny was. The last precious rays of sunlight filtered in through a window, obscuring her face when she moved the right way. Before, when Mika used to paint, she might have snapped a photo of it, sketched Penny in pencil, using the sharpest point on the upward curve of her happy mouth. Instead, Mika thought about the weather outside, the coming evening, the rain pattering on the windows, the strangeness of meeting Penny then and now. Both felt like the first time.

"I always wondered about you," Penny admitted like a dirty secret. Penny was in her bedroom. Pink cherry blossom wallpaper behind her. When Mika had been pregnant, Caroline promised to integrate Penny's Japanese heritage into their lives. A letter arrived describing a cherry blossom–themed nursery and a sushi-making class the couple had enrolled in. Mika was pretty sure most of what the Calvins learned about Japan was from a Wikipedia page.

"Here I am. Did your . . . Did Thomas and Caroline tell you anything about me?" Beyond the screen were two crumpled tissues Mika had just pressed under her armpits.

"Not much." Penny sipped from a steaming mug. Coffee? No, tea. Mika wished she'd grabbed a glass of water. Near Penny also were a little bowl of pretzels and a notepad with a pen. Penny came better prepared. "You were super young. Nineteen. Just starting college and didn't want a baby."

Want? It wasn't so much she didn't want Penny. It was that she couldn't have her. What she wanted was Penny to live and grow with a family better than hers. *Better than me.* She loved Penny and was ashamed she couldn't take care of her. That she wasn't enough for her. *What do you know about raising a baby?* The ghost of Hiromi's words haunted her.

"Anyway," Penny went on, setting the cup down. "They never tried to hide it from me. I mean, hello!" She pointed to her face. "It was kind of a given. Half-Japanese kid. White parents. I actually thought all kids were adopted for a while." Penny snickered. "Like there was a place where parents went and picked out babies. But then my friend Sophie—I've known her since kindergarten—said she had this weird turned-out-toe thing she'd inherited from her father. I went home and asked what I had from my parents. They

explained things like a sense of humor, kindness, etc."
Penny balled her hands into fists and bumped them
against the table. Mika straightened. Had she been
that self-aware at sixteen, at eighteen? She remembered being excited, vulnerable, alone. Unprepared.
No, Penny had been raised differently. She was so . . .
self-assured. "But I was like, no, *physically*, what part
of me comes from you? Then they explained it all. We
didn't have the same blood type. Or hands. Or feet
or anything. Someone else in the world possessed my
DNA. Since then, I've always thought about it. About a
part of myself that might exist elsewhere. I mean, who
am I?"

Mika clutched her kneecaps. *Who am I?* Mika
couldn't answer it for her daughter. She couldn't even
answer it for herself. Another shortcoming.

"Whew." Penny finished. "I feel like I'm doing all
the talking. Sorry. I'm used to being the center of attention." She pointed to her chest. "Only child, you
know."

"It's fine," Mika assured her. It was more than fine.
Listening to Penny, seeing her, it felt as if Mika had
been retrieved from the bottom of the coldest part of
the ocean, and she could feel the sun again. "I like
hearing about you."

"Good." Penny lightened. "I want to know all about you too."

Mika thought on this. She folded her hair behind her ear. She saw the dishes stacked in the sink, the piles of boxes, the letter on the counter stating her cell phone payment was past due. "There's not much to tell. I'm afraid I'm kind of boring, really."

"You still live in Oregon?"

Mika nodded. "In Portland." A place boasting more strip joints per capita than any other city. But it also had a donut shop that sold zombie eclairs and the largest continuously operated outdoor market in the United States. People came to buy hemp and jewelry and eat street food. One out of four cars had a bumper sticker that read: KEEP PORTLAND WEIRD. "I live in the Alberta neighborhood." A quintessentially Portland place. "There are some shops down the streets. Goat yoga studios owned by bearded hipsters who sell sustainable organic orangutan-safe coffee on the side, that kind of thing."

"That's so cool." Penny smiled. "Your house looked super pretty." *Super.* Penny used the word a lot, and it fit her. Into everything. Bigger than life. "Well, the garden, at least. That's all I could see on Instagram."

Through the window, Mika could see the backyard,

the falling fence, the unmowed grass, the overturned lawn furniture, and the discarded beer bottles full of slugs. Then she realized Penny had said *your house*. As in Mika's. She sought to correct her. "It's not really—"

"I can't wait to get my own place," Penny cut in. "I'm going to apply all over the West Coast and East Coast. Nowhere in the Midwest. Don't get me wrong, I love living in Dayton, in Ohio, I mean. But it's so small, you know? Sophie and I are going to be roomies wherever we go." At last, a similarity. At sixteen, Mika and Hana worked at a Taco Bell. They'd listen to hip-hop while dumping bags of meat into warmers, chattering about their futures, bonding over being Asian American—how many times they'd been asked, "Where are you from?" *Someday I'm going to travel and paint*, Mika would brag. She'd concocted so many plans. Riding motorcycles across South America. Drifting through the Venice canals on a gondola. Eating chocolate croissants in Paris. "What else?" Penny tapped her fingers. "What about your job? And, oh my god, was that your boyfriend in the picture?" Leif, she meant. Mika hadn't seen him in two years. To say things ended badly was like saying Van Gogh was just a painter. "He's cute. You travel too? Where'd you go to high school?" Penny stopped. Took a breath. Clearly gearing up for more.

Mika laughed. She put out a hand. Deflected. "Wait. Stop. I want to hear more about you."

Penny's brow furrowed. Mika had a picture of her making that very gesture. It was one of her favorites. Caroline had sent a snapshot of Penny holding an empty cone, a double scoop of ice cream melting on the pavement. She wore a little white dress with hand-stitched flowers, her hair caught in a summer breeze. "I run cross-country. I read a lot. But not anything, you know, super noteworthy or important. Though recently, my dad gave me a copy of *The Loneliness of the Long Distance Runner*. I think he bought it on the title alone, and I thought it would be super grim. But I ended up kind of liking it. There was this whole antiestablishment theme."

"I've never read it."

"It's good. You should pick it up. What was high school like for you? I'm so curious."

Mika pulled at her ear. She'd been a misfit and lonely growing up. The void had been filled by Hana and painting. At night, she'd steal away, huddling under her comforter with a flashlight, pencil, and drawing pad. She'd started sketching her own hand, then the hands of others, exploring the warped veins in her mother's fingers, the age spots on her father's. Art was like air to Mika. Her ikigai. It carried her through the darkness toward the dawn. But Mika didn't paint anymore. That was *before*. Why bring it up? "I went to a magnet school. It was for students who didn't necessarily fit into regular academia." Most kids napped during classes, and the teachers turned the other cheek. "I loved the Beat Generation when I was younger—Jack Kerouac, Gary Snyder, Neal Cassady." Penny took another note, mouthing the words *Beat Generation*. "My good friend, Hana, attended with me. She was there when you were born, as a matter of fact."

"She was?" Penny lit up.

"She was." Penny stayed silent. Mika hesitated to add more. What might she say? *The nurses hated us because we kept ordering food. I still pee a little every time I laugh too hard. My breasts are like sock puppets. I grieve every day.* She settled on, "She held you. After I did, I mean."

Penny thought for a moment. "Do you think I could see a picture of her?"

"Sure. I don't have one handy right now." There was one in a frame on the mantle pushed behind some gourd vases. But they were dressed up as nuns for Halloween, a bong on the table between them. "But I'll send you one."

"Awesome." Penny smiled at Mika.

Mika smiled back.

"Where do you work?" Penny asked finally.

"I'm kind of between things right now." At Mika's answer, Penny chewed her lip—her face caught in a fragile moment of hoping for more but expecting less. Mika imagined that expression shifting, morphing to one her mother sported all too often around Mika. Blatant disappointment. What made a perfect mother? A perfect woman? Whatever it was, Mika understood it was the opposite of herself. "I mean, I recently left my old job to branch out on my own." She closed her eyes. She was thirty-five. A third of her life was over. She was supposed to have done something by now. What corner had she painted herself into? She opened her eyes. The lie tripped out, stumbling over her tongue. "I love art, and . . . and I'm looking into gallery space, hoping to find some artists to represent and start my own business. It's in really early stages . . ."

Penny positively glowed. "That's amazing."

Mika blushed. Felt too embarrassed and unsure to fess up. Plus, she wanted Penny to keep looking at her in that way. As if she was good and kind and special. A tiny white lie never hurt anyone, anyway. "Well, I guess . . ."

They bounced questions off each other for a while. Made small talk. Penny was a medal-winning runner. The scholarship kind. Her friend Sophie ran track too and had six siblings. "Mormons, you know?" Penny said. Mika did not. But she smiled like she did. Before they knew it, an hour had passed. Their conversation dwindled.

"Can we talk again?" Penny asked.

"I'd like that," Mika said, meaning it. In the beginning, her expectations had been low. She only wanted to know Penny was safe and loved. That she hadn't ruined Penny's life. But now, she couldn't tamp down the desire to speak to Penny again. It was part of the human condition to want more.

"Keep in touch," Penny said, putting her pointer finger up as Mika reached out to end the call.

Mika paused, not understanding the motion. "What?"

"It's something my mom . . . ." Penny looked down, her eyelashes creating half-moon shadows on her cheeks. Then she glanced up, watching Mika closely. "Something we used to do. We'd extend our pointer fingers and tap them together. It's silly . . ."

"It's not silly." Mika swallowed. She pressed her finger to the screen. Penny did the same. "Keep in touch, Penny."

ADOPTION ACROSS AMERICA
National Office
56544 W 57th Ave. Suite 111
Topeka, KS 66546
(800) 555-7794

Dear Mika,

I hope you're doing well. Enclosed are the requisite items in regard to the adoption agreement between you, Mika Suzuki (the birth mother), and Thomas and Caroline Calvin (the adoptive parents) for Penelope Calvin (the adoptee). Contents include:

- An annual letter from the adoptive parents describing the adoptee's development and progress
- Photographs and/or other memorabilia

Give me a call if you have any questions. (Sorry if the above sounds formal, legal speak, you know?)

All the best,

Monica Pearson
Adoption Coordinator

Dear Mika,

I can't believe it has been six years already since Penny came into our lives. Time has flown by. Penny has grown so much. She is a precocious and athletically inclined child. The other day she nearly beat Thomas in a foot race! I feel like if we projected her brain onto a screen, all we would see is the word *go*.

A month ago, she gave us a little scare. Penny stopped responding when we called her name. The pediatrician referred us to an audiologist. We spent an entire afternoon at the children's hospital. They ran a battery of tests, placing big headphones on her ears and instructing her to press buttons when she heard certain sounds. Then we waited in a small room for the results. We were so nervous. Thomas wouldn't stop bouncing his knee and kept going on about flying Penny to California. He was looking up specialists on his phone when the audiologist came in. "All of Penny's tests checked out. It seems your daughter has selective hearing," he said, emphasis on *selective*.

In the parking lot, we pasted on our most serious expressions and had a conversation with Penny about the importance of paying attention and what a big deal this was. All the testing could have been avoided, we explained. In the car, Thomas started laughing, and so did I. We couldn't stop. One thing is certain, our lives will never be boring with Penny in them. As always, pictures are attached. Including a self-portrait Penny created with mustard and a couple pieces of bread.

Big hugs,
Caroline

Chapter Five

For three weeks, Mika and Penny chatted nonstop. They stayed up together, night after night, their conversations following a labyrinthine path. Penny would text: Can you talk? And Mika would reply, Sure! It wasn't that she had nothing to do. It was that she was doing nothing.

They celebrated each other's accomplishments, cracking bottles of apple cider for Penny and champagne for Mika. Penny won a big cross-country race, and Mika pretended to find the perfect gallery space for a new artist she wanted to showcase. They'd have an official opening in a few weeks—so exciting, she couldn't wait. In reality, she'd been applying for higher-paying jobs, but still no callbacks. She watched the money trickle from her account with a resigned panic.

Penny broke up with her boyfriend, Jack, after he kept wanting to hang out in places with mattresses. When Penny asked about Leif, Mika said he'd taken her on a romantic dinner, on a hike, to a museum exhibit . . .

With each lie, Mika painted her life in brighter colors—a successful job, a dedicated boyfriend. For the last sixteen years, it felt like she'd been living in exile. With Penny, she'd disembarked from her current life and boarded a new ship, sailing toward a destination she'd always dreamed of but could never quite reach. Next stop: love, career, family, home. A life she might have had, before she had Penny, before she quit painting. It made Penny feel good. And Mika too. It was much easier to talk about things as you wished them to be. For the first time in a very long time, Mika was content. Fulfilled.

"Ugh, sounds like Charlie let Tuan pick the music again," Hana griped outside of Charlie's freshly painted front door. Tonight was Charlie and Tuan's house-warming party.

The couple had moved in a month ago. Mika and Hana had helped prep the house for its debut—weighing in on such important matters as what picture to hang over the fireplace, how the furniture should be laid out, and once cleansed the whole place with sage after the light kept flickering in the kitchen. Tuan had come home around the time they were smoking out the corners of the living room. *Did you check the bulb?* he'd asked. *Of course we have, Tuan,* they said. *Don't you think we tried that first, Tuan? We're not stupid, Tuan.* When he'd left for a bike ride, Charlie changed the lightbulb, and they swore to never tell.

Through the door, Mika could hear the low tones of R&B, i.e., slow jams—the music Tuan liked to play for parties *and* make love to afterward, according to Charlie. There were some things Mika could go a lifetime without knowing. Also heard was the murmur of conversation and the clink of glasses. The party was in full swing. Naturally, Mika and Hana were late.

Footsteps pounded on the pavement behind them. "Mika. Hi. Sorry, I'm late. Traffic was a bitch. Not as bad as LA, though." Hayato was dressed in a collared shirt and slacks, his work lanyard still around his neck, a big black swoosh prominent over his name and title. Tucked under his arm was a bottle of wine.

"You made it!" She and Hayato had texted since church. They had spent a whole Saturday exchanging stories about their Japanese mothers. Checking off the commonalities—refusing to use the dishwasher, elaborate bento boxes for lunch . . . that sort of thing. Now, Mika hugged Hayato, then turned to Hana. "Hayato, Hana. Hana, Hayato."

Hana and Hayato exchanged how-do-you-dos.

"Funny." He pointed to the plant in Hana's hands. Mika and Hana's housewarming gift was an artichoke agave with the words NICE HOUSE, SUCCA scrawled across the pot.

Hana frowned. "Twenty bucks says Charlie puts it in her guest room."

"The guest room is where bad gifts go to die," Mika explained to Hayato. Popular items included: the eleven-by-fourteen-inch portrait from her mother-in-law of Tuan when he was a baby, a giant crystal cross and pot-pourri holder from Charlie's mother, and an acoustic guitar—a gift from Tuan to himself. Also tucked away in a closet was a stuffed bunny with the softest floppy ears. Charlie had found it in a children's boutique store. She'd shrugged at the time, murmuring, "Someday." Hiromi adored Charlie. Charlie did everything right and in the right order. As soon as she finished her undergraduate degree, she hopped straight to her graduate degree—a master's in teaching. The day she got a job, Tuan proposed. They married a year later. And now, they had bought a house and were planning a family.

Why can't you be like your friend Charlie? Hiromi often said. *Be* was Hiromi's favorite word to invoke around Mika. *Be silent*, Hiromi would command, her breath stale, when Mika was little and cried. *Be a dancer,*

Hiromi would say, cinching the obi around Mika's waist until her breaths were wisps, prepping her for odori. Be. Be. Be. Be for me. Be anything but yourself.

Hayato laughed, gaze landing at the door with the iron knocker. He removed his lanyard and stuffed it into his pocket. "This is your friend's place? It's nice. You sure it's okay I'm here?" The house was beautiful. Built in 1909 on a corner lot, it had been fully updated outside and in. A huge wraparound porch accessorized with Adirondack chairs and original leaded-glass windows dominated the front. Charlie and Tuan had spent hours landscaping the yard, choosing plants native to the Pacific Northwest—high grasses, maples, and bushy ferns.

"Of course it's fine," Hana said. "Charlie is great. She's married to Tuan, and he's a gem. They're totally in love." Hana put her hand on the doorknob and turned. Light flooded onto the porch. She paused and dropped her voice to a whisper. "Listen. If either of you gets hungry, I have sandwiches in my purse."

"You brought sandwiches to our best friend's house-warming?" Mika whispered back, entering alongside Hana, Hayato at her elbow. The door swung closed behind them.

"You know she never has enough food at these things," said Hana. Hayato's eyes glimmered with amusement.

Blond with big brown eyes, Charlie sailed across the

room. "You're here." Hana and Mika had met Charlie freshman year. Charlie was a sucker for underdogs, which explained her attraction to Hana and Mika. Of course, Mika and Hana had imprinted on her like a set of wolf cubs.

Charlie lived across the hall, and as she was to most of the students in the dorm, Mika was a kind of fascination, being pregnant in college and living in student housing. A day after she returned from the hospital, Mika's milk came in. Charlie had spotted Hana and Mika in the bathroom, frantically stuffing Mika's bra with toilet paper.

Mika had been foolish to think once she signed the adoption papers it would all go away, that things would go back to how they had been before. Instead, they got worse. The milk was her body's signal. Giving your baby away wasn't a natural process. *I can't make it stop,* Mika had cried.

You should get some breast pads, Charlie calmly suggested, shower kit in hand. *My sister had a baby last year. That's what she used.* After, Charlie had called her sister and found out how to make Mika's milk stop.

Now, a serial hugger, Charlie wrapped her arms around Mika, then Hana, then Hayato. "You're Mika's friend from church? Mika mentioned you just moved here," Charlie said, squeezing Hayato. She was small but surprisingly strong. Spin classes three times a week, and Krav Maga twice, will do that to a body. "Are you interested in acquiring a large crystal cross slash potpourri holder? Might look nice in your place."

Hayato coughed into his hand. "Not really my aesthetic, but thanks."

"Shoot." Charlie pouted.

"Sorry," Mika said to Hayato.

Charlie shrugged like it didn't hurt to try.

"Happy housewarming." Hana handed off the plant.

Charlie studied it as Mika scoped out the marble island. There was plenty of booze accompanied by an unenthusiastic buffet of appetizers—sliders on brioche buns, fruit skewers, some vegetables, and dip. Mika knew tucked in the pantry was a can of ranch Pringles and desserts with irresponsible amounts of butter for when everyone left. Then the three women would cozy up on the couch. Tuan would rescue his guitar from the guest room and play the only song he knew, "Stairway to Heaven."

"Tuan," Charlie called. "Come see the gift Hana and Mika brought us."

Tuan joined the group. He was Vietnamese, tallish with a runner's body and flop of black hair he was perpetually pushing back. "Hey, Tuan." He shook Hayato's hand, introducing himself.

Charlie tapped her lips. "I know just the place for this. The guest room needs a plant, don't you think?" she asked her husband.

"I don't know." He pushed his hair back. "Maybe the mantle?" Charlie sent Tuan an I-want-to-punch-you-in-the-nuts glare. Tuan half smiled and kissed Charlie on the nose.

"Place looks nice," Mika chimed in.

"Thanks!" Charlie turned a megawatt smile on Mika. It was an open concept. The kitchen boasted stainless-steel appliances polished to a high shine and marble countertops. A gray, L-shaped couch dominated the living room. In the fireplace, a log burned. Lights were controlled by dimmers to create ambiance and mood—this evening's aesthetic: low and warm with a touch of romance. Wines and beers showcased regions throughout the world. Once upon a time, Mika drank beer. But never after college. Nope, those days of kegs and red Solo cups were gone. She bypassed the brown bottles and poured herself a healthy glass of wine, big enough to slay any bad memory.

• • •

Two, three, four glasses of wine later—who was counting really?—Mika was deep in conversation with Hayato. They sat on the couch close together. A few feet away, Hana slow-danced with a coworker of Tuan's. Hayato had just filled Mika in on his job, creating marketing materials and designing shoes for Nike. Hayato swirled the wine in his glass. "What do you do for work?"

Mika waved a hand. "Unfortunately, I am unemployed."

"Oh?"

At his sympathetic tone, she said, "It's fine. Totally fine." She had the money from her parents.

"Where have you been applying?"

Mika sipped her wine, the chardonnay growing warm because she refused to put her glass down. "Nowhere great." In the few weeks she'd been searching, she hadn't found anything even remotely appealing. "But I've decided to see this as an opportunity. You know, if one door shuts, another opens."

"I like the attitude," Hayato said. "Take a look at Nike and see if anything fits your qualifications. I'm happy to put in a good word."

"Wow. Thanks, that'd be great," she said, grateful yet struggling to picture it. The moment lapsed into silence. She rested her head on the back of the couch and peered at the ceiling. She thought of Hana and her career, Charlie and her marriage. How her friend's stones had reached the other side of the river.

Charlie's voice cut through the room. "Heads up," she called to Mika. "Your phone is ringing off the hook." Charlie tossed the phone to Mika, just as the ringing cut off. Three missed calls from Penny.

"Will you excuse me for a moment?" she said to Hayato before standing and slipping out the back door. Penny had left two voicemails. Mika shivered against the cold spring evening and pressed the phone to her ear, listening to Penny's first message. "Hey, it's me. Give me a call when you get this. I have a surprise for you."

Then the second message. "So, I couldn't wait. I am dying. *Dying.* Remember how I told you for my sixteenth birthday my grandparents sent me a check for, like, five hundred dollars, and I've been trying to figure out what to do with it?" There was a pause. Probably for Penny to take a breath. Mika often found herself winded after Penny's calls. "I was going to put it toward a new phone, but then I had a brilliant idea! I'm going to visit you for my spring break!"

Mika put a hand out against the fence, steadying herself. Portland didn't have many earthquakes, but she was sure a tremor just shook the ground.

Penny went on. "We'll officially meet in two weeks! I can't believe I bought a ticket. Oh my god, my dad is going to totally regret giving me my own debit card.

Don't worry, I'm going to tell him tonight. I can't believe I'm coming to see you! I can't wait to see your house and gallery. I'll totally be there for the grand opening. And I want to meet Leif!" Squeal. Actual squeal. "I'm so excited."

Mika listened to the voicemail three more times. The words didn't change. But they did sink in with a sickening effect. Her lying heart twisted in her chest, then twisted once again with guilt. Oh god, Penny was coming to Portland. Penny, whom she loved. Penny who thought Mika was a totally different person. She peered up at the sky. Waited to see if thunderous clouds were rolling in. If bare-chested men on massive horses would stampede across the skies. Nothing. Check. Not the end of days. Good to know she was the only person biblical-level fucked.

Chapter Six

Mika barreled through the house. First stop, Hana. "Excuse me." She yanked Hana's arm, separating her best friend from the blue-haired woman she slow-danced with.

"Hey." The woman frowned. "You told me you were single."

"I am," Hana explained sheepishly.

Panic inched up Mika's spine. The words from Penny's message flashed across Mika's mind like warning signs before a cliff. *I'm coming to see you. Two weeks.* "Emergency. Code red. I need you."

Hana's brow hiked up. "I'm intrigued. Lily—"

"It's Lola." The blue-haired woman's frown intensified. Hayato was still in the living room and engaged in an animated conversation with Tuan plus some other dudes.

"Lola," Hana said, giving her a salute. "It's been real."

Off they went, Mika steering them toward Charlie's bedroom. Inside, Mika shut the door, muting the party. "Listen." Mika turned the volume up on her phone, hit play on Penny's message, and set it on the king-size bed. Penny's sweet voice filled the dim room. As they listened, Mika's stomach plummeted. She should've known this would happen. She had years of experience of everything going right and then suddenly wrong. Nothing was ever certain.

"Penny's coming to visit. This is great!" said Hana. Then at Mika's expression, she amended, "This is not great?" Hana's brow darted in. "Hold up. Did she say your gallery? And what was that about Leif?"

Mika sat on the bed, more of a collapse, really. She cupped her knees, flexed her hands. It didn't make anything better. "That's what I need your help with. I may have improved the truth in our conversations." She pinched her fingers together. "A little."

Hana squinted her eyes. "How little?"

"You know . . ." Mika brushed her shirtsleeve, started to sweat anew. "I said I graduated from college with an art history degree." Once, long ago, she'd dreamed of finishing her art degree and back-packing through Europe or South America. Instead, she'd gotten a degree in business. It had taken her eight years instead of the usual four.

"Okay." The set of Hana's face made it seem not so bad.

She sucked in her cheeks. "Maybe with honors."

Hana laughed, *the bitch*. "What else?"

"I dunno. My own gallery and house, traveling the world, super-successful boyfriend, I think I even said I bike everywhere."

Hana's eyebrows inched up. "So, you're a lying liar who lies?"

"Again. I prefer the term 'improving the truth.'"

Hana screwed her face up. "But why?"

It was hard for Hana to understand, Mika supposed. Other than terrible housekeeping skills, Hana really had nothing to hide. She had a great job. Women threw themselves at her. How could Mika explain? "Safe space?" Mika asked.

"You know it," Hana answered immediately.

"It's who I want to be. Who I thought I could be . . . before." A safe kind of hope existed in fiction. The possibilities were endless. Her life different. A more positive timeline. If only. If only . . . Plus, she wanted to give Penny what she had to outsource sixteen years ago to Caroline—a good mother, a fit mother.

"Mika." Hana sighed. Finally, she stood, approaching the door as if to leave.

Panic sliced through Mika like a santoku knife. "Where are you going?"

Hana turned. "I'm getting Charlie. We're going to need backup."

• • •

A few minutes later, Charlie, Mika, and Hana sat in Charlie's bathroom—because Hana had her best ideas in the tub.

"You told her you were backstage for the opening performance of *Hamilton*?" asked Charlie. She sat on the closed toilet, laptop and Excel spreadsheet open. And because Charlie was Charlie, she'd decided to sort Mika's lies by category—School and Career, Hobbies, Love Life, etc.

Mika frowned. "It's not like I said I was *in* the production. Just that Leif whisked me away to New York and surprised me with backstage passes to meet the cast on opening night."

Hana sprawled in the clawfoot bathtub, wineglass in hand. "That is oddly specific."

"The devil's in the details," Mika replied.

"I'm filing it under Hobbies," said Charlie.

Someone shouted in the living room. Apparently, board games were happening. "Are you sure you shouldn't be out there with your people?" Mika asked Charlie.

"You are my people," Charlie said pointedly. "Besides, it's fine. Tuan is covering for me. He totally understands."

"Tuan is awesome." Mika wished she had a partner like Tuan. He had once entered some bicycle race across California. He was in position to win some big money but had quit because he missed Charlie "too damn much." To be loved like that, Mika thought, a little melancholy. Once, she believed she was in love. Freshman year of college. She'd been foolish then. So naïve. So easily taken advantage of. With a shake of her head, Mika squashed down an image of Penny's biological father. No, she didn't like to remember him.

Charlie made a dismissive gesture with her hand. "You're not missing anything. Every time he walks past me after I've gotten out of the shower, he goes 'boobies.'" She held her palms aloft as if handling two melons. "And then I spend an inordinate amount of time trying to hit him in the genitals with his own arm." She grinned, the lovesick fool.

"Focus." Hana lounged in the bathtub again. "What else?"

Mika scrolled through her memory. Another hour passed. The party quieted, the front door opened and shut. Tuan knocked and said he and Hayato were headed to a bar down the street. The list grew.

School and Career
Majored in art history
Internship with a local art museum
Hired by a local art museum
Slowly advanced to a curator
Saved enough money to become an art gallery owner
Grand opening (two weeks from now!)

Hobbies
Travel (has been all over Europe and South America)
Bicycling

Love Life
Boyfriend: Leif, entrepreneur
Leif proposes regularly, but Mika isn't ready to
settle down

Charlie offered to make some sort of flowchart. Mika declined. Finally, Charlie drew in a deep breath.

She shut her laptop with a decisive click. "The way I see it, there are two options."

"Okay," Mika said gravely.

"One, you tell Penny the truth. Come clean."

Mika considered it for less than a second. "Yeah. I'm not super jazzed about that."

"Or two. We create this life for you."

"I'm listening," said Mika. Her throat knotted. A wanting grew in her chest, making it ache. Since placing Penny for adoption, Mika had dreamed of meeting her someday in person. Granted, the fantasy usually involved Mika on her way to some fabulous destination, maybe the installation of her first piece of art at the Met, with a brief stopover in Dayton. Just enough time to have lunch and see Penny's face glow with pride at having come from Mika—to be made of her. Penny would never look at Mika like that if she knew Mika's life resembled a late-stage Jenga tower.

Hana piped in. "How are we supposed to do that?"

Charlie puffed out her cheeks. "Well, most of this seems kind of manageable. Like the house—"

"Mika lives with me," Hana helpfully added.

Mika blinked, saw Hana's house. The lawn with weeds and assorted thorning plants. The inside full of boxes and stacks of dusty magazines. The fridge with an odd smell. Mika's level of shame hit an all-time high.

"Yes, and you live in a house," Charlie enunciated slowly. "Or I'm pretty sure it is. Is a condemned building still considered a domicile?"

"Hardy-har-har," Hana deadpanned.

Mika lay her cheek against the cool tub. It reminded her of slipping her hands between the cold sheets in the hospital the day she surrendered Penny. Touch has a memory, it turns out. She concentrated on something else. The here and now. Hana's gold hoop earrings. Tuan's razor balancing on the edge of the sink. Charlie shaking her head.

"Forget it," Charlie announced. "We'll call it a house. All we need to do is tidy it up a bit." Charlie had always been an optimist. "Hobbies-wise, Tuan bikes, and I'm pretty sure he can give you some pointers, some terms to use."

"What about the gallery space?" Hana asked. Contrary to Charlie, Hana had always been more of a pessimist.

"I don't know," Charlie said. "But we can figure it out. Now, about the Leif situation . . ." Charlie pursed her lips, thinking. Penny had seen pictures of Leif. There was no way Mika could hire an escort, even if she could afford it, which she couldn't. Charlie inhaled as if preparing to summon some sort of ancient demon. "You should call him."

Mika screwed her face up. "Boo." Leif didn't know about Penny. She'd been careful to keep that part of her life secret. She'd have to tell him. She'd have to see him again. Preferably the rest of her life would pass without Mika speaking to Leif.

"Easy," Charlie said. Two words described the relationship between Mika and Leif best: scorched earth. All their friends knew not to enter that hostile territory lest they be burned. "Tuan sees him all the time." Mika said nothing about Tuan's friendship with Leif. She knew the two were still buddies. Tuan made friends like pants picked up lint. Charlie continued, "He's doing really well for himself since weed was legalized. He's got his own store and everything."

Mika hoped Leif was doing good in the same way she hoped to get genital warts. Just then, her phone rang. An unknown number flashed on the screen. "It's from Ohio," Mika whispered, recognizing the zip code.

"Is it Penny?" Hana asked.

Mika shook her head. "No." She'd filed Penny in her contacts.

"Don't answer it," Hana said.

"Answer it," said Charlie.

Mika slid the button to accept and put the phone on speaker. "Hello?"

"Hi. Mika Suzuki?"

"Speaking," she said, an awful knot of dread forming in her stomach.

"This is Thomas Calvin. Penelope's father." His voice was deep, a little forbidding. Too severe, *grave*. An antidote to Penny's liveliness. *This* was the man who raised Mika's daughter?

Mika said nothing. She stood abruptly. Wine sloshed from her cup, and she licked her fingers clean while balancing the phone in her palm.

"Hello. Are you there?" said Thomas.

"I'm here," Mika replied, cheeks aflame.

"Can you speak now? Is this an okay time? It sounds like you're in a tunnel. There's an echo."

"I'm in my gallery."

Hana gave her two thumbs up.

Charlie hid her face in her hands.

"Look, I apologize for calling out of the blue. Penny informed me she's planning on visiting you. I didn't even know you two had been speaking. I didn't even know she knew your name." Mika winced. *Oh, Penny, what have you done?* It had never occurred to her to ask what Penny's adoptive father knew, how he felt about them talking. Their conversations had been singularly focused on each other. Their similarities, how they were both emotional eaters—happiness, sadness, boredom: all of them deserved pie. How they loved dogs but were allergic, even to the ones with hair instead of fur. They'd blocked out the rest of the world, only existing for each other. "Forgive me, but I'm shocked. It's not like her to keep secrets from me. And now she's purchased a plane ticket to Portland. I'm . . . well, I'm concerned she hasn't thought things through."

"What's there to think about?" Mika said, automatically defensive. Her cheeks heated with insecurities. Was Thomas questioning Mika? Who she was? Her qualifications to be in Penny's life, to be a mother?

"Everything," he answered sharply. "She spent all of her birthday money on the ticket. She was supposed to be putting that money toward her college fund." He paused, words hanging in the air. "I'll just . . . I'll tell Penelope we've spoken, and now isn't a good time for her to visit. Okay?"

"Yes," Mika said.

"Excellent," Thomas said, and then he was quiet.

"I mean no," Mika said abruptly, surprising herself.

"I'm sorry?" It was clear people did not disagree with Thomas often.

"It just so happens my schedule is clear," Mika said brightly. Penny wanted to come to Portland. And Mika wanted to meet Penny in person. "I'd love to meet Penny. Get to know her better in person."

"You're serious?"

"Absolutely."

"Ms. Suzuki—"

"Mika, please."

"Ms. Suzuki, I appreciate you wanting to help. But with all due respect, you don't know my daughter. Penelope is impulsive. She needs direction. She had other spring break plans, other plans for that money . . . Like I said earlier, I just don't think she's thought this through."

You don't know my daughter was the only thing Mika heard. And it cut her deeply. She struggled to conceal the hurt, to maintain an even tone. "You know, when people are running toward something, it often means they're running from something."

"What's that supposed to mean?"

She thrust out an arm. "It's just a general life observation. Maybe it's more than impulsivity. Perhaps Penny is working through some things." Mika remembered herself at sixteen. Drawing, hanging with Hana, searching for a better life. Isn't that what everyone does? What Mika's parents had done when they came to the States? What Mika did in college? Mika had yearned for more. So did Penny. And Mika understood deeply the emotional pull of something greater, how irresistible it could be.

He sighed, softened the teensiest bit. "That may be true. She . . . I thought everything was okay. But her mother"—Mika swallowed against the word *mother*— "wrote her this letter to be opened on her sixteenth birthday. She won't let me read it, but ever since, she's been acting differently. This trip . . . seeing you, meeting you, could raise a lot more questions than it answers."

"Thomas. May I call you Thomas?" Mika began to pace the length of the tiny bathroom. Three steps forward. Pivot. Three steps back. "I appreciate your concern. But I won't turn Penny away."

"If she comes." His tone changed. "She won't be alone. I'll be accompanying her."

"Wonderful," Mika said, feeling perversely good and sporting an outraged gleam in her eyes. "The more, the merrier. Please give Penny my best. I look forward to meeting you both. Have to run now." Mika was sweating. So much. "Nice talk."

"Wait—"

She hung up.

"Whoa," Charlie breathed out.

"Holy shit," Hana said.

"So, option two?" asked Charlie, smoothing her hands over her laptop.

"Option two," Mika said, still staring at her phone.

Hana held her wineglass aloft. "I'll cheers to that."

Chapter Seven

Much happened over the next forty-eight hours. Penny sent her flight details. Then followed up with a text. Ugh, my dad is coming too. But I'm sure we'll be able to ditch him. He wants your email. Can I give it to him? He is BEYOND. Sorry. Mika agreed Thomas could have her email. What else could she do? Soon enough, Thomas sent a confirmation he'd be on the same flight with Penny. He also included a suggested itinerary, leaving on the track changes in the Word document so they could discuss, i.e., negotiate, the schedule. Fucking lawyers.

Details were agreed upon.

Day One (Sunday): Arrive on flight 3021, at 10:21 a.m. It would take them approximately fifteen minutes to go from their gate to the baggage claim, where Mika would pick them up. Bags in hand, they would proceed directly to lunch. *Penny insisted on food trucks?* Thomas had written, baffled by such a notion. After lunch, Penny and Thomas would spend the afternoon at the hotel resting and have dinner in because, apparently, Thomas was a cantankerous old man living inside a cantankerous younger man's body.

Day Two (Monday): They'd visit the Portland Art Museum, where fake-Mika had interned, and have dinner at Mika's house, where fake-Mika's charming boyfriend Leif would join them.

And on it went. Day Three (Tuesday): Dinner at one of Portland's Michelin-starred restaurants. Day Four (Wednesday): Lunch with Hana . . . culminating on Day Five (Thursday): Mika's faux gallery opening. The one she'd rambled on to Penny about. *I have the best artist. He's brilliant. I can't believe he hasn't been snatched up by another gallery. How lucky am I?*

Mika vacillated between panic and excitement. Fourteen days, scratch that, *twelve* days. She had less than two weeks to fake her life. Less than two weeks until she met Penny in person again. The countdown had begun.

Charlie and Hana promised to aggressively support her. They cleared their evenings and weekends to help her prep. Charlie even intended to ask the tech guy at her school to engineer some photographs of Mika around the world. The house. The hobbies. All handled. Or would be handled. Two pieces were still missing. The gallery space and Leif. Of the two, Leif seemed easier, the lowest-hanging fruit.

And Leif wasn't answering Mika's phone calls or texts. *Bastard.* She'd tried a half dozen times. Nothing. He'd read her texts. She was sure. The little bubble with three dots appeared and reappeared like he was deciding what to say, then settled ultimately on passive-aggressive silence. He'd left her no choice. She stood on Northwest Twenty-Third Avenue, a hip, high-end shopping district. When Tuan gave her the address, she'd been surprised. She'd thought his store would be somewhere deep in North Portland near some skeezy strip bar named Pirate's Booty. The outside didn't look like a weed shop. The windows were covered with beige bamboo shades. The name, Twenty-Third Marijuana—not super inventive, Mika thought smugly—was spelled in wooden letters and softly lit underneath. Mika sighed and opened the door. *Whatever.*

A huge white dude with neck tattoos stood near the entrance. "ID."

Mika fished her license from her purse. "I'm here to see Leif."

He shone a light on her ID, looked at her, looked at the ID, then handed it back to her. "See Adelle." He pointed to a cool white chick with a Bettie Page haircut. "She handles his schedule. You want to buy anything, it's cash only. ATM is located in the corner."

"Thanks." Mika stuffed her license back in her wallet and wandered toward Adelle. Leif owned this? This cross between an Apple store and a spa? New age music played. Enya maybe. Glass counters framed in light wood showcased all sorts of paraphernalia—bud, balms, baked goods. It was busy. The store hummed with traffic—conversations revolving around different kinds of highs. "You want something mellow?" she heard a clerk say.

"Yeah," the kid wearing a University of Portland sweatshirt replied. "Just something totally chill."

Adelle held a clipboard and was scribbling on it. At Mika's approach, she glanced up. "What can I help you with?" She wore a tag with the word *Manager* on it.

"I'm here to see Leif."

Adelle tilted her head, chewed on a piece of gum. "Do you have an appointment?"

"Um, no."

"Sorry. Leif sees people by appointment only. And he's not in anyway." She went back to her clipboard. There was a tattoo of a koi on her arm and some kanji.

"That's a nice tattoo. What does it say?"

"Oh!" Adelle glanced up. "'Fearless.'"

Nope. Mika had taken calligraphy for a decade. It was the kanji for *weasel*. "Look, I know Leif is here. The truck he converted to run on recycled vegetable oil is parked out back." Mika straightened, feeling brave and assertive. "Please tell him the woman who once shaved his back is here."

Adelle's mouth opened and closed. She popped her gum. Then she picked up a phone and hit a button. "Yeah, hi. Sorry to bother. Someone is here to see you." She appraised Mika. "Asian, short, and kind of angry . . . Sure." She hung up. "You can go on back." She gestured to a white door with an EMPLOYEES ONLY sign. "His office is the last one on the right."

Mika hefted her purse over her shoulder. "Nice to meet you." She was through the door before Adelle could answer.

Leif's office door was open a crack. Mika didn't bother knocking. He didn't bother getting up from his desk. She focused on his office first. Not much to look at. Pretty simple with a white desk and giant computer. No windows. Then with no other place to go, her eyes focused on Leif.

He leaned back in his chair, adjusting his big body. His new, *slimmer* big body. Gone was the pudgy stomach, the fullness in his face. Now his cheeks were sharp angles under a five-o'clock shadow. His long blond hair had been clipped and lay in a purposeful wreck. Her heart stopped for a moment. The first time he'd kissed her, he'd asked permission. With gentle hands that grew plants, he'd cupped her cheeks. *I want to kiss you right now, can I?*

"Well, well, well." His voice sliced through Mika's memory. "Look who decided to grace me with her presence."

"Dale." Leif's real name. He hated it. "It's nice to see you."

His lips turned up in a rakish grin, revealing whiter teeth than Mika remembered. "Mik." She hated the nickname. It was too close to Mickey. "Wish I could say the same."

She faked a smile. He faked a smile. It was a duel of sorts. Mika stepped inside the office, undeterred. She folded herself into a chair. "Make yourself at home," Leif snorted.

"This is a nice place," she said tightly.

"I did the construction myself." Leif puffed up a bit. "Solar panels on the roof keep our energy bills to under one hundred dollars a month. We're a zero-waste facility too. We compost almost everything."

"Wow. A long way from sleeping on a futon and

playing Frisbee golf all day." She paused. Stuck her nose up in the air. "I've been trying to get ahold of you."

"I know. I've actively been avoiding you." He leaned farther back in his seat and spread his legs wide. *Dick.* This was not her Leif. Her Leif watched *The Blair Witch Project* stoned in his underwear. His top three values were: unbanking, tiny houses, and Hacky Sack. Her Leif hated Ronald Reagan. Ate burritos in hot tubs and had a friend called Mustache whose real name he did not know. Her Leif always made sure the front door was locked, the windows too—mostly because he feared someone might steal his stash. But it made Mika feel safe. And he didn't mind that she liked to keep their bedroom door open when they had sex. One of her quirks, Leif always thought, like how she hated the song "Return of the Mack"—who doesn't love that song? And whenever she got fired from a job, her Leif would put on clothes that were too small for him and dance around the apartment singing "fat guy in a little coat." This was new Leif. New Leif wore tailored jeans and stacked leather bracelets and drank green juice. New Leif probably spent most of his time working out while polishing his anger toward his ex like a wicked dagger.

She fluffed up her tone. "I need a favor."

Leif blinked at her. "No."

She waited for him to elaborate. And waited. So, not going to happen.

"Have a nice day." He picked his phone up from the desk and started to scroll through it.

"Leif." Mika worked hard to keep her voice steady. "You owe me. For Puerto Rico."

He dropped his phone and pressed a hand to his fine T-shirt-covered chest. Did Leif have pecs now? "I owe you?" The rise in his voice made Mika flinch. "How so?"

Anger shot through Mika as sharp and hot as electricity. "I transported drugs for you," she hissed. At the airport, he'd thrust the baggie at her, eyes glittering like someone who had discovered something new and entirely unknown, something that would change the course of the world itself. *Just put them in your bag, babe. Please, this could be the key to getting my business off the ground—a new strain. We could be rich.* And she'd done it. Sweating through security and the whole flight.

"Seeds," Leif said as if offended, as if she was overreacting. "They were seeds." He ran a hand through his hair. Shook his head. Gathered himself.

Once home, Leif had been moody, pouty. *You never support my dreams,* he'd said.

Flummoxed, Mika answered, *But I carried seeds for you.*

Leif devolved to downright petulant. *But you didn't want to. I don't think I can be with someone who isn't on my side.*

Are you kidding? Mika spat out, thunderstruck. *You're breaking up with me because I transported drugs for you but didn't want to?* It went very bad very quickly from there. So maybe she'd accused his parents of being first cousins. Then when that didn't cut deep enough, she'd called his dreams stupid. *Why do you have such a hard-on for tiny houses?* she'd said, stuffing her clothes into plastic garbage bags with hurricane force. She'd called Hana to pick her up. *You'll never open a weed store. It's absurd. Thirty-two and still chasing rainbows.*

At least I have dreams, he'd said.

On her way out, she'd slipped the seeds that meant so much to Leif in her pocket, then filmed herself flushing them down the toilet. She sent the video to Leif. He sent a single word back—Bitch. To which she replied, Fuck off immediately and forever, Leif. And that's where they left things.

Shame burned Mika's face. She smoothed her hands over her knees. "Look, I'm sorry I implied your parents were first cousins and . . . for everything else. I realize

now how unsuited we were for each other." Their relationship had been like a minor traffic accident. They'd
rear-ended each other, then been bound together in a
way neither had ever intended. They weren't built to
last. Most of the time, Leif had been high (sometimes
he'd take pills too). Mika had been emotionally closed
off. Leif didn't know about Penny, but she was always
there, a plate of glass between them. He sensed it from
time to time. When Mika would go silent. When she'd
stare vacantly into a pot or pan, burning food. But she
couldn't bring herself to tell him. Let him see all those
dark spaces within her. What would he think? Anyway,
Leif wanted to be numb; Mika already was. She hadn't
felt alive since . . . well, for a long time.

"You're right about that." He shook his head, sig-
naling one thousand regrets.

They sat for a moment. Silence, thick and heavy,
settled in the room. "I need your help," she said at last.
Her stomach dropped. He had her where he wanted
her, belly up and waving a white flag of surrender. If
he said no again, she'd go home and concoct a new story
to tell Penny. *Leif was in a boating accident. He's missing at sea, presumed dead. It's sad, but I'll move on.
Do you know any single male thirty-somethings?* But
then again, she wanted Penny to see her with Leif. To
see Mika loved by someone. Worthy of their affection.

"Sixteen years ago, I gave a baby up for adoption." The words were out before she could snatch them back.

She stared at him. Tried to read his face. The muscle in his jaw worked. At length, he stood abruptly and grabbed his keys from the desk.

"Please, Leif." Mika stood, blocking his exit.

He peered down at her. "C'mon, Mika." His voice was velvet and way too nice. "I haven't eaten. Let's go get a bite. My treat."

Mika was rendered speechless. She didn't know what to do with this new Leif. Didn't know what to do with herself. "Okay," she said uncertainly.

His mouth turned up, a cross between a rake's smile and old Leif's. "Thought so. You never turn down a free meal."

She hated it when he was right.

• • •

Leif guided Mika to a diner down the street. She ordered a double stack of pancakes and a side of bacon. Leif had a salad, no dressing, and seemed confused when they didn't have bone broth. In between bites, she told Leif about Penny, about the lies. All of it. When she finished, Leif picked up his glass of water, drinking and watching her over the rim. "Well?" Mika tore apart her napkin, balling the pieces up and lining them up along the edge of the table like tiny soldiers.

He placed the water down, wiped a hand across his face. "Jesus, give me a minute. You've hit me with a lot of information. I always felt like you were hiding something." Leif processed things out loud. "I thought maybe you weren't into me and were into Hana . . ."

Mika raised a mystified brow at him. He was serious. He couldn't be serious. "Really? That was your go-to? That's been living in your head this whole time?" Such a guy thing to assume. *She's not into me, so she must be a lesbian.* "Please tell me your ego isn't that fragile."

Faint pink lines slashed his cheeks. "You're right. Sorry. But it wasn't all in my head, though, right? You weren't into Hana, but you relied on her in a way you never relied on me."

"That's true, I guess." Mika turned to Hana when times were hard. Every year around Penny's birthday, Mika would pack up. *Girls' trip,* she'd say. Then spend the week at Hana's, ignoring Leif's phone calls and opening herself to the unfairness of life. The inexplicable sorrow.

"What about, I mean, can I ask about Penny's biological father? Does he know about her?"

"He doesn't get to know about her," she said sharply.

"Okay," Leif said carefully, watching her.

"He's not the issue," Mika said in a tumbled rush. "The issue is Penny, and she's coming to town, and she thinks you're my adoring boyfriend."

"Mika," Leif said, with such naked grief on his face, Mika had to turn away lest she become undone. The waitress brought the check. Leif withdrew a wad of cash from his wallet and set it on the tray. "I need some air." He walked out, Mika catching the door and chasing after him as he went. This part of Twenty-Third wasn't too busy. A bicyclist shot by. A mom meandered past with a toddler.

"Leif," she said as he paused at the corner. "I can't do this without you." Her throat bobbed. "I need you . . . I need *this*."

Five whole agonizing seconds he stared at her, head cocked to the side, eyes searching. "Alright," he said, although it sounded very much the opposite. "I'll do it."

Mika smiled ear to ear. "You will?"

"For the record, this goes against my better judgment." He opened his hands. "But if it means that much to you . . ."

"It does. More than anything."

"Tell me what I have to do then."

She gave him the date and time, and he wrote it down on his phone. "Maybe wear a suit or something. I'll send you a write-up with everything I've told

Penny. But the highlights are: we're madly in love, I'm starting up my own gallery, and you're in agriculture, but I didn't specify which type." She paused. "Then I can make excuses for you the rest of their visit."

He sighed. "Okay. Done."

"Also, you took me to *Hamilton* opening night." She paused. "We met the cast."

"Wow."

"It was super romantic. You surprised me, and after, we kissed in Times Square."

"I'm impressed with myself."

She squinted at him. "It's going to be okay."

Leif spun his keys. "Chances are fifty-fifty this explodes in your face." He tongued his cheek. "What are you doing for a gallery space?"

"I don't have that part figured out yet. I thought I'd tell Penny it's being renovated or something."

"She's going to want to see it."

"I don't know." Mika flicked a hand. "I can tell her there is asbestos or something." How easy was it to lie now? Too easy. She consoled herself with the thought that the lies weren't significant. It was the love she and Penny shared. That was real. That's what mattered the most.

"I might have a space for you. It's a place I own in North Portland . . . a warehouse. I thought I'd use it as a grow house. But then all these artists started opening up studios down the street because the rent was cheap. I decided to go with what the universe was telling me and flip it to studios." Mika blinked, surprised—an industrial zone turned artist lair. Leif scratched the back of his head. "Anyway, a buddy of mine is an artist, and he's been using the space. Would probably let you display his work if you wanted."

Without thinking, Mika flung her arms around Leif. "Thank you." She pressed her face into his chest. He still used the same soap. But he didn't have the bit of fat around his midsection anymore. She missed his love handles. He'd confessed once kids made fun of him in school—pinching and poking at his sides. She should've told him how much she loved his body. How the sex was always better when your partner was a little flawed. It made her less inhibited. She didn't mind Leif seeing all her jiggly parts then.

"You're welcome." He returned the hug with one arm.

Mika pulled back and squinted against the sunlight. "Hey, do you remember that time in Whole Foods when you asked the checkout person to type in the bar codes because you didn't want lasers touching your food?"

"I do." His eyes glinted with humor.

"That's the most annoying you've ever been."

He stepped away from her. "I'm going to have Adelle send you some literature on lasers and food handling."

"Do that." Mika was halfway down the street before she turned and yelled, "And while you're at it, tell her the kanji on her arm means 'weasel.'" She gave Leif a jaunty wave. "Let me know about the gallery."

Chapter Eight

"Wakey, wakey." The next Saturday morning Mika stood over Hana's bed, holding two cups.

Hana groaned. "Go away."

"Get up, lots to do today," she chirped. "I've got a whole life to fake and only"—Mika checked her wrist where there was no watch—"eight days to do it. I. Am. Freaking. Out. Also, your boob is out."

Hana grumbled and sat up, adjusting her shirt to cover herself. "I'm putting a lock on my door. Are you wearing overalls?"

"You like?" Mika posed.

"I do not. We need to do something about your wardrobe before Penny comes. I don't think your Walmart chic is going to cut it."

Mika handed Hana a cup. "Not to worry. Charlie is going to outfit me in her best I-am-a-kindergarten-teacher business casual clothing—aka my Ann Taylor nightmare. Clothes make the woman. Or unmake her. Let's go. We're about to embark on a no-expenses-paid trip to cleaning the house."

Hana took a drink and spit it back into the cup. "What the fuck?"

"It's tepid apple kombucha. I got it from the goat yoga studio down the street."

"It's disgusting."

"It's what Mika 2.0 is drinking now. She is very into probiotics and healthy living. She cannot get enough bicycling, especially the tiny seats that implant themselves in your rear end. She enjoys those the most." Mika set her cup down, squeezing it between a bread maker in a box and four dead plants. She stooped and picked up a T-shirt, shaking it out. "This shirt smells like smoke and bad decisions." She tossed it to Hana. "Put it on."

"Please stop referring to yourself in the third person." Hana threw an arm over her eyes.

"Hana," Mika said mock-seriously. "Let's take life by the short and curlies."

"Oh my god, never use that term again."

"C'mon, I have donuts in the kitchen."

That got Hana moving. She wandered from her room, shirt sans pants. She leaned against the counter and nibbled on a maple bar. "What's the plan?"

"Charlie and Tuan are on their way over with a truck. And so is Hayato because he doesn't have anything better to do. We're going to start by—" Mika searched for the correct phrase. *Performing an exorcism? Burning everything to the ground?* "Decluttering. Then this afternoon, we'll work a bit in the yard. We won't get it all done today."

Hana put her maple bar down on a saucer she'd purchased from an estate sale across the street. She touched a box, curled her hands over a stack of *Architectural Digest* magazines. They had her ex-girlfriend Nicole's name on them. "I don't know," she said, a stubborn edge to her voice.

Mika gently pried Hana's fingers from the magazine stack. "Maybe we start small, like with the shoes in the oven?"

Hana inhaled through her nose. "Okay. Okay."

Mika coaxed Hana into putting on pants, and twenty minutes later, Charlie and Tuan arrived in a bright green truck: B.J.'S JUNK AND HAUL. Hayato appeared around that time too, saying something about moving and how it was the worst. They didn't correct him. Hana had been living in the house for years.

They worked through the day. Cleaning out the fridge of petrified meatloaf, chunky milk, and congealed kimchi. Opening boxes, unpacking them. Placing items to keep on the cleared kitchen table and items to discard in the truck Tuan had borrowed. It was more of a mess than when they started. Tuan installed a bicycle rack, and Charlie brought clothes for Mika to wear, plus some bike outfits.

"Penny isn't going to go through my drawers," Mika said as Charlie stuffed jerseys and Lycra shorts into her dresser.

Charlie held up a handful of garments. "This is confidence spandex."

When the house grew too warm and stifling, they moved outside to the lawn. Charlie slapped on a pair of garden gloves and started weeding. Tuan and Hayato pruned the giant oak in the front yard—each fall, it dropped so many dead and dirty leaves, the neighbors complained.

Mika wandered to the backyard to find Hana. "Charlie wants to run to the garden store and pick up some annuals? At least, I think that's what she said. I'm assuming she meant flowers. Want to come with? What are you doing?" Hana had her back to Mika and a hose in her hand. Mika circled around to Hana's front, dehydrated grass crunching underfoot. "I'm pretty sure that tree is dead." Hana was showering a small, brown, malnourished maple.

"Nicole and I planted it. It was the first thing we did when we moved in."

Mika eyed it warily. "I don't know if it's salvageable."

Hana shook her head. A tiny crease between her eyebrows. Sadness. "I'm going to love it back to life."

Charlie tromped toward them. "Forget the garden store." She pulled off her gloves. "I'm beat. Anyone ready for a drink?"

Hana dropped the hose. "I'll get the glasses."

At the end of the day, muscles Mika didn't even know she had ached. She lay in bed, watching her ceiling fan turn in lazy circles, didn't even have the energy to take off her shoes—her mother would die. The kitchen and family room were a mess, but all the boxes were gone. Progress. Her phone chimed. She fished around her bed for it. Two texts. The first from Leif. An address followed by: Stanley is cool with you displaying his work, but he's working in there this week, so you won't be able to get into the space just yet.

The other message was from Penny. So excited to see you, just over a week to go! FaceTime tomorrow?

Mika replied, Yes, FaceTime tomorrow. Super excited too. Spent today getting my place ready for you to see. Mika's eyes fluttered closed. Her phone beeped. Penny again. I hope you're not going to any trouble. All Mika could do was laugh.

• • •

Five excruciating days later, Hana, Charlie, and Mika gathered for dinner in the newly cleaned house. The floors had been scrubbed. The walls painted. The lawn had been mowed, and little flowering plants bordered the walkway to the front door. Tuan had even repaired the crack in the ceiling. They'd arranged the furniture around the fireplace and set pictures on the mantle of Mika all over the world— doctored by the tech guy at Charlie's school. There was a cozy armchair you could imagine reading books in on a rainy day. Her bedroom had a fresh white duvet and a little crystal lamp with a dish for jewelry on the nightstand.

The kitchen counters were cleared, and it was airy and light, with a big window overlooking the backyard. They'd strung the fairy lights up again and sprayed down an old picnic table, setting it with hurricane vases and white candles, re-creating Mika's Instagram picture. New gleaming small appliances graced the granite countertop. All thanks to Hana's late-night QVC purchases. *I was making Nicole a home*, she'd said as they plugged them in. A delicate green fern and a white orchid adorned the middle of the dining table. It was all fresh-baked bread and nights by the fire and sunny days making jam. Mika's heart lifted into a smile when seeing it. She could have raised a baby here. Could have come here after traveling the world or a hard day at work in her gallery. The process reminded Mika of when she'd been in high school. She used to buy paintings from the thrift store because she couldn't afford new canvases. She'd strip them down or paint over them. Create something new. Something better.

"Not bad, not bad at all." Charlie slumped back against the couch. Tonight, they were having pad thai and pho. One last hurrah before Penny came.

In between bites of noodles, Mika glued pictures into a scrapbook for Penny. Charlie and Mika had spread out photographs on the coffee table to pick through them. Hana had been oddly distant the last hour, focusing on her wine, opting to drink her dinner.

"Oh! Definitely put this one in." Charlie handed Mika a picture.

The glossy snapshot was of her at Penny's age. Sixteen and in front of an easel, a charcoal sketch behind her. Now, Mika rubbed her fingertips together, remembering the gritty charcoal between her fingers. How good it felt to create. That burst as if you were going to come out of your skin. Mika placed the photo back on the table. At the portrait, Hiromi had brought her eyes close to the paper and sniffed. *You drew this? You didn't trace it?* Mika had spent a good portion of her childhood convincing her mother she could draw, then her first college year persuading Hiromi she deserved to. "Not this one."

Charlie frowned. "Okay . . ." she said carefully. To Charlie, it was a mystery—why didn't Mika paint anymore? Only Hana knew the truth. "You were so good."

Were. The operative word. All that, the painting, the traveling, was a ghost life now. Something that could have been but wasn't ever meant to be. "Is there one of my parents?" Mika asked.

Hana refilled her wine.

"Here." Charlie handed over another photograph. This one of Mika, age six, with Hiromi and Shige, posing around a brand-new box television. Shige had bought it to watch Kristi Yamaguchi skate in the Olympics. Three years later, they would watch the Supreme Truth terrorist attacks in Japan on it—Hiromi stayed up all night calling relatives, weeping with them. Mika's hands were folded neatly in front of her in the photograph, and her hair sported the classic Asian kid bowl cut. Behind her, Hiromi wore a pair of acid-wash mom jeans and gold glasses with a rose-colored tint, her hand clutching Mika's shoulder like a warning—*Do not go far from me.*

Mika placed the snapshot in the scrapbook. "Perfect." Penny might ask about her biological grandparents. Mika would make up some excuse—*They're on a cruise, maybe you'll meet them next time.* Except Mika knew that, despite what Penny might believe at this moment, there would be no next time. Her daughter was coming to meet her biological mother, get answers, and then she would become caught up in her real life again and leave Mika behind. Mika knew enough about herself to know she was only to be loved for a season, not a lifetime.

There were many photographs of Hana and Mika in high school. Mika stared at one. Of the two downtown. Hana's arm slung around Mika, protesters behind them, hands clutching a SÍ SE PUEDE sign. They'd skipped school to attend a farm worker demonstration. Mika wasn't sure what they were protesting—it was more Hana's thing—but it felt good to yell. To chant. To make a scene. Hana had helped Mika find her voice. It was loud and powerful. She stuck the photo in the album.

Next, Mika picked up a Polaroid Hana had snapped of her. It was her first day of college, and she was smiling as if it were Christmas morning. Hiromi thought

Mika would major in business and live at home, but art and the dorms had always been her intention.

Hana and Mika had filled out their financial aid and housing paperwork together and received Pell Grants. The night before she moved into the dorms, Mika had watched the clock, waiting for nine p.m. to strike, the hour Hiromi usually turned in. When her mother was the most tired. The least likely to be up for a fight. As her father shut off the television, Mika steeled her nerves and announced that she was moving out *and* majoring in art. Hands balled into fists, she'd been ready to set her life down for her dream.

Ungrateful, Hiromi had called her. She was in her house robe. Shige wouldn't look at Mika. *This girl thinks she's going to be a painter*, Hiromi had spat out to Shige. Then turned her wrath on Mika. *You'll never be an artist. You'll waste your life. Go.* Hiromi had flicked a hand at Mika, the vibration of her mother's anger so heavy it might have knocked the teeth from Mika's mouth. *You hate it here so much, then leave. Maybe I'll finally get some sleep.* Mika had packed and spent the night at Hana's. It had rained. Mika swiped away tears and comforted herself that she didn't want to stay at home anyway, waste another moment living with a woman who wished to annihilate her. She had aspirations of grandeur. A girl broken and breaking out.

The dorm room was the first time Mika felt like a real artist, the dingy walls, the hissing radiator, the wardrobe bursting with black clothes. She was always five minutes early for everything. God, she remembered always watching the clock, unable to wait for her real life to begin. She paid so much attention to the minutes and hours. In fact, she knew the exact time Penny was conceived. Had turned her head and seen the clock on the nightstand. 12:01 a.m. The digital numbers the same color red as the dot a sniper uses to mark their target. But Mika didn't pay too much attention to time anymore. She let it happily pass by. She pressed the photo into the album, casting a thumbprint over her shining face with a sigh.

The last photograph they included was of Mika, seven months pregnant with Penny. She was smiling and curled into an armchair like a small animal, hair swept up into a pair of space buns.

Hana swirled the wine in her glass, something percolating in her facial expression. "Excuse me," she said, then disappeared out the back door.

Of course, Charlie and Mika raced to follow her. They watched Hana through the window as she stomped to the sad malnourished maple, the one she had planted with Nicole. She bent, grabbed the trunk with both hands, and pulled. It didn't budge.

"Do you think we should get her a shovel?" Charlie whispered.

"No, I think she's having a moment," said Mika.

Hana let out some sort of weird, sad, half battle cry. She placed her hands around the trunk again and pulled and pulled until finally, the dead roots snapped and gave way. Hana tumbled back with the force of it, landing on her ass. She sat for a moment, chest heaving, cheeks flushed, and eyes wild. Then she glanced up, connecting eyes with Mika and Charlie through the window.

Charlie held up her wineglass. So did Mika. They clinked them together, a silent cheers. "To new beginnings," Charlie said.

"To high hopes," Mika added.

Chapter Nine

On Sunday, Mika waited at the Portland airport in baggage claim. Five times she'd checked her phone already, tracking Penny and Thomas's flight. It had been early, landed twenty minutes ago. But no sign of them yet. What if Penny had changed her mind? What if Thomas had changed Penny's mind? She scanned the crowds. A young kid, parents smiling behind him, ran toward an older couple. "Grandpa, Grandma!" he cried. A slim guy dropped his duffel and embraced some dude in a beanie. A dark-haired girl with a bounce in her step walked alongside a tall, handsome man. It all came together in her mind, a car crash of a revelation.

Penny and Thomas. They were here. Finally.

Mika's smile widened. A warm feeling spread inside

her, serotonin peaking. Penny saw Mika and raced forward. Mika thought of movies she'd seen in which children take their first steps, parents holding out their arms. Penny stopped short of Mika, and they stared at each other. *There should be some other music playing*, Mika thought. Piano. A love song. The day suddenly took on a hazy, soft quality as if in a dream.

Penny spoke first. "Can I hug you?" she asked shyly.

"Yes, please." Mika opened her arms, and Penny stepped forward into them. She kept her touch light even though she wanted to squeeze, to hold on tight, to never let go again, to live there. Mika was filled with so much desire to love she might burst.

Thomas sauntered over to them, and it was like a dark cloud had shifted over the sun.

Penny pulled away. Thomas nudged his daughter. "This is the first time I've ever seen you speechless," he said, warmth in his tone. Maybe he wasn't so bad after all.

Mika forced herself to make eye contact with him. She should have braced herself. Sharp cheekbones. Light green eyes. Messy dark hair on the longer side but trimmed nicely, with the slightest hint of salt and pepper. Thomas was attractive. *Hot*. So much no. Nope. Never. Mika chastised herself. Feeling deeply uncomfortable, her face grew warm.

"Thom, so nice to meet you. Mika." She stuck out her hand.

"Thomas," he corrected, all that warmth for Penny bleeding from his voice. They shook hands, his grip firm and sure—Mika's clammy and soft, dead fish–like.

"I'm so terrified and thrilled right now. I'm not even sure where to start." Penny's nails were short and painted bright pink. She wore a ring on her right middle finger and twisted it.

Mika turned her attention to Penny, still feeling the heat from Thomas's stare. "Let's get your luggage and some food. Sound good?"

"Perfect," Penny said.

Mika smiled. So did Penny. It was like looking in a mirror. Like seeing Mika at age sixteen, seeing herself young and hopeful, seeing her *before.*

• • •

You sure you don't want some help?" Thomas shifted impatiently in the parking garage. Cars beeped, and engines started. A faint scent of exhaust clung to the air. The weather was okay, though, the sun shining. It was one of those days that made it hard to be in a bad mood. Well, hard for some people. Thomas seemed to have perfected quiet and brooding no matter the weather. *He's a real trouper that way.*

"No, I've got it." Mika fumbled with the keys. She'd borrowed Charlie's car, a used Volvo, to drive Penny and Thomas around in. It was an upgrade from her own rusted Corolla with duct tape holding together a side mirror after an unfortunate collision with a tree. Only, the battery seemed to have spontaneously died on the key fob, and Mika had to do things the old-fashioned way, i.e., use the actual keys. She'd managed to unlock the doors but couldn't find the trunk release. "It's fine."

"Yes. You've said that six times already." Thomas shifted on his feet.

"I just never use the trunk, that's all," Mika said, half inside the car, bent over the front seat and acutely aware her ass was in the air, and both Penny and Thomas were watching her. "Hold on, I think I've almost got it." But really, she had removed her phone and was texting Charlie. How do you open your fucking trunk?

"Here, let me." Thomas's voice was closer. Mika put her phone facedown and straightened. They were nearly chest to chest. Thomas's mouth twisted in the dimness of the garage. "May I?"

"Oh, um, sure, I guess," Mika said, visibly embarrassed with herself. She shuffled back next to Penny near the trunk.

Thomas folded his long body and peered into the

cab. "Here it is," he said way too quickly. Through the back window, Mika watched him pull a lever. The trunk popped open.

"He's awesome with cars," Penny said. Thomas came back, a smirk on his face, exuding superiority.

He eased open the trunk. "Thought you said you never used this?" he drawled.

"What?" Mika came to his side, careful to keep a foot of distance between them. *Great.* Charlie had forgotten to clean out the trunk, which contained: an emergency roadside kit, some dry cleaning, and a box full of CDs, marked "To donate."

Thomas picked a CD from the top of the pile. "Slow jams, music to make love to," the cover read. He tilted his head at her, squinting his eyes the tiniest bit.

Mika plucked the CD from his hands and threw it back on the pile. She shut the trunk. "I think we'll just use the back seat for your bags."

A tiny pouty dent formed between Thomas's eyebrows. "Put the luggage in the back seat? The wheels are dirty."

"Bags in the back seat are fine. I'll sit with them. I fit easily into small spaces," Penny said, sharing a smile with Mika. They were the same height, just under five-two. Mika didn't know how tall Caroline was, but

Thomas was over six feet at least. Now it was Mika's turn to feel smug. *I gave her that, her height, her slight frame,* she thought.

Thomas made a noise in his throat. "Great."

"Great," Penny said as Thomas began to place the bags in the back seat. "Let's go to lunch. Fair warning, I've been on a wicked training regimen, and I am taking a break. I'll be playing it fast and loose with food today." She rubbed her hands together, an I-came-to-play smile on her face. "Get ready to see some things."

• • •

Thomas visually shuddered when Mika pulled up to the curb, parking near Cartlandia, a mecca of food trucks. Seeing this, her happiness index level upped. *His favorite meal is probably untoasted bread.*

"I think there's something for everyone here," Mika said as they stepped from the vehicle. The air was spiced with curry, miso, and roasted meats. Over thirty food trucks were permanently parked in the space. White tents had been pitched with folding tables underneath.

Penny and Mika strode forward, and Thomas followed behind, arms folded—a sign of his peaceful protest. They agreed to take a reconnaissance lap, scoping out what might be good. Penny and Mika happily chattered between reading menus. Turns out, Penny *hated* Jack Kerouac. She'd downloaded a copy of *On the Road* and started reading on the flight.

"I'm sorry," she said. They'd stopped in front of the Ball-Z food truck, which served up ball-shaped dishes of the world. "I mean, I get why you probably liked it. But he's super sexist. The representation of women is terrible except when he talks about his mother, whom he seems to respect."

"But didn't you like the energy in the words? He wrote the novel in three weeks. Isn't that amazing? It's so visceral. It made me regret ever standing still." *On the Road* made Mika want to explore the world. Have rolling bones and chase her dreams. "It's what originally inspired me to travel and study art."

"It's just not inclusive enough for me. The whole Beat Generation was basically a bunch of white men having a serious bromance."

"Point taken."

"But I'm glad it worked for you."

"It served its purpose."

They moved along, Thomas a foot or two behind. Mika pictured a cartoon she once saw, where a rain cloud trailed the main character. Back where they started, Penny tapped her lips. "Do you think the ramen is good?"

"Oh, it's the best. I eat it all the time. I'll have the same. Why don't I get it, and you two find a seat? Thomas, what do you want?"

"I'll take whatever you recommend." She'd recommend something for Thomas, alright. You couldn't go wrong with ramen. But maybe she'd ask for double ajitsuke tamago, a soft-boiled egg soaked in mirin. It was delicious, but the custard yolk might be off-putting to Thomas. He shifted, removing his wallet from his back pocket, and then offered Mika a couple of crisp twenties.

Mika put up a hand. "My treat." No way she'd let Thomas pay for her. The cash hung in the air between them. Mika thought Thomas might try to wrestle the bills into her hand. "I insist." Mika fluffed up her tone and smiled overbrightly. "Be right back." She scooted off.

Mika ordered and handed over her card to be swiped. She couldn't afford the meal and could practically hear the change plopping from her bank account. *Should've taken Thomas's money.* It wouldn't be the first time she'd cut off her nose to spite her face. The order came up fast, and Mika balanced everything on a tray. Thomas and Penny had found seats under the tent, their backs to Mika. She paused out of eyesight but within earshot.

"Isn't this fun?" Penny asked Thomas, voice full of

trepidation. Mika recognized the tone, the one you used with your parents when you desperately wanted them to approve. She'd used it on Hiromi many times. *Mama, I drew you a caterpillar, do you like it?* Mika, at age seven. *Hmm, looks more like a worm, I think*, Hiromi had replied.

"I'm enjoying spending time with you," he said placidly.

"But not the food trucks?"

"What do you want me to say? I am convinced they're on wheels so they can make a fast getaway when the health inspector comes. In fact, I bet I can look up their food safety rating online."

Penny giggled. "Please, don't." She waited for a beat. "Are you still angry with me?"

Thomas put his phone down and tapped his long fingers against the table. No ring on his left finger, Mika noted. "No, I'm not mad. I wasn't really mad before either. I just wish you hadn't lied to me."

"But are, like, your feelings hurt?"

"It's not your job to worry about my feelings. It's my job to worry about yours." Well, that was kind of nice. "What do you think of her?" Her, he meant Mika.

"I like her so much. And it's nice. We like the same things." At this, Mika lightened with the promise of a wish suddenly fulfilled. She wanted to be friends with

Penny. It's what she had wanted with her own mother. Warmth. Comradery. A place to rest, to come home to.

"So, she's like a sixteen-year-old girl?" Thomas asked drily. Mika shifted on her feet, the tray getting heavy, but couldn't bring herself to interrupt them. She felt like an intruder—on the outside looking in.

"Dad—"

Thomas cleared his throat. "Sorry. Go on."

"I don't know. We talk about books and boys and our dreams."

"I want to talk to you about those things."

"It's just not the same." Penny shifted. "Look, one mom died, and the other gave me away. I have serious issues. I need something . . . someone."

"You've got me," said Thomas.

Penny flicked a hand. "Typical men, thinking a penis solves everything."

Thomas coughed into his fist and patted his chest. "Penny, please."

"Just try to lighten up a little. Be cool."

"I feel like I've been very pleasant. But don't you think it's odd she didn't know how to pop the trunk of her car?"

"Ready to eat?" Mika cut in. She set the tray down on the table, and Thomas cracked a faint smile.

Mika placed bowls of steaming ramen in front of each

of them. Penny hesitated, eyes bouncing between the fork and wooden hashi. Finally, she chose the fork with a furious blush. Mika pulled her lip between her teeth and set down the hashi she'd grabbed, opting for the fork as Penny had. "These always give me splinters."

"Yeah?" Penny's eyes flashed cautiously to Mika's, then back to her bowl. She had a smattering of freckles on the bridge of her nose that spread into the apples of her cheeks. Penny's father had freckles on his arms.

"Oh yeah, these cheap hashi are the worst."

"Hashi?" Penny asked.

"Chopsticks in Japanese."

Penny seemed inordinately pleased by this. "Hashi."

Thomas flexed his hands, veins protruding. "You know, I think I changed my mind. I'm getting the curry too. What the hell, right?" He stood. "Pen, how about an oatmeal chocolate chip cookie, your favorite?"

Penny nodded. "Sure, that sounds good."

"I'll be right back." Thomas squeezed Penny's shoulder, then leaned down and placed a kiss on her shiny dark hair.

She swatted him away. "Stahp."

"You want anything?" Thomas asked Mika.

So much, so much, Mika thought. But she shook her head and said, "I'm good. Nothing for me, thanks."

ADOPTION ACROSS AMERICA

National Office

56544 W 57th Ave. Suite 111

Topeka, KS 66546

(800) 555-7794

Dear Mika,

It's been too long since we've chatted. I do hope you're doing well. Once again, please find the enclosed requisite items in regard to the adoption agreement between you, Mika Suzuki (the birth mother), and Thomas and Caroline Calvin (the adoptive parents) for Penelope Calvin (the adoptee). Contents include:

- An annual letter from the adoptive parents describing the adoptee's development and yearly progress
- Photographs and/or other memorabilia

As always, I'm here should you have questions.

All the best,

Monica Pearson

Adoption Coordinator

Dear Mika,

Ten! Penny is ten, and I am pretty sure our little fourth-grader has one purpose in life, and that is to create chaos. Two months ago, she decided to walk everywhere backward. And now, most recently, she has decided to take up baking. Inspired, I'm sure, from watching *The Great British Baking Show.*

She sends Thomas to the store with lists of groceries, with dreams of whipping up all sorts of things—chocolate chess pie, pecan shortbread tea cakes, something called a caramel-apple skillet buckle? You name it, she wants to try it. Every afternoon, as soon as she gets home from school, she is preheating ovens and setting mixing bowls on the counter. She then leaves the sink piled high with dishes and the floor coated in flour. We critique what she makes as if we were on the show. *It's a nice bake, a little soft in the middle, but the presentation is excellent, and the flavor is good.* I have to admit, Penny is a *terrible* baker. But we eat whatever she makes and smile so wide our cheeks hurt. But what can I say? I am a sucker for Penny. I always want her to follow her dreams. Pic of her most recent creation included. I think it was supposed to be a hedgehog cake?

Big hugs,
Caroline

Chapter Ten

The next morning Mika waited for Penny and Thomas in their hotel lobby. She stood by a velvet couch that probably cost more than Hana's mortgage and became acutely aware of her chipped fingernails and her hair that hadn't been trimmed in who knows how long. The elevators dinged, the doors opened. Penny and Thomas emerged.

"Hey," Penny said brightly, skipping toward her.

"Morning." Thomas shuffled over. He and Penny both wore sweatshirts, jeans, and tennis shoes.

"You ready?" Mika buttoned up her coat and headed for the door. "I thought we'd walk. Rain isn't forecast until this afternoon," she said, but mostly it was because she couldn't afford the gas and didn't want to pay twice for parking. "The museum is only a few blocks from here." As she slipped through the revolving door, her phone buzzed. Mika checked the caller. *Hiromi.* She declined, sent her mother to voicemail, and slipped the phone back into her pocket.

A few steps from the hotel, Penny said, "It's so pretty here." A grating wind swooped by from the Willamette River, and all three of them hunched, letting it roll over their backs. "I wandered around a little bit last night, and there are all these lights wrapped around the trees in the square."

Thomas furrowed his brow. "You left the hotel?"

"Just to go to the mall across the street," Penny said breezily.

"Penny—" Thomas started.

"I bought these socks." Penny stopped in front of an art deco building with a set of mythical-looking iron gates. She pulled up her pant leg. Blue socks with cat faces adorned her delicate ankles. "Cute, right?"

"Very cute," Mika said with a smile.

Thomas glowered at Mika but spoke to Penny. "I would appreciate it if you would tell me the next time you decide to leave the hotel."

Penny was unfazed. She tucked her pant leg back down and said, "Aye-aye," giving Thomas a salute, which made him peer up at the sky in a god-give-me-patience sort of way. They started off again. The red brick of the Portland Art Museum came into sight.

A little farther down the Park Blocks was a college, Mika's alma mater. She could just make out the art building. It wasn't much to look at. A gray cube. But it was a place where beautiful things happened. And Mika had wanted to be a part of it so badly she physically ached. The weather had been similar—static gray sky, moist air—the day she met Marcus Guerrero, a fine arts professor. She'd knocked on his door, yellow slip in hand. He'd answered, paint flecks on his light blue T-shirt, a red bandana holding back his dark hair, a miasma of smoke and coffee clinging to him.

The registrar says I need permission to skip Painting I and II. She thrust the form at him, shifting back and forth on her feet. She'd been braver then. Headstrong. Willing to do anything. Whatever it took.

He stared at her so long and hard she started to turn away. His hand fell from the knob, and he ambled back to his desk to sit in an old office chair with green leather and wooden arms—it had probably been around since the college's inception in the forties. He leaned back, way back. *Alright,* he said. *Show me what you've got.*

Mika swallowed. *What?*

Your portfolio, he said, the slightest accent carving

his speech. Marcus was a legend among the art students. Rumors swirled about him. He was a Gulf vet and kept a Purple Heart in his desk drawer. His father was a famous shipbuilder, and he'd grown up in the Mediterranean on yachts. But really, he had been poor, the son of migrant fruit farmers. He grew up in Florida and spent his youth picking bananas.

I don't have one.

Then paint something. He nodded to the corner of his office. An easel had been crammed between two shelves bursting with palettes, tubes of paint, jars of brushes, turpentine.

Right now? Mika remembered flexing her fingers, feeling queasy.

He stretched, laced his fingers together, and cradled the back of his head. *Right now.*

"Wow." Penny's voice brought Mika back to the present. "You interned here?" she asked, gazing at the building, awestruck.

Mika made a noncommittal noise in her throat that passed for affirmation. Then she added, "Right after college. Not for very long. And it was years ago. I'm sure everyone I've worked with has moved on."

"So, you had me freshman year of college," Penny said, piecing together Mika's fake timeline. "Then graduated and went on to work at the museum. That's pretty impressive. This girl in my class, Taylor Hines, had mono freshman year of high school and had to repeat it. But you had a baby and managed school and a career still."

Mika flushed at the compliment. What would Thomas and Penny think if they knew the truth? It had taken Mika eight years to graduate. She flunked freshman year and lost her Pell Grant, then had to go crawling back to her parents for help. *Good news,* she said shortly after everything had happened, *I've switched my major from art to business. Can I have some money?* Society applauded doing the impossible. Trying hard. Pulling yourself up by your bootstraps. It's the American way. But Mika couldn't reach her feet. Plus, there was an expectation that Mika's life was better without Penny. That the sacrifice had been worth it.

At the ticket booth, Mika and Thomas both reached for their wallets. "You bought lunch yesterday, and you're having us over for dinner tonight. I insist." He paused, waiting, staring Mika into compliance. This didn't work on Penny, Mika had observed, but worked on Mika rather well.

"Um, sure, I guess. Thank you." She tucked her wallet away, a little relieved. She still didn't have a job.

Thomas purchased tickets, and they were given

a map of the galleries, though Mika didn't need it. Inside, she inhaled, finding comfort in the smell, which she couldn't quite place but was endemic to buildings this large. She visited the museum regularly. It was so quiet. No place to hide from her thoughts, but it felt safe too. Somewhere she might mourn or dream, then leave it all behind. Having Penny beside her now in this sacred space made Mika feel complete.

They wandered up the marble steps to the European galleries, bypassing the Asian galleries, which, as always, had been stuffed to the sides—museums usually favored dead white men.

She guided Thomas and Penny on a mini-tour, passing a painting of Icarus. Mika often contemplated the mortal who flew so close to the sun that his wax wings melted away. She wondered, if Icarus had known his fate, would he have still done it, flown so high? Would the climb have been worth the fall?

As they paused in front of a Monet, Mika described Impressionism. "See the small, thin, and slightly visible brushstrokes? That's a hallmark of Impressionism. Monet painted outdoors—plein air, it's called, a method to capture the light and essence of the landscape in a single moment." Her arts curriculum in college had included art history courses. Talent wasn't enough. To be an artist, you had to be a sort of keeper too. Had to have studied the greats, learned their techniques. It was a lot like jazz, mastery before improvisation. And like Hiromi in her garden after the last winter frost, Mika had dug in, only to abruptly quit halfway through Impressionism, before she'd even known she was pregnant with Penny.

"It's cracked." Penny scrunched her nose up.

Mika smiled. "Craquelure. It's from the varnish drying out. It happens with age."

Penny wandered off and stopped in front of a Degas. Head tilted up, she gazed at the pastel on paper, sniffled, wiped her nose. Thomas was still entranced with the Monet. Mika wandered to Penny's side. "You okay?" she asked quietly.

Penny kept her head bent. "Yeah. I'm fine. It's just my mom . . . she used to have a lot of silly nicknames for me. She'd say: 'Hey, sugar plum fairy' or 'baby turkey' or 'little dancer.' This reminded me of that." The Degas was of a singular ballet dancer, nimble fingers adjusting the tulle skirt at her waist.

"That's nice." Degas was where Mika had left off in her studies; "little dancer" was what Caroline had called Penny. Mika wondered at the significance of that. An ending and a beginning. If it was all meant to be. Or if she was just searching for a sign . . . grasping at air, like Icarus as he'd fallen.

Penny's smile was faint. "It's a stupid thing for me to cry over."

"I don't think so," Mika whispered. "You can talk about her." Caroline, she meant. "Don't be afraid to. You can talk to me about anything." *I'll always listen. I'll always be here. I'll always believe in you.*

"Thanks." Penny stepped away and found a bench to sit on around the corner. Mika joined her. To passersby, they looked like mother and daughter, Mika thought. Guilt stabbed at her insides. Caroline and Thomas had run the marathon with Penny, while Mika had been on the sidelines. "She was really amazing. She liked Kahlil Gibran and E. E. Cummings. Her wedding band is inscribed with: 'I carry your heart in my heart.'" Penny twisted off the ring she wore so Mika could see the inside of it, the Edwardian font. She shoved the band back on her finger. "But it was hard not having a parent who looked like me, and I feel like I can't say that around my dad because he's still so sad about it all."

Mika's stomach bottomed out. Thomas and Penny were still grieving. "It was hard being adopted by white parents?" Mika asked, focusing on the former rather than the latter.

Penny sat back and swung her legs up, so she sat cross-legged on the bench. "I dunno. My parents tried to do Japanese things with me. They enrolled me in some classes, and we went to festivals in Dayton. But there was always a disconnect. I think they were uncomfortable when people asked questions about us. Like, 'Where'd you get her from?'" Penny paused, picked at one of her nails. "Kids used to make fun of my eyes in elementary school. They'd sing that song from Lady and the Tramp, 'We Are Siamese,' and pull their eyes up."

The ache inside Mika grew worse. It was a kind of beautiful agony, having a child. Feeling their emotions as well as your own. "Assholes."

Penny half smiled. "Sometimes Dayton feels so small, and I feel so big in comparison. Does that make sense?"

"It does," Mika answered right away. She saw herself superimposed on this young person, her daughter. Mika had felt that way in high school too. Bursting at the seams to go to college and live on campus, out from under her mother's thumb, away from Hiromi's destructive perfectionism. Now, she wanted to caution Penny. *Move forward slowly. Don't take such big steps. It's not a race. You don't have to have it all figured out right now.*

"Plus," Penny said, "everywhere I go in Dayton, there is a reminder of her, of them, of us as a family.

But we're not a family anymore, or we are, but it's so different, and I'm confused about what it all means. I don't know." Penny scuffed her feet against the shiny floor. A flock of women wearing purple hats passed by, chattering about a Picasso in the next gallery over. "I heard he was a terrible womanizer," one said. Mika watched them go, watched as Thomas rounded the corner.

"Hey. You disappeared," he said, stopping in front of them. "You okay, kiddo?" His brow dipped.

"Fine." Penny's face, her smile, was bright and blinding. *Convincing.* "Better than fine," she added. "Great." She flashed her grin to Mika. And Mika's heart thudded against her chest.

Penny gazed at her with such tenderness, such gratefulness, that something fractured inside of Mika and melded together. Something that had maybe been broken for a long time. If only she could tell the scientists in the world, *Stop studying, I've found the key to fusion.* It lay in the bond between parent and child.

Chapter Eleven

M ika bustled around the kitchen six hours later, cracking open the oven and checking the home-made macaroni and cheese. Leif peered over her shoulder. "Jesus, how much cheese is in that?" The white béchamel sauce had just started to bubble up.

"Over one and a half pounds of cheddar and Gruyère." Another expense. As it turned out, faking your life cost a lot. Mika shut the oven and skirted around Leif to the fridge to get a bin of salad. "I got the recipe off Martha Stewart."

Leif rubbed the curve of his bicep. "Remember when Martha Stewart and Snoop Dogg were friends?" Mika chose not to answer. She dumped the salad into a silver dish. He picked up one of the decorative lemons from a fruit bowl. "Fake," he murmured. He placed it back and turned to Mika. "Do you think I should have dressed up more?" He wore a collared shirt untucked and a pair of jeans.

Mika set down the salad tongs. As if she wasn't nervous enough already, Leif was making it worse. "Leif."

"Whoa. Haven't heard that tone in a long time. Takes me back." He mock-shivered.

Mika narrowed her eyes at him. "Are you high right now?"

Leif huffed. "Of course not. Now that I'm a professional, I can't get high off my own supply."

Mika groaned. "That is your final drug reference for the evening."

"You brought it up," he teased. He lowered his body, bracing his hands on his knees so they were face-to-face. "It's going to be fine. I promise. I memorized all the notes you sent me. And you look great. Very Julia Child about to make a roast chicken."

The tension eased from Mika's shoulders. "Thanks," she said, then eyed the clock on the oven. "They'll be here in twenty minutes."

"So, how are they?" Leif straightened, taking a fake lemon from the bowl and rolling it between his giant palms. "What's she like in person?"

Mika didn't have to think about it. "Amazing. She's amazing." She beamed, dazzled by her daughter. "I'm

excited for you to meet her, actually." Penny was someone Mika wanted to share with others. Maybe that's how
Hiromi felt back when Mika danced, the insane urge to
call people, brag about the person you created. *Everything they do is because of ME.*

"And the dad?"

Mika deflated at the mention of Thomas. "He's
tough. I can't tell if he doesn't like me or if he just doesn't
like the world. It's clear he loves Penny, though." She
thought of him at the food trucks, hands spilling over
with oatmeal chocolate chip cookies, the careful way he
watched his daughter as if he couldn't stand the thought
of her ever hurting.

The doorbell rang. "Shit, they're early." Mika stared
at Leif like he knew what to do. "I still need to finish the
salad."

"You get the door. I'll finish up." He shooed her away,
and Mika ran to the door, forcing herself to slow a few
steps before the threshold. She tucked her hair behind
her ear and pasted on a bright smile before swinging
open the door.

Thomas and Penny stood on the front step, their Uber
pulling away behind them. Thomas wore a navy suit,
no tie, and Penny sported a skirt and blouse. "Shoot,"
Penny said. "I knew we shouldn't have dressed up. I told
you," she said pointedly to her dad.

Thomas flashed a grin, the picture of cool evil in his suit. He ran his eyes up and down Mika's jeans and T-shirt. "Better to be overdressed than underdressed."

"You guys look great." Mika forced a smile, opening the door wider. Thomas hesitated. "Come on in. Leif's in the kitchen, and dinner is almost ready."

"Are we early?" Penny asked, stepping into the house. "I told Dad we should have walked around the block or something."

"You're right on time," Mika said.

At last, Thomas strolled in. Hands in his pockets, he looked around. He stopped right under where Tuan had repaired the crack in the ceiling. Mika had a sudden vision of the plaster splintering and falling. "Leif, meet Penny . . . and Thomas," she said, corralling the two toward the kitchen.

Leif set down the knife he'd been cutting vegetables with, wiped his hands, and offered one to Thomas. He shook with Thomas first, then Penny.

Penny, with the energy and exuberance of a squirrel, pumped Leif's palm up and down. "This is awesome. I've heard so much about you."

"Likewise." Leif smiled and turned to Mika, disentangling himself from Penny. "Why don't you three head outside? We thought since the evening is nice, we'd eat on the patio. I'll bring the food out."

"You will?" Mika asked, stunned. The only food Leif had ever brought to Mika was from a paper bag.

"Of course. Go on. Men belong in the kitchen as much as women."

Mika smiled for Penny and Thomas's benefit, then turned to Leif. "Tone it down," she coughed into her hand. She led Thomas and Penny through the living room.

Penny paused to gaze at the photos on the mantle. "All your travels," she said warmly. Mika stopped too, shoulder to shoulder with Penny. There Mika was, or at least an avatar, smiling in the Pompeii ruins, in the House of Mysteries. Behind her, a fresco with distinctive red paint—cinnabar. Next photo over, she was in the Louvre grinning in front of the *Mona Lisa*.

Thomas nosed in, eyes squinting. Could he see what Mika saw? That the light wasn't quite right? That the shadows and highlights violated the laws of physics? "Let's go outside," Mika said. She ushered them out the door, face blooming pink.

In the backyard, the fairy lights Mika had hung reflected and glowed in Penny's dark eyes. "It's exactly like your Instagram photo!"

Thomas toed the hole in the ground where Hana had pulled up the tree. "You have gophers here?"

"What?" Mika frowned, her face only starting to

cool. "No. Just doing some landscaping. You know houses, the work is never done."

"You should put some dirt in that. Someone could trip and twist an ankle," said Thomas.

"Isn't this nice, Dad?" Penny said. "It's still snowing outside back home. I didn't know Portland had such warm springs."

Mika swallowed. "It's rare. It seems you brought the sunshine with you." She stared at Penny tenderly and tried to manage her happiness levels. How right this all felt, having Penny here. How domestic.

They settled at the picnic table. Leif appeared with the macaroni and cheese plus salad. They dished up. Mika had lit the candles in the hurricane vases, and they ate in silence by soft candlelight for a bit.

"So, how did you two meet?" Thomas asked, wiping his mouth.

"How'd we meet?" Mika's eyes leaped to Leif, the bite of macaroni she'd just taken lodged in her throat. *Shit.* They'd never discussed their couple's origin story, the fake one. The real one was Hana had gone to buy drugs from Leif, they'd all gotten high, and Mika had hooked up with him. Casual sex turned to regular sex, and then Mika was cohabitating with Leif. It occurred to Mika how so in little control of her life she'd been the last few years. Falling into jobs.

Into a relationship with Leif. Into the next day and the next.

Leif set down his fork. "You know, Mika tells it better. You go ahead." He grinned at her, a dare in his brown eyes.

"Well." Mika gripped the edge of the table. Her stomach flipped, and a rush of blood slid up her neck. "I was out to dinner with a couple artist friends from . . ." She paused, searched her memory for a place, a destination, *anything*.

"Greece," Leif interjected easily. "They were from Greece, right?"

"That's right. And Leif was there too? I can't remember why though?" She scrunched her nose up and stared at Leif.

Leif sipped his wine before answering. "For work."

"What is it you do?" Thomas asked Leif. "Penny said something about agriculture but didn't know any specifics."

"I am in agriculture. Mika thinks it's pretty boring, so I'm sure that's why she didn't get into specifics. I work mostly in the biochemistry field. I do freelance consulting with universities, a government contract here and there, that kind of stuff." Mika breathed out. That sounded good. Believable. "What about you?" Leif asked Thomas.

Thomas put down his fork and knife. "I'm a copyright attorney. I have my own practice in Dayton. A far cry from the firefighter I wanted to be when I was ten," he joked.

"Not everyone can follow their passion. But I think it's important to take risks. Take the Portland Naked Bike Ride, for example—"

"Penny," Mika said a little too loudly. "I almost forgot I have a gift for you."

"You do?" Penny brightened.

"Be right back." Mika grabbed the scrapbook from the house and returned, placing it in front of her.

"Leif, would you mind getting dessert?" Mika stared at Leif as Penny touched the corner of the album.

"Course not," Leif announced. He knocked the table once and stood. Mika mouthed a silent thank-you at him.

"It's nothing big," Mika said as Penny slid a hand over the linen cover. "Just some pictures of me when I was your age . . ."

Thomas was quiet for a moment, then said, "This is nice of you."

Penny looked up, her eyes shining. "Yeah." She flipped through the pages.

When Penny stopped at a snapshot of Mika when she was sixteen, Mika spoke up. "God, I was so awkward at sixteen. Not nearly as confident as you. You have your parents to thank for that, I think." Thomas's eyes flashed toward Mika, the corner of his mouth curling into a genuine smile of appreciation. Mika cleared her throat. "I'd convinced my parents to let me get a perm. Only we couldn't afford to do the whole head, so I only had my bangs done."

Penny laughed, then sobered. "Is there a picture of your parents?" She asked it quietly, as if she were afraid to but couldn't afford not to.

"There is," Mika said, glad she'd included one. "Toward the back, I think."

"Do they live nearby?" Thomas asked, his deep voice startling Mika.

"They do, but, um, they're on a cruise right now," she told Penny.

Penny nodded but kept turning the pages one by one, soaking it all in. She stopped at a page, and Mika rose in her seat to see what had caught her attention. The photograph of Mika pregnant.

"I'm in there," Penny said, tracing the outline of Mika's swollen belly with a finger. "What was it like? Being pregnant with me?"

Thomas's eyes darted toward Mika, and her heart buoyed in her chest. "What was it like?" she repeated, tapping her lips, pretending to conjure the memory. Even though she didn't need to. It was always alive inside of her, tangled around her bones, threatening to drag her under. All those months of growing a baby she wasn't sure she would hate or love. She shouldn't have ever had any doubts. When she'd pushed Penny out, it had been love at first sight, flowing as naturally as the blood in the cord between them. But how could she tell Penny that? And in front of Thomas? "Well, I was pretty sure you were trying to kill me." She injected humor into her voice. "Food didn't stay down the first trimester. Then the second trimester, I had heartburn so bad it felt as if I'd swallowed a small volcano. I couldn't sleep without being fully upright. And the final act, the third trimester, the simple notion of bending down and putting on shoes nearly suffocated me." There wasn't a part of Mika's body Penny hadn't colonized.

Penny laughed, and Thomas grinned too. "You've been feisty from the beginning," he said to his daughter.

Penny laughed again. So did Mika, her face lifted to the crescent moon. She tried to tell herself this moment didn't mean that much. That her heart didn't suddenly feel open and endless like the summer. That it wasn't like she was eighteen again and just starting out. When the world had been at her feet. When her life had been thick paint, vibrant colors, and bold strokes.

Chapter Twelve

The following evening, Mika hurried to meet Thomas and Penny at their hotel again. They'd planned dinner at a restaurant a block down. She'd managed to find a parking spot on the street right before the sky opened up and huge fat drops of rain poured down. By the time she skated through the lobby doors, her hair was plastered to her head. "I'm here," she said to Thomas, rushing over and slipping a little bit. "Sorry, I'm late. Traffic was terrible, and I couldn't find parking. Where's Penny?" She searched the lobby.

"She should be down any minute." Just then, Thomas's phone buzzed. "Hold on," he said to Mika. "It's Penny." He answered, "Hey, kiddo. Mika is here. You about ready?" He listened carefully for a minute. "You did? Did you bring anything with you? No, of course not. It's no problem, you know that. I'll run to the store right now. Want anything else? Okay, I'll be up soon. Just hang on. Hey, it's fine, it's fine. Yes, I'll explain it to her. Yes, I'll be *nice*," he said a little more quietly. Finally, he hung up. "Well, Penny isn't coming. It's that time for her."

Mika's brow darted in. "Time? Oh!" Understanding dawned. "It's that *time* of the month."

He scratched the back of his head. "She needs me to go to the store for her."

"Um, there's a Target down a block east. I'll show you." They borrowed a couple of umbrellas from the concierge. Ten minutes later, they were in the same Target Mika had been in when Penny first called. *Is this Mika Suzuki? This is Penny Calvin. Penelope Calvin. I think I'm your daughter.* Thomas perused the shelves and shook his head, just so disappointed in the selection. "Excuse me." He flagged down an employee in a red shirt and asked about a particular brand of tampon. Supersized. The employee said they'd check and scurried off.

Thomas stuck his hands in his pockets and rocked back on his heels. "Penny is particular."

Mika had to admit she felt a little charmed by the whole scene unfolding in front of her. "Is she?"

"Yeah," he said with a shrug. "She likes a certain

brand. If they don't have them, we might have to go to another store. What?" he said at her wide-eyed stare.

"It's just . . . I'm very impressed. My dad never went to the store for feminine products." Hiromi would buy them and slip them to Mika in a dark plastic bag as if some dark underworld bargain were taking place. Once, she'd sent Leif. He'd FaceTimed her, and they got into a whole thing about organic options. She'd hung up on him, content to bleed out on his couch. It would have served him right.

Thomas scratched his jaw. "It's nothing to be embarrassed about. I never want her to be ashamed of her body." He paused as if considering if he should say more. Finally, he decided to keep speaking. "I threw her a period party."

"I'm sorry, what?"

He laughed, focused on his shoes. "Yeah. She got her period a year after Caroline died, and I searched the internet. I think I googled 'single dad, daughter got her period first time' or something. All these suggestions popped up about a party welcoming her into womanhood. I invited some of her friends over for a surprise party."

"And she liked that?" Mika had been mortified when she'd started her period—embarrassed and confused.

Hiromi had never discussed that it would happen to Mika, so she'd been surprised, to say the least.

Thomas shook his head. "She didn't like it. She wouldn't leave her room. I sent her friends home. After a while, she came down and asked that I never throw her a period party again. I guess maybe the cake and streamers were too much." He shuffled his feet.

The Target employee returned with a carton of tampons, the right kind. They paid and walked back to the hotel. On the eleventh floor, they knocked on Penny's door. "Kiddo," Thomas said.

Penny opened the door, bathrobe on, and television blasting in the background, some reality show about housewives. "I don't feel like seeing anyone," Penny said, holding out her hand. Thomas placed the bag in her open palm. She went on. "You guys go out to dinner. Don't waste the evening because of me. I'm probably going to clean out the minibar of anything chocolate or salty." Then she shut the door in their faces.

In the elevator, Mika said, "We can pass on dinner. I think I'll just head home."

Thomas folded his arms and scratched his jaw. "I'm that bad company, eh?"

"No. Of course not," Mika sputtered, caught.

He stared at her. "How about a drink? In the lobby?

I think maybe you and I should talk, get to know each other better. For Penny's sake." They reached the lobby, and the doors slid open. Mika searched and searched for an excuse, thought about just flat-out running away—but that seemed like the more humiliating option.

Thomas waited outside the elevator for her. "Mika," he said flatly.

"Thomas."

"Please have a drink with me."

"Fine." Mika inhaled and slipped past Thomas. "One drink."

They strolled through the lobby to the hotel bar. As Mika had been conditioned to do, her eyes sought out the paintings. Typical abstract hotel pieces with monochrome swirls, something chosen for the aesthetic. *Couch art*, Marcus, her professor, used to call it.

Thomas stopped at a little table in the corner and pulled out a chair for Mika. At the sound of wooden legs scraping against the tile, Mika remembered Marcus's office again. The first day she'd met him, the easel made a similar noise as she had dragged it out to set it up with a blank canvas from the closet.

What should I draw? she'd asked over her shoulder. Sunlight streamed in through the window, dust particles suspended in it.

If you're asking me that, you don't belong in advanced painting classes, he answered.

She nodded vacantly and chose a piece of vine charcoal from the shelf. Placing it against the canvas, she drew an arching line and winced. Too heavy. Too broad. No purpose. She erased it with her hand and started again, summoning her anatomy knowledge from the books she used to get at the library. Marcus smoked while she worked. Halfway through, he turned on music, some soft folksy ballad. An hour later, she was done, fingers black, bloodless, and aching.

Marcus cut the music off. *Who is she?* he asked.

My mother. Mika found a towel and wiped her hands on it. She'd sketched Hiromi. Her hair set in a smooth dome, eyes brutal and unforgiving, double lines bracketing her mouth like parentheses of disappointment.

Don't ever ask someone what you should paint again. A crinkle of paper, and Marcus handed her the signed form. *Enroll in my Painting III class. I'll teach you.*

Mika grasped the form and left his office, sat on a bench for a while. It was the first time anyone had said she showed any promise. She felt powerful. Fully alive. Marcus loomed large in her memory.

Now, Mika settled into her chair, Thomas adjacent to her. He flagged down the bartender and ordered a scotch neat. Of course, he did—anything to make more hair grow on his chest. Mika's heart raced, and she ordered a glass of cab. Awkward silence descended as they waited for their drinks.

"Will Penny be okay?" Mika asked.

Thomas eased back in the chair, spreading his legs. "She'll be fine. The first day is always the worst for her."

"That's good." It occurred to Mika how much she didn't know about Penny. Once upon a time, she'd convinced herself it would be okay never truly knowing her daughter. It was enough to know Penny was alive and well. She'd been a fool. Now, Mika was greedy and jealous of Caroline and Thomas, all those moments they'd had with Penny. She tried to muscle down the envy, but it refused to stay pinned. The thought of never seeing Penny again, not being a part of her life as Mika anticipated might happen, seemed unacceptable now. The waiter returned. With a flourish, he placed two cocktail napkins down and their drinks on top of them. They sipped and listened to the man playing the piano—a famous sonata by Mozart.

"Will you tell me more about Penny?" Mika played with the base of her wineglass, turning it halfway around, then halfway back.

Thomas tilted his head. There was a small votive candle on the table, and it cast shadows underneath his sharp cheekbones. "We sent letters every year."

The packages from Caroline burst with photographs, drawings, even a clay dish Penny had made in elementary school. And the letters were long and descriptive. Mika had no trouble imagining her daughter's life, how well she was doing, how well she was being taken care of. And she was always comforted by Caroline's words, written with the familiarity of one mother to another. But then Caroline had died. Thomas's letters were short, straight to the point—a razor's edge of uncertainty. "You did," she said carefully. "But I'm sure you couldn't put it all down."

Thomas sucked in an uneasy breath. "Well, you already know about the period party gone wrong. What else?" He shifted in his seat, thinking. "Her letter-writing phase."

"Letter-writing phase?" Mika warmed and leaned in.

"I took her to a counselor after Caroline died. The counselor suggested Penny write letters to express her feelings. She'd write something like: 'Today I feel sad, I miss Mom.'" Thomas tipped his drink to his mouth. Mika watched as he swallowed, his Adam's apple working. "Then I'd write back: 'I'm so sorry, kiddo. I miss her too.' It was kind of this safe space where we could talk. We used the technique for a couple of years off and on. It was pretty effective. One day, I think she was thirteen, maybe, I asked Penny to shower and tidy up her room. Pretty innocuous." He waited for Mika to nod in agreement. "She came back to me a few minutes later with a letter that said something like: 'I'm feeling really mad and sad right now, so please leave me alone until further notice.'" He paused and sipped his scotch.

Mika smiled. "Did you leave her alone?"

Thomas sucked in air through his teeth. "That probably would have been the smart thing to do. But I followed the counselor's advice and wrote her a note back. Something like: 'Thanks for communicating with me. It's okay to feel mad and sad sometimes. I'm here if you want to talk.'" His eyes clouded with humor, and his mouth twisted into a smile.

"Not the right thing to do?" Mika asked.

"Not even close. She came storming out of her room. I swear she was gathering dark forces to descend upon me. She slammed the note down and had revised it." He paused. "She'd underlined the 'really' and crossed out 'mad' to add 'angry.' Then over the whole thing with a Sharpie, she wrote: 'Go away' in capital letters."

"Wow," was all Mika said quietly. Sometimes the whole thing, the pregnancy, the birth, and even now, seeing Penny, felt unreal. As if Mika were watching someone else's life unfold. In a way, she was, she supposed. She couldn't quite get a grip on the fact that this *was* her life.

Thomas knocked back the rest of his drink. "Yeah, she's always been this way. Small but fierce, scrappy. I'd bet on her in a fight. What were you like as a kid?"

"Me?" Mika straightened. She thought of the Mika *before*. Hiromi called her daughter oversensitive. She viewed Mika as strange, foreign, her differences as betrayals. "I was shy, I suppose, but with visions of grandeur." She wanted to be something great someday. "Until I met my best friend, Hana. I took more risks then." Felt like she was indomitable. In high school, they went to house parties on the weekends. Getting drunk with students and their parents who subscribed to the "if my kid is going to drink, they might as well do it under my roof" philosophy. Then she doubled down in college. Lost her virginity the first week there to some guy whose last name she couldn't remember. She had fun and liked having sex, the feeling of a body against hers.

Mika blinked.

Marcus was there again, just on her periphery. They were alone in the classroom, the door shut. She was nearly halfway through her freshman year. Aside from painting and art history, she'd enrolled in philosophy. She was

in the midst of existentialism. Sartre and Kierkegaard—
*Life can only be understood backwards, but it must be
lived forwards.* And studying ancient arts, the Greeks,
the Romans, Byzantine to late antiquity. Icons. The
Virgin Mary. Under Marcus's tutelage, she'd mastered
traditional techniques—scumbling, wet on wet, glazing,
chiaroscuro.

Your paintings lack life, Marcus was saying. He
dipped a brush in black ink and slashed a line through
her study of an orange. *There is no story. What is your
story?* It was a kind of agony, disappointing Marcus.
Look at Peter's painting—he gestured to a canvas
leaning against the wall, his graduate student's art, a
portrait of a pop star, holding an apple in the Garden
of Eden—*it's derivative as shit, but it still has a narra-
tive. Come on,* he said, *can't you see? The story is your
power.*

"Penny was anything but shy," Thomas said, pulling Mika back to the present. "She . . ." He shook his
head.

"What?" Mika leaned forward. Somehow, they'd
drifted closer to each other, their knees bumping.

"I forgot about this, but when she was a toddler and
potty training, she liked for us to watch her poop."
Mika burst into a laugh. Thomas answered with a grin.
"I don't know. It was probably because we made a big

deal out of it. Caroline had read this book about how you're supposed to celebrate when they go. We did this whole cheering thing. But Penny would get super serious when she had to shit, and she liked to lock eyes with one of us. She'd say, 'Watch me, watch me.'" He grinned. "It got to be a thing, and finally, Caroline was like, 'We have to stop this. We'll be watching her poop when she's in college.' Penny hates this story, but it's one of my favorites."

Elbow on the table, Mika rested her chin in her hand and studied Thomas in repose. "What else?"

"Well, in fourth grade, she got seriously into ventriloquism." He mock-shivered. "So creepy. I'm glad that's over. She got into magic soon after."

"Naturally," said Mika, and they shared a smile, a half-laugh. She sighed. She'd been wrong about Thomas. He didn't have the emotional range of a potato. "You guys were good parents. You're a good dad." Mika hadn't meant to say it, but the words came pouring out.

Thomas huffed out a laugh. "Thanks. I operated without a manual for a while. I look back at after Caroline died, and I'm ashamed of how much I didn't know. I pretty much relied on Caroline to do most of the parenting. Then when she passed away, I felt so out of my element . . ."

An ache speared through Mika's chest. "How bad was it?"

He frowned. "I did her hair. It wasn't too bad for the first time. She cried at the end of the day when I tried to take the bands out, so I used scissors and ended up lopping off a section of hair. I had to take her to a hairstylist to get it fixed. She pitched a fit when they suggested cutting it into a bob to even it out. So, we made a compromise, short in the front and long in the back."

Mika made a face. "That sounds an awful lot like a . . ."

"A mullet," Thomas said, light eyes intent on her. "I gave my daughter a mullet."

Chapter Thirteen

"So, what have you told her about me?" Hana asked. It was Wednesday, the night before Mika's gallery opening. Thomas and Penny were planning on meeting Hana for the first time. Mika had chosen Lardo, a hip sandwich restaurant on Hawthorne that wouldn't hurt her bank account too much.

Mika smirked, scanning the crowded restaurant for a free table. "Oh, you know, the usual, how you had a crush on our freshman English teacher and would talk to her endlessly about *Smallville* and how Kristin Kreuk"—the doe-eyed female lead, aka Lana Lang—"carried the show."

Hana's mouth quirked into a smile. "Ah, Mrs. Sampson. I barely kept myself from breaking into song whenever I spoke to her. I wonder what she's up to now."

A family of four cleared their table, and Mika darted to claim it. They sat down to wait for Thomas and Penny before ordering.

"What else did you tell her about me?" Hana drummed her fingers against the table.

Mika glanced at the neon sign on the wall they sat under. It said: PIG OUT. "You know, the usual. Since high school and through college, we've been friends, and that you were there for her birth. She's probably going to want to know about it." Mika removed a napkin from the dispenser and started shredding it. "I'm sure she's going to ask all about us and that time of our lives. So just downplay what kind of students we were, okay? How much we partied, how many times we skipped school."

"Mika," Hana sighed, a sympathetic look in her eye.

"I want her to be proud of where she came from. I want to be someone she looks up to." *I want to be the person I was before but better,* Mika thought. Maybe this was her chance at redemption. Absolution. A way to go back in time and make things right. It was a twisted logic, but there it was—her chance to gain back what she had lost.

"You don't want her to know you nearly pooped pushing her out?" Hana said drily.

"Oh my god, you promised we'd never talk about that."

Hana shrugged.

"Love your face," Mika said.

"Love your face too," Hana answered back. "Even though it's a lying, wrong face."

"Please don't make me feel worse." She felt bad enough already lying to Penny, but it was better than the truth. She'd promised to always protect Penny. This was Mika's way.

"Sorry," Hana said. "I just wish you could see how great you are."

Mika opened her mouth to answer, but the bells over the door jingled. Thomas and Penny stood at the entrance. "That's them," Mika said, sticking her hand in the air and waving the two down.

The father and daughter smiled at the same time.

Hana whistled low. "Hot dad alert."

"Hana," Mika said, cheeks flaming as Thomas and Penny inched closer.

"What?" Hana touched her chest. "Even though I'm a lesbian, I can totally objectively appreciate handsome men."

"Hi." Thomas smiled warmly at Mika. He stuck out a hand for Hana to shake. "Thomas." Introductions went on from there, and they found their seats, Mika and Hana sitting on one side and Thomas and Penny on the other.

"What's good here?" Thomas asked.

"Definitely the Dirty Bastard Fries," Hana said. "They're hand-cut and cooked in bacon fat, then tossed in fried herbs and parmesan."

Thomas took everyone's order and moved to the counter to place it. When he came back, they made small talk for a while. Mostly around Hana, her work as an ASL interpreter for bands. Penny was beaming. *So impressed and impressionable*, Mika thought. It made her think of how she was with Marcus, what a neophyte she'd been, how much she'd wanted his approval, she'd been like a cat twining itself around his legs—it still made her stomach hurt, her desperation. Now, they stuffed themselves on fries and pork sandwiches. Thomas wiped his mouth and balled up his napkin. "I can't eat anymore," he declared, rubbing his flat belly. His T-shirt rode up, revealing the thinnest strip of skin. Mika found a spot on the wall to focus on.

Hana leaned forward, elbow on the table, chin in her hand, and gazed at Penny. "So?" she said.

"So," Penny parroted back.

"What do you want to know?" Hana asked.

Penny blushed at Hana's directness. "You were there the day I was born."

"Oh yeah, I was totally in the splash zone," said Hana.

Mika grimaced at the visual and reevaluated her choice in best friends.

Penny twiddled her thumbs. "Will you tell me . . . Will you tell me about the day I was born?" She looked to Hana, to Mika, asking them both.

Mika sat back. The food in her stomach soured. It was hard to remember that day. Harder still to talk about it. About how the pregnancy tore her life in half. How when Penny was born, Mika had been dizzy with love, then heartbreak. How she'd sunk like a stone after. It was painful, letting that curled ribbon of time flatten.

"Penny," Thomas said softly. "Maybe we should save this conversation for another day."

Penny deflated. "Sure, right. I totally understand." But it was clear she didn't.

Under the table, Hana squeezed Mika's knee reassuringly. "It was raining, I think," Mika's best friend said carefully.

"It was," Mika confirmed, her voice light, faint. She'd gone to her ob-gyn the day before and had been miserable. *I just want her out,* she'd said, flushed and crying. *I just want this all to be over. I want my life back.* It felt as if Penny were clinging to Mika, knowing they'd soon be torn apart.

"Mika had an epidural," Hana added. She nudged Mika. "Remember how the nurse suggested it was too early for an epidural, and maybe you should try breathing?"

A ghost of a smile appeared on Mika's face. "She was offering me snowballs. I wanted a grenade."

"It was pretty boring after that. We slept for a while," Hana said. Mika remembered Hana at the end of her hospital bed, body slumped down in a chair.

"Hana slept," Mika qualified. "I tossed and turned, couldn't get comfortable." She had cried. From being exhausted, from the pain, from the emotional gutting.

"Then, early in the morning, Mika started pushing," Hana said. In between bearing down, Mika had said, *I don't want to hold her.* Then changed her mind. *I want to hold her, don't let them take her before I get to hold her.* "Mika held you first, but I held you right after," Hana chimed in. "Your face was all red and scrunched up."

"Sounds beautiful." Penny laughed.

"It was, it really was," Mika said, and that was the

truth. Her gaze fluttered to Thomas. A half-smile tilted the corner of his mouth, same as Penny's.

"We were right outside, in the hospital waiting room," Thomas interjected. And Mika found a certain distant comfort knowing Penny had changed hands to her adopted parents. There wasn't a point where she hadn't been loved and looked after.

"I know," Penny said. "Mom wrote to me about it in her letter." The letter that Caroline had written for Penny's sixteenth birthday. The letter that launched Penny's search for her birth mother.

"She did?" Thomas's eyebrows darted in. Ah, Mika remembered, Penny wouldn't let Thomas read the last words Caroline had written to her daughter.

Penny waved a hand at her father, dismissing him. "Changing subjects now. I'm dying to see your gallery space," she said to Mika, her dark eyes intense. "Can we go tomorrow? Give me a tour before everybody else gets to see it?"

Oh, Mika thought. "Oh!" Mika said. Leif had sent the address last night. Had said she could get inside anytime the next day. She'd cleared her calendar to check out the space, whip it into shape, but she hadn't expected company. She glanced at Hana. Amusement tilted the corners of her friend's mouth. "Sure!" she agreed, backed into a corner. She would come up with an excuse later.

"I hate to cut this short." Hana pushed away from the table. "But I've got a roller derby game."

"Roller derby?" Penny echoed.

"You guys want to come? It's violent and bloodthirsty, might be up your alley," Hana said, and Penny lit up like a Christmas tree. "There's open skate afterward."

Penny gripped the table. "Yes, yes, so much, yes."

• • •

Thomas, Penny, and Mika sat in the stands and watched Hana skate into the rink twenty minutes later. Thomas eyed the women decked in short shorts, tank tops, skates, helmets, and protective eyewear. "We don't have roller derby in Ohio," he murmured.

"What's Hana doing?" Penny asked.

Mika sat back in the bleachers. "She's the jammer, so she'll start behind her team," Mika began, explaining how points were scored when one jammer lapped a member of the opposing team. For an hour and a half, they rooted Hana on, wincing when someone elbowed her and booing when the ref called a track cut, penalty. By the time Hana's team, Asian Invasion, defeated their rivals, Fresh Meat, Penny was bouncing in her seat. Hana called Penny down to the rink, and Penny leaped up to join her for open skate.

"Want to watch from the beer garden?" Mika asked, pointing to the rink's end, where there was an open area with picnic benches and a bar.

Thomas rubbed his knees. "Should I be worried about this? Do I need to have my insurance card ready?" In the rink, Hana was outfitting Penny with a helmet and knee pads.

"No," Mika said. "She'll be fine. Hana will just show her some moves and introduce her to some of the girls."

Soon enough, they were settled in the beer garden, a frosty IPA in front of Thomas, a glass of hard cider in front of Mika, watching as a girl with full arm tattoos and safety pins in her ears showed Penny how to block.

Thomas wiped at the condensation gathering on the outside of his glass with his thumbs. "You know, I had reservations about this trip."

"You don't say?" Mika teased him with a smile. She sipped her drink.

Thomas's gaze grew serious. "I'm sorry. I've been a grouch. It's been a bad . . . Shit, I don't know, I guess it's been a bad few years. I thought Penny was doing okay with everything. It's been just us two for so long. She never even asked about you. It shocked the hell out of me when she announced she'd found you and was planning to visit." He rubbed his chest. "I don't think I've adjusted. Plus, there is this whole letter Caroline wrote to her. She won't let me read it. I'm trying to respect her wishes, but damn, it feels like all Penny does lately is keep secrets from me." Thomas stared into his drink.

The corner of Mika's mouth twitched uncertainly. "So, Penny is keeping secrets and trying to establish herself outside of you. Sounds an awful lot like a teenage girl to me." She placed a hand to her chest. "I speak from experience."

If anything, this made Thomas broodier. His brows knit together more tightly. "Well, shit, I don't like any of that."

"She's a good girl. A good person, your daughter."

He nodded thoughtfully. "I used to think Caroline was the best thing that ever happened to me, but then Penny came along, and I felt guilty because she . . . well, because she *is* the best thing that ever happened to me."

Mika said nothing. Though she thought, *Same.*

"She's growing up, I guess, that's all," said Thomas.

"She is. But she's making good choices too. Like how she handled everything with that boyfriend . . ." Mika trailed off at Thomas's confused expression.

"What boyfriend?"

"Shit." Mika chewed her cheek. "I shouldn't have said anything. Please don't tell her I told you."

Thomas crossed his finger over his heart. "I won't say a word."

Mika tried to remember their phone conversation about him. "Jack or James, I think his name was."

"Jack," Thomas confirmed. "She talks about him sometimes."

"Well, I guess they were together, but she broke it off with him." Mika leaned forward and whispered. "Because he kept wanting to hang out in rooms with mattresses."

Thomas's lip curled, and so did his fist. "That motherfucker."

Mika placed a hand over his, then pulled back. Heat spread up her neck. "Calm down, and leave his mother out of it. Penny has a good head on her shoulders." *I want someone who thinks I'm beautiful because of my mind,* Penny had said after she'd broken up with him.

Thomas flexed his fingers and relaxed. "Well, okay then." He gulped down his drink. A half-laugh rattled out of him. "I'm not used to this. It's hard to share her."

"I can imagine," Mika said, the slightest edge to her tone. She'd shared Penny from the beginning.

"Right. Sorry." Thomas gave Mika an embarrassed

smile. He was wearing a hoodie today, DARTMOUTH ROWING etched across it. He looked younger than his forty-six years.

"You mind if I ask you a question?"

Mika finished her beer. "Go ahead."

"Do you regret it?" Thomas asked.

Mika tilted her head. "Regret what?"

"Penny," he said after a second. "Giving her away, I mean."

Mika stilled. *Surrender. It's the act of giving yourself over to forces greater than you*, Mrs. Pearson had said. "It was the right decision at the right time, and even now . . . I wouldn't have wanted anyone else to raise Penny. She is exactly who she should be." Mika paused, then said, "But yes. There's always some regrets, aren't there?"

Thomas's eyes clouded in thought, then he said, "That's all part of the universal experience of having a child."

At Thomas's alluding to Mika being Penny's parent, warmth spread in her chest. Just then, Penny skated up. Her face was flushed, her eyes shining. Her hands held a T-shirt from the gift shop. "I'm totally buying this." She held it up in front of her. Emblazoned across the chest was THESE WILL ROCKURFACE OFF in old English.

Thomas laughed, then quickly sobered. "No. Absolutely not. Try again."

Penny pouted. "But—"

Another thing I missed, Mika thought. She may have been able to choose who raised her daughter but not what clothes she wore, or what toys she played with, or what bedding she slept under. Over the years, she'd pause in kids' departments, running her hands over baby booties or toddler swimsuits or graphic tees, and she'd think about what Penny might be wearing. So many things she missed. So many things she lost.

Mika popped up. "C'mon, I'll help you pick something else out."

Time for a do-over.

Chapter Fourteen

ight a.m., and Mika was awake, texting Penny. You sure you want to see the gallery today? It's really a mess. A spear of shame struck Mika, but she quickly shoved it back into the hole it crawled from. I promise it'll look great by the time you show up tonight! she added.

Penny texted back almost immediately. No problem at all. I could even help you get it set up! I don't mind getting my hands dirty. Text me the address? With a defeated sigh, Mika did but asked Penny to give her a few hours' head start. She texted Leif to confirm Stanley, the artist, was expecting her. He replied with a thumbs-up.

On her way, Mika's phone dinged with a text from Hana. Penny is awesome, she said. Know what else is awesome?

Mika had gone to sleep before Hana had gotten home, then left before Hana had woken up. Usually, the two were on the same schedule of late nights and later mornings. But lately, Mika had been getting up earlier, mostly to maximize time with Penny while she was in Portland.

Mika tapped out a response at a red light. Let me guess. Cheesecake for breakfast? Sweatpants? Interpretive dance?

The light turned green, and her phone rang. She glanced at the screen. Her mother calling. *Again.* Her heart dropped. No doubt Hiromi was wondering if Mika had found a job yet. She declined the call. Soon after, her phone lit with a new voicemail alert. Another red light and Hana had texted back. Yes, all those things, plus Garrett has chronic diarrhea. He has to quit the tour to take care of his IBS. She followed with a sad face emoji, then a party hat emoji. This means I will be going on tour with Pearl Jam.

Mika replied, First, please don't ever tell me about Garrett's bowel movements again. Second, I am very happy for you.

Idea! Hana said. You should come with me as my emotional support animal. Free hotels, meals, backstage passes . . . What do you think? We'd leave in a couple weeks.

Mika pulled up and parked outside a run-of-the-mill warehouse. A sign advertised First Thursdays every first week of the month, a time when people came to drink wine from plastic cups and hop from booth to loft, previewing up-and-coming, but mostly starving, artists.

She let herself in through a heavy door. On the wall was a register listing different artists in residence. CREATIONS BY DAPHNE, SUITE ONE. ZEN PRODUCTS, SUITE TWO . . . STANLEY WOLF, SUITE TEN.

Mika headed up the stairs, knocking on the door of suite ten before stepping inside. "Hello," she called. Metallica played on an old stereo and assaulted her ears. It smelled like the time Mika burned a pot on the oven. All around were heaps of twisted scrap metal—rebar, steel bands, iron bars. Natural light from four huge windows filled the space. A man held a blowtorch in the corner, sparks flying from it as he worked on a sculpture. The blowtorch cut off. The guy raised his mask and clicked off the music.

"Hullo, hullo! You must be Mika?" He crossed the room, stripping off gloves. "Stanley." He stuck out a hand for Mika to shake. He was white with bright blue eyes and a shock of dyed black hair. One of his ears was pierced, a feathered dangle earring hanging from it.

Mika shook his hand and smiled. Then she stepped

back to peer up at a seven-foot sculpture. It was hard to decipher what it was supposed to be. A man, maybe? But his back was hunched and twisted. "This is interesting. It's charged with such a strong emotional quality."

Stanley blushed. "Leif told me you're looking to set this space up as a gallery."

Mika moved more fully into the room. "I am, and if you're up to it, I think this will definitely work." The space was oozing with potential. A half dozen more sculptures were grouped in the corner, bodies bent toward each other, like lovers taking refuge under an awning during a storm. If they cleared Stanley's equipment, the sculptures would stand out in the vast room, illuminated by the ceiling's canned lights. She glanced at Stanley. "You sure you don't mind? Me displaying your work, taking over your studio today?"

"Nope." Stanley threw his gloves on top of an eclectic mix of materials, including a set of oils and an easel. Mika stared at the paints and clenched a fist to keep the tremors at bay, a combination of fear and longing. There was also a bottle of turpentine, and she became paralyzed for a moment. Became utterly still as if a beast in the woods were stalking her.

"I'm pretty much done here. So, it's all yours. There are some cans of paint and rollers in the corner. Leif thought you might want to give it all a fresh coat. I'll let you do your thing," Stanley announced.

Jarred, Mika smiled vacantly, heard herself mutter a thank-you to Stanley. The door slammed. She swallowed, shook it off, and rolled up her sleeves. Time to work.

• • •

Two sweaty hours later, Penny texted that Uber had dropped her off. Mika hopped downstairs to meet her.

"Hiiiii," Penny sang, skipping over. "What do you think?" She held her arms out. Today she wore a jean jacket and the new shirt Mika had purchased for her underneath. They'd exchanged the ROCKURFACE OFF shirt for an Asian Invasion tee—the logo a pair of chopsticks stuck in rice.

"I like it," Mika said. Seeing Penny happy made her happy.

Penny scrunched her nose. "I tried to convince Dad to buy me hair dye last night. I feel like this whole look could be elevated if I had a blue streak here." She picked up a lock of hair framing her face.

"Don't do that on your own. I bleached my hair in high school, and it took a year to go back to normal. If you decide you really want it, be responsible and go to a professional."

Penny nodded gravely. "Good call."

"How'd you sleep?" Mika asked as she led Penny up the stairs to the gallery.

"Like a dream," Penny answered. "I'm so excited to see your space."

Mika tugged on her ear. "There's still a lot to do . . . Don't get your hopes up too high." At Penny's concerned face, she added, "I'm just feeling the pressure to get everything right. The opening is tonight."

"I get it. I'm the same way before a track meet. Anxious and excited, you want everything to go perfectly."

"Exactly." Mika opened the door, and Penny entered.

"Whoa!" Penny exclaimed, bypassing Mika.

"What?" *That bad?* Mika tried to imagine the space through Penny's eyes. Despite her efforts over the last few hours, the area was still messy. The welding equipment lay heaped in a pile in the middle of the floor, along with various art supplies.

"Needs some tidying up," Penny said, circling the space.

"Yeah," said Mika a little dejectedly.

Penny stared at Mika a moment. "Well." Penny clapped her hands together. "Between the two of us, I think we can have it all cleaned up in an hour or two."

"You sure you don't mind?"

"Of course not!" Penny said. "Where do you want to start?"

Mika tapped a finger against her lips. "Let's clear all this equipment out." Mika crossed the room to open what she assumed—*hoped* was a closet. She peeked inside. Dusty, empty space. She flung the door wide.

Together, they worked tirelessly for the next sixty minutes, hauling welding equipment and scrap metal to the closet. Sweat dotted their brows. "This in the closet too?" Penny asked. At her feet were the painting supplies.

Mika flexed her hands, trying to dispel a tremor. She focused on a couple of stubby graphite pencils. Marcus did drawings in pencil. A single shard of broken pottery that, if you turned your head just right, resembled a beating heart. A rotten bunch of bananas. A dry well. Near the end of winter term, Marcus had won an award for the pottery drawing.

Congratulations, Mika grinned at Marcus, a little out of breath from racing across campus to see him after her art history class. They'd moved on from the Virgin Mary. Now they focused on the Renaissance, where women were draped over chairs, painted in half shells, or floating on clouds with the light focused on their hips, their thighs, their breasts—ready to be feasted on, devoured. Mika was in his office and thrust a gift at him, an electric pencil sharpener topped with a red bow. It had been a running joke between them that Marcus used an old sharpener that you twisted by hand.

Thanks, he replied with the slightest smile, picking at the ribbon.

What are you going to do with the award? I think you should hang it by your desk. Mika gestured at the plaque from the Southwestern Institute of Art.

I don't know. I'll probably end up using it as an ashtray, he said, scratching at the overgrowth around his chin.

Well, you should definitely celebrate, Mika added.

Actually. Marcus eyed Mika. *We're going to gather at Pete's apartment tonight for drinks. I didn't want to do anything, but he insisted. Why don't you come?*

Mika had blushed furiously and beamed, instantly thinking about what she might wear. *I'd love to. Thanks.*

"Mika?" Penny was in front of her.

Mika tried to twist her mouth up into a smile. "Sorry, got lost in thought. You mind putting them in the closet?"

Penny nodded mutely and scooped up the paints, disappearing into the closet. Mika broke a pencil under her heel and kicked it into the corner. She wandered to the sculptures and mentally sorted through them, where they should be placed, how they should be sequenced. She chose one, the most hunched, and pushed it closest to the entrance. She was on number four by the time Penny finished with the painting supplies.

"Wow," Penny breathed. "That's very effective."

Mika stepped back and wiped the sweat from her brow. Each subsequent sculpture bent slightly less than the previous, like a film of still snapshots of the same twisted figure slowly unraveling to stand upright. "I think it looks good too." This time Mika smiled for real. Proud and so happy.

They moved the final sculptures but left the one draped in heavy canvas. "I think Stanley is still working on that one," Mika explained, wiping her hands on her jeans. "I'll touch base with him later and see where we should place it. We make a good team," Mika said, and Penny smiled. "You want something to drink? I saw a vending machine down the hall."

"Sounds good," said Penny.

They used the loose change from the cup in Charlie's car to buy waters and a few bags of chips, then sat cross-legged on the gallery floor. "What's your dad up to today?" Mika asked, arranging the food around Penny like an offering.

"I don't know. Probably working or something. I actually asked him not to come."

"You did?"

Penny bit her lip, fingers still on a package of Doritos. "Yeah. I thought it would be nice if it was just the two of us. I love my dad, but . . . he can be a bit of a wet blanket."

Mika smiled. "Not going to argue." But then she thought of Thomas at the roller derby rink, watching Penny with such devotion, such admiration, such pride. "He does seem like a pretty great dad, though."

A wisp of a smile appeared on Penny's face. "He is. Especially when I was younger. He used to read to me every night. It was kind of our thing. I loved 'Goldilocks,' and he'd always read this line about her long beautiful *dark* hair that shone in the sun, then he'd look at me and say: 'Just like you.' Then when I was older, I flipped back through the book and reread it. He'd changed the words from 'light' to 'dark' and colored in the pictures of her hair with a Sharpie."

"That's really sweet," Mika choked out.

"We haven't been as close lately," Penny said, brushing a crumb from her knee. "I'm not sure if it's me changing or him or both of us. Probably mostly me. Sometimes I just stare at my reflection and think: 'Who are you? Who are you?'"

Who am I? That question again. Mika had seen a documentary once that cataloged the lives of adopted children, how their lives might have differed had they been raised by biological parents, nature vs. nurture. What made Penny, Penny? How much of her was defined at birth, and how much was determined through the years? What parts had Mika given her daughter? Thomas? Caroline? Her biological father? And did it even matter? "You know," Mika said slowly, "if it makes you feel better, I don't think any of us know who we are. I've spent my entire life trying to figure it out."

Penny hiked up her chin. "That does make me feel better. At least a little less alone, I guess."

"You're not alone." Mika reached over and squeezed Penny's hand.

Companionable silence settled between them until Penny stood up abruptly. "I can't believe this trip is almost over."

"I can't either," said Mika, standing too. The days had flown by. Tomorrow, Penny and Thomas would leave. Mika imagined what would happen after Penny's departure: Penny would call a few more times, make an effort at keeping in touch. But then the calls would slowly fade into oblivion. And this ghost ship of a life Mika was sailing on would come to port. She'd go back to her real life. But who was Mika in real life? And who was she now with Penny? Without Penny? "I wish we had more time," Mika said, and at the words, a jumble of emotions knotted and lodged in her throat—relief at the charade being over and sorrow at letting Penny go again. She knew one thing for certain: Mika in real life was very, very sad.

"It's funny you say that," Penny remarked casually. "There's a great summer running program here at the University of Portland." She paused, eyes trained on the floor. "And I applied for it last night."

"You did?" Mika kept her voice level, though she was feeling so much. Surprised. Terrified. *Thrilled.*

"Yeah. I like Portland." Penny gazed at Mika, searching her face. "And I really like you. I feel like this all fits me here."

"I hadn't considered you wanting to come back." Mika's mind spun in a dizzying circle. She wanted Penny to stay forever. It was her dream come true. *Keep her. Never let her go again.* But what about all the lies? The gallery? The boyfriend? She might be able to sustain them. Penny would be busy with her running program. They'd get together in the evenings, the occasional weekend. If Penny wanted to meet her grandparents, Mika would pretend they were on another cruise or visiting relatives in Japan. *They do that every summer,* she pictured herself saying. *Buy tickets early in the year, nonrefundable.* And as for her relationship with Penny . . . she'd keep building it, feeding it, growing it. She'd focus on what was real: Sharing her thoughts and feelings with her daughter. Supporting her, listening to her, loving her. "What does your dad say?"

Penny sucked in a breath. "He's actually cool with it. Well, he's pretending to be cool with it. When I told him it was nearly the whole summer and students stayed on campus in the dorms, he kind of clenched up, but then, like, visibly forced himself to relax." Another pause. "So, would you be okay with it? With me coming back? You'd want me to?"

Penny's question felt loaded with an especially loaded word—*want.* "Of course I want you to come back," Mika answered automatically, her soul taking over any rational thought.

"Can I just say something?" Penny asked, voice reedy. And Mika nodded and wondered when girls learned that they had to ask permission to speak. "I'm just so happy being here with you. And I haven't been happy for a long time."

Something in the center of Mika's chest felt warm and gooey. "I'm so happy too."

Chapter Fifteen

Arms full of wine bottles and plastic cups, Mika shouldered her way into Stanley's studio again later that evening. "Here, let me." Leif jogged over, relieving her of the load.

She followed him to the back where a long folding table had been set up, white cloth draped over it. He arranged the wine and started uncorking it. "Leif. I cannot thank you enough." Mika viewed her and Penny's handiwork, impressed and proud. The sculptures told a story now. The only thing left was Stanley's final piece, still draped in canvas in the center of the room.

"You haven't seen the best part. Check it out." Leif showed her a little acrylic stand with business cards, her name imprinted on them: MIKA SUZUKI GALLERY, then her phone number. Over the table was a banner that said the same but no phone number. "Adelle helped make them. She's great with design."

"Oh, wow." Mika picked up one of the cards, running a padded fingertip over the sharp corner. This was as close to her dream as she'd ever been. Back when she painted, she had yearned to see her name on an exhibit—imagined her own work under the spotlights. Shaking hands with admirers. Discussing how she used light to capture the subject. And though this was slightly different, seeing her name in a studio, with the word *gallery* next to it . . . it was, well, it made her emotional. She peered up at Leif, words tangled in her throat. "Leif . . . thank you. I don't know how I'll ever repay you."

"It's cool." He thumbed his bottom lip, trying not to smile.

"It's not," Mika said. She pressed on. "I shouldn't have said the things I said when we broke up. I'm sorry I called your dreams stupid. They're not."

"I did some shit that wasn't cool either. I shouldn't have asked you to transport seeds for me." He opened his arms. "Truce hug?" He did his Chris Farley voice.

"Truce," Mika said. They smiled at each other and embraced.

The door opened. Mika tore herself from Leif. Thomas, Penny, *and* Stanley shuffled into the gallery.

She rushed to them. Thomas wore his suit from the other night, and Penny still wore her roller derby T-shirt. "This is amazing. We walked around outside for a few and saw all the artists putting up their tents. It's such a creative, happy vibe," Penny said. "And I think in honor of your new show, I should have a glass of wine."

"Not going to happen," Thomas said, humor in his light eyes as he stared at Mika. Her mind blanked. Their gazes held, stretching into an uncomfortable silence until Leif interlaced his fingers with Mika's and squeezed.

"Hey, nice to see you again." Leif shook Thomas's hand in a way that seemed almost protective. "Glad you could be here to support Mika."

Stanley clapped his hands together. "Well, since everyone has arrived. You all ready to see the pièce de résistance?" His accent was bad, so bad.

Mika slinked away from Leif's hold. "Yes, please." Then she whispered to Thomas and Penny, "I can't wait to see. Stanley is a talented artist."

Stanley moved to the sculpture and stripped the canvas with a whoosh. Mika squinted, unsure what she was seeing at first. Metal twisted together to form the head of a dog but the body of a man? Yes. And . . . a penis. Mika's brain caught in a hamster wheel. It was all she could see—a very large, very erect penis.

"Penny, close your eyes," Thomas said quietly.

"No way," Penny said.

"Well, what do you think?" Stanley stood proudly by the last sculpture. "I'm destigmatizing the male form."

Leif out and out grinned. "I love it, Stanley. You've outdone yourself."

Mika tried to hide her surprise. She swallowed. "Yes, I can see it." What could she say? "The welding work is phenomenal. You can really feel the strength of the animal. Don't you think?" Mika wasn't sure who she was asking, but her eyes connected with Thomas's.

Thomas shifted, sliding his hands into his pockets, eyes crinkling with humor. "Yes, very . . ." He couldn't even. He coughed into his fist. "Sorry, thirsty." He thumped his chest. "I think I'll get a drink."

Penny stepped to Mika's side. She locked arms with Mika, bringing her in close. "I don't really understand art, but I think this is great. If you love it, I love it," Penny said unconditionally.

"You do?" Mika asked, voice softening.

"Of course I do. All of this exists because of you," Penny said. And they squeezed each other in a kind of half-hug.

The night went on. Stanley's art received a lot of attention. Bad or good, it remained to be seen. Hana made an appearance but left to go skip around the booths. The gallery grew hot and crowded, and soon all the wine had been consumed. "I have more in my car," Mika said.

"I'll help you." Thomas had removed his suit jacket and rolled up his sleeves. He followed Mika down the stairs and to the parking lot. Cold night air greeted them, and Mika slowed for a moment to let it press against her warm face. The sun was setting, and the aisles of vendor and artist booths were cast in a red glow. There was a hint of rain and the buzz of conversation in the air.

"This feels good," Mika said, fanning her cheeks.

"Yeah." Thomas ambled beside her, hands in his pockets. "I don't know, something about all that art . . ." He trailed off.

Mika glanced up at him, alarmed. His mouth was set in a firm line. "What?"

"It was rubbing me the wrong way." The corner of his mouth curled, and his eyes twinkled.

"Ha, ha."

"Sorry." Thomas held up his hands. "I couldn't help myself. I'll try *harder*."

"Keep laughing, buddy. And I'll have a serious bone to pick with you." Mika smiled wryly.

He placed a hand over his mouth and laughed. Mika

liked the sound, low and husky. "You're right. I'll try not to be so cocky."

They came to the car, and she opened the door to the back seat. "Is that all out of your system now?"

Thomas shook his head. "Actually, I've got about an hour's worth of material. Surprisingly two jokes center around ghosts."

"Who knew copyright lawyers were so funny?" She grabbed a bottle of wine. "My feelings might be hurt, but I know this all comes from your lack of knowledge of fine art."

"Ouch." Thomas winced. He wrapped his fingers around the base of the wine so they were both holding the bottle. "Have I hurt your feelings?"

"No." Mika felt herself flush. "Of course not. Stanley is an excellent welder, but his concepts need developing." Or just burning. Some things shouldn't see the light of day. Better to start fresh.

"It's a beautiful exhibit, Mika," Thomas said thickly.

Mika's heart skipped a beat. For a full sixty seconds, neither spoke. Thomas's lids lowered. Blink, and she might have missed it. The heat in his eyes. The pulse hammering in his neck. The telltale signs of desire. What would happen if she closed the gap between them? The air was charged with possibilities. She shook her head. *This is ridiculous.* She was ridiculous. Entertaining the thought of Thomas's lips on hers. She let go of the bottle, the zap of electricity shorted out, and she toed the gravel on the ground. "Th-thank you," Mika stammered out. Her eyes drifted to the back seat of the car, to the bottles of wine. "Um, I have half a dozen more, mostly reds, but . . ." Her throat was dry. "But we should be able to get them all between the two of us."

"Sure. Right." Thomas stepped back. They loaded up with the drinks, then set off back to the gallery.

Between steps, she stole glances at Thomas, examining his relaxed face. Had she imagined it? The heat in his eyes? *Definitely.* He had said something nice to her, that was all. When would she ever learn? She'd done something similar with Marcus. Projected her feelings, read too much into his smiles, his kindness. She'd confused lust with love. Let her desire eclipse reality. Let herself become lost in it.

The night of Marcus's party, she'd arrived early. After knocking on the door, she'd appraised her outfit. The tights, plaid skirt, and fine turtleneck sweater made her feel older, but really, she'd been a little girl playing dress-up. Peter, the graduate student hosting the party, had answered the door, Marcus behind him in the empty apartment.

I'm early, she had said, twirling to go, *I'll come back.*

Marcus grinned, grabbed her arm, and pulled her through the door. His eyes were red and hazy. Drunk, already. *You're right on time,* he said, spinning her around. He placed a hand on her back and swayed to the music. She rested a hand on his shoulder. It was the first time she'd ever touched him. She remembered the sinewy feel of his muscle under her fingers, his hot skin burning through the fabric of his shirt. Right behind her, another few people came—graduate students, a colleague or two of Marcus's.

Peter brought Mika a drink, something strong in a red Solo cup, then she was dancing with Marcus again. Laughing. She felt his attention like a physical force, a boulder rolling into her, a hand turning her into a new direction. She'd been smitten from the beginning, falling under his spell. Thinking of koi no yokan—the sensation upon meeting someone that falling in love with them is inevitable.

Cool wind swept through, forcing Mika to the present. She bowed her head in the fleeting shame. "So," Mika said, squinting against the dying sunlight. "Penny told me she's applying for a summer program here."

"Yes," Thomas intoned. "She announced that to me this morning."

"She said you're okay with it."

Thomas let out a little laugh. "I don't think I have

much of a choice." Their pace slowed. "But I am okay with it. I think this has been good for Penny." He grew thoughtful. "For us. Plus," he added. "You'll be here."

Mika couldn't help a smile from creeping across her face. Thomas trusted Mika to look after Penny. "I'll take good care of her."

They came to the warehouse, and Mika used her back to push through the door. She tromped up the steps, aware Thomas was behind her. They deposited the wine on the table, and Leif set to uncorking it. "You're all flushed," he said.

Mika's stomach flipped. "It's warm in here."

Leif eyed her suspiciously, then Thomas, who stood over her shoulder. "While you were gone, Stanley got a commission."

"He did?" Mika poured herself a healthy glass of wine.

"Some hipster wants him to sculpt himself as a centaur," Leif said.

Mika nearly choked on the sip she'd just taken. She patted her chest. "My god."

Penny joined them. "I feel like we should toast to the evening. Leif, would you mind pouring me a glass of that cabernet?"

"Penny. No," Thomas said again.

Penny shrugged. "Never hurts to try."

"Mi-chan." Mika shook her head. She could have sworn she'd just heard her mother. She couldn't have possibly, though. What would Hiromi be doing here? "Mika." Her name again, this time unmistakable.

Mika's blood ran cold as she straightened and slowly turned on one foot. There was Hiromi, hair slicked back into an unforgiving dome, knee-length skirt, and purse slung over her elbow. "Mom," she said, stunned, poleaxed really. "What are you doing here?" The chatter in the gallery died away. It was like they were in a bubble suddenly—Leif, Penny, Thomas, Mika, and Hiromi.

"What are *you* doing here?" Hiromi flung back.

"Hi," Thomas cut in. "I'm Thomas Calvin. Penny's dad." He stuck out his hand, and Hiromi stared until he dropped it.

Penny stepped forward too, a hesitant smile on her face. Mika could only watch as Hiromi and Penny looked at each other, *saw* each other for the very first time. Noticed how they shared the same cheekbones, the same tiny nose and bow-shaped lips. How their hands were similar too, thin with longish fingers that tapered into oval nails. How if time fast-forwarded a few decades ahead, Hiromi might be an age-generated portrait of Penny, of Mika—because blood always tells. Mika knew the moment it registered for Hiromi. Her mother's lips parted. Her black button eyes watered. She couldn't stop staring at Penny.

At her granddaughter.

"This is so amazing! I thought you were on a cruise," Penny said, totally uninhibited. Why wouldn't she be? Penny was used to being loved, to having others love her in return. She didn't know Hiromi didn't want Mika to have her, didn't know that instead of "baby" or "her," Hiromi called Penny "it."

"Cruise?" Hiromi's raven brows darted in. "I've never been on a cruise."

"Hey, kiddo," Thomas said, calling Penny softly back to him.

Mika's stomach plunged, an elevator with its cables cut. "Mom." She couldn't think of anything to say. "How did you know I was here?"

"I followed you. You haven't been returning my phone calls. I was worried. What's going on?" Hiromi's eyes fell on the business cards on the table. Then on the banner above the table. MIKA SUZUKI GALLERY. "Is this what you spent the money I gave you on?" she asked, gesturing at the gallery, arm encompassing the terrible art. "You're supposed to be looking for a job."

Mika saw Thomas's brow dip in confusion. Saw Penny's smile dissolve. Saw the questions forming in their eyes.

"Okāsan," Mika said, inching forward, hand out to guide her mother away. "Let's talk outside."

Hiromi sidestepped Mika. "What's he doing here? I thought you broke up with him?" She stared at Leif, face twisting as if staring at a plate of food she did not like.

Mika rubbed her brow. Feeling the pieces fall around her. How could she pick them all up with only two hands? "We did. But . . ."

At that, Thomas's light eyes flared.

"We're working things out," Leif interjected, trying to help in the worst possible way.

Hiromi snorted. The noise said it all. "And who is this?" she flicked a hand at Penny, and it seemed to fall on Mika's daughter like a physical blow. Penny flinched. "Mi-chan?" Hiromi pressed. Hiromi knew exactly who Penny was. It was unmistakable. But this was Hiromi's efficient way. Refuse to acknowledge Mika had had a baby. Wield her words like a pair of garden shears. Clip Mika down to a nub.

"Mika?" Thomas pressed.

But Mika didn't have an answer. She couldn't answer. At the prospect of lying again or telling the truth, Mika's mind came to a crashing halt. Her world had spun out of control. Cold spread through her, in her feet, into her hands, into her bones. All over. She was frozen.

Thomas cleared his throat. "This is Penny. Mika is her birth mother." He paused, put an arm around Penny, pulled her in. "It sounds as if you and your daughter need to talk, and I think we should let you." Thomas moved to go, but Penny broke from her father and stepped over to Mika.

"Looking for a job? Why would you be looking for a job? You quit to open the gallery. This *is* your job," Penny said, brow furrowed. "I'm so confused. You said you took out a business loan for the gallery. But you borrowed money from your parents? Did you lie about that? Why would you lie about something like that?" Her voice cracked, pleaded.

Mika's shoulders hunched with heaviness, with the past catching up with her. She regretted so many things in that moment. Under Penny's scrutiny, what else could she do but tell the truth? "I didn't quit my job," she said in a whisper. "I was fired." Penny stood stock-still, but her face was open, willing, wanting this all to be a misunderstanding. Mika cleared her throat. "I borrowed money from my parents to make ends meet."

Penny shook her head. "I still don't understand."

Mika rubbed her lips together. "Um . . . I didn't tell you the truth about a lot of things, actually. I don't have an art history degree. I barely graduated college with a business degree, and it took me eight years. Since then,

I've hopped around jobs. The gallery is Stanley's, he rents from Leif, they let me borrow it for today. And Leif and I aren't a couple. We were, but we broke up." She opened her hands, smiled helplessly at Penny. "I can't seem to hold on to anything."

"Mika," Leif said softly, sadly.

"So you're a liar?" Penny flicked out, eyes blazing.

Thomas, Penny, Leif, and Hiromi all looked to Mika, and Mika looked away, sick. She couldn't say it aloud, so she dipped her chin in silent confirmation. *Yes, I am a liar.*

"C'mon, kiddo," Thomas said. "I think we're done here." Mika glanced up as Thomas peeled Penny away, tucking her under his arm again.

"Why would she do that?" Penny whispered up to her father. A tear slid down her cheek.

"I don't know," Thomas said. "But let's go back to the hotel. We'll talk there." Thomas made eye contact with Mika. He nodded once, eyes exacting and unforgiving—a set of closed doors. "Goodbye, Mika."

Penny let her dad lead her away, and Mika stood there, rooted to the spot. Watching as they walked out of the gallery, out of her life. The day she left the hospital after she'd had Penny, a nurse had pushed her out in a wheelchair, depositing her on the bench right outside the maternity ward, Hana beside her with their backpacks. They sat for a while. Mika staring off into space, flexing her empty hands. Doctors and nurses came and went. A new mom rolled out, her baby in the car seat with balloons tied to the handle. The dad pulled up to the curb and gently assisted them into the car.

Everyone just going about their business. *Nothing to see here.* Their worlds turning, while Mika's had stopped. She'd been pregnant, had given birth to something alive and wonderful, had held on to it for a few precious hours, and now it was gone—her baby. And Mika was left with no reminder of what had been except some cramping and bleeding.

If we don't go soon, we're going to miss the last bus, Hana gently pressed, her voice a tinny wobble. A gust of wind tore at her hair. The light leached from the sky.

Yeah, okay, Mika had murmured.

Now, all around them were people again. Viewing the art as if none of this was happening in the corner of the gallery. As if Mika's heart wasn't breaking all over again. She focused on Hiromi. Even though it should have been drilled out of her, it was still Mika's natural instinct to search out her mother.

Hiromi opened her mouth, clicked her tongue. "Mi-chan," she said with such utter disappointment it made Mika tunnel even deeper into herself, into a space where no one could follow.

Someone squeezed her shoulder, Leif probably, but Mika couldn't feel him through all the layers of pain. Mika wanted to scream. Mika wanted to run after Penny, cling to her like ivy. But Mika didn't move an inch. She didn't make a sound. She did as she'd been taught. Hold in the pain. Be silent. Don't make a scene.

ADOPTION ACROSS AMERICA
National Office
56544 W 57th Ave. Suite 111
Topeka, KS 66546
(800) 555-7794

Dear Mika,

I've tried calling but haven't been able to get ahold of you. Caroline Calvin passed away. I'm sure this is difficult for you. I want to assure you Penelope is in the best of hands with Thomas. They have lots of extended family supporting them through this time. Do you remember seeing pictures of Caroline's parents? They live in the area. Please call me if you need anything or just want to talk. I am here.

All my very best,

Monica Pearson
Adoption Coordinator

P.S. I've included the funeral pamphlet, which contains some lovely words from Thomas about Penny.

Caroline "Linney" Calvin
1972–2016
Dayton, Ohio

Caroline Abigail Calvin passed away on January 21, 2016. Caroline was born on September 19, 1972, and grew up in Dayton, Ohio. She married her childhood sweetheart, Thomas Preston Calvin, a copyright attorney, in May of 2000. She worked as a pediatric nurse and was known for her bedside manner. Patients often commented on her kindness and willingness to sit and chat for a while. "She always had time for us," a patient's mother said.

Caroline dreamed of having a family and fulfilled that dream when she and Thomas adopted their daughter Penelope in 2005. After that, Caroline left her job as a nurse to raise Penny. Upon learning of her terminal cancer diagnosis, Thomas took a leave of absence from his job. The three traveled but spent most of their time with family, which was the most important thing to Caroline.

From Thomas: Caroline loved a well-done hamburger, making quilts, gardening, and poetry. She was also obsessed with bargain hunting—she never passed on a deal. But most of all, she loved our daughter, Penelope, who made her smile up until the very end. From the moment we adopted Penny, we instantly experienced more than a lifetime of love, at least that's what Caroline always said. I can't count the number of times she'd look at me and say, I'm so happy right now. In her last moments, Caroline assured me that her heart was full. With her final words, she wished for Penny and anyone else who mourns her to know that no matter what, love always returns.

Chapter Sixteen

Mika was at home, in her bed, sleeping—*dreaming*. She was ten, in a kimono and on a stage, a single light illuminating her. The auditorium had red cushioned seats and was empty, except for the two seats in the front row occupied by her parents. The back of the auditorium blew away, chunks of wood splintering in the air as if a bomb had been detonated. Not a bomb, but a storm. A tornado, and caught in its swirls were apple pies, plastic red Solo cups, tubes of paint, broken bits of pottery. Mika's mouth opened in a scream, and she felt herself falling down the tunnel of her own throat.

The dream shifted to reality, to a memory.

She was back in Peter's apartment, at Marcus's party. Bodies crammed into the small space. Mark Morrison played on the loudspeaker, "Return of the Mack."

Mika leaned against the wall, watching Marcus across the room grind against a graduate student. Her eyes and body were heavy. She thought it was from sadness, but later on, she'd realize it was from something else. She blinked, slow lidded, and droopy. When she opened her eyes, Peter was in her direct line of vision.

Hey, he said with a wolf's grin. *I brought you another drink.* He'd been refilling her cup all night. He tipped it up to her mouth. Mika turned her head, and beer spilled down her cheek, soaked the front of her black sweater.

I don't feel good, she said.

Peter hooked an arm around her waist, promising to take her somewhere quiet. She stumbled and leaned into him. Then they were in his bedroom. He laid Mika down, and she watched through a haze as he closed the door. Locked it. The noises from the party silenced. She drifted off. And woke to Peter on top of her, pinning her to the mattress.

She tried to push him off, but her movements were slow, sludge traveling down a wall. *No,* she said, then louder, *No.* His hand smelled like turpentine as he held it over her mouth and squeezed her cheeks, eliciting hot tears. All she could do was watch him through a watery haze, his face fragmented, a cubist painting. Not Marcus, but Peter above her. It wasn't right. It wasn't what she wanted. She watched the time on his nightstand clock, the minutes ticking away. 12:01, 12:02, 12:03, the exact time Penny was conceived. Then her eyes rolled up to the ceiling. The bed creaked like a *chop, chop, chop* . . . pieces of her falling away. In a single moment, her life bifurcated, even slices of before and after.

Mika startled awake with a gasp. Her fingers searched her throat, fluttered over her hammering pulse. The memory fled, and she closed her eyes. Breathed deeply and heavily. She was safe. It was over. Thoughts jumbled up, reality picked away at the miasma of dreams and memories—nightmares. Penny. Thomas. The art gallery. A new cord of panic twisted around her lungs and pulled tight. *Their flight leaves at eleven fifteen.* She might be able to catch them at the airport. She dressed, pulling on sweatpants and a sweatshirt discarded on the floor. When she came out of her room, Hana was in the kitchen. Mika didn't say a word as she frantically searched for her keys.

"Well, good morning to you too," Hana said, sipping a cup of coffee.

Mika didn't stop looking. Under a stack of papers. In the couch cushions. Where were her fucking keys? Her chin quivered. "Penny and Thomas are leaving today, and I fucked up so bad. I need to get to the airport and try to find them, but I can't find my fucking keys." Mika jammed her palms into her eyes until she saw white spots.

"You mean these?" That's when she noticed Hana wasn't the only person in the kitchen. A slight, petite, brown-haired girl held her hand aloft, keys dangling from her fingertips, metal glinting in the bright morning sunlight. "I'm Josephine, by the way," she said, smiling, showing off a dimple in her left cheek. Hana grinned too.

"Thanks." Mika snatched the keys and shoved her feet into her shoes near the front door.

"You want me to drive you?" Hana chased Mika out the front door.

"No." Mika waved a hand. "It's fine. It will all be fine."

The drive to the airport passed in a blur. Weaving in and out of traffic, some honking. Her heart pounding as if she were a person drowning in the ocean. She parked in the departures drop-off-only lane and jumped from her car. Everywhere were signs that read: LOADING AND UNLOADING ONLY, DO NOT LEAVE CAR UN-ATTENDED. A security guard in a bright yellow vest blew his whistle. "Ma'am, you can't leave your car here."

Mika didn't listen. Too intent on searching the outside for a splash of dark hair, for a tall man with a set of broody eyes. They weren't outside. She ran through the double glass doors and vaguely remembered the airline they were flying. *Alaska.* She scurried to the ticketing booth, scanned the lines. No Penny. No Thomas. What time was it? She found a digital clock behind the counter, 10:35 a.m. She ran to the departures board but couldn't remember their flight number. But she was able to connect the dots with the flight and destination. There it was. In big capital letters: BOARDING. A hand cupped her bicep and pulled her. "Lady, you can't leave your car."

She jerked her arm away. Her chest felt tight. What was happening now seemed inevitable. A crash course of events set for sixteen years in the future. She couldn't help but think of watching Mrs. Pearson taking Penny away at the hospital. Her hands clutching the tiny bundle. Her baby. This was it. Penny was gone. *Again.* Bereft, her knees buckled. It rolled over her, a cold blue tide. "Penny," she whispered.

"Seriously, lady," the security guard said. "I'm going to tow your car. Then I'm going to have to call the police." Mika stood woodenly. Her body wouldn't work. The security guard shifted closer to her. He waved a hand in front of her face. "C'mon. Don't make me call the police. My shift just started. If you go back to your car right now, we'll forget the whole thing ever happened."

Finally, Mika nodded vacantly and staggered away, spirit separating from her body. It was much the same as when she'd left Peter's apartment the morning after. He'd been sleeping, and Mika had woken to his arm thrown across her. She eased from his hold, sat on the edge of the bed, and examined her lower half—the damage. An animal assessing itself—if it was too wounded to run. Her skirt was still on, but her tights and underwear were gone. Her thighs were tender, black and blue with the marks of fingerprints. She stood and wavered but managed to tiptoe to the door. Heart pounding at every little noise. Afraid she'd wake him. Persephone skirting Cerberus.

She inhaled her first deep breath as she burst out of the building. Then stumbled through the campus. Torn tights. Torn skin. Torn soul. Her body a small apocalypse. The rest she remembered abstractly. A jagged yellow line of sick, pale sunlight. Wind so sharp it rippled the short grass and burned her cheeks and whipped her bare thighs. Two black splotches—crows fighting over a discarded container of watermelon. A flash of blue from a light atop a special telephone. If Mika picked up the receiver, someone would come escort her to safety. She considered it but discarded the idea as easily as a gum wrapper. *How many sexual partners have you had?* The police might ask, even though it was nobody's business.

And Mika would say eight, two of which she could not remember very well. But she did remember Peter. Remembered saying no. Yet who would believe her? This girl who wasted her life painting, spent her nights at frat parties, and once gave a blow job to a guy in a backyard. When did a woman's decision to have sex become a barometer for honesty? Mika didn't know the answer. She just knew it to be true.

A car horn blared, and Mika startled. She was back in the airport, the guy in the yellow vest scrutinizing her from the curb. *Go*, he mouthed and pointed to the exit.

She drove far enough to park in the cell phone waiting lot, then hit the steering wheel before collapsing against it. She was lost again. Lost and alone.

How did everything always go so wrong?

She leaned back. She'd lied to Penny. Her intentions had been good. But that didn't matter. What mattered was Penny had been hurt. That was the last thing Mika wanted. Wasn't that how this had all started? All she'd wanted was to protect Penny from the truth, from learning about Peter, about herself, from the knowledge that the world could be such a terrible and cruel place. She had wanted to show Penny that the adoption had been worth it for both of them. Penny received a loving family. Mika achieved her dreams.

She rolled down her windows, let the morning chill

the tears on her face. Smelled the rain and the fresh-cut grass. Then she drew out her phone, and before she knew it, she was calling Penny.

"You've reached Penny. Leave a message." Penny's voicemail picked up. She was probably in the air by now.

"Penny," Mika scratched out, cords in her throat tightening. "It's me. Of course, you know it's me. I'm so sorry. So sorry," she repeated. Then paused, gathering herself up. "I owe you an explanation. When you contacted me . . ." She gripped the seat, and the leather turned to flannel, the rough feeling of Penny's hospital blanket under her hands as she held her baby close and fed her a bottle. Mika kept talking, letting the truth spill out. Babbling on about how she'd been so surprised when Penny called. How she'd assessed her life and came up with hands empty. How everything seemed to snowball after that. A minute passed that felt more like an hour, and Mika finished with another "I'm sorry." She was prepared to spend her life apologizing. "I don't know what I was thinking. I just . . . I guess I just wanted you to be proud of me. Please call me. *Please.*" She pressed the pound button. A disembodied voice directed her to hit one to send the message now. She hesitated; the unholy truth felt riskier than the lies. She drew her finger closer to the button, a knife above a wound ready to lance it. She hit the one and slumped down.

It was done.

A breeze ruffled her hair, and she brushed it from her eyes. She sat for a while more, watching the gray sky, listening to the sound of planes departing, feeling as if she'd time-traveled. She tapped out a text to Hana. I need you. Hana responded almost instantly. I am here. Waiting for you. Josephine is gone. Come home.

Mika put her car in gear and drove home. To Hana, to a place where Mika always felt perfectly loved. As promised, Hana was waiting, her arms open, and Mika fell into them, finding comfort in her bony shoulder. They had the same body shape and fit together perfectly—filling all of each other's hollow places. This is what she longed for from Hiromi. But her mother was too hard of a person. Hard flinty eyes, hard callused hands, just hard. Maybe that was the key to parenting: you couldn't keep your children from being hurt, but you could give them a soft place to land.

Hana whisked Mika inside and sat her down on the couch. "Come on, tell me all of it. I'll make you an omelet."

"We don't have any eggs," Mika said and started to cry all over again. She pulled a throw blanket to her and blew her nose into the soft chenille.

Hana pulled Mika's hands from her face and held

her, stroking her hair. "It's okay," she said over and over until Mika breathed a little easier.

"Sit. I will find something to soothe you . . . and some tissues," Hana said. Twenty minutes later, Hana placed a cup of noodle soup in Mika's hands. She waited for Mika to take a couple of bites, then encouraged her to sip the broth. "Now," she said. "Tell me what happened."

Mika told Hana how it had all blown up in her face. About Hiromi showing up at the opening and exposing Mika. Of chasing Penny and Thomas to the airport and the rambling voicemail she'd left. "You think they'll get back in touch?" Hana asked.

Mika shrugged, resisting the urge to check her phone and see if Penny had called or texted. Of course there wouldn't be anything this soon. Penny and Thomas were flying right now. "Honestly, I'm not sure. I don't know if the truth or lies are better." She turned the mug of soup slowly between her palms.

Hana pursed her lips. "Do you want me to cancel the Pearl Jam tour?" She was supposed to leave in three weeks.

"What? No," Mika said, swiping under her nose. "Don't be silly. You should definitely go. No need for both of us to be sad sacks."

"But you need me . . ."

"No. Absolutely not. I forbid you to even think of it." Mika set her cup down on the coffee table. Pain still zinged through her abdomen, but she ignored it. "Now, enough about me. Tell me about Josephine."

A smile broke across Hana's face, along with a furious blush. "Not much to say. I met her last night at Sheila's"—a hipster hole-in-the-wall gay bar. "She's an artist. She does things with mixed media and her hands you wouldn't believe." Hana wriggled her fingers.

"TMI." Mika waved a hand even as a grin flickered over her face.

"Just saying." Hana shrugged. "I don't know, all this cleaning out of the house, it's been a game changer for me, I think."

"You're happy," said Mika.

"I'm happy," Hana said.

"I'm glad," Mika told Hana. "Love your face."

"Love your face more," Hana said, then added quietly, "I won't go if you don't want me to."

Mika shook her head but couldn't form the words to say no because her throat knotted. She knew Hana meant it. She would stay. And Mika's heart threatened to burst at the simple promise.

Chapter Seventeen

Mika didn't leave the house. For seventy-two hours, she subsisted on Thai takeout, Diet Coke, and a steady stream of *Law & Order: SVU*. Every time she blinked, she saw the gallery opening on the inside of her eyelids. *Blink.* Penny's face when Hiromi thrust out a hand and said, "Who is this?" *Blink.* Thomas wrapping his arm around Penny as she tucked her chin into her chest—shrunken, sad, dejected. *Blink.* Penny tipping her head up to her father, tears sliding down her cheeks as she asked him, why—why did Mika lie? The images, the pain, never dulled.

She checked her phone and email every five or so minutes—no messages from Penny or Thomas. She tried to put the two out of her mind but found her thoughts drifting toward them if she wasn't careful.

She missed Penny's smile, her whirlwind energy. And she missed Thomas too, his charming grumpy vibe, the way he loved Penny. A ship had arrived on the shore she shared with Penny and Thomas. It had come to retrieve Mika, take her back to exile, where she belonged.

Hana appeared in the doorway of the room, threading a gold hoop through her ear. She was going out with Josephine again. Third time this week. "More *SVU*?"

Mika shifted on the couch. She wore an old Grateful Dead shirt she'd stolen from Leif and a pair of loose sweatpants. Her phone was close by on the coffee table among the litter of takeout containers, soda cans, and bags of chips—last night, Mika hit rock bottom and snacked on the corn nuts stuffed in the back of the cupboard, a relic from the previous owner of the house. "Yep. Season eleven, the episode where Stabler and Benson suspect a sugar daddy of murder when a young woman's body is found stuffed inside a suitcase."

"Ah, a tale as old as time." Hana dropped a compact into her purse. "You sure you don't want to come with?"

"Pft," Mika said. "I wouldn't dream of crashing your date."

"So, this is your plan for the evening, television and

takeout?" Hana picked up a container from the coffee table and sniffed it.

Mika rolled to her back and eyed Hana. "Yes, and contemplating a bunch of stuff that makes me realize the banality of my own existence."

Hana set the takeout container down. "Well, while you're spiraling, do you think you could eat something with a vegetable in it?"

"Pad thai has vegetables," Mika said with mild offense.

Hana snorted and opened the door. "I'm spending the night at Josephine's. I'll see you in the morning."

Mika gave her two thumbs up. She listened as Hana's car pulled away and curled onto her side. Her phone pinged with an incoming text, and her heart quickened. Hope was like that, a helium balloon tangled in branches, refusing to stay down. The last few times this happened, it had been Hiromi or Leif or Charlie or Hayato. She was an equal-opportunity decliner, swiping right on each. Still, she picked her phone up, poised at the edge of disappointment.

Penny.

Her name lit up the screen. I listened to your message, she had texted. When can we talk?

Mika bolted upright and shut the television off.

Right now? she answered Penny. She stood and started pacing, phone in hand. Five agonizing minutes later, it rang. She answered right away. "Hi," Mika said.

"Hi," Penny said, not her usual bright self. She'd done that. Mika had dimmed Penny's light. So much of Mika's sense of worth hung on how her daughter felt, about life, about her. "So . . ."

"So, you got my voicemail." Mika kept her voice even, airy. As if to say, *Go on, punish me, hit me if you want, I can take it.*

"Yeah. I listened to it as soon as we got home." Three days ago? Penny had heard it three days ago? "It took a while for me to sort out everything I was feeling."

A lump formed in Mika's throat. "I understand."

"I don't understand," Penny said sharply.

"Okay," Mika said. She stood and walked to the kitchen, retrieved a glass from the cabinet, and filled it from the faucet. When was the last time she had water? Phone pressed between her shoulder and ear, she asked, "What don't you understand?"

"Why you didn't keep me?" Desperation sharpened the edges of her words.

Mika startled, not expecting that question. But she supposed they'd been working up to it. It had always been on the fringes of her and Penny's relationship, a pair of hands pulling it apart. "I couldn't," she said, leaving the kitchen to sit down on the edge of the couch, thinking of how unequipped she'd been at the time. Mika remembered the Instagram posts she'd seen. All those women, new mothers with babies. The comments sections littered with seemingly positive reinforcement. *You got this! You're one tough mama! Dig deep!* Encouraging each other to push themselves beyond their limits. The messaging was pervasive. A good mother wouldn't abandon her children. Wouldn't abandon her biological duty. If she did, there must be something wrong with her. Or with her offspring. Did Penny feel that way? That her DNA was messed up?

For one whole minute, Penny was silent. "Did you want me?"

"I *did* want you." Mika inhaled. Exhaled. She'd wanted Penny despite Peter. Despite Hiromi. Despite her mother's quiet discontent. "I wanted you. But I wanted things for you. Better things. I wanted you to have a big house, a family and parents and cousins and grandparents. I wanted you to go to a good school with new supplies and clothes. I wanted you to have everything I never had and would never be able to give you. That's how much I wanted you." For Mika placing Penny for adoption had been the ultimate act of love. Penny deserved better. Penny remained silent on the other end of the line, but Mika could hear her breathing, each exhale and inhale like a metronome. "I know this is all so messed up. I lied to you, and I will be forever sorry." She forged on. "If you . . . If you can find a way to let me back into your life, I promise I won't ever lie to you again."

The stony silence carried on for another beat. "Was it because you were ashamed of me?" Penny asked finally.

Mika straightened. "No!" she blurted. *How could Penny think that?* "It's the opposite. I didn't want *you* to be ashamed of *me*." Mika felt the tightening constraints of motherhood. To be strong enough. To be smart enough. To be enough. But she couldn't relay that to Penny. How she felt something inside her was missing, derelict. "My life isn't pretty. It's a real shit show." That garnered a soft laugh from Penny. Mika ran with it. "I mean, I keep a bag of chocolate chips open on the counter so I can reach in whenever I walk by and have a handful."

Penny laughed again but sobered quickly and turned sad, wistful almost. "Was any of it real?"

Guilt and sorrow raced through Mika like a set of bloodhounds. It had all been real to Mika. The hugs. The warm feelings. The wanting. The love. That was all true. But she could see what she'd done. By lying,

Mika had rendered their relationship meaningless, at least to Penny. "Honestly, I kind of mixed things up, blended the truth with fiction. Hana is my best friend, and she does love roller derby. But I don't live on my own. I live with Hana because I can't afford a place, and she's a terrible hoarder, or at least, she was—she's doing better, actually. Leif is my ex-boyfriend. He doesn't have a degree in biochemistry but does have a love for it; he applied it toward growing marijuana. He owns a dispensary in Portland. He wears mostly hemp and believes in unbanking."

"That actually makes a lot of sense now." Penny's voice warmed.

"When we dated, he used a crystal for deodorant." Mika paused. "It didn't work," she said as if whispering a secret in Penny's ear. Penny giggled. Mika flopped backward and played with the drawstring on her sweatpants. "What else do you want to know? I'll answer any of your questions."

Penny grew quiet. "There is something." She hesitated. "I wanted to ask in Portland, but it never felt like the right time."

"Shoot," Mika said.

"My father . . . I mean, my biological father. Do you . . . know him? Like his name or anything."

Now Mika grew quiet. She imagined telling Penny about Peter, the rape. Mika winced against that word. *Rape.* Such an ugly term. She had trouble using it in conjunction with what happened to her. Though her body remembered the violence, her mind refused to capitulate. *Not me. It could not have happened to me.* She wasn't the only one who had trouble using the word. Media, news outlets, they preferred *sexual assault.* It seemed nicer, gentler somehow. A woman might recover from an assault, but she might never survive a rape. And deep down, Mika was haunted by her inactions that night. Her paltry no. The way she lay limp. The way she couldn't be an agent in her own salvation. How could Mika explain it to Penny? She separated her daughter from the event. Did it help that when Penny was born, she looked nothing like Peter? She took after Mika's side. Would she have reacted differently if Penny's skin were lighter, her eyes rounder and green, her hair brown rather than black? *No,* Mika thought with absolute certainty. *I would have loved her the same.* She used to gaze down at her swollen belly and whisper to it, promising, *He'll never know you.*

"Are you still there?" Penny prodded.

"Just thinking," Mika said. "I'm . . ." She swallowed. Sometimes she looked Peter up online. He was an artist in New York now, with a family, and it was confusing to Mika how he might be tender with others when he'd ripped into her like a piece of rotten fruit. He hadn't made it big yet, but he made a living at it, with the occasional freelance commission landscape. "There are things in my past that are difficult to talk about." It occurred to Mika that Penny was a victim of Peter's too. They both had burdens to carry. But it didn't have to be Penny's yet. Someday she'd consider telling Penny. But before that, she would fill Penny's head with how good she was, how beautifully strong, *how loved.*

Penny would understand, even though that was where she came from, it wasn't where she was going. "For right now, you know everything you need to. I know this isn't fair to ask, but you're going to have to trust me to tell you things when I'm ready and respect what I can't talk about yet." Mika felt it then. A subtle shift in their relationship from friendship . . . to what? She wasn't sure. But it was more. A recognition that Penny was only sixteen and Mika was thirty-five. Nearly two decades of life experiences separated them. She wouldn't lord it over Penny, but she would use it to protect her daughter at the very least.

She heard Penny take a steadying breath. "Okay," she said finally. "I can accept that."

Mika sighed with relief. "Someday, I hope you can

forgive me," she said. "I imagine you're still angry, and that's okay—"

"I am," Penny cut in. "But . . . not so angry I never want to speak again. I still . . . I still have so many questions. I want to trust you, but I'm not sure I can."

"Okay. You need time. I can accept that," Mika said, echoing Penny's words. "I hope you can forgive me for giving you up for adoption too." Might as well go for broke.

"Oh," Penny said. "As far as I'm concerned, there's nothing to forgive. It's like asking you to apologize for the sky being blue, or for me being Japanese, or born a woman. Some things just are. This is a part of me."

Tears sprang in Mika's eyes. "Thank you," she said.

"Yeah," Penny said. A beat passed. "I should probably get going. It's late here."

Mika sat up and swiped under her nose. "Sure. Of course. Do you think . . . Could we talk again soon sometime?"

"Want to give me a call next week?" Penny asked.

"Yes," Mika answered, and she tried not to sound too eager, too desperate. They said goodbye. And after, Mika sat for a while, mentally sorting through their conversation, then her life. After Peter, after Penny, she didn't think much of the future. Couldn't imagine life anymore, all of the beautiful infinite possibilities. But now . . . *now* she went to the kitchen and retrieved the garbage can from under the sink. With a single swipe of her arm, she swept the contents off the coffee table, dumping it into the bin. She picked up the throw blanket she'd been hibernating under and folded it, placing it over the armrest of the couch. That done, she sat again and peered at her phone. At all the missed calls from Hiromi. Still not ready to speak to her mother, she hit call back on another person's phone number.

Hayato answered on the third ring. "Hey, you."

"Hey," Mika said cheerily. "How are you?"

"Good. I'm good. How about you?" In the background, she could hear a television, the voice of a famous newscaster.

"I'm doing okay." Mika smiled. "I was hoping I might be able to buy you a drink and talk to you about a job."

Chapter Eighteen

"What's your favorite movie?" Penny asked the following week. The urge to say something more refined sat on the tip of Mika's tongue—*The Shawshank Redemption*, *Schindler's List*, *The Godfather*—but she settled for the one she watched over and over with Hana. "*Dumb and Dumber*," she answered.

Penny hadn't seen it and watched it over the weekend. "Why is it your favorite movie?" she pressed Mika on their next call.

"I don't know. It's funny, right?" Mika said. She leaned against the kitchen counter. The phone pressed against her ear. She'd just had her first interview at Nike and was still in her collared top and pencil skirt,

sans shoes. Over sugary drinks, Mika had unbur-
dened herself to Hayato, telling him about Penny, the
adoption, the lies, and her crumbling finances, then
asked him to help her with a job. He'd been happy
to. And upon his advice, she'd scoured Nike's career
page and applied for the first position, administrative
assistant II, she qualified for. Hayato helped move her
application to the top of the pile.

"Hilarious," Penny agreed.

Mika thought more about Penny's question. "It was
kind of an escape for me. I didn't have an easy childhood. My parents are very traditional, and there wasn't
much room for humor in our home."

"Were they angry when you got pregnant with me?"
Penny asked.

"I actually don't know." Hiromi's face flashed in her
mind. She still hadn't spoken to her mother. Which
wasn't unusual. They'd spend days, weeks, even months
not talking to each other. But eventually, Mika would
always come back. She remembered Hiromi breaking
down over a bunch of bananas soon after they'd moved
to the States.

Stop buying so many, Shige had said, eyeing the rot-
ting fruit on the counter.

I can't, Hiromi had said. *I don't understand why*

they come in such big quantities. Who needs a dozen bananas?

You never split the bunches in Japan, and Hiromi had assumed it was the same in America. She decided to complain to the store manager. In broken English, she begged him to put out smaller quantities. He'd laughed and said she could do it herself. Hiromi thought he was making fun of her. But Mika understood and showed her mother. It's what kept Mika tethered to Hiromi. The thought that they might be lost without each other.

"My mother was disappointed," she said to Penny now. She paused. Felt her mother's derision beating down on her like a hot desert sun. *What do you know about raising a baby?* "Very disappointed."

"Sometimes that's worse," Penny said.

"Yep." Mika expelled a breath.

More time passed. Mika had a second interview at Nike. Penny was wrapping up her school year. There were parties and a dance she went to with friends. They FaceTimed during Hana's last roller derby game before she left on tour with Pearl Jam. Mika was hired at Nike and had a dizzying tour of the campus by a very competent yet brisk HR employee. That night she sent Penny a photograph of her work ID with the words It's official. When Mika had faked finding a gallery, they'd toasted on screen, popping bottles and giggling. This time, Penny replied with a party hat and streamers. That's all. Penny was more subdued with Mika. Their relationship was no longer a house catching flame but one being painstakingly rebuilt—what happens after the fire.

Two weeks later, Mika smoothed down her black dress pants and peered at the latest text from Penny. Happy first day of work. Call me after?

I don't know when I'll be home, but I'll give you a ring, Mika tapped out. She tucked her hair behind her ear, a little overwhelmed at being in the middle of the Nike Worldwide Headquarters campus. Two hundred eighty-six acres. Seventy-five buildings. Thousands of employees. No biggie. Her phone rang. Noting the caller, she answered with a relieved smile. "Hi."

"Hey, you finding your way?" Hayato asked. "I can step out and walk you to the Serena Williams Building."

"I'm good," she promised.

"Perfect, I'm so glad this all worked out," Hayato said.

"Yeah, thanks again for putting a good word in. I don't know how I'll ever repay you."

"Buy me lunch and maybe a few more chocolate martinis, and I'll say we're even." He paused. "It's just a shame we're not in the same department. But let's have lunch together today. We can meet at noon in the cafeteria—do you know where that is? In the Mia Hamm Building?"

She did know where the cafeteria was, although she had no idea who Mia Hamm was. "I'll see you there."

"Alright. Have a good first day. I can't wait to hear all about it," said Hayato. They hung up, and Mika set off into the Serena Williams Building—she did know who that was. The day passed in a blur of introductions and setting up her computer. She met Hayato for lunch. They sipped Diet Cokes and nibbled on salads. He showed her his office, an open concept with large drafting tables. Several easels had been set up, and on them were artboards—pictures of shoes designed with bursting flowers and emblazoned with the iconic swoosh.

"Our Summer Collection for next year," Hayato said, stuffing his hands in his pockets. "I've been staring at the renderings for days. Something isn't right about the design. It's supposed to be a play off this artist who does huge flower backgrounds behind famous people's portraits."

"It's the colors," Mika said automatically.

"What do you mean?" Hayato looked at her sharply.

She stepped forward. She knew of the artist. He'd been up-and-coming when she'd attended college.

Now he was just up-and-up. "I know the artist." She blushed. "Well, I know of him. He uses traditional colors in modern portraits. For example, when he painted that portrait of the woman refugee from North Korea, the one who escaped with her baby? He used the same colors from the fourteenth-century painting *Flight into Egypt* by Giotto to evoke . . ." She shook her head. "I don't think you need to go that deep. But anyway—old colors, new ideas, same problems."

Hayato nodded thoughtfully. "We should use some retro Nike colors."

Mika shrugged. "You could try."

Hayato grabbed a set of colored pencils from a cache of art supplies on his desk. He chose three and scribbled on the artboard. Mika felt something rise within her. Envy. The desire to draw and let it swallow her up. She wondered if Hayato could see the deep hunger in her eyes. After Peter, all the colors she had once painted with were gone. Afraid she'd run into him, she had dropped her art courses and switched majors. *I lost everything. Time. Myself. My future.* How could she not feel as if something had been stolen from her? First, her body. Then, her painting. And last, her baby.

"Like these?" Hayato asked, eyes blazing with inspiration.

"Sure." She smiled encouragingly.

"You really unlocked this for me. How do you know this?"

She shrugged. "Anyone would."

"No, not anyone. But thank you."

"Of course. Always happy to help you exploit art for profit," she joked. Then realized it sounded kind of mean. Had she been keeping herself from the thing she loved for so long, she'd become bitter? "Sorry."

He shook his head as if dazed. "No, it's okay." He laughed it off. "Lunch again tomorrow?" he asked, walking Mika out, and she agreed.

After work, she stopped and purchased a few groceries. She wandered the aisles and checked her bank account. Lunch with Hayato had put a considerable dent in it. She decided she could afford some ramen and maybe some Lucky Charms but passed on the wine.

Once home, she called Penny. "Hey," Penny answered. "How was it?"

Mika slipped off her flats and unbuttoned her pants. "Good. It's mostly spreadsheets and scheduling meetings for my boss." Mika's boss was a nice man named Augustus, Gus for short. His face was round, his complexion ruddy, and the slightest southern accent bent his speech. He had a wife whom he adored and packed him lunch every day. And he didn't mention anything about Mika being Japanese but did make sure he pronounced her name right.

"So," Penny started. "I have some news. I got an acceptance letter today from U of P."

Mika stopped. The running program Penny had applied to before when she'd visited. Mika had remembered it but was careful not to ask. She didn't want Penny to feel any pressure. "Did you?" Mika asked, keeping her voice light but still injecting the right amount of curiosity.

"I did," she said. "And I think I want to come."

"That's fantastic." Mika tried to sound casual. Cool. "Would your dad be okay with you returning?" Thomas was a subject that didn't come up much during their conversations. Although, Penny had reassured Mika, he knew they were speaking again. What did Thomas think of Mika now? She remembered the night of the gallery opening, the bottle of wine between them. The way he'd spoken to her, voice as rough as crushed velvet, *It's been good for her. For us.* She'd lost Thomas's respect, his hard-won trust. And he didn't seem the kind of man who forgave easily, especially when it came to Penny. All at once, Mika admired that trait. It was something they shared. But she hated being on the receiving end of his disappointment, his derision.

"Oh yeah," Penny huffed out. "He said it was my decision. But in the same way he said, 'Go ahead,' when I wanted to try riding my bike without training wheels for the first time. Like he wished I wouldn't, but there really wasn't any way to stop me."

"When does the program start?" Mika asked.

"Third week of June. I have a couple weeks in between when school dismisses here and the start there. I'll probably come a day or so early to settle in and maybe spend some time with you?"

"Yes. Absolutely." Mentally Mika ticked off the days. It was the end of May. "We could go to the Asian supermarket. Maybe another roller derby game. You can meet my other friends, Charlie and Tuan."

"That would be great," Penny said. There was a pause before she went on. "Do you think . . . I might be able to meet your mom and dad?"

A new heaviness settled across Mika's chest. "I don't know, Penny. I'll check with them, but I don't want to make any promises. My mom and I . . . we have issues." Hiromi's unhappiness hung like a dark cloud over most of Mika's childhood. How could she willingly thrust Penny under that same shadow?

"That's okay," Penny said, and from the tone of her voice, Mika could tell it was not. "I get it. I mean, she would barely look at me at the gallery opening."

Mika bit her lip. "I'll talk to my mom. Let me see what I can do."

"Alright," Penny said thickly. "It's not a big deal." But Mika could tell it was. She vowed to make it happen. Didn't Penny know? Mika would do anything for her.

• • •

Mika waited two whole days before calling her mother. It was Friday evening when she sat on the couch and dialed Hiromi. She turned the television down as the line rang.

"Mi-chan," Hiromi answered. "Is this my daughter? I wasn't sure I still had one."

"Okāsan." Mika rubbed her brow. "How are you?"

Her mother chatted on about a windstorm coming through and how her father had eaten something disagreeable. Of course, they didn't discuss the art opening or what had happened that night. In the tenth grade, Mika had been caught shoplifting. She'd taken an item of clothing from the line of a white pop star who dressed up in a kimono and outlined her eyes in kohl—she said it wasn't appropriation but appreciation. Mika may not have wanted to belong to Japan, but she didn't believe Japan belonged to the singer either. Anyway, Hiromi had picked her up from the security office. The whole car ride had been silent. Then at dinner that night and for the next three days. That was the root of their real issue. Silence. Intractable, the emotional killing kind.

Mika settled back on the couch, closed her eyes, and remembered her promise to Penny. "Okāsan," Mika interjected. "I've got a job now, and I've been talking to Penny again."

The other end of the line went quiet. Mika checked to make sure they were still connected. They were. She put the phone back to her ear and spoke. "She's coming to town again in June for a cross-country training camp. She's a runner, has won all sorts of medals and awards," she said warmly. "And she'd like to meet you." Mika gazed at the popcorn ceiling while she waited for her mother to answer.

"I have to go," Hiromi said finally. "Your father needs me." *Click*. She'd hung up, and that was it.

• • •

Eventually, June came.

"I can't wait. Two more weeks," Penny chirped happily on the phone one night. "I've got a bunch of new running gear. And I'm rooming with this awesome girl from California named Olive."

"Olive like the fruit?" Mika asked. She was at home. Was spending more and more hours at home these days.

Opting for quiet meals in lieu of dinners out. Water instead of wine. All to tuck a few extra bills away in her savings account. For once in a very long time, Mika was planning for the future. Living for Penny.

"Yep. Hold on." There was some shuffling. And Penny talked to someone there. "I'm on the phone, Dad." So, Thomas. Mika listened carefully but couldn't hear what Thomas said back, just the dull sound of his voice. "I'm talking to Mika. Yeah, got it. Money is on the counter. Go, I'll be fine. I'm just going to get a pizza or something. Sorry." Penny came back. "You'd think he's never left me alone in the house before." Mika couldn't help but imagine Thomas in his suit again, on his way out on a date. What kind of woman would Thomas go out with? Was Thomas some sort of sex-crazed superhero widower who masqueraded as an awesome dad by day? "He'll be back in, like, a couple hours. He has some big deposition tomorrow and had to finalize some details, but I'm sure he'll call three times. Once to tell me he's at the office, then to tell me he's almost done at the office, and finally, to tell me he's on his way home from the office." Right, so Thomas wasn't a sex-crazed superhero widower. He was just working late. "Anyway, so what was I saying? Oh yeah . . ." Penny went on, and Mika happily listened.

On Saturday, Mika pulled up to her parents' house

and honked. Her mother opened the front door right away, followed very slowly by her father. The sky was bright blue. Not a cloud in sight.

"Mi-chan," Hiromi scolded, coming down the cement walkway. She flapped a dish towel in her hands like it might dampen the noise.

Mika climbed from her car and stepped around the hood, a piece of paper in her hands. She thrust it at Hiromi. "Here."

"What's this?" Hiromi asked, scanning the piece of paper.

"It's a check." Mika had written it that morning for one hundred dollars, five percent of what she owed her parents from the church loan. "I'll give you more once I get paid again."

Hiromi harumphed but stuck the check in her pinafore apron pocket. "What's that?" She gestured at the back of Mika's car. The windows were rolled down and half sticking out of the back seat was the bushy head of a maple tree.

"That is a tree I'm going to plant in our backyard." In the hole where Hana had torn the dead, malnourished tree from. "I feel like watching something grow." She grinned at her mother, at the day, at her life.

"You have to water it every day," Hiromi warned.

Mika rolled her eyes. "I know."

"At least twenty minutes."

"Got it." Mika rounded the hood again. No way would she be roped into going inside. Let her get away now. *Please.*

Hiromi rubbed a leaf between her pointer finger and thumb. "This one has white spots on it. Might be a fungus."

"It's fine." Mika opened her car door and sat in the driver's seat. She started the engine, and Hiromi knocked on the window. She rolled it down. She missed driving Charlie's car around, with its automatic windows and air-conditioning. Maybe in a year or two, she might be able to afford a new used car.

Hiromi peered in the car, then at Mika. "Your father and I want to meet her, the baby," she said, dropping her voice as if the subject were taboo.

Mika stared at her mother a moment, confused. She opened and closed her mouth. Penny, she meant Penny. But Penny wasn't a baby anymore. That baby, the one Mika had given away, was gone. She shook off the thought, not ready to examine it. "You want to meet Penny?"

Hiromi nodded once. "You can bring her to dinner here."

"Or we could go out to a restaurant," Mika suggested. She hadn't been inside her parents' house in years.

"No, too expensive," Hiromi said with finality. "Bring her here. I will cook."

"Okay." Mika could only agree. And she did it for Penny. Penny who wanted to meet her biological grandparents. Penny who wanted to see where Mika grew up. "I'll tell her. She'll be so happy."

Hiromi did not smile. "Don't forget to water the tree."

Chapter Nineteen

One week before Penny was to arrive, Thomas texted Mika.

He opened with a Hi. Mika was at work and stared at her phone next to her keyboard. She checked around the office. Everyone was busy, filing or plinking away softly on keyboards. Of course, they couldn't tell the adopted father of Mika's daughter was texting or that the two hadn't spoken since the gallery opening where Hiromi had brought the world down around Mika's ears.

Hi, she typed back, bending down, hiding in her cubicle.

It's Thomas, he wrote.

She tapped out, Yes. I know.

Three dots inside a gray bubble appeared on the

screen. Right. Sorry. Penny's flight arrives Sunday. Can you pick her up? I'd rather she didn't have to take an Uber or cab alone, he said.

She straightened. Already planning on it. Penny and Mika had agreed—Mika would pick Penny up from the airport, then drive her to the dorms at the University of Portland and help her settle in. If Penny was feeling up to it, they'd have dinner somewhere and hang out for a bit.

She's never flown alone. I offered to fly with her. She declined. Then he added, Her no was quick and emphatic. Mika pictured him in his office. Sitting behind an enormous mahogany desk. Suit and tie on. Frown firmly in place. Did he hate her?

Gus, her boss, passed by her cubicle. Mika dropped her phone and swung back around, putting her hands to the keyboard. She waved at him. "Don't work too hard," he said with a genuine smile. She smiled, laughed a fake laugh, and waited until he was gone before replying to Thomas. I've got it covered.

Twenty minutes later, he responded. Are you sure? It's not an inconvenience?

Really, it's no problem. We've got the afternoon planned. Hookers, drugs, the whole shebang. Mika chewed her lip. That was a joke. Too soon?

Another few minutes passed, and Mika continued

the spreadsheet she'd been working on. Thomas texted. Way too soon. So he hated her. Definitely hated her.

Please don't worry, she responded. She's in good hands. I promise.

Have her text me when she arrives, was all he answered.

• • •

That Sunday, Mika pulled into the arrivals terminal at the airport. Penny stood at the curb, waving to her with one hand, the other clutching the handle of a burgundy suitcase. Today Penny's hair was whipped up into a glossy ponytail. Mika popped the trunk and got out of the car. They both said hey at the same time and hugged, falling into each other's arms easily. Mika held on for a second too long. Then she slung Penny's suitcase into the back, and they climbed into the rusted Corolla.

Penny buckled her seat belt. Either she didn't notice the spider crack in the windshield or the tape holding the side mirror together, or she was politely ignoring it. "Whew. I almost didn't make it. My dad dropped me off this morning, and I swear he was going to cry. I'm pretty sure he was considering kidnapping me. Can you kidnap your own child?"

Mika checked her rearview mirror. "He's texted

multiple times." Once to remind Mika when Penny's flight arrived, *She gets in at 12:15*, and then an hour later, *Penny's flight is delayed*. Mika had responded with encouraging words, hoping to calm him. She'd earned back Penny's trust, but Thomas's was harder won. *Fair enough. I know. No worries. I'm already at the airport in the cell phone waiting area*, she'd written—the same place where she'd idled and left her rambling voicemail. *I'll be here whenever Penny is ready.*

"I know. He's the worst. I texted him as soon as the wheels touched down," Penny said, then fanned herself. "It's hot. Will you turn up the air-conditioning?"

"Sure," Mika said. "Roll down the windows."

Penny flushed even more and cranked the window down. They veered right off Airport Lane, passing some hotels and a Swedish furniture store. Mika watched Penny, eyes bouncing back and forth between her and the road. Penny pulled down the visor, her face half in shadow. The wind in her hair, the smell of summer, made Mika think of herself as a teen. When she'd driven streets aimlessly or hung out at the first twenty-four-hour Starbucks with Hana. *Looking for trouble*, Hiromi said once. But really, they'd just been looking, period.

Penny applied some lip gloss from her bag. Mika

didn't remember her wearing makeup before. Mika pursed her lips but didn't say anything. They coasted down Eighty-Second and into the north side of town. The University of Portland was located in the St. Johns neighborhood on a bluff overlooking the Willamette River. The campus might have belonged somewhere on the East Coast with its stretching green lawns, brick buildings, and white trim. A sister school of Notre Dame, a sign boasted at the entrance. Penny produced a stack of papers from her backpack, one with a map on it. "It says we're supposed to go to Corrado Hall to check in and receive room assignments." She pointed to the right, and Mika steered her car down a small road.

They found parking nearish the dorm. Mika popped the trunk and removed Penny's suitcase. "Here, these are for you too." She dipped into the back seat and pulled out a new pillow and a set of twin sheets she had purchased and washed. The pattern was cute, tiny yellow chrysanthemums.

"For me?" Penny squinted against the afternoon sun.

"Yep. I know they said everything was provided, but I thought you'd like something with a higher thread count and a new pillow. Bedding is very important," Mika said, as if imparting ancient wisdom.

Penny took the sheets and pillow, staring at them.

"Thanks. That's really sweet. But can you afford this?" She hurried on to explain. "I mean, your car . . ."

"Shh." Mika patted the car near a little rusted dent. "You'll hurt her feelings. If you're asking if I bought sheets and a pillow instead of eating tonight, the answer is no. I can afford it. I promise." Just two days ago, Mika had even given her parents another check. Hiromi had taken the piece of paper, eyeing it suspiciously as if anticipating it to spontaneously combust. Then she had stuffed it in her apron pocket and asked about the baby and when Mika would bring her. They'd scheduled dinner for next week. Penny was elated at the prospect of meeting her biological grandparents. Mika less so. Way less so.

Penny smiled and hugged the bedding close to her chest. Mika locked the car and came back to Penny's side. "Ready? Hey, you alright?" she asked, seeing Penny worrying her lower lip.

"Yeah. It's just . . ." Penny hugged the bedding to her tighter, like gathering a blanket around oneself before a storm. "Runners will be here from all over the country. Everyone is so good . . . That's why they, like, got into the program."

The glaring vulnerability stirred something inside Mika. She grabbed Penny by the shoulders. "You're going to be great," she said. If only such a power as a mother's confidence in her children existed, the world might be different. "Say it. Say: I'm going to be great."

"I'm going to be great," Penny mumbled, pink with embarrassment.

"What's that?" She shook Penny, spoke louder. Students paused in their wanderings to stare, the deranged Asian and her mini-me. "I can't hear people who don't believe in themselves," she all but yelled.

"I'm going to be great!" Penny near shouted.

Mika smiled and released her. "That's better." Together, they walked to the dorm. In the lobby, a gold-and-purple banner read: WELCOME TO UNIVERSITY OF PORTLAND. A girl with long curling hair checked them in. "Penelope Calvin. You'll be in room 205, just up the stairs and to the left." She handed them a set of keys and motioned for the next in line. Amid other families, they climbed to the second floor and found Penny's dorm room. The hall was crawling with people, teenage girls *and* boys, Mika noticed, making themselves at home in the rooms. "You didn't mention this was a coed thing," said Mika, eyeing a room where a boy with sunken eyes and floppy kiddie pop star hair spread a plaid comforter on his bed while his mother deposited drinks into a mini-fridge.

"Didn't I?" Penny put the key into the lock, turned, and pushed her way into the dorm room. "Funny. I thought I did."

"You most definitely did not." Mika dragged Penny's suitcase into the room. There was a single window, and on either side of it two tall beds with ladders, a desk under each, and a wall of cabinets. There was a shared bathroom outside in the hall, but the room had a sink and a little mirror above it. All in all, it was on the nicer side of dorms. Mika's dorm room had been in an older building and slightly larger than a shoebox, but it had felt enormous, so full of potential. Penny dragged her suitcase to the center of the room and unzipped it, clothes bursting free, mostly running gear, stretchy tank tops, and small shorts. On top was the roller derby T-shirt Mika had bought her. Penny shook it out, then carefully refolded it, placing it in one of the wardrobe drawers.

Penny's roommate arrived, a freckled redhead whose name, Olive, fit her perfectly and who seemed to be the human embodiment of an exclamation mark—her body long and taut and filled with energy. "Oh my god! We're going to have so much fun! What summer training schedule did you do last year?! On Mondays, I did an eight-mile fartlek, then on Tuesdays, I did a five-to-seven-mile easy run with eighty-meter strides, and on Wednesdays, I did hill repeats . . ."

Mika didn't understand any of it, but Penny nodded like an eager puppy. She half listened as she tucked the sheets around Penny's lumpy mattress.

"Hey." The boy with the pop star hair leaned against the door, hands half jammed in his pockets. Cool. So cool. Mika nearly rolled her eyes. "Devon." He jutted his chin up.

"Penny," Penny said, preening. Olive introduced herself in much the same way.

"Listen, a bunch of us are going to get dinner and play Frisbee after. You two want to come?" Devon said.

Penny glanced at Mika uncertainly. "I kind of had plans . . ."

Mika held up her hands, grinning through a burst of disappointment. "No worries. We can catch up later."

"Really, you don't mind?"

"Of course not." Mika forced a smile, burying her emotions under a happy facade.

"Cool," Devon said. "I'll just meet you outside."

"Thanks." Penny threw her arms around Mika. "I'll call you." Then she and Olive started chatting about strides, and Mika waited a beat, watching the two girls with a sort of sad fascination, then left.

The door was open a crack, and Mika heard Olive say to Penny as she left, "Was that, like, your mom? She's super pretty."

"Kind of. She's my biological mom."

"Got it. You have layers," said Olive. "You can tell me over dinner."

Mika left and wandered around the campus for a few minutes, feeling like a weird old lady, even though she was only thirty-five. She thought of herself before and after, and a sharp bolt of longing shot through her chest. How much she'd changed but wanted to stay the same. She sat on a bench. A wide green expanse of lawn stretched before her.

Mika. She heard her name drift by on the summer breeze. She blinked, wondering if it might be real. *No,* just a memory. It appeared before her like a hologram. It was spring of her freshman year, and she could still hide her belly under oversized sweatshirts. But she had started feeling the extra weight, the press of Penny against her ribs, and had sat down on a cement half wall to catch her breath. *Mika,* the voice called again, this time closer. She looked up. Marcus. *I wasn't sure it was you.* He stopped in front of her, a messenger bag slung over his chest, paint splattering his hands. *Where have you been? You dropped my class.* She stared up at Marcus, rendered mute. The sun blazed behind him, cut a path across his cheekbone. It reminded her of Rembrandt's self-portrait. *Is everything okay? You didn't find another mentor, did you? Because if you're taking Painting IV from Collins . . .*

Mika dragged her backpack to her lap and wound her arms around it. *I'm . . . I'm not . . .* she tumbled out. Then she felt it. The phantom press of Peter's hand against her mouth. The smell of turpentine. She couldn't speak. Her heart hammered in her chest, threatened to beat right out of it. Penny kicked. She stood, nearly knocking into Marcus, who had drifted closer. *I'm not painting anymore,* she said, shoving away from him. *I'm not good enough . . .*

That's not true. You have the most raw talent I've ever seen.

She stared at her feet. At her muddy sneakers. She'd thrown out the outfit she'd worn to the party. Vowed not to wear heels or skirts or makeup again. She didn't want to be pretty anymore. Was afraid to be. Being pretty was an invitation. No, she corrected. Being a woman was an invitation. Marcus stepped closer.

I have to go, Mika mumbled before taking off in a jog. She ran through the flat blue morning, all the way back to her dorm room. She locked the door and slumped down against it; felt as if the ceiling were sliding down, as if the walls were constricting. Her hands shook, her heart beat fast, her breathing faster. She didn't know how long the episode went on. Only remembered waking later in bed, groggy and hungry. It was her first panic attack.

Now, Mika sat for a bit longer, letting the hologram fade. Those months after the rape, it had felt as if she was outside of herself. As if her spirit had detached from her body and floated around it. Most of her memories weren't from her own eyes but as a specter peering from above.

After a while, Mika drove home and applied one of the face masks she'd planned for her and Penny tonight. When it started burning, she removed it and snapped a picture of her red face, sending it to Hana. How bad is it? Mika's face had begun to cool by the time Hana replied. Have you seen The Man in the Iron Mask? Mika smiled, and her phone rang, Hana's name flashing on the screen.

"Hey," she answered. She sat on the couch and brought her knees into her chest, looping an arm around them.

"Isn't Penny in town?" Hana said. It was quiet where she was. "I thought you two were going to have dinner and hang after. I remember you telling me some big plans for a restaurant that cuts meat in front of you and a spa evening."

Mika played with her toes. "She ditched me for her golden retriever roommate. She promised we'd catch up later." Mika wasn't sure how she felt about it. Months ago, she'd been a star in Penny's universe.

"Oof," Hana said. "So, you've been usurped?"

"I'm afraid so," Mika said glumly. Maybe this was how Thomas felt. Pity party, table for one. She'd like to cry, but it might burn her face more.

"I have some news that might cheer you up."

"I could use some news to cheer me up."

"Pearl Jam is playing Seattle in two weeks on Thursday, then breaking for the weekend. I'm going to hang with Josephine Friday night, but I've reserved Saturday night for my main bitch. Get ready to make some bad decisions."

Mika unfolded her legs and leaned back into the couch. Mentally she cataloged her schedule. She'd blocked out next weekend for Penny—they were going to dinner at Mika's parents'. Thomas would be in town the weekend after, so Penny would likely be tied up with him all day Saturday. And when he left on Sunday, Penny was taking a bus with her team to run sand dunes at the coast. *Sand dunes.* Which sounded as absurd to Mika as someone suggesting Russell Crowe reprise his role in *Les Misérables*. "That's actually kind of perfect and sounds so good. Can't wait. We should invite Hayato and Charlie, maybe hit up some clubs."

"Definitely."

They chatted for a while longer. Mostly about how things were going with Josephine. It seemed to be getting serious. After, her phone chimed with a text.

Everything okay with Penny? It was Thomas.

Got her all settled in her dorm and met her roommate, Mika answered.

She texted me, but it was just a thumbs-up, said Thomas. At that, Mika laughed but didn't respond. She thought about Thomas. About being a parent. How once you and your baby were inseparable. Mika had felt that way when she carried Penny, even though she'd known she wasn't keeping her. She'd read an infant doesn't know where it ends and its mother begins. To the baby, the two are one—like the salt and the sea.

Chapter Twenty

Monday morning at work, Gus, her boss, poked his head into her cubicle. "Knock, knock," he said. "How do you feel about working some extra hours this week? I've got to finish putting together a collaboration model for one of our stakeholders. Shelly was working on it but had to take leave for a family thing, it got punted to me, and I could use some extra help!" He spoke with gusto and held up his hands to emphasize his point.

Mika set her phone away from her and straightened up. "Sure. That'd be fine." She could use a distraction. She'd been a bit lonely without Hana. Focusing a bit too much on when she'd see Penny again, on Friday, when they'd have dinner at Mika's parents' house—the thought alone was enough to wind her up. How would she feel stepping foot in her childhood home again? How long had it been since she'd been inside? At least a decade.

And most importantly, how would Hiromi treat Penny? Mika thought of Hiromi lying in wait. She vowed not to let her daughter be cut by her mother's sharp edges.

"Great! Everything should be on the shared server. Go ahead and take a look and let's meet after lunch to go over it." He took off, and a faint smile appeared at the corner of Mika's mouth. She dove in. Even came in early on Tuesday and Wednesday to get a head start. But she did manage a lunch with Hayato, where they stalked Seth, the new guy he was dating, online.

Friday passed in a whirlwind. At 3:05, she emailed Gus to say all the completed documents were ready for his review. He fired off an immediate response: Good work, take the rest of the day off. You earned it.

So Mika was a little early to pick Penny up from campus. She expected to idle at the curb, maybe text Hana to say she couldn't wait to see her next weekend. She did not expect to see Penny canoodling—Mika wasn't sure she'd ever used the word *canoodling* before, but she was now and couldn't be more surprised or unhappy about it—with Devon, the floppy pop star–haired kid. The two stood way too close. His hands on her hips. Penny's hands on . . . *his chest?* Mika couldn't believe it. And her first reaction was to make it stop. She laid on the horn. Pedestrians halted in their tracks. Penny pushed away from Devon, and he had the grace to step back as well, running an embarrassed hand through his hair. Penny mumbled something to him and stooped to pick up her backpack before walking to the car.

"Hi," Mika said as Penny climbed in.

"Hi. You're early." Penny slumped down in her seat and covered her burning face with her hands. "Don't take this the wrong way, but that was super mortifying."

"Sorry about that. My hand slipped," Mika said a bit too quickly. "Old car, sensitive horn, you know?" Actually, the horn was really hard to push. She'd spilled something on the wheel who knows how long ago and ever since it'd been stuck. Good to know it still worked. Mika pulled away, keeping Devon in her sights in the rearview mirror. "So, um, new friend?"

Now off campus, Penny shifted in the seat to sit upright. She hesitated a moment. "He's kind of my boyfriend."

A yellow light changed to red, and Mika braked. "Boyfriend? Is this a recent development?" *So fast,* Mika thought. But who was she to say anything? She'd moved in with Leif after sleeping with him for only a month.

A smile flitted across Penny's face. She sat on her hands. "As of last night. We made it official. We're going out."

Mika was unfamiliar with teenage dating rituals, but she knew enough to know "going out" meant serious. At least it did when she was sixteen. She chanced a glance at Penny. "That's a big deal." The light turned green, and Mika sped up to merge onto the highway.

"It's really not," Penny said, playing it cool. "Look, can we keep this quiet? Just between us?"

"You mean, not tell your dad," Mika clarified as they went over a bridge.

Penny gave one nod, confirming. "He'll be all weird about it since Devon and I are in the same dorm."

"I don't know . . ." Mika trailed off. She wanted to create a safe space for Penny. And Devon didn't seem so bad. Puppy love, Mika would call it. It would either be over in a few weeks, or it wouldn't. *What would be the harm?* Besides, she rarely spoke to Thomas. If he didn't ask, she wouldn't bring it up. Is a lie by omission still a lie? Mika wasn't sure. She'd flunked philosophy. "Okay, I won't say anything." Mika wondered if Caroline and Penny had secrets. If Caroline had ever checked Penny out from school early and taken her for ice cream. *Don't tell your dad*, she might have said. *This will be just between us girls.* A part of Mika yearned for the same. For that bond.

"Thank you," Penny said. "I appreciate you trusting me." Mika almost said, *I trust you, not the world.* But she clamped down on the urge. "So, tell me about your parents. Anything I should know before I meet them?" Penny asked.

They were outside Portland now, in the suburbs. They passed the Korean mart that didn't check IDs. The twenty-four-hour Starbucks where Mika and Hana had huddled together to weep on 9/11. The junior high school where Mika used to walk carrying a cigarette in one hand and her dreams in another. She'd sit on the bleachers and wish herself somewhere else. Inhale and believe she was meant to do great things. That she *could* do great things. "I'm nervous," Penny added as Mika turned down a side street. A few kids played in the road with a hose.

"Don't be nervous," Mika said, parking in front of her parents' house. Seeing the forest green shingles, she felt a sudden acute pain, the sore spot of her childhood being poked. "They're not huggers. If they bow or incline their heads, just do it back." *I love you* was never spoken in Mika's home. Loving was in the doing. Working to provide an income. Making homemade meals. Obeying your parents. "And if my mom asks if you want something to drink, don't drink the bottled water. It's not new. She refills old bottles and puts them back in the fridge." Hiromi didn't wash the bottles between refills. "In fact, anything bottled, always check the seal. One time she bought generic lemon-lime soda for my birthday and used it to fill an old liter of Sprite."

"Okay," Penny said carefully, eyeing the giant satellite dish on the side of the house. They walked slowly to the door and paused again in front of it. Mika saw the curtains move. Her mother was watching. "Did they ever ask about me?"

Mika studied Penny's anxious face. She didn't want to lie but knew the truth would hurt her. She decided on neither. "I never really volunteered any information. Talking about you was difficult for me." She paused. "Ready?"

Penny dipped her chin. "Ready."

Mika placed her hand on the knob and turned to Penny. "One last thing. Just remember we can leave anytime. You say the word, and we're out of here. This is all in your control." Was she saying it for herself or for Penny?

"Got it," Penny said.

Mika opened the door. Shige and Hiromi were waiting on the other side. Mika toed off her shoes in the makeshift genkan, and so did Penny. Mika hurtled back in time. To when Shige had purchased the house. She held her mother's hand while they toured it, the FOR SALE sign still planted on the lawn. Hiromi's nose inched higher and higher each room they peered into. Everything was wrong. The doors opened and shut instead of sliding in and out. Hiromi didn't care for the shower-bath combo in the master bedroom, or the pantry in the kitchen, or that the backyard faced north—the laundry would never dry that way.

Now, Mika smiled uneasily, wondering if Penny could feel it, how the walls pulsated with Hiromi's unhappiness. "Okāsan, Otōsan." *Mother, father,* Mika said. "This is Penny." She almost added *my daughter* but stopped short.

Hiromi and Shige bowed their heads, and Penny responded in kind. "It's nice to meet you," she said.

Silence then, as they all stared at each other. Her mother had dressed up. Wearing her nicest clothes, a semi-fitted dress, two pintucks at the waist. And her father in a suit. Both wore house slippers. The shag carpet had been freshly vacuumed, and the table was set with a dozen elaborate dishes—sesame tofu, rice scooped into perfect balls, asparagus in dashi—all of Mika's favorites. Hiromi must have cooked for hours.

Her mother spoke first. She opened her hands. "Mi-chan says you a runner."

"*You're* a runner," Mika corrected her mother.

"That's what I said," Hiromi said. "Shige, isn't that what I said?"

"I *am* a runner," Penny cut in. Hiromi fixed an assessing stare on Penny. "I'm here doing a summer training camp at the University of Portland. My school is a division one school. I made the varsity team my freshman year."

"You're fast?" Shige asked, a glint of approval in his eyes.

Penny nodded. "Fast and consistent, that's what's important."

"You must be good to be in a program at the University of Portland. I read it's a sister school of Notre Dame," Hiromi said, impressed.

"I try," Penny preened. Taut silence again. They could have been strangers on a bus, the interior filling with recycled air.

"Are you hungry?" Hiromi finally asked.

"Sure," Penny blurted. "I mean, I could eat, or we could wait. Whatever you prefer."

"Let's eat, let's eat," Shige said as if he were behind the whole meal. They shuffled to the table. Penny, Mika, and Shige sat down.

"Do you want something to drink? Water, ocha?" Hiromi asked, watching Penny like some sort of curiosity.

"Water is fine," said Penny. She removed the napkin from the table and spread it over her lap.

"From the tap," Mika clarified.

Penny grinned, and Mika smiled back. Hiromi filled waters and brought them to the table. "I made all Mika's favorites from when she was a little girl," Hiromi said, sliding into a chair. Automatically Mika, Shige, and Hiromi pressed their hands together and said: "Itadakimasu."

Shige picked up his hashi and began to place some teba shichimi, chicken with a seven-ingredient spice rub, on his plate.

"Go on," Hiromi said. "Try the asparagus; I made the dashi myself."

Penny peered down at her lap. Hiromi had only set the table with hashi. Mika popped up from the table and opened the utensil drawer in the kitchen, fishing out a couple of forks. She handed one off to Penny, then kept one for herself.

"You never use hashi?" Hiromi said as if insulted.

"Okāsan," Mika said in warning. She wondered if her mother blamed her for Penny not being Japanese enough.

"I will show you. This is how I taught Mi-chan." Shige scooted closer to Penny. "Go on," he said, his voice rich, warm, and coaxing.

After a beat, Penny picked up the hashi. Mika's mind tripped, stumbled into a forgotten past. To when they still lived in Japan. In Daito, a small city inside the Osaka Prefecture. She'd been wearing a yellow jumper, kneeling at a low table. A bowl of edamame was in front of her, and she was practicing her hashi. Her parents were in the other room. Arguing. Mika stood and crept over. Her feet just outside the yellow blade of light streaming through the cracked door. *I don't want to live in America,* her mother had said, voice thick with entreaty. She'd been dressed in a full kimono.

Once a month, she met a friend, a fellow maiko, for lunch in Kyoto. The two would don their best kimonos and bring their children. Mika remembered playing with a little boy on the restaurant's floor, her mother's feet clad in tabi and zōri. They'd returned to find Shige home early. His head hanging low.

You have to find another job with another company, Hiromi insisted, like it was a done deal.

Her father waved an angry hand. He'd been younger too. The lines on his face not as deeply etched. *There aren't any other jobs. This is our only option. We are moving. End of discussion.*

Mika leaned against the wall. The house was steel-framed, built to withstand an earthquake or a wife angry with her husband. *What will I do there?* Hiromi asked plaintively.

You will do your job. You will be a good wife to me and a good mother to our daughter, Shige replied. And Hiromi shut up. She did not have the cultural permission to disobey her husband.

"See, you're never too old to learn something new," Hiromi said now, and Mika realized the comment was directed at her. It never failed. Hiromi could always make Mika feel small, as insignificant as a sneeze.

They ate, Penny using the hashi with all the finesse of a doe on ice. But she persevered, and Hiromi watched her with unblinking eyes as if trying to absorb her. In the living room, a phone rang and rang again. "Shige," Hiromi scolded.

Shige retrieved his phone. "All day, I get calls from telemarketers. They want me to buy this or that." He silenced it.

"You can block the calls," Penny said. "Here." Shige handed over his phone, and Penny tapped a couple of buttons. "You can also add your number to a do-not-call registry," she said, handing the phone back to Shige.

"You are smart." Hiromi smiled and squeezed Shige's forearm.

After dinner, Mika paused in the paneled hallway, watching as Penny wandered through the house, her desire to open the doors Hiromi kept neatly shut burning in her eyes. Penny had come to uncover things. "Which one was your room?" Penny asked.

"That one." Mika pointed to a door with a brass knob to Penny's right.

"Can I see it?" Penny asked. Around the corner, Hiromi puttered in the kitchen to the tune of clanking dishes and running water. Shige retired to his armchair, watching the evening news at half the volume he usually did.

"Yeah, I guess," Mika said because she couldn't say no. Directly across from them was the lime-green-tiled bathroom where Mika's father used to unclog the sink with a pair of hashi, all while muttering that Mika had too much hair and used too much mascara. Penny pushed the door open and stepped inside. It was the same. Puke green shag carpet from the living room and hallway. An old milk-glass light fixture that cast a warm yellow light. Just enough space for a futon shoved against a wall and a desk. Mika used to sit at that desk and draw for hours. "There's not much to look at," Mika said now. Years ago, Hiromi had stripped the *Tiger Beat* posters off the walls, the portrait drawings Mika had done.

Penny walked the meager perimeter. "This is where you slept?"

Mika watched her from the doorway, the sight of her old room grabbing her by the throat. "Yep."

"But you had a bed, right?" Penny stopped near the lumpy navy futon. Above her was Mika's kindergarten school picture. The first day Hiromi had stood off to the side of the classroom while the other mothers gabbed about their summer trips to Sunriver. She could not find herself at home with them, those moms with skin the color of milk who jazzercised and worked late hours and made meals in the microwave.

"That folds out into a bed," Mika pointed out.

Caroline had shared pictures of Penny's room. Cherry blossom wallpaper, which she'd seen in the background of their video chats, still looking pristine and perfect. White substantial furniture. A bed with a frilly canopy. Mika had imagined Caroline and Thomas would give Penny all the things Mika could not afford. But then she remembered Penny at the dining table with Shige, learning to use hashi. *Some things money can't buy.*

"You studied here." Penny was at the desk, fingers trailing over the fake painted grain.

"'Studied' is a generous term." More like plotted her escape. Now, she felt embarrassed she'd ever reached so high. It was the folly of youth, she supposed, to think you were bigger than you were.

Penny gave Mika a half-smile, then pulled open a drawer. Inside were Mika's notebooks. Her sketch pads. "Can I look?" Penny asked. In her hands was an Arches drawing pad. Mika had paid in change for the sixteen-page notebook. In it was a series of gouache portraits, mostly profiles of people she knew. The first was of Hana, hair twisted back in braids, cheeks turned up to the sun. "Oh my god, are these yours? Did you paint this?"

Mika took the notebook back, snapped it closed, and shoved it back in the drawer. "It's not that big of a deal. The proportions are all off." She heard the echo of her mother. *Who is that supposed to be, your friend? You made her face too full. She looks fat.*

This is why she hated coming here. The walls held too many memories, too many words Mika never wanted to hear again.

"I knew you loved art and painting, but I thought you just, like, *appreciated* it, not that you could actually do it," Penny said, gesturing at the closed drawer. "Those are insanely good."

"It was a long time ago."

"*You* should have been exhibiting in the gallery." Penny folded her arms and her face twisted into a frown.

"I don't paint anymore." A knot rose in Mika's throat, and her eyes stung.

"Why did you stop?" Penny's gaze cut to Mika, cut through Mika.

Mika looked at her feet and crossed her arms. "I grew up. Money became a thing." *Life beats you down and forces you to discard foolish pursuits for more practical ones.* Penny chewed her cheek. She opened her mouth to say something, but Mika beat her to it. "I gave it a go for a while and took some classes freshman year, but it didn't pan out." *What's your story?* Marcus had asked her.

"You had me freshman year," Penny said. Mika saw the conclusion her daughter was drawing. That Mika had quit because of Penny.

"I quit before I had you." Mika touched an end of Penny's hair, let it slide through her fingers. "Then after, I didn't want to paint anymore. What can I say? I gave all my colors to you." She leaned in so they were inches apart, sought to assure Penny that her mother's failures weren't hers to bear. "I'd do it again." Penny smiled. Mika sighed, tired now and emotionally wrung out. "We'd better say goodbye. It's getting late." She slipped from the room and found her mother in the kitchen. "We have to go," Mika announced.

Hiromi set down a tray of milk puddings. Her cool, disappointed eyes trained on Mika. "I made dessert."

Mika wiped under her nose, saw Penny approach out of the corner of her eye. "Traffic might be bad, and I'm tired."

Penny stepped forward. "It was nice to meet you, Mrs. Suzuki. Thank you so much for having me over for dinner. I really loved it."

All at once, Mika felt guilty. "We'll come back," she promised.

"Next Saturday," Hiromi blurted. "I'm making tsukemono. I could teach you."

Penny's chest swelled with excitement. "Really? I'd like that." She cocked her head at Mika.

"Next Saturday? Your dad is coming into town," said Mika. *And I am going to get balls-to-the-walls drunk with Hana,* she mentally added.

Penny frowned, thinking. "Shoot. That's right."

"What about a weeknight?" Hiromi said. Mika had forgotten her mother had the tenacity of a bulldog when she wanted something. She remembered her mother white-knuckling the wheel while driving across town in twelve inches of snow to take Mika to dance practice. "Shige would pick you up."

Penny perked up. "Yes, I want to do that very much." Too late, Mika realized she hadn't been invited.

Hiromi's lips twitched into an almost smile. "I'll give you my phone number. I know how to text now. I'll wrap up dessert for you." Hiromi and Penny exchanged phone numbers, then Hiromi packed up a milk pudding in a sour cream container for Penny.

In the car, Mika drove, winding through the suburbs. She flicked on her blinker to turn onto the main road leading to the highway. "How was that? Okay? Too much?" she asked, staring straight ahead. It was dark now, the brightest stars twinkling in the sky.

"They're great," Penny said as she opened the sour cream container and peeked inside. "Your dad is so sweet, and your mom is intense but in a good way, like my running coach back home. Is it really cool if I go there on my own this week?"

Mika paused. She worried Hiromi might trample Penny's fragile spirit. But Mika's mother had been different with Penny. Warmer. Lighter. More willing. Mika sped up to get on the highway. She swallowed back her hesitation and said, "Sure. Of course." Who knew? Maybe this time would be different.

Mika focused on the road, the sky, the infinite dark. She wondered about starting over. If it was possible to begin again. More than anything, she wanted it to be true.

Chapter Twenty-One

"That'll be twenty-seven bucks. You want to open a tab?" The shirtless and very hairy bartender shouted over the music, sliding three tequila shots across the wood top to Hana, Mika, and Hayato. Heavy bass rocked the floor, and strobe lights flashed. Tonight was eighties night. Pop remixes from Whitney Houston and Cyndi Lauper blared over the sound system.

Hana wedged herself between black vinyl stools and handed over her card to the bartender. "I've got it. You can leave it open," she shouted at his back.

The three took their shots and clinked them together. "Kanpai!" Hayato yelled, squeezing a lime between his teeth and downing the shot. Mika and Hana followed suit, liquid burning their throats. They shouldered their way through the crowd, passing a couple of drag queens outfitted in leotards and a mural of Lady Gaga swathed in robes holding a baby Jesus.

"We should hit up the Golden Eagle after this," Hana said, naming a gay bar in Northeast Portland. "It's more laid back, mostly bear gays who like rockabilly."

Hayato caught Mika's hand and twirled her around. He'd embraced the theme and wore a white *Miami Vice* suit with a teal shirt underneath. "I want to dance."

Mika had gone full *Flashdance*, with a long off-the-shoulder sweatshirt-like dress, leg warmers, and heels. She followed Hayato to the dance floor. Dudes in cages swung around poles, body paint glowing in the black light. For a while, the three stayed together, but soon enough, Hayato and Hana coupled off. Mika took a breather, finding a slice of wall to lean against. "Love your outfit," a slim blond guy in the exact same costume said as he passed by. In her bra, her phone buzzed. She fished it out, surprised to see Thomas's name flashing on the screen. She plugged her ear and started toward the courtyard. "Thomas?" she yelled over the noise.

"Mika, you there?"

"Hold on." She made it to the courtyard. Little groups congregated, smoking and chatting. She shuffled to a corner, nearest the street. The night was hot and stifling. "Can you hear me now?"

"Yeah. Look, I'm sorry to do this, but there's been a gas leak in my hotel."

"Oh, no."

"It's okay. Well, it's not okay, actually. I've been calling around trying to find another hotel, but everything is booked for some comic convention." Right. Portland's Comic Con was this weekend. As if on cue, a couple dressed in matching Thor costumes wandered by on the street. "Do you know of somewhere I could stay? Anyone who has an Airbnb that's somehow vacant?"

Mika put a finger to her lips. "No. Sorry."

"Shit."

Although . . . Hana *was* staying with Josephine, and her room had been unoccupied for some time since she'd been on tour. "Ugh, this may be weird, but Hana's not home lately. I have an extra room." Mika let the offer dangle.

Thomas hesitated. "I don't know."

"Forget I even suggested it." Mika banged her head against the brick wall.

"No, it's a great offer. It wouldn't be weird? You'd be comfortable with that?"

"It will only be weird if you make it weird," she said. "I'm cool with it as long as you and Penny are."

Thomas snorted. "I'd rather not bother her. She was excited about going to the *Rocky Horror Picture Show* with some new friends tonight. But I'm sure she'd be fine with it. Anyway, I don't want to worry her."

Mika straightened. "Alright. I'll come pick you up then." She'd driven tonight and parked on the street, planning to Uber it home if need be. But she hadn't had that much to drink. "Text me what hotel you're at and give me a few minutes to say goodbye to my friends."

• • •

Thomas had booked a hotel near the University of Portland and was waiting outside when Mika pulled up. She didn't bother getting out of the car, just popped the trunk—successfully this time—for Thomas's suitcase.

"Thanks," Thomas said, climbing into the front seat.

"Of course." Mika pulled into traffic.

"This is a different car," Thomas observed. Out of the corner of her eye, she saw him press his fingers against the worn seats.

"This is my real car," Mika explained. "The one I drove you and Penny around in belonged to my friend Charlie. She loaned it to me for the week."

"Right," Thomas said. "It's nice."

Mika laughed. "It's terrible. Tape, glue, and a prayer are holding it together, but we've been with each other a long time." She patted the dashboard with affection.

"No, it's great, really. And the smell is unique, like . . ." He searched for the word.

"Mildew. I left the windows down in the rain." They stopped at a red light, and she caught Thomas staring at her exposed shoulder. She tugged the dress up. "I was downtown. It was eighties night at the Cockpit." Thomas said nothing. "So, Penny is at the *Rocky Horror Picture Show*?" She'd been a couple of times with Hana. Had dressed up in fishnets and red lipstick way back when. Mika wondered if Devon had gone too. She imagined the floppy-haired pop star kid in a pleather corset and smiled to herself.

"Yep. I didn't know what it was. I mean, I know the movie, but apparently, it's a 'whole thing,'" he said, making air quotes. "She has a unique talent for making me feel very uncool." Thomas's mouth twisted into a half-frown.

A minute later, they were home. Mika showed Thomas around and put fresh sheets on Hana's bed. She toed off her heels, slipped on a pair of sweats, and gathered her hair into a high bun. "You want something to eat, drink?" She moved to the fridge and peered inside.

Slim pickings. A few groceries for salad. A couple IPAs that were Hana's. "I have lettuce, beer, or water."

"Beer would be great." Thomas stood in the middle of the living room, hands jammed halfway in his pockets. Mika uncapped the beer and handed it off to Thomas before curling into a corner of the couch with a glass of water. Thomas settled on the other end, legs splayed. Mika studied his profile, the hard planes of his cheeks, his straight Roman nose. He had perfect proportions to model for a sculpture.

He stared at the door to Hana's room. "Where is Hana anyway? You never said."

Mika stretched, hooking her toes on the coffee table. "Well, she's home this weekend but staying with her girlfriend. She's been on tour with Pearl Jam the last month or so."

"Well, that's awesome."

"Yep. She's an ASL interpreter."

"That's right, she told us about it when we went to her roller derby game."

"It's pretty amazing to watch her work, the way her body moves. It's like performance art. She invited me on tour, but I said no."

His mouth twitched. He sipped his beer. "How come?"

Her brows knit together. "I've been on tour with her before. It's crazy and wild fun, but I decided to hang here to . . . fix things with Penny and focus on my job."

Thomas nodded thoughtfully. They both understood. Penny was always a reason to stay. "Penny said you had a good conversation after." He waved a hand around as if to wrangle the messy past, the art gallery opening, Mika's lies, her chaotic voicemail to Penny.

"She did?" Mika swallowed a bit and briefly averted her gaze. She placed her glass of water on the table. She'd been waiting for Thomas to bring up the gallery night, the aftermath. She and Penny had had it out. Did Thomas want his own reckoning?

Thomas settled deeper into the couch, spread his legs a little wider. "Yes. Literally, she said: 'We had a good conversation.' That's all."

"It was a good conversation, I think. An honest one, at least," Mika clarified.

He was silent for a minute. "You know, Penny let me hear your voicemail."

Mika's stomach soured. Shame coated her insides.

"It was a brave thing to do, lay it all on the line like that," Thomas said seriously, light eyes intent on her.

Surprised, Mika's eyes widened, then she scoffed, feeling an uncomfortable prickle. "I wanted to make it right, that's all." She wouldn't call it brave. She remembered running from Peter's apartment. Hadn't stopped running since—afraid of time and herself, worried she might get hurt again. But now, she seemed to have slowed down to let Penny in. She blinked against the sudden vulnerability, the fear. "Thank you, though. And thanks for letting her come this summer."

Thomas's turn to scoff. "I don't think I could have stopped Penny even if I'd tried." Thomas slugged the rest of his beer and sat back with a sigh. "I was wary when you two started speaking again."

Mika let out a long breath. "I understand."

"She said you took her to meet your parents. I was nervous about that too. Last time I saw your mother . . . she basically stared at Penny like she had three heads."

Mika hesitated for a second. Wondering how much to tell Thomas about her relationship with her mother. How much should she let him in? "My mom didn't want me to have Penny," Mika admitted softly. Thomas sharply inhaled. "She, um, didn't think I could handle being a parent and wasn't supportive during the pregnancy."

"I'm sorry," Thomas said, and there was a trace of something in his eyes. Sadness? Pity?

"It's alright," Mika said. "It's in the past now." Not

really, but Mika didn't want to dig too deep. Whatever she unearthed would be too messy. Too hard to clean up. "I was worried about Penny meeting my parents also. But it went well. Better than I thought. My mom likes Penny, I think."

"She called me after and was really excited. Said she's going to make something with your mom . . ."

"Tsukemono. Pickled vegetables," Mika filled in.

"Penny also said this is the first time she's ever felt Japanese."

Mika froze momentarily, taken aback. "Wow. I'm sorry." She apologized because she knew what it felt like. To try to give your kid everything and know you came up short. That you weren't enough. That they needed more. Children were the worst and best things that could happen to a person.

Thomas shrugged. "None of this is easy."

"It's not," Mika agreed. "Thomas," she said, and she waited until she had his attention. "I'm working hard at my relationship with Penny. I shouldn't have lied. I was insecure about . . . a lot of things," she admitted. "I wanted to be worthy of Penny." *Of you. Of everyone. The world.* But she didn't add that.

He nodded long and slow and said, "I believe you." He picked at the label of his beer with his thumbs. "Although, I could have told you from the beginning, lying to your kid isn't a good look." He tapped his chest. "Personal experience."

"Oh?"

"We had a cat, and when Penny was five, it disappeared. Caroline and I woke to these awful screeching noises early one morning. Coyote got it, I think. But instead of telling Penny that the cat was dead, we told her it had run off. She'd search for it all the time. Until one day, she found its collar with a little blood on it. Probably scarred her for life. Caroline had trouble talking about the hard stuff. Even when she found out she had cancer. She didn't want to tell Penny right away. I went along with it. But hindsight is always twenty-twenty. We should have told Penny about the cat. We should have told her about her mother." Thomas grinned ruefully, and the weight of it hit Mika full in the chest. "Though I'm definitely not telling her how much I drank in college." He hunched forward, letting the empty beer bottle dangle between his fingers. "Anyway, parents lying to kids is not a new thing. You didn't invent it, so don't punish yourself too much."

Mika didn't know what to do with Thomas's kindness, how to repay it, so she said, "There's more beer in the fridge if you want another."

Thomas unfolded from the couch and pointed to her near-empty glass of water. "Refill?"

"I'd better not," she told him. "I purposely dehydrate myself before bed."

Thomas used the counter to snap the cap off the bottle. "I'm afraid to ask."

Mika stretched, languid, and tired. "If I have too many liquids, I pee all night." A weak bladder had been a gift from pregnancy. A reminder that Penny's body used to be inside Mika's. Mika might have forgotten the details of those nine months. Most things fade with time. Even the things you try desperately to hold on to. But her body always remembered. Maybe that's what makes you age. The weight of events drooped your shoulders, carved lines in your face. Yeah, that was it. The mind may forget, but the body always remembers.

Chapter Twenty-Two

Mika sipped a cup of coffee in the kitchen and watched Thomas emerge from Hana's room, pulling a navy T-shirt over his head. She spun around and blinked, seeing the flat plane of his stomach, the little strip of hair that disappeared into his waistline. His happy trail.

"Morning," Thomas said, voice rough with sleep.

"Hey." Mika winced at the shrillness in her tone. "I made coffee." She retrieved a mug from the cupboard and slid it toward Thomas.

"Thanks." He poured himself a cup.

"Creamer is in the fridge." Mika leaned against the counter and crossed her arms, mug still in one hand. She'd dressed in leggings and an oversized T-shirt.

Any other morning, she'd be wandering around in her undies.

"Black is fine." He sipped the coffee and set it down. A bowl with three oranges was on the counter, and he frowned at them, the phantom taste of something sour twisting his lips.

"Is my coffee that bad? There's a goat yoga studio slash café down the street," she offered.

"No. It's not that. I . . ." He hesitated.

"What?"

Thomas clamped his lips shut and shook his head. "Nothing." He glanced at the oranges again.

"Tell me."

At length, he said, "It's the oranges. They're all wrong."

"Okay," Mika said slowly.

"I hate the navels." He visibly shuddered and paled.

"You mean these?" She picked up an orange and studied the belly button. The bowl used to house fake lemons.

"Yes," he said soberly.

"Huh." She placed the orange back in the bowl, belly button down. Then she turned the rest, so they faced the counter. "Any other food aversions I should know about?"

"No, but I'm also afraid of geese." The color returned to Thomas's cheeks. Mika was prepared to let it go, but then he said, "I'd rather not talk about it."

"Now I have to know." Mika eyed him over the rim of her mug.

He leaned against the counter. "Bad experience as a child. I had a stuffed goose that I loved until my brother chased me around the house with it, threatening to peck my eyes out. Then, when I did actually see a flock of live geese in person, they chased me. Haven't been able to tolerate them since."

"I love all these glimpses into your personal life. It's very psychologically helpful," Mika teased. They smiled at each other. Light came through the kitchen window, hanging thick in the air like stirred honey. Mika cleared her throat. "So, uh, what time does your flight leave?" Penny was running sand dunes. Through Hana's open door, she could see Thomas's bag was already packed.

He checked the watch on his wrist. "Flight doesn't leave until later this afternoon. I'll probably head to the airport early and find somewhere to camp out. I'm rewatching all of *The Lord of the Rings*."

Mika's jaw dropped. "Wow. That might be the saddest thing I've ever heard."

Thomas leaned forward, elbows on the counter. "I'm thinking of learning elvish."

Mika blew out a breath. "Scratch what I just said. *That's* the saddest thing I've ever heard."

A half-laugh rattled out of Thomas. "It's a very popular language."

"Yes. Among lonely virgins who can't grow facial hair," Mika blurted, then her cheeks burned. Had she really just said that?

Thomas's mouth remained a straight line, but his eyes glittered with humor. "That's a really harmful stereotype." He paused. Thought about something. "I could fix your hole for you."

Mika swallowed. "Come again?"

Thomas dipped his chin toward the window, the one facing the backyard. "The hole in your yard, as a thank-you for letting me stay the night." Mika flashed back to when Penny and Thomas had come to dinner. When Thomas had toed the ground and asked if she had gophers. Right.

Mika smoothed her lips together. "That's okay. I actually already filled it in." She'd planted the maple tree there, the one Hiromi thought had a fungus.

Thomas wandered to the window. "Looks good."

She considered Thomas. Their conversation last night. How today felt like a fresh start and in the spirit of that . . . "Okay," Mika said, knocking back the rest of her coffee and placing the mug in the porcelain sink. "Let's go, sad guy."

Thomas turned to her. "What?"

"I'm taking you out."

His eyebrows pinched together. "I know we've had our differences, but I feel like murder is a little far."

"Hardy-har-har," Mika deadpanned.

Thomas set his cup down. "Where are we going?"

Mika grabbed her keys and opened the door wide, her smile even wider. "You'll see."

• • •

"Donuts?" Thomas shifted on his feet, hands stuffed into his pockets. "This is better than Mordor and learning elvish."

Two guys in skinny jeans ahead of them turned and let their eyes travel from the tips of Thomas's shoes to the top of his silver-streaked hair. "Could you tone down *The Lord of the Rings* jargon?" asked Mika. "I might know someone here." *Here* was Voodoo Dough-nuts in Old Town. The first few years, the donut shop had been open only from nine p.m. to two a.m. In col-lege, Hana and Mika would stumble in, liquor soaked, to binge on frosted vanilla donuts dusted with Cap'n Crunch and bacon maple bars. The shop soon opened during the day, and now here Mika and Thomas were, waiting in line for a much-coveted pink box of donuts. "We're working on your spontaneity."

The line moved. Mika and Thomas shuffled forward. "I'm very spontaneous," Thomas said proudly, rocking back on his heels. "On the weekends, I don't make my bed. And sometimes Penny and I have breakfast for dinner." He raised his eyebrows in a take-that kind of way.

"Whoa!" Mika held up her hands, then clutched her chest, pretending to be aghast. The two guys in front of them snickered. "I think my heart just stopped from shock." Thomas cracked a slow sheepish smile. She elbowed him. "C'mon, let's get all sugared up and paint the town red." The line moved again, and they were inside. The floor was pink, yellow, brown, and beige linoleum tiles. The walls were painted yellow and pink. Truly hideous. But it smelled amazing, like swimming in a vat of sugar and cinnamon and bread rising. They ordered half a dozen of the most popular donuts from a dude at the counter with a handlebar mustache, then wandered back to the car. They settled in, pink box of donuts on the console between them. Mika waited to start the car, eyes on the waterfront before them.

She popped open the box and picked an Old Dirty Bastard, a raised yeast donut with chocolate frosting,

Oreo cookies, and peanut butter. "I still wish you would have let me buy you a T-shirt." At the counter, Mika had tried to foist a T-shirt onto Thomas. It featured the Voodoo Doughnut logo, a version of Baron Samedi with a banner that read: THE MAGIC IS IN THE HOLE. As with the oranges, Thomas had visibly blanched. He didn't wear any sort of shirt with a graphic on it. Much too wild. A quirk of Thomas's Mika might have found alienating but now thought of as kind of endearing.

"You're treating me to breakfast with a side of heart attack, that's enough." Thomas plucked an Apple Fritter from the box and took a healthy bite. "Oh my god!" he said, cheek full of dough, eyes nearly rolling to the back of his head. "That's the best donut I've ever had."

"Right?" Mika's grin split wide. "I know. I used to come here all the time with Hana."

Thomas swallowed. "So good." He picked out a Key Lime Crush and finished it in two bites. He licked jelly from his finger. "Let's bring Penny here next time I visit. She's such a foodie and hasn't ever mentioned it. She'll think I'm cool because I knew about it before her."

Mika grinned. She glanced at the clock on her dashboard. It was still early. Thomas's flight didn't leave for another six hours. She considered where to take him next. The Freakybutttrue Peculiarium, the farmers market, more food . . . what would Thomas like to do? She stared at the water, the boats whizzing by and drifting in the current. She started the car. "You ready to go?"

Thomas made some sound of agreement. At least, Mika thought so. It was hard to tell with his mouth full of Cap'n Crunch donut.

Thirty minutes later, Mika pulled into a gravel parking lot shaded by towering fir trees. A convenience store with a handmade sign that boasted: THE BEST DELI SANDWICHES THIS SIDE OF THE RIVER PLUS KAYAK RENTALS.

"Kayaking?" Thomas said, but in a different way than he'd said *donuts* earlier. On the way, he'd polished off two more, and a faint coat of powdered sugar dusted his knee.

"Kayaking." Mika nodded. She remembered Thomas had rowed in college.

"I haven't been out on the water for . . ." He shook his head. "Jesus. I don't know how long." He cracked his knuckles, dark brow furrowing. "Yeah, okay. I'm excited." They rented the kayaks, then met up with a stocky, bearded guy on the sandy shore who fitted them with a waterproof bag, life jackets, and a red whistle. "Just in case you run into Roslyn," he said.

"Roslyn?" Mika asked, slipping on her life jacket.

"Yeah. Alligator, we think she was some kid's pet." He laughed it off and waved a hand. "Anyway, you probably won't see her, but if you do, you'll have the whistle."

"Whistle, yeah," Mika said, pausing as she zipped the jacket.

Thomas grabbed the whistle and looped it around his neck. "Anything else?" He was ready, nearly bouncing on his feet. Hadn't looked at his watch once since they'd arrived or mentioned traffic and the airport.

"Nope. Kayaks are yours for three hours," the guy said.

Thomas thanked him and trudged to an orange kayak. Mika followed, jacket still undone. "Um, Thomas. I think we should go somewhere else."

"What? Why?" He whipped around.

"Because of . . ." She lowered her voice so the bearded guy wouldn't hear, but he was already climbing back up the steps to the parking lot. "Roslyn."

"The alligator? Wait, are you scared?" he asked, disbelieving. As if he ate alligators for breakfast.

"Of course I'm scared."

"I see." Thomas tried to hide his smile. "I'm sure he was just joking. The whistle is if we capsize or get lost. Plus, don't you think if there really was an alligator, there would be signs posted?" True. That did make sense. "And they'd give us something more than a whistle?" Even more sense. Thomas gazed across the water, sadness softening his eyes. "But if you *really* don't want to . . ." He trailed off, hung his head, and rolled his eyes up, regarding Mika through dark lashes, a sad puppy if she'd ever seen one.

"Ugh, alright," said Mika. "But if we run into anything remotely scaly, I am pushing you in front of me."

Thomas crossed his heart. "I will beg any creature we encounter to take me first."

They loaded into the kayaks and shoved off using their paddles. Thomas took the lead, his bow knifing through the glassy water, with the air of a seasoned professional. She watched the muscles in his arms move and flex as he used the oars to steer. Farther and farther from the dock, they drifted, paddling aimlessly. And Thomas was like a kid on cupcakes, his excitement like a lasso—ensnaring Mika.

"Penny would love this," Thomas called to her.

"Yeah," Mika agreed with a smile, picturing it: the three of them paddling through the water, Penny's infectious laugh floating down the river, always so ready for adventure. Mika snapped a few pictures, sent them to Penny, and then put her phone back in the wet bag.

Thomas kayaked farther down the river. Mika was content to trail behind him, following his lead. Every so often, he paused and turned back to make sure she was keeping up. A boyish grin transformed his features—he looked years younger, carefree. The sun was beating down, the birds were chirping, and it felt like they were the only two people for miles.

When they reached a patch of lily pads, Mika rested the paddle on her knees and leaned back, happily drifting in the water and basking in the sunlight and Thomas's happiness.

Bonk. Something jutted against the back of Mika's kayak. She spun toward the sound. *Roslyn?* The kayak rocked, tilted. Mika panicked and shifted her body weight, making a jerking motion. The kayak tipped, taking Mika with it. A strangled scream erupted from her throat just as she hit the water. She was submerged for a second. Head bobbing to the surface, she gasped. Through the curtain of her soggy black hair, she spotted Thomas paddling toward her.

"You cross paths with Roslyn?" He glided right up next to her and pointed at something with his oar. Mika shoved the hair from her face. Nearly at eye level, staring at her, was a beaver. Its nose twitched, revealing long yellowing teeth. It studied her for a moment, then turned, tail slapping the water as it swam away. "Little furry to be an alligator," Thomas said matter-of-factly.

Mika glared at Thomas, turned her back, and swam

to her kayak, trying unsuccessfully to hoist herself into it. Too late, she remembered basic pull-ups made her scream. Getting her wet, clothed body back in the kayak was nigh impossible. In the end, Thomas had to get in the water and help her. Together they swam, guiding their kayaks to a nearby sandy alcove. They trudged to the shore, wet clothes clinging to their bodies. Thomas whipped off his shirt, and Mika found the ground suddenly fascinating. He wrung it out into the sand and slipped it back on. Mika crossed her arms over her chest and shivered. The day was warm, but they were in the shade. Each breeze a tiny cold whip against her skin.

Thomas's light eyes swept down Mika and back up. "Hang on," he commanded. He tromped into the forest and returned with dry twigs, leaves, and some bark. Mika watched as he used the nylon rope from the whistle and made something resembling a bow with it. Finally, he squatted down, assembled some other contraption, moving the bow back and forth. The leaves began to smoke and catch fire. Thomas blew on it, and the blaze increased. He dumped a couple bigger pieces of wood onto the fire.

Mika stepped forward to splay her hands above the flames. "This is very Bear Grylls of you," she said pointedly.

"That guy? His stuff is all staged." Thomas seemed a little offended.

"Oh?" she asked. Thomas merely nodded—enough said. "So how does one learn to conjure fires from sticks, leaves, and nylon rope?"

"I was an Eagle Scout," he said with a shrug. He paused. "Stay here. Warm up. I'm going to get more wood."

"Eagle Scout," Mika whispered to herself, watching Thomas gather logs from the tree line. "Course you were."

A few minutes later, the fire blazed in a full roar. They slipped off their shoes and propped them up to dry. Mika's cheeks grew toasty warm. Thomas sat across from her, knees up, elbows resting on them. Mika listened to the chirp of the birds and stared at the fire, transfixed by the flames. "Sorry about the beaver."

"Don't worry about it. I'm sure beavers get mistaken for alligators all the time." Thomas looked away. He pressed his lips together, mouth working not to smile. She watched as he hung his head. His shoulders shook. He was laughing—*at her.*

"You're hilarious," Mika said flatly.

He smirked at her. "No. I get it. I totally do. He was terrifying. I see why you panicked. Definitely not an overreaction."

Mika dug her toes into the sand. "The beaver was big."

"When I retell the story, I will cast the beaver as massive, at least a hundred pounds," Thomas promised.

"I'm pretty sure they don't get above fifty pounds. But I appreciate your mutant beaver take." Mika also appreciated the way his damp T-shirt clung to his shoulders. She found a stick and jabbed at the fire, shifting her gaze away. "You should know that, in the instance of another extra-large beaver that might be an alligator, I will gladly throw your body in front of mine. It would be a shame for Penny to lose a parent, but . . ." Mika paused, realized what she'd said. She scrambled to make it right. "Shit. Sorry," she said feebly. She'd forgotten. *Caroline.* She stared at him helplessly.

Thomas looked at her over the fire with a fervent gaze. "It's alright," he said finally, expression inscrutable.

Mika dug her hands into the sand and fisted them. "No, it's not. I am an insensitive asshole. I'm sorry," she said stupidly. "Penny said you don't like to talk about it. I understand. You're not over it."

His eyes flickered, and a few tense beats passed before he answered. "Do you ever get over someone you love dying?"

"No." Mika peered away.

The lighting was just right. The surrounding trees mirrored in the water, their leaves bright and green, grinning at summer. Soon they'd curl, turn brown, wither away with fall. Most lives were drawn with fragile lines. The panic attacks worsened after Mika had Penny. At first, Hana had been patient and kind. Sitting by Mika's side while she fractured and short-circuited, fragmented all over the place.

I think I'm dying, she'd say to Hana, gasping for breath. But really, Mika had thought, it was her soul trying to reenter a body that didn't fit anymore. Half a dozen times later, Hana's patience thinned. She turned lovingly mean. She forced Mika's feet into shoes, her body across campus to the free counseling services. There Mika had met Suzanne, a graduate psychology student who approached Mika as though she were a skittish whipped horse. Suzanne taught Mika how to breathe through the fear. When Mika calmed, she had clenched her fists and pounded her knees and said, *I just need to get over this.* It was something her mother had instilled in her. To rise above adversity. Just as there were narratives for good mothers, there were narratives for good victims too. Don't let it define you. Be brave. Not a victim.

Suzanne leaned over, macramé necklace swinging

in the air, and with all the sympathy in the world and maybe a little pity, she said, *Babe, this isn't something you get over. This is something you go through.*

Now, Mika repeated it. "It's something you go through," Mika whispered to Thomas.

He stared at her, gaze sharp and fiery. "That's exactly right." A sad ghost of a smile appeared on his face. "Caroline had this running joke. Now that I think of it, it was kind of morbid. But she used to tease me that I was trapped in a coma dream. Sometimes she'd hug me from behind and say, 'Wake up, Thomas, I love you. I need you.' Then she'd laugh like it was the funniest thing. When she passed away, I was by her side. There were all these nurses around, but I couldn't help myself. I whispered in her ear, 'Wake up, Caroline. I love you. I need you.'" He paused. His eyes were red and liquid. Mika's were too. "I've never told anyone that."

"After I had Penny, I used to talk to her," Mika blurted. *Hi, baby, you are two weeks old today, and I hope you are doing okay. I'm not doing so hot myself . . .* Mika would say. It was all she could do to keep from self-destructing completely.

Thomas bobbed his head in agreement. "I used to talk to Caroline too. Then it became less and less. Until one day, I didn't talk to her at all." He cleared his throat and wiped under his nose. "Anyway, it's something I've been through. I'm on the other side now. I don't carry all that around with me anymore. I'm thankful for Caroline, for the life we made together, for Penny. I don't have any regrets. But . . ." He took a breath and went on. "Penny said I don't like talking about her?"

"Yeah."

"That's my fault." He tossed another log onto the fire. "I was so pissed after she died. So lost in my own desolation, I didn't make it easy for Penny."

"What was she like?" The words slipped out, and Mika wished she could take them back. She wanted to like Caroline but also felt a deep hunger to find faults within her, this phantom other mother to Penny.

At last, Thomas smiled again. "Caroline was pretty amazing. As a person, she was sweet and giving, and kind. She'd stay after shifts and visit patients who didn't have a family when she was a nurse. She was a great wife and mom. We made a good team. I wish she was here to see Penny. How good she is."

"She sounds perfect." Mika tried to keep the envy from her voice. How could she ever compare?

Thomas studied Mika. "She wasn't, actually. Far from it. She had a temper and used silence like a weapon." Mika thought of her mother's quiet unhappiness. Of Penny's refusal to talk about Caroline. Of her own unwillingness to step forward after Peter. All the ways women wielded or kept silence. How dangerous it could be. "Once, she didn't talk to me for two days straight when I had too much to drink with some buddies."

"Yikes," Mika said.

He nodded and poked at the sand with a finger. He smiled wryly. "She liked being in control. She cleaned obsessively and was a bit of a perfectionist. Sometimes I thought I wouldn't ever be good enough for her. But she loved me anyway, and I loved her."

Mika peered at Thomas. She thought about love, its different forms—what it felt like to have it, to lose it. They had that in common.

An engine's roar sounded and closed in. Birds startled from their trees. A fishing boat motored to a stop and idled just off the shore. "Hey!" The bearded guy from the kayak rental place cupped his hands over his mouth and yelled, "Your rentals are overdue, and there are no fires on that beach. It's public land."

Thomas and Mika hauled to their feet. Thomas threw sand on the fire, and the bearded guy brought the boat closer. Together they loaded up their kayaks.

"Sorry," Thomas said, wind breezing through his hair on their way back to the dock. "We had a run-in with Roslyn."

The bearded guy barked a hearty laugh. He raised his arm to point at a vine maple growing in the sandy bank. Its branches arched over the water, and from them hung a stuffed muddy alligator, a piece of cardboard around its neck, the name *Roslyn* Sharpied on it. "Roslyn strikes again," he said.

• • •

Mika waited, back turned while Thomas changed out of his damp clothes into clean and dry ones in her car. He emerged with a sweatshirt. "Here," he said, handing it over.

"Oh, thanks." Mika slipped it on, Dartmouth rowing emblem over her chest.

She drove him to the airport, and they said goodbye. Mika offering to wash the sweatshirt and send it to him. But he said he'd get it when he came back into town in a few weeks. At home, Mika showered. When she emerged, a text from Thomas waited.

Flight is about to board. Thanks for this morning. I forgot how good it feels to be out on the water.

She remembered Thomas in the kayak. His faint grin was contagious, overconfident, eyes on the winding river. She knew that look. Knew that feeling. It was the same as when she gazed at paints. Like something belonged to you. Anytime, she answered.

It was really amazing. You just get busy with family and all, but I feel like I still got it, he replied.

Yeah, you're for sure the GOAT of kayaking, she shot back.

He replied with a single word, GOAT?

She tightened the knot on her robe before clarifying. Greatest of all time.

I am sensing sarcasm. Are you still upset about the beaver? he teased.

I don't know what you're talking about, she answered with a growing smile.

Thank you, he simply said.

Don't mention it. I'm glad you had fun, she replied.

She picked up her clothes from the floor, including his sweatshirt, and dumped them into the wash. Back at her phone, Thomas had texted again. Seriously, I owe you one.

ADOPTION ACROSS AMERICA
National Office
56544 W 57th Ave. Suite 111
Topeka, KS 66546
(800) 555-7794

Dear Mika,

How are you?! Can you believe how fast time passes? Penny is thirteen, and it has been such a joy watching her grow up with you. As always, enclosed are the requisite items in regard to the adoption agreement between you, Mika Suzuki (the birth mother), and Thomas Calvin (the adoptive parent) for Penelope Calvin (the adoptee). Contents include:

- An annual letter from the adoptive parent describing the adoptee's development and progress
- Photographs and/or other memorabilia

Give me a call if you have any questions.

All the best,

Monica Pearson
Adoption Coordinator

Dear Ms. Suzuki,

Penny celebrated her thirteenth birthday last week and is in the eighth grade. She is doing fine and excels in most of her classes. She is thinking of joining a running team and has asked for a kitten for Christmas. I've included some pictures of her recent science fair project.

All best,
Thomas

Chapter Twenty-Three

Mika peered at the mound of oranges.

"Am I missing something?" Penny tilted her head, then her mouth formed a little O. "Did you see a giant spider? I saw this news story once about tropical arachnids hitching rides in fruit shipments."

Mika shook her head, stepping closer to the oranges to avoid a dad with three rowdy kids in his cart. Uwaji-maya, the Asian market, was loud, bright, and bustling this Saturday morning. "No. No giant spider."

Penny pursed her lips. "Shoot."

Mika picked up an orange to examine it, turning it in her hands. "Did you know your father doesn't like the navels of oranges?"

"Oh, yeah. He's a total weirdo." Penny shifted, setting down the basket filled with Meiji chocolate bars, Pocky sticks, and White Rabbit candy—totally a balanced diet. Then she turned a section of the oranges so they were all navel or butt up.

Mika retrieved her phone from her back pocket and snapped a photo. "Should we text him a picture?"

"For sure," Penny said with a bit of a grin, picking up the basket.

Mika hit send with a wicked smile. They laughed and shopped some more, Penny marveling at the packages of dried squid, live uni in tanks, and mountains of bok choy. Drinking up the sights and smells like a stalk of bamboo starved for rain. Thomas texted back with a photograph of a beaver, but somehow, he'd colored the eyes neon green. Mika opted not to show Penny. How would she explain? *I thought I saw an alligator, and it was really a beaver. I tipped my kayak, and your father had to fish me out.* First, the whole thing was embarrassing. Mika felt her cheeks heat even thinking about it. Second, the oranges were something the three of them shared, but the joke about the beaver . . . that was Mika and Thomas's. The whole scenario might seem off to Penny—weird or, worse, *intimate.*

As they checked out, Mika insisted they try some takoyaki. "Fried octopus, street food," she explained to Penny as they slid into chairs at the food court. In Japan, it was rude to walk and eat. Mika placed the ball-shaped snacks in the middle of the table and pointed out some of the ingredients—doughy balls with a chunk of octopus on the inside, tempura scraps, pickled ginger, and green onion. Penny broke apart a pair of wooden hashi and dug in. Mika loved how fearless her daughter was.

Penny chewed slowly, thoughtfully. "This is good. I like it," she announced. As soon as she was done with the first, she popped a second in her mouth, then announced, cheek full, "I'm thinking of sleeping with Devon."

Mika choked, coughed, and spluttered, then gulped some water.

Penny watched her with a side-eye. "You okay?"

Mika patted her chest. "Sorry. *Sleeping* with him?" she said carefully, throat still burning a little. Maybe she'd heard incorrectly. Maybe she'd heard correctly and didn't understand. Maybe sleeping together didn't mean the same thing as Mika thought it did. Maybe it was more of a slumber party–type thing now in teen-speak, like wrapping yourselves up in sheets and lying side by side silently in the dark with absolutely no touching.

"You know, sex," Penny said, her voice dropping.

Mika sipped her water again and tried to muster an encouraging smile. "That's a big step." It was the only thing she could think to say in the moment, other than reminding Penny she was sixteen. A baby. *My baby.*

Penny balled a napkin up and fisted it. "I'm ready. I'm sure I am. Like, I think I love him."

Devon might not feel the same, but Mika didn't have the heart to say that, didn't have the heart to break Penny's heart. To voice her fear that Penny may not be loved in the way she wanted or should be. So instead, she said, "Love isn't always a requirement." She regarded Penny, thought about her daughter, her worldview—how it was small and singular and a little naïve. Is that what Hiromi had thought of Mika when she was a teen? Mika shifted in her seat. How deeply unsettling to think you might be like your own mother.

Penny bit her lower lip, raising her lashes to shyly meet Mika's eyes. "Can I ask . . . I mean, what was your first time like?"

Mika focused on a tanuki in the home goods section. The dancing raccoon's eyes were crossed and between his legs hung an enormous set of testicles—you know, for good luck. "My first time?" She blinked and saw the Cheerful Tortoise, a bar on campus. Remembered her hips swinging like a pendulum, smiling at a cute guy through the crowd. His name was Jordan, a political science major. He wore Birkenstocks with socks, shared an apartment with four other guys, and in his room, instead of a lamp was one of those outdoor floodlights. "It wasn't super memorable or romantic. But it was fun," Mika answered honestly with a wistful smile. "It hurt a little." She felt her cheeks burn, felt Penny's attention intensify. She hadn't told Jordan she was a virgin until after. He insisted on going slower, trying again. They listened to Wilco while he went down on her. Mika studied the table. "Penny," she said, going for a calm, nonjudgmental tone. "Are you sure? About Devon? You haven't known him very long." A handful of weeks, Mika wanted to add. One thousand percent, she felt like a hypocrite. But god, why have children if you couldn't save them from your mistakes?

"I have," Penny said, resolve in her eyes. Eyes that hadn't seen nearly enough. "We spend a lot of time together, almost all day, every day. Plus, you know, I've done tons of other stuff."

Mika stiffened. "I don't need to know." The fewer details, the better.

"I'm ready. I know I am," Penny insisted.

"Okay." At Mika's capitulation, her softening, Penny did too.

"Devon is a good guy. We've talked a lot about it. He hasn't been pressuring me or anything."

"Okay," Mika said again. She inhaled, accepting the inevitability. This was going to happen. There was something timeless about kids not listening to their parents. And Mika felt very much part of that infinite loop. "What about protection? Have you discussed that?"

Two bright splotches appeared on Penny's cheeks. Maybe she was thinking about Mika, how she'd gotten pregnant so young. How she didn't want to be the same as her birth mother—a teen with limited choices. "He said he'll wear a condom, and I've been on birth control for a couple years . . . bad periods."

"Sounds like you've got it covered, then." Mika moved to stand and clear the table. Hiromi had never spoken to Mika about sex. And what she had learned in high school revolved around saying no, pregnancy, and STDs. Nobody told her how fun it could be. How complicated too.

"We do. I promise," Penny assured, staying seated. "Hey, but you think you could keep this quiet? Between us?"

Mika paused, the paper plate and used hashi in her hand. "You mean not tell your dad?"

Penny waved a hand. "It's not a big deal. Look, there are just some things he doesn't need to know."

Mika sat back down in her seat. Penny wanted Mika to lie to Thomas. *I can't.* The thought struck Mika like a lightning bolt. "I'm not super comfortable with that, Penny. You don't have to have the virginity conversation with him, but you need to tell him about Devon, that you're dating someone at least. I mean, I know from experience the truth has a way of revealing itself," she tried to joke.

Penny's face hardened. She looked everywhere but at Mika. "I should probably be getting back to the dorm."

"What?" Mika flinched. Penny had the weekend free. She was going to spend the night.

"Yeah, I just remembered I promised Olive we'd work on some of our times together."

"Seriously?" Mika quirked a brow.

"Seriously." Penny stood and grabbed her shopping bag, white-knuckling it. "Ready?"

They walked to the car, the shadow of Penny's anger trailing behind them. Mika was at a loss for words. *What just happened?* The ride itself was worse. Silent and pulsating with Penny's discontent. Mika swore she heard a ripping sound, a tear in the fabric of her and Penny's relationship. How would she stitch it back together? Mika parked her car at the dorm and turned to her daughter, speaking to her over the console. "I—"

Too late. Penny slammed the door.

• • •

Hours later, Mika was no longer confused. Able to replay the conversation multiple times in her head in the quiet of her house, Mika vacillated between being deeply hurt by Penny and angry at her.

"She's mad at me?" Mika huffed out to herself, feeling unspeakable things about Penny. Things like how stubborn and petulant her daughter could be. But then . . . "She's mad at me," she said more quietly. She thought about calling Thomas. Conferring with him on how to best approach Penny. But it was Penny she really wanted, *needed* to speak to. So, just as the sun was going down, Mika dialed her daughter. She didn't want to go to bed with this unresolved. Wasn't there a saying about never going to sleep angry? Anyway, Mika didn't want to hide, to cower under Penny's changing weather patterns.

The phone rang a few times, and Mika braced herself, steadied her nerves.

"Hi," Penny said. That was all.

"I don't want you to be mad at me," Mika blurted. She winced and waited. *I gave birth to her. I should be a natural at parenting.*

"I don't want to be mad at you either," Penny admitted.

Mika inhaled and stared out the living room window at the dark pavement outside. "Well, now that we've established that . . ." She trailed off. "I want you to be able to tell me things. I want to be a sounding board, a safe place for you, but I'm also your—" She stopped short at saying *mother*. "I'm an adult, and it puts me in a difficult position lying to your dad."

After a beat, Penny sighed. "I get it, I guess." *Where is she?* Mika tried to picture Penny in the hall of her dorm. Nose scrunched, a little red from crying, maybe Devon watching. "I'm going to tell my dad about the coed housing and Devon. Not because you told me to—"

"Of course not," Mika interjected.

"But because I want him to meet D." She sighed again. "He's probably going to do that thing where he says he's not mad. He's just disappointed." Mika's lips tipped up. It sounded exactly like Thomas. "I don't think I am going to tell him about the sex part, though," Penny said, as if drawing a line in the sand.

Even though Penny couldn't see it, Mika nodded firmly. "Your body, your choice."

"We really do like each other. I know I'm a teenager, and that's probably all you see—"

"It's not all I see," Mika said. "I believe you're smart and savvy and know your own heart."

"Thanks. That means a lot."

"I recognize this is awkward." Mika had to swallow against a sudden thickness in her throat. "Promise me you'll come to me if you need anything. It's okay to say you want to and then change your mind. Even if it's in the middle of it, and you think he'll be angry. A real man won't be." Mika curled her empty hand into a fist. Remembered pressing it against Peter's chest. *No.* A fierce protectiveness rose inside of her.

"D isn't like that," Penny insisted. "I'm sure. I want to."

"Alright," Mika said softly. Penny kept her on the phone a little longer, regaling Mika with tales of FaceTiming with Hiromi, how they had a whole conversation with Hiromi's thumb over the camera. And Mika felt light again, like seeing the first slice of the sun after a great and terrible storm.

• • •

Thomas called Monday afternoon just as Mika had swung her purse over her shoulder to head across Nike's campus to meet Hayato for lunch. They had big plans to peruse photographs from the latest royal wedding while eating chocolate pie. Big plans.

Thomas didn't give Mika a chance to even say hi. "Penny has a boyfriend," he said without preamble.

"She told you." Mika passed a set of dudes nearly one and a half times her height and smiled at them, pretty sure they were famous basketball players.

"She wants me to meet him next time I'm in town. Have you met him?"

"Not officially. I've seen him a few times." Mika stopped outside the double glass doors leading into the Mia Hamm Building and waved to Hayato, who was already waiting for her. She held up a finger asking for one minute. He mouthed *No problem* and messed around on his phone.

"Does he appear to have any deviant tendencies?" Thomas asked in a flat voice.

Sometimes Thomas sounded as if he were stuck in a black-and-white movie. He probably wouldn't like it if Mika called him "old-timey." She scrunched her nose. "You mean was he carrying a switchblade and looking for trouble?"

Thomas dragged in a breath. "I wish I could laugh right now."

"I'm sorry." Mika folded in her arms. There was a giant water feature nearby, complete with a spraying fountain. Ducks swam and bobbed on the choppy surface. "I'm glad she told you, though. We were eating takoyaki—"

"Takoyaki?"

"Fried octopus balls."

"Huh?" She pictured Thomas's glower, the expression on his face when he was confused and slightly angry about it.

"Not actual octopus balls, like their testicles . . ."

Mika held the receiver away from her face and stared at the sky for a moment. She was drifting too far off course. "Never mind. We were eating, and Penny was telling me about Devon and how they were getting more serious. When I learned that, I encouraged her to tell you about him."

Silence then. "So," he drawled out. "You've known a while Penny was seeing someone?" Thomas asked.

Mika let out the faintest sigh. "Only a couple of weeks. She asked me to keep it a secret. I'm sorry. She got so mad at me when I said she should tell you." Mika remembered Penny's anger. How she'd worn it like a beat-up pair of leather boots. Used it to stomp all over her. "I wasn't comfortable with you not knowing anymore." More silence. "Don't be angry," Mika finished.

"I'm not," Thomas said after a moment. "I'm glad she's talking to someone I can trust."

Mika felt it then—the sensation of placing a heavy weight down after carrying it for a very long time. She mumbled a thank-you.

Long after they'd hung up, through lunch with Hayato and the rest of her day, Mika's head rang with those four precious words: *someone I can trust.*

Chapter Twenty-Four

Three days later, Thomas texted Mika. I'm thinking of growing a mustache.

Mika sat in a glass-walled meeting room, papers fanned around her. Gus liked her work on the collaboration model so much he'd asked her to help on another. *I know you can handle it,* he'd said, voice brimming with confidence.

Please don't. Mika thought an immediate response necessary.

You're right, he said two hours later. I should definitely get an ear piercing.

Penny would hate that, Mika said as she left work.

To which he said: All the more reason to, then.

If you're going to do it, better to really commit and get both ears pierced, don't you think? Mika answered when she got home. She popped a meal in the micro-wave and sat down to eat, phone on the table in front of her, awaiting Thomas's reply.

It's a bold statement, he said just as she took her first bite.

She chewed thoughtfully and answered, You could pull it off.

Eight days later, on Thursday, Mika was just shut-ting down her computer when Thomas texted again. The boyfriend is taking Penny on an all-day date Sat-urday. Hiking at some waterfall. I asked her if I could tag along. Even offered to pay.

Mika waved to Gus through the glass walls of his office. "Have a good weekend," he called, poking his head out. She wished him the same. I hope you were joking, she responded.

Half joking, he shot back almost immediately.

So not coming this weekend? No church? Mika asked, sitting in her car with the windows rolled down. It was still bright out. And blistering hot. She waited for him to reply. They'd actually made plans for the weekend together. On Sunday, Penny, Thomas, and Mika were supposed to attend services with Hiromi and Shige.

Still coming. Still going to church. But I'm going to keep my flight arriving tonight, too late to switch.

Mika chewed her thumb, thinking. Saturday she had plans to go to a winery with Charlie, Tuan, Hayato, and his new boyfriend, Seth. Hey, I have an idea, she typed.

I love ideas, said Thomas.

Since Penny will be busy on Saturday, why don't you come out with my friends and me? We're going to a winery in the afternoon, then maybe some bars after, which will mostly entail a lot of dudes with ironic facial hair.

Mika's toes curled in her shoes, the action of some- one about to skate on thin ice. This was different than last-minute kayaking. This was inviting Thomas out to meet her friends, to be a part of her life. Yet some- how . . . it also felt natural, right. Her chest squeezed, waiting for Thomas to respond.

I've always longed to immerse myself in ironic facial hair culture, he said.

Mika smiled warmly. Now is your chance. Seize the day. You in?

He responded instantly. I'm in.

• • •

What should I wear? Thomas wrote Saturday morn- ing. Suit and tie?

Mika grinned. Each time Thomas texted, she got a

little excited but pretended she didn't. Those weren't butterflies fluttering in her stomach. Not at all. Did you happen to bring a tux?

Seriously? he asked.

No, she replied, although she wouldn't mind seeing Thomas in a tux. Thomas in jeans and a T-shirt was just fine too. All too well, she remembered watching him walk from Hana's room the morning after he'd stayed over, that little slice of stomach as he pulled his shirt on. I mean, if you wore a beret, I wouldn't hate it.

I'm wearing jeans, Thomas said.

Maybe a jaunty scarf around your neck? Mika asked with a smile, a bite of her lip.

I'll see you at one, Thomas answered.

Mika picked Thomas up at his hotel and drove them to Charlie's. "I'm sorry Penny didn't want to hang out with you," she said. They passed a bank, a guy on a unicycle.

Thomas stretched his legs. "I shouldn't feel bad. This is how it's supposed to be, I guess. You go along guiding your kid in one direction, then find out they want to go off on their own, jump ship. You hope you've given them enough wisdom to be okay."

Mika frowned. "Sounds like you basically train something you love to eventually leave you."

Thomas's eyes bored into Mika's for a few heavy beats. She felt the heat of his stare on the side of her face. "Exactly."

"I'm not sure I like that." She shifted, focused on the road. Out of the corner of her eye, she saw Thomas smile crookedly.

When she pulled up, the grape-colored tour van was already waiting, along with Charlie at the curb. Charlie waved at Mika behind the wheel; her smile grew wider seeing Thomas in the passenger seat. As soon as Mika was out of the car, Charlie trotted over to her.

"Mika," she said in a voice that was a touch higher and giddier than usual. "This is a surprise. I didn't know you were bringing anyone. Hi, I'm Charlie." She stuck out a hand.

Thomas shook her hand. "Thomas," he said.

"Ah, Penny's dad. Lovely to meet you," Charlie said, her smile blinding.

"I figured it wouldn't be a problem since we paid for eight." That's how many the van seated and the group minimum. The friends had divided the payment equally among each other.

"Oh, it's no problem," Charlie said. "No problem at all. The more, the merrier, I always say." She stared at Thomas expectantly.

Thomas shifted on his feet and looked away.

"Should we get going then?" Mika interjected.

"Um, oh yeah," Charlie said, springing to life. "Let's go. Everyone is already on board. Not that you're late or anything. Besides, I always say better late than never . . ." She trailed off. "Go ahead. After you."

They started toward the van, Thomas in front of them. Mika paused, her foot on the step leading up. *What is wrong with you,* she mouthed to her deranged friend.

Charlie's mouth split into another broad smile. *Oh my god,* she mouthed back. They boarded, and Charlie announced, "Look, everyone, Mika brought a friend." And Mika was thankful for the dark interior, that it might hide her embarrassed blush. She shouldn't have invited Thomas. What had she been thinking? She'd acted on impulse, something she hadn't done in a long time, since before Penny, before Peter.

Mika flopped down into a black cushioned seat, and Thomas settled in next to her. "Sorry," Mika said. "Charlie is being weird. Maybe she started drinking early."

"It's fine," Thomas said, kind of stiff.

Well, they were off to a torturous start. Hayato cleared his throat. Introductions went around from there. Tuan to Thomas. Thomas to Hayato. And Seth,

Hayato's new handsome blond boyfriend, to everyone. "Nice to meet you, man," Seth said, shaking Thomas's hand.

"You too," Thomas said.

They pulled apart. Seth sat back down next to Hayato. The van was moving and everyone just kind of sat there, staring at Thomas. "Hey, I think you've got something," Seth spoke into the silence to Thomas, "in your collar there." He flicked the back of his own shirt.

Thomas frowned and felt along the nape of his neck, coming back with a tag between his fingers. "Right. New shirt," he admitted flatly. "I bought it this morning at a shop near the hotel. Apparently untucked is the look these days . . ." He drummed his fingers on his knees.

"I like it," Charlie interjected. "Tuan should get the name from you."

Tuan leaned in and asked about the store, what hotel he was staying at, if Thomas liked the area. Mika heaved an unsteady breath and turned to Hayato and Seth. Easy conversation took hold, and sixty minutes later, the van wound up a hill, following the route like a lazy cat's tail.

The van slowed and stopped with a hiss. They

shuffled off and outside into the bright late afternoon sun, where a sommelier greeted them. She wore a fleece vest with the winery's name embroidered on it and escorted them to an overlook, beyond which the valley stretched, rows and rows of verdant grapevines. A gentle breeze twisted through Mika's hair. The sommelier announced that the lunch and tasting would begin soon and invited them to play one of the games on the lawn—croquet, horseshoes, even a giant Jenga tower.

"Check it out." Seth squeezed Hayato's hand. "Cornhole. Anyone want to play?" Seth glanced around the group, obviously searching for a partner.

Thomas stuck up his hand. "It's been a while, but I used to play all the time in college."

Seth kissed Hayato and Hayato patted his bum. "Good luck, babe."

Mika gave a half-salute to Thomas. "Have fun."

They were off, setting up the boards and beanbags. It didn't take long for Charlie, Tuan, and Hayato to close in around Mika. "Whoa." Mika stepped back. "Personal space much?"

Charlie smiled benignly. "He bought a new shirt," she stated.

Mika shrugged. "Yeah, so?" The sommelier set up the wines, glasses, and plates at their table a few feet away. "Hey, Tuan, don't you want to take Charlie for a walk in the vineyard before the tasting starts? It looks super romantic."

"No." Tuan's smile was anticipatory. "I am here for this."

"Let's talk about Seth instead," Mika said.

"Seth's great. I am into him. I am pretty sure he's into me," Hayato said, then added, "You know what I buy new shirts for?"

Thomas's laugh tripped over on the wind; it wrapped around Mika, threatened to carry her away. She dug her feet into the ground. "You buy new shirts all the time," Mika said pointedly. It was true. They spent their lunches going through websites, riffling through men's and women's wear, deciding what colors suited their Japanese complexions best—never yellow.

"For dates," Hayato clarified. "I buy new shirts for dates."

"That's not what this is." Mika's denial was quick. Too quick. "He's Penny's dad."

Charlie tilted her head. "So?"

"So?" Mika parroted back. "It's a line I'm not willing to cross. Besides, I'm not even sure if he wants to cross it . . ."

"Oh. He does," Hayato said all-knowingly. "New shirt. And untucked too. Men wear untucked shirts to draw attention to their . . ." He glanced down authoritatively.

Mika rose up on her tiptoes. "I think our table is ready." In another life, she might have dreamed of someone like Thomas. A family with Penny in it. But this was the universe tempting Mika again, a tidal wave waiting to drown her. She wouldn't dip her toes in the water a second time.

Mika left and sat at the table alone until Charlie joined her. They watched Thomas and Seth for a minute. Mika focused on Thomas, how he'd rolled up his shirtsleeves, the flex of his wrist as he threw.

"It's a little scary, isn't it?" Charlie asked.

"Again, I don't know what you're talking about." Sometimes it was even scarier to admit you were afraid. But the truth was . . . the truth was Mika *was* afraid. Ever since Peter, she'd been subsumed by futility, too scared to paint, to travel, to love, to laugh, to take risks. She'd folded up like a piece of origami. Making herself smaller and smaller, a piece of paper slipping through the cracks of life.

"It's okay to want things, you know?" Charlie said quietly. "And it's okay if it gets messy. Things have a way of working themselves out."

Spoken like a true optimist, Mika thought. "But what if they don't?"

Charlie arched a brow, didn't back down. "But what if they do?"

Touché. The two fell quiet. Mika watched Thomas again. She thought of Penny, of that day in the art museum, of peering at that painting depicting Icarus's fall. She let herself contemplate falling. Could it be worth it?

• • •

"We'll be featuring a pinot and pie tasting today." The sommelier held up a bottle and poured splashes of ruby gold into each glass. "You may notice the fresh fruit aromas." She swished the wine and smelled to demonstrate. "Raspberry and strawberry are accented by herbs and savory spices on the nose."

"Cheers!" Charlie held up her glass. The six sipped and spat. "Oh, I almost forgot," Charlie announced. "I brought party favors." She dashed from the table and returned with a bag. She dipped into it and produced a stack of black felt hats.

"You weren't joking about the berets," Thomas whispered. Mika snickered. He'd kept his sleeves rolled up, and there was the slightest glinting of sweat along his hairline from playing cornhole with Seth.

Charlie half rose from her seat and handed out the berets. She loved party favors, costumes, themed foods—anything a little extra. She passed one to Mika with a smile.

"You'll look great in this." Charlie smiled, giving Thomas a beret.

"Do I have to wear it?" Thomas asked, rotating the beret around his finger.

"No," Mika said, and at the same time, Charlie said, "Yes."

"When in Rome." Thomas fitted the beret on his head, and Mika had to admit, it looked pretty dashing on him. Charlie sat back down next to Tuan with a smile.

"I also brought a game," Charlie said happily, taking a stack of index cards from the bag. Groans circled around. "Shut it. We're going to bond meaningfully. Starting with . . ." She turned over the first index card and read from it. "'Your house, containing everything you own, catches fire. After saving your loved ones and pets, you have time to safely make a final dash to save any one item. What would it be? Why?'"

They paused as the sommelier introduced another pinot, something energetic with dark fruit and woodsy spice notes. Tuan took a sip of the dry wine and swallowed. "I'll go first," he offered. "Just one thing?" he asked.

"Just one thing and why," Charlie confirmed.

"Definitely my Bumblebee Transformer. I've had it since I was twelve, and I want to give it to my kids someday," Tuan said.

Charlie smiled, and Hayato offered to go next. "I guess I'd rescue my manga collection," he said.

"I'm with you two," Seth said. "Childhood memorabilia all the way. I'd take my baseball cards."

Thomas's turn. He stretched out his legs, knee colliding with Mika's. Her stomach flipped. "Well, most of my important documents—insurance papers, passports, birth certificates, that sort of thing—are actually in a fireproof box," Thomas said sheepishly. The group gave him a collective thumbs-down. "Okay. Okay." Thomas held up his hands. "I'd take my wife's ashes. For obvious reasons."

Mika felt as if she'd been doused in cold water. She didn't blame Thomas for wanting to save his wife's ashes. But she couldn't help but feel Caroline's presence lurking. Caroline, the ideal wife, the ideal mother, the ideal woman. All the things Mika could not, would never be.

"What about you, Mika?" Charlie asked.

Mika stared out into the valley. She thought of the packages from Caroline. The letters and photographs of Penny stuffed in her dresser drawer. Everything else she might live without—clothes, makeup, etc.

"Pictures." She paused, stomach bottoming out. "Of Penny. Which reminds me, I should probably make digital copies. Hana is bound to burn our house down someday."

Thomas smiled at Mika, and she felt the warmth of it radiate through her skin.

"I'd also take my guitar," Tuan added. "While our house burns, I would serenade you."

Charlie seemed extraordinarily pleased by this.

Mika pretended to puke in her lap. "If you say you watch her sleep, I am going to throw myself from this overlook."

"That's just hyperbole and very bad," Charlie said to Mika with a frown. She sighed. They waited as the sommelier poured glasses of their final tasting—another pinot characterized by its elegance and soft finish.

"Alright. Next question." Charlie picked up an index card and read it. "'For what in your life do you feel most grateful?'"

"Good friends," Hayato said.

"New friends," Seth said. The two kissed.

"Charlie, obviously," Tuan said.

"Oh, we're definitely playing slow jams tonight," Charlie said, kissing Tuan right on the lips. "What about you?" Charlie turned toward Thomas and Mika.

"That's easy," Thomas said. His lips had the slightest stain of purple. "My daughter, Penny."

Mika stretched out her legs, her gaze connected with Thomas's. "Same," she said. They smiled at each other. Conspirators. Their love for Penny tucked between them.

Chapter Twenty-Five

Charlie and Tuan were tipsy and slow-danced at the Allison, a cute hotel near the vineyard where they'd decided to have dinner. A few yards away, Hayato and Seth chatted up the bartender.

"Hey." Thomas slid into the booth beside Mika.

"Hey," Mika said back. "Where have you been?"

Thomas smiled. His eyes were slightly glazed, courtesy of the three wineries they'd visited. "I did something." He shifted and pulled a stack of index cards from his back pocket and placed them on the table.

"You didn't!" Mika said, eyes wide, then darting to Charlie. Her face was firmly planted in Tuan's chest. "You stole them," she accused, mouth ajar. "I'd never have expected such deviant behavior from you."

"Totally unpremeditated. Perfectly defensible in

court." Thomas's smile spread. "Anyway, I was going to the bathroom and saw the van parked outside. The door was just open. I mean, if Charlie didn't want her cards stolen, she should have guarded them better."

"True," Mika agreed sagely. She put a finger to the top card and slid it off the pile. She flipped it over. "'Take four minutes and tell your partner your life story in as much detail as possible,'" she read aloud. Thomas smiled lazily, and she felt it all the way to her toes. Mika set her phone on the table. She scrolled through and found the timer app, setting it for four minutes. "You first," she told Thomas.

Thomas stretched out in the booth, making himself comfortable. He scratched his jaw. "I was born in Dayton, Ohio. My parents were married for twenty-three years, and I have an older brother." He leaned forward, and beneath the table, his thigh pressed against Mika's. Neither moved away. "I had a pretty normal childhood, I think. Football games in the winter. Baseball games in the spring. My dad loved sports and having sons to take them to. I think he was disappointed when I got into rowing in college. He had a heart attack and died when I was nineteen."

"I'm sorry," Mika said. There were two minutes, twenty seconds left on the clock.

"Thank you," Thomas said. "Anyway, I met Caroline

shortly after that. We hooked up at a party, and I cried after. I thought she'd never want to see me again but . . . she was so fucking nice about it. And it felt so good to know I wasn't alone." Mika's stomach twisted, seeing the pain on Thomas's face. "We got married soon after we graduated and did the rest of schooling together. She helped me study for the LSAT. I helped her study for her nursing certificate. We also started trying to have a family. My parents had me when I was young, and it was the same for Caroline. Caroline had it all planned out. Get pregnant early, have a few kids, then retire soon after they went to college. We were going to travel together." Thomas wasn't looking at Mika. He rubbed his forehead. "We blamed it on stress at first, not getting pregnant. School, exams, all that. A year went by, and another. Caroline's doctor recommended a specialist. A few tests later and the results were inconclusive. I still remember Caroline's face, her frustration, her heartbreak. She felt betrayed by her body. 'It's my biological right,' she'd said. I was more relaxed about it. Taking on the mantle of 'If we're meant to be parents, we will be.' But Caroline had a goal. She wanted a baby. She wanted to be a mother. After a lot of discussions, we decided to look into adoption. There were a couple of false hopes. A woman in New York who was pregnant but decided to keep the baby. A teen in Florida who had surrendered her six-month-old but wanted him in foster care with the hopes of reuniting and—"

The timer went off. "Keep going," Mika said, wanting to hear more. Wondering about Caroline's infertility. *Betrayed*, that was the word Thomas said Caroline used. Mika had felt the same about her body. How it had accepted Peter's baby when Mika had said, *No, I don't want this.* And then there was Caroline, who had said yes, but hers wouldn't comply. She felt as if they had something in common now, both viewing their bodies as hostile landscapes. Caroline's from infertility. Mika's from rape.

Thomas shook his head. "No. Your turn now." He patted his chest. "Rule follower, remember? Tell me about you. I want to know about baby Mika." He set the timer for four minutes and started it.

"Well . . . ." Mika took a sip of wine. "I was born right outside of Osaka."

"Wait." Thomas paused the clock.

"Hey. No fair." Mika frowned.

"You weren't born in the States?"

"No. We moved here when I was in kindergarten." Mika had been as thin as a twig, as small as a leaf when they'd left Japan. She started the timer again. "My dad worked for a tech company. It went under soon after the economic bubble burst in Japan." Shige became a casualty of the employment ice age. "He was lucky another company offered him a position in the States." Mika had another memory. She was in their car, on the highway, on their way to the airport. Semi trucks whizzed by, and they passed a vineyard. Grapevines hung heavy with grapes the size of golf balls, white paper bags covering them to protect from birds and weather.

"We brought our own food on the plane." Hiromi wouldn't eat any of the nuts or chocolate biscuits, even though they were free. She eyed anything American with a sense of distrust. Mika had watched through the window as they landed. The brown water of the Columbia River as the plane descended, the current flowing west. She went on. "My mom wasn't excited about moving to the States, but I was. A new place, a new world it seemed like." That was where Mika's and Hiromi's paths had diverged. Mika had gone running headfirst. Hiromi couldn't even bring herself to take a few timid steps. "We rented an apartment the first couple of months. My mom didn't leave it. She'd give me a few dollars and send me to the store. A police officer stopped me once and brought me home." Mika paused, eyeing the timer. Less than one minute left.

"What happened?"

Mika screwed up her face. "He called social services. It was a whole thing. They couldn't find a translator, but they did get ahold of my dad at work. He was able to defuse the situation. When they left, my mother still didn't understand. 'In Tokyo, kids ride the subway alone,' she said. 'She's my daughter. Who are they to say what I can do with my own daughter?'" Mika watched the time dwindle. Three. Two. One second. The clock beeped. "Time's up," Mika said before Thomas could argue. She grabbed another card from the pile. "'What do you fear most in life?'"

Thomas thought about it for a moment. "That's a tough one. I guess I fear dying young, like my father and Caroline, leaving behind so much unfinished business. Maybe that's where my need to control everything comes from." He glanced at Mika. "You?"

Peter came to her mind first, but she dismissed the thought. She didn't fear him. She feared the violence. She feared it might happen to her again. But there was a bigger, more immediate looming threat. "I guess I fear my mother." Sometime during Mika's conversation with Thomas, refilled wineglasses had appeared on their table. She drank.

Thomas leaned forward. Now their knees and elbows were touching. "I'm going to need you to elaborate."

Mika inhaled, the knot of resentment toward her

mother tightening. "Maybe I fear being like her."
Wasn't there a saying about sons committing the sins
of their fathers? More like daughters and mothers. "Or
I just fear her in general—her disapproval, it's like a
curse. When I was growing up, nothing ever felt good
enough for her. The house we lived in. My father's job.
Me. I don't know. She should have stayed in Japan, I
guess." Hiromi wanted to live in Japan. For her daughter to be Japanese. But Mika was Japanese American,
and it was the American part her mother hated most.

Thomas tilted his head. "Maybe she didn't know
how to handle it, moving to another country."

"She absolutely did not." It was all Mika could think
to say, but then she added quietly, "I'm pretty sure
my mother hates me." *You'll waste your life,* Hiromi
had said about Mika painting. But really, Hiromi had
meant, *You've wasted mine.*

"Maybe she doesn't know how to love you," said
Thomas.

"Is there a difference?"

"I think so." A pause. "Parents make mistakes," he
added.

"This isn't the same as throwing Penny a period
party." Mika shook her head, frustrated. She thought
of her relationship with her mother. Punctuated by
silence. When she'd been caught shoplifting. When

she'd come to her mother in her broken need. *I'm pregnant.*

"I know it's not the same. All I'm saying is, you go in full of earnest conviction and hope for the best and plan to pay for their therapy later in life when you've fucked it all up." He paused. "That was a joke."

"Ha." Mika thought about what parents passed down to their children. *Peter, the attack was in her DNA now,* Suzanne had explained. *It's coded in you. It has rewired your central nervous system.* What happened to Mika was embedded. What had Hiromi passed down to Mika, then? What crosses had Hiromi brought to bear upon her daughter? Same as Mika, Hiromi had her own dreams—raising her family in Japan, a life that had been promised, then ripped away by circumstances out of her control. Maybe her ikigai wasn't being a housewife. Hiromi had been a maiko. She'd lived in a house she loved, she had a *before.* Her own ghost life. "This is a very sobering reality," Mika said.

Thomas's knee pressed into hers. She raised her eyes to his. Then under the table, she felt him graze her hand. Automatically, she opened her fingers, and Thomas slid his between hers. They sat for a moment holding hands, hanging on to each other. Charlie's words came back to her. *It's okay to want . . . It's okay if it gets messy . . . Things have a way of working themselves out.*

After a moment, Thomas held up his wineglass with his free hand. "To the ties that bind."

Mika clinked her glass to his. "To the ties that bind."

• • •

The happy glow stayed with Mika in the van. She sat next to Thomas in the back. And somehow, her head found its way to his shoulder. Outside the window, the stars blurred together like in a Van Gogh painting. She listened to Tuan and Charlie kissing. Hayato murmuring to Seth. To the sounds of traffic and the rattle of the windows disturbed by the rushing air.

At Charlie's house, Hayato and Seth loaded into an Uber. Thomas asked if Mika wanted to share one. "Sure," she agreed. Actually, it didn't make any sense. Mika lived on this side of the river. Thomas's hotel was downtown on the other side, the same boutique hotel he always stayed at. But she wanted to linger in his company a little longer. And if Thomas knew that it was out of Mika's way, he didn't show it.

They sat in the back seat of an SUV on the way to Thomas's hotel. She watched the city lights play on Thomas's face as he confirmed with the driver where they were going. Music played, a heady beat with lots of bass. The car careened over a speed bump, and Mika jerked. Thomas reached out. His hand cupped her knee. He turned to her. "Okay?"

"Fine," she said, mouth dry, completely boneless.

His hand stayed put, and as they glided over a bridge, it inched ever so slightly up. Again, he peered at her. "Okay?"

"Okay," she whispered back, and his eyes glittered, emeralds in the night. Warmth pooled in her belly.

He held the door open when they reached the hotel. "Want to come up for a nightcap?" he asked.

One more drink wouldn't hurt. Again, she agreed, and she felt a ripple, a rush of air, the rest of her defenses falling. Icarus taking flight.

As if under a spell, she followed him through the dim lobby and into an elevator. The lighting was brighter in the six-by-six-foot space. It sobered her up a little. An older couple rode with them. Thomas stared straight ahead, and Mika let her eyes wander down his body, stopping at the hem of his untucked shirt. Adrenaline and anticipation pumped through her veins. The couple deboarded, and the air suddenly felt heavy, laden with magic. Music spiraled from the speakers. A classical piece Mika recognized but couldn't name.

Up they went.

Floor five.

Six.

Seven.

"Mika," Thomas said, eyes shining and not with drink. Then his hands were gripping her hips. She tipped her chin up. They met in the middle, mouths open and wanting. Five tense hours of lust and want pouring out of them and into each other. He crashed into her, and Mika welcomed him, wrapped a leg around his waist, as he pressed her against the back of the velvet paneled wall. Her hands fisted in his hair. *Ding. Twenty-first floor,* an automated voice announced. Somehow, they stayed fused together. Stumbling down the hall, hand in hand. It was a long corridor. Too long. Thomas gave up on walking and sought Mika out again. Her back was against the wall, hotel room doors flanking them as Thomas took complete possession of her mouth.

He broke the kiss, taking a breath, and murmured into her neck, "I feel like I'm attacking you."

"Issokay," Mika moaned. And it was. God, she wanted him. She was on fire.

He nicked her ear with his teeth, tightened his grip. Mika moaned again as he sucked on her neck. She tilted her head to give him better access. She'd like more of that. Yes, please, and thank you so much. Through slitted eyelids, she glimpsed one of the hotel room doors.

Remembered Penny opening it in her bathrobe, hand outstretched for a box of tampons. Reality dawned, quick and unforgiving. Thomas was Penny's dad. She snaked her hands up to Thomas's chest, gripped his untucked shirt. "Wait. Stop."

Her mind spun in dizzying circles as he stepped away. "Right. Sorry," he said.

"No, don't apologize," she said quickly. There was two feet of space between them, but it was bigger than that, Grand Canyon wide. "I just think we should talk."

He ran a hand through his hair. "Yeah. You're probably right. Let's get a drink."

Mika nodded. "In the lobby. A drink downstairs at the bar," she qualified. Thomas plus Mika plus bed didn't equal a great idea right now.

He studied Mika with a tense brow. "Downstairs it is."

• • •

In the bar, Mika took the chair opposite Thomas, as far away as she could get without sitting at another table. He remembered her order from last time, a local red wine, and placed it again with the waiter. Soon enough, they had their drinks. They stared at each other for one whole long minute. Thomas's hand flexed around his glass. Mika squeezed her thighs together, thinking of that same hand on her thigh, her hip, what it might feel like creeping under her shirt.

"Thomas," Mika said seriously.

"Mika," Thomas parroted back, voice still thick with desire.

"We kissed." She sat up a little straighter.

"We did." When had Thomas become so agreeable?

"I liked it."

"Me too." He sipped his scotch, eyes on Mika. "I'd like to kiss you more."

She ran her tongue over the edges of her teeth. "I feel the same." Thomas smiled slyly. "But what about Penny?" There, she'd said it. She'd poked the elephant in the room.

He sighed. The lust blinked out of his eyes. "What about Penny?" he murmured to himself.

Mika fingered the base of her wineglass, unease making her stomach sensitive. "I'm working hard at my relationship with her. I don't want to lose her. But you and me . . ." Mika let it show in the rasp of her voice, her thirst for him.

"I feel it too," said Thomas. "There is obviously something between us." Some of the tension dropped from Mika's shoulders. It wasn't all in her head then. It was mutual. Thomas *liked* her.

He reached across the table and grasped her hand,

turning it to caress the inside of her palm with his thumb. "If you want to tell Penny, we can. But I think we should keep it between us for now. Clearly, we're attracted to each other, and we have a good time together." He licked his lips. "Let's explore this on our own. See if it's something real, then if it is—"

"We'll tell her," Mika cut him off.

"We'll tell her," he agreed solemnly.

Mika gave Thomas a slow nod. "Alright."

He smiled at her. She smiled back. Fuzzy contentment ballooned around them. They finished their drinks, then Thomas kissed her long and sweet outside the hotel. He held the door open as she climbed into a taxi. "I'll see you tomorrow," he said, leaning down.

"Tomorrow?" she asked, heavy-lidded and tired.

"Church? With Penny and your parents?" Thomas reminded her.

Mika's eyes flared open. "Right," said Mika. Thomas kissed her again and closed her taxi door. Mika touched her lips as the car pulled away, a single heady thought rolling around in her mind—*perhaps, perhaps, perhaps.*

Chapter Twenty-Six

The following day Mika woke to a text from Thomas. I fell asleep thinking about you last night.

Mika rolled onto her back. Her head throbbed a little, but it was nothing compared to what Thomas's words did to the rest of her body. Her phone chimed with another text from him. Did I really steal your friend's card game?

She grinned. Yes. You also wore a beret.

I'm sure the beret enjoyed itself very much, Thomas said.

I am sure it did. She pictured Thomas putting it on, his easygoing smile. Mika dozed for a moment, wishing Thomas was beside her, until her phone chirped again.

I'm picking Penny up soon. Will you send me the address for your church?

Mika bolted upright. Church. Thomas meeting her parents. Penny would be there too. A simple event suddenly seemed very complicated. Would Penny be able to sense the shift in Thomas and Mika's relationship? Her phone sounded again. A follow-up message from Thomas. You there? Penny is looking forward to it.

I'm here, Mika replied, picking clothes up off the floor, smelling and discarding them. She tapped out the address. C u soon.

• • •

Freshly showered, a cup of to-go coffee in hand, Mika pulled up outside her parents' church and waved to Thomas and Penny standing out front.

"Hey," she said, getting out of the car. The tips of her hair were still wet, and the coffee sloshed over the cup. Mika licked the rim.

"Hey," Thomas said warmly. They leaned into each other as if to hug but stopped short. Penny stood by. Watching. Instead, Thomas put his arm around Penny, pulling her in close.

"Dad." She rolled her eyes and sidestepped him. "I'm going to go see if Hiromi and Shige are inside." She skipped in through the doors.

Mika and Thomas followed her at a slower pace. He looked fantastic in a dark blue suit and tie, and Mika couldn't help but think what was under it. She thought back to the hotel elevator, the hallways. How his thick veined hands had gripped her hips. How he'd licked a pathway up the side of her neck. Speaking of her neck, she caught sight of herself in a glass door, a distinct red mark near her collarbone, a burn from Thomas's scruff. She slapped a hand over it.

Thomas smirked. *Smirked.* "Sleep well?" he asked, totally unrepentant.

"Like a baby," Mika retorted, rubbing the spot, then letting her hand fall away. "How about you?"

"Tossed and turned a little bit but managed to get some rest."

"I found them." Penny had breezed back. "They're already sitting down but saved seats for us in the second pew. C'mon," she said in a you're-not-moving-fast-enough way. Mika didn't tell Penny her parents always arrived early and sat in the same spot. "Now remember, Dad, they're not really the touchy-feely type. If they bow, just parrot it back."

"Got it," Thomas said. A lock of hair fell over his forehead, a spill of ink that Mika wanted to brush away.

They came into the sanctuary, and Mika's parents stood in the pew waiting. The first time Mika had attended services with her parents, the old pastor had invited them to a New Year's potluck the following week.

Hiromi had been quietly excited. After months of living in the United States, drifting in aloneness, their little family had found somewhere to belong.

The days before the New Year's potluck, Hiromi had spent all her time preparing an osechi ryori to bring and share. Mika helped her mother pack food, the pieces—sweet-rolled omelet, fish cakes, pickled lotus root—slotted like tiny jewels into the lacquered boxes. The day of, she helped her mother dress in her finest kimono. Shige wore a suit. When they arrived, it was like a record scratch. None of the congregants wore kimonos. Still, they stayed the whole time. The congregants were friendly and warm, and welcoming. After, Mika helped her mother out of the kimono. Watched as Hiromi carefully folded it in at the sides, then over like a piece of origami, and put it away in a plastic tub in her closet. She never wore it again.

Thomas greeted Mika's parents. "It's so nice to meet you. Thank you for being so welcoming to Penny."

"Of course, of course." A polite smile touched Hiromi's lips.

Shige stuck out his hand for Thomas to shake. If Thomas was surprised, he didn't show it. He easily shook Mika's father's hand. Pastor Barbara stood at the pulpit, and they settled into their seats. Mika sat next to her mother. And Penny between Mika and Thomas.

Mika had never brought anyone to church before with her. Never Leif. Or Hana. This was new, wild, uncharted territory.

"It's so nice to see everyone today, including some new faces in the crowd," Pastor Barbara said.

Hiromi nudged Mika. "He's very tall," she said under her breath in Japanese.

"Hai." *Yes*, Mika answered.

"Too tall," Hiromi said again in Japanese. "Too hard to look him in the eye when you speak. Ideal height for a man is less than six feet. Your father is five-seven."

Mika didn't know what to say, so she said nothing. The sermon went on, and they sang a couple of songs about friendship. Announcements were last. "Obon is fast approaching. Which we still need dancers for."

Hiromi nudged Mika again. "You should do that," she said in English, and it was on purpose. So Penny would hear. When Mika quit dance, it was the first time she'd defied her mother. She'd refused to get in the car and go to practice, scrunching up her face and twisting her arm from her mother's hold. She'd stomped her foot and shouted no.

Now, Mika said quietly, "I don't think so."

Penny turned, her mouth open as if to say something, but stopped short as the pastor finished up. After the service, Penny and Mika gleefully gorged themselves on sweets. Pastor Barbara came to introduce herself. "Thank you for joining us today," she said to Thomas. Thomas sipped some green tea. His stance was casual and relaxed, though he stuck out like a birch tree among bonsai. On the flip side, Penny was in her element; she couldn't stop smiling.

Mrs. Ito, Hiromi's arch-nemesis, approached them. She bowed to Hiromi. "Suzuki-san, how are you? I came to meet your guests."

Mika scooted closer to Penny. "Mrs. Ito, this is my daughter, Penny, and her father, Thomas."

Mrs. Ito's mouth opened and closed. Then she smiled. "Oh, I see. It's one of those big sister, little sister things."

"Nope," Mika spoke up. "I got pregnant when I was eighteen and placed the baby for adoption. Penny is my biological daughter."

"My granddaughter," Hiromi stated proudly, and Mika gave her the side-eye. Well, okay then.

"Thomas is her adoptive father," Mika added.

"Well," Mrs. Ito said, a gleam in her eye. *What great gossip! How soon could she get away to tell the others?* "Isn't that wonderful? I should have known. You do resemble each other." Mika used to hate it when people said she looked like Hiromi. All she could see was her mother's flaws. "And it seems you both have the same healthy appetite." Mrs. Ito's eyes dropped noticeably to the plates in Penny's and Mika's hands.

Out of the corner of her eye, Mika saw Thomas tense and shift uncomfortably. She gave him a slight shake of her head. Better to not get involved.

"Penny is a runner," Hiromi interjected. "She needs the energy. And Mika is still young. She can afford to eat what she wants a little longer. You know, she has a big job at Nike now." Mika would not classify her job as *big*, but she knew better than to correct Hiromi when she was on a roll. "She walks around that campus all day. I worry she doesn't eat enough with how hard she's working. In fact, I wanted to bring her some butter cookies from last week's service, but I noticed your son Kenji took them all home. I don't know why he needed so many. He still lives alone, yes? Perhaps they were for his cats."

Mrs. Ito's eyes glinted. So did Hiromi's. As the two petite Japanese women stared each other down, Mika had a sudden vision of the movie *Gladiator*. The part where Russell Crowe faces off with Joaquin Phoenix in the last scene. *My name is Maximus Decimus Meridius* . . .

"Will I see everyone at Obon?" Pastor Barbara blurted. Over the years, she'd had her hands full with Mrs. Ito and Mrs. Suzuki. Mika wondered if all mothers did this, tried to prove themselves for a job description they didn't write.

"I don't think—" Hiromi started with a frown. Penny hung her head. Mrs. Ito smiled, the grin of the victor.

"We'll be there," Mika chimed in boldly, Hiromi's insecurities becoming her own. "And we're going to dance."

"We will?" Penny asked, surprised.

"Yes." Mika nodded once. "I'll teach you all the steps you need to know over the next two weeks in the evenings." She nudged Penny. "Okay?"

"Okay." Penny lit up from within. "Dad, you have to come back for it."

Thomas lit up too. His eyes bore into Mika's, and they shared a secret smile before he turned back to his daughter. "I wouldn't miss it for the world, kiddo."

Chapter Twenty-Seven

Wednesday, Mika left work at five o'clock on the dot. She picked Penny up at the dorm and waved to Devon as Penny climbed into the car. They ordered takeout, and, munching on spring rolls, Mika gave Penny the lowdown on Bon-Odori. How the movements were passed down from generation to generation. How many believed you danced with your ancestors on that sacred day. Could Penny picture it? The ghosts of ages past at her elbow? Tracing her hands as she raised them to the sky?

"Hold on," Mika said, stopping as her phone chimed with an incoming text. It was from Thomas. A picture of one of the note cards, which said, "Do you have a secret hunch about how you will die?"

You took them home? Mika replied. Stealing from the bus is one thing, but this is next-level depravity. She glanced at Penny practicing the movements, watched as she twirled, her hair spreading out in a dark fan. I'm sure it will be something humiliating like accidental drowning in a toilet, she tapped out. You?

He must have had his response at the ready. Bear attack, definitely.

Mika laughed out loud. I didn't know there were so many bears in Ohio, she responded.

You have no idea, Thomas said.

Penny paused, a quizzical smile on her face. She had caught the look in Mika's eyes, the coy smile. "Hana," Mika lied, putting her phone down. "Sorry," she said, throat thickening with conflicting emotions. She shouldn't have lied about that. Felt guilty but wasn't prepared to explain her relationship with Thomas to Penny. "Try that step again. This time keep your eyes on the horizon instead of looking down." Penny nodded and resumed practicing.

On Friday evening, Mika and Penny rehearsed again. "Want to hang out tomorrow?" Penny asked as she got out of the car.

"Yeah," Mika said. "Give me a jingle. I'll be around."

"Cool," Penny said, slamming the door. Mika's

phone rang, and Thomas's name flashed on the screen. She watched as Penny disappeared through the swinging door, then answered.

"Hi," she said finally.

"Hi," Thomas answered back.

"I just dropped Penny off at the dorm. Um, if that's why you're calling and couldn't get ahold of her." Mika kept the car parked. The last ray of sunlight dipped below the horizon. With the dark came quiet, a stillness Mika always loved.

"I talked to Penny earlier today." There was a clinking sound. Ice cubes hitting the inside of a glass.

"You did?"

"I did. I wanted to talk to you." Thomas paused. "Is that okay?"

A faint smile appeared at the corner of Mika's mouth. "That's okay."

"Good."

"How was your day?" Mika asked. She lay back in her seat, content to stay awhile.

Thomas sighed. "My day hasn't ended. I'm still at the office. I might sleep here tonight."

"You sound tired," Mika said.

"I am. This case I'm working on is taking more time than I thought. I'm representing a design company that's suing a larger big-box store for the use of one of their prints. It was supposed to be cut-and-dried. Usually, big companies settle rather than go to litigation, but apparently, this corporation has decided this is the hill they're going to die on," he answered. "Anyway, you ready for another card?"

"I'm ready," Mika said. The streetlights blinked on, one after the other.

"'Share with your partner an embarrassing moment in your life,'" he said.

Mika groaned. "Pass."

"You can't pass," he stated. "But I'll go first if that makes you feel better."

"I'm all ears."

"I lost a bet in college and now have a small tattoo on my hip."

"Of what?"

"A Tyrannosaurus rex trying to tie his shoes." He paused. "My friends thought it was hilarious . . . because, you know, T. rexes have short arms."

A laugh bubbled from Mika. "Oh. I get it."

"Now you," he said.

"Well." She stalled for a moment, running a hand over her steering wheel. "My father took us camping when I was ten." Hiromi hated it. "I think he was trying to assimilate. You know, do things Americans do. I had to go to the bathroom really bad, but the campground was pretty rustic. There weren't any toilets." She stopped, cheeks blazing. "Do I have to do this?"

"Oh, yeah," Thomas said warmly. "I can't go back to work until I hear the rest."

"Ugh, fine. I slipped on my father's shoes and headed out into the woods, popped a squat, only . . . I didn't account for the length of his shoes and ended up going all over them." Mika closed her eyes, letting the heat of embarrassment wash over her.

A laugh rattled out of Thomas. "What did your parents do?"

"Nothing," Mika said. "I buried the shoes and pretended not to know anything when they searched for them in the morning." Somewhere in the Mt. Hood National Forest, a pair of Adidas slides had found a permanent home in a shallow grave.

After that, there were no more texts. Mika called Thomas or Thomas called Mika. He left messages for Mika during the workdays. *Hey. Thinking about you. The funniest thing just happened . . . I wanted to tell you . . .* They ate dinner together on the phone and talked late into the night, the note cards a pathway they walked down together.

"Is there something you've dreamed of doing for a long time?" he asked late one night.

Mika curled on her side. She lay in the dark of her

room. Outside her window, the moon was a hangnail in the sky. "Once upon a time, I wanted to travel. I'd go to Paris first. To see the Louvre, the Musée d'Orsay."

"Why haven't you done it?" There was rustling on the other end of the line. Was Thomas in bed too?

"I don't know," she said, sticking a hand under her pillow. She wondered what it might be like if Thomas was in bed beside her. How it might feel to rest her head on his shoulder. How his warm breath might stir her hair. It would be nice to have someone to lean on.

"Is it a money thing?" Thomas asked.

"No, more like a circumstances thing." Peter had taught her the world was a cruel and unfriendly place. There were too many shadows where people hid. Too many sharp ledges to fall from.

"Care to elaborate?"

"Not really. What about you?"

"Travel sounds good. Lately, I've been thinking about closing the practice. It was the right thing for a family, but now I'm finding I have more time for myself, and I'm in a financial position to pursue something else. Though I'm not sure what."

"Professional kayaker?" Mika asked with a grin.

"Maybe. I haven't given up on elvish either," he said. There was a shuffling. The sound of paper. "'Would you like to be famous? In what way?'" Another card.

Thomas answered first. "I don't think so. I'm pretty content right here, right now, where I'm at. You?"

Mika's hands curled, remembering the feel of a brush in them. "I don't know about famous, but successful, well known at least. I used . . . I used to paint." *You have the most raw talent I've ever seen,* Marcus had said. She sighed. "It was just a hobby."

"Doesn't sound like it." Thomas's voice deepened. "Paris makes more sense now. I could see you and me there," he added.

Mika's heart lodged in her throat. "You already have the beret," she said, though it made her wonder. Dared her to dream. She'd always pictured herself alone on the cobblestone streets. But maybe someone else was there. Holding her hand. Sipping coffee with her under a red striped umbrella. Kissing her outside the Louvre.

"It's a date, then. You, me, and Paris."

Thomas's words beckoned Mika, luring her in like a siren's call. She breathed in and out. "Alright, Thomas," she agreed, drowsy and happy. "You and me. Paris, here we come." She fell asleep with a smile on her face.

• • •

Time tumbled on. Mika and Penny had an old lady day. They completed a one-thousand-piece puzzle, snoozed on the couch, played bingo at a local hall, and ate dinner at five p.m. Penny perfected the Bon-Odori, and they celebrated with a sleepover. Eating hot tamales and Red Vines while watching an infomercial couple they were obsessed with.

"They look like brother and sister," Mika said, transfixed.

"And what are they selling? Powdered supplements? So people don't have to eat vegetables?" Penny remarked.

"I can't stop watching them."

"I know, right? It's like I'm hypnotized."

Forty-eight hours before Obon, Thomas called Mika. "Hi," she answered. "What are you doing?" She was sitting on the couch, legs curled underneath her. A single lamp on, and the sun setting outside.

"I just got home, actually," he said. "And I'm going through a pile of mail I've neglected all week."

"Want to call me back?"

"No. I—" He stopped short.

"Everything okay?"

"Fine," he said after a long, long pause. "There's a letter from Adoption Across America."

"Oh?" Mika sat forward. What a strange and kind of beautiful reality she was in.

"It's probably the reminder that my annual report is due to you."

"I can't wait. I'll be watching my mailbox for your next five lines about Penny." It came out sharper than she'd expected, a decibel higher too. Thomas's succinct letters had been in such stark contrast to Caroline's. Between the lines, Mika could almost hear Caroline whispering to her, addressing Mika's heartache. *Do not worry. I am taking care of our daughter. Be easy now. I love her as you love her.*

Thomas sucked in an uneasy breath. "I'm sensing a tone. You didn't like my letters?" he asked. There was a frown in his voice. Confusion.

She played with her toes. "Caroline's letters . . . they were longer. They made me feel more a part of Penny's life."

"And mine didn't?"

Mika exhaled. "No, they didn't." She resisted the urge to apologize. To make excuses for Thomas. To say, *It's okay. I'm sure you were going through a lot.* Six months ago, she would have placed the issue to the side, but Thomas and Penny, this whole thing that had happened and was happening between them, made Mika feel bigger. Braver. More willing to demand things. To want things.

The line grew quiet, and Mika knew he was choosing his words carefully. "Shit. I'm sorry." He paused, voice unsteady, a mix of regret and angst. "That kind of stuff doesn't come naturally to me. I'm used to contracts and brevity. Why use six words when two will do?" He paused, huffed out a laugh. "But that was thoughtless of me. I've been an asshole."

"I wouldn't call you an asshole." Not now anyway.

"Forgive me?"

Mika breathed in slowly. It didn't necessarily heal the hurt. There would always be a gaping wound at missing her daughter's life. And Thomas had contributed to it by withholding. But still . . . the wind in Mika's angry sails deflated. "It's already forgotten."

"Okay," Thomas said evenly, although it sounded like he didn't believe her. "You ready for another note card then? It's the last question."

Mika sat back on her couch, hooking her toes on the coffee table. "I'm ready."

"'Finish this sentence: I wish I had someone with whom I could share . . .'" He trailed off.

Mika answered immediately. "The small things. Like bad days, good days, favorite television shows, embarrassing stories." She stopped on a blush. Because the truth was, the truth was, Mika *had* been sharing those things with Thomas. There was no denying it now. Thomas was taking up space in Mika's life. She was in deep. Her hand flexed, feeling a phantom heat. Icarus approaching the sun. Touching it. How good it felt. The light. The warmth. How could she not want to bask in it forever?

Thomas replied, and she felt the weight of his words as heavy as a hug. "Me too."

Chapter Twenty-Eight

The night before their performance, Mika and Penny drove across town to Shige and Hiromi's house. "I haven't gotten the kimonos out in years," Hiromi explained as she pulled the plastic tub from her closet. There was a quickness to her movements, a lightness in her air. As if her hip, knees, and back no longer ached. As if she were young again. Had Mika ever seen her mother so excited? Then Hiromi added, "Since Mika quit dancing." Ah yes, there was the expected verbal jab. When Mika had danced, there had been a shine in Hiromi's eyes. Pride. How quick Mika had been to pierce it out. *You two are like fire,* Shige had said. *You burn everything down.* She told herself she quit dancing to focus on other pursuits, on painting, but it really had been to spite Hiromi, to hurt her as she had hurt Mika.

"Here, let me." Mika stepped forward, relieving Hiromi of the tub, setting it on the quilt on her parents' bed. She peeled the lid off, and the smell of mothballs clouded the room.

Penny stuck her nose in. "They're beautiful." On the top was the kimono Hiromi had worn to New Year's at the church years ago when Mika had been six. Light pink ombré that tapered to purple with hand-stitched cranes. Mika remembered being a child and pressing herself against her mother's thigh, the feel of the embroidery against her cheek.

"The yukata are on the bottom," Hiromi said. For Obon, they'd wear lighter-weight cotton kimonos. As Hiromi removed the kimono, her hands trembled. Perhaps at the memory that she'd once been a maiko, that she once had shone brightly. Hiromi pulled out three yukatas, then helped Mika and Penny dress. First were the plain white undergarments, then the actual yukata.

"Arms up and out," Hiromi instructed Penny. Mika saw herself at age thirteen—holding her arms out straight, the edges of the kimono sleeves tucked into her hands, fabric pooling around her feet, finding it impossible to keep still. But Penny held herself rigid as if she'd turned to stone, taking in every word Hiromi said as if it were gospel. Hiromi folded the waist of the kimono up so that the hem hit Penny right at the ankles. "Now, I wrap it," Hiromi said. With expert hands, she tucked the right of the yukata around Penny's left hip, then did the reverse. She used a purple cord to secure the yukata closed. Last was the obi. Again, Mika recalled herself as a child, feet shifting from having to stand still too long, breaths stolen as the obi was tied tightly around her waist in a perfect bow. Now, Hiromi did the same to Penny. Tears gathered in Mika's eyes. She didn't know why. But then Penny's eyes connected with hers. They were liquid too. Mika's heart swelled to at least twice its size.

"How do I look?" Penny asked uncertainly.

"See for yourself," Hiromi said. In the corner of the room was a full-length mirror. They shuffled to it.

There they were. Hiromi was still in her plain clothes, but Penny and Mika were in full yukatas, long dark hair around their shoulders, a cascade of nightfall. "We'll pin your hair up for the festival," Hiromi said and went back to the tub to withdraw a hana kanzashi, a traditional flower pin. "This was my mother's," she said, twisting Penny's hair up and securing it.

"What do you think?" Mika asked. They gazed into the mirror—three generations of Suzuki women. Mika could almost see the gardens in Japan, where she and her mother had once spent their afternoons. The rows of manicured trees. The temple bells ringing. The sound of the loudspeaker announcement at the train's approach. Once upon a time, Mika thought she didn't share anything with Hiromi—they had been aliens to each other, orbiting different planets. How wrong she'd been. And now, they had something new in common, the currents of motherhood pulling them in the same direction. To Penny. To a child whom they both adored. Who inspired the kind of love that guts you—was this how Hiromi felt about Mika?

Shige knocked on the door. "I stopped at the store." He held out his hand to reveal a bundle of pine sticks. Joy spread across Hiromi's face.

"What is it?" Penny asked.

"Mukaebi. Welcoming fire," Mika explained. "It's to guide spirits home."

In the backyard, Shige set the bundle to flame and placed it in a copper dish. They huddled around, Mika's feet over the stain where Hiromi dyed Shige's hair once every other month. In Japan, they would have gone to their ancestral home to light the fire. They would have visited graves, cleaned them, and set watermelon and sweet treats on the shouryoudana. They would have celebrated with family and food. But living in America, they made all sorts of cultural compromises.

They watched the sticks burn, and the strands of tradition pulled down through the generations, stitching the four of them together. Mika studied Penny, the lick of fire against her cheeks. Her face turned up to the sky. The way their shadows grew into the night, into the inky darkness stretching from their bodies like skeletons. She wondered if Penny was thinking of Caroline, of summoning her home. If she was any closer to the answer to her question. *Who am I? Who am I?*

• • •

Flight is delayed, Thomas texted early the following morning, the day of Obon. I'll meet you there. Hiromi dressed Mika and Penny again in yukatas. Mika's mother spent extra time fussing over Penny. Who would have known Hiromi would make such a wonderful Obāchan? They drove separately to the festival. At the Portland Buddhist temple, the courtyard had been transformed. The atmosphere was cheerful— taiko drummers pounded away on a yagura stage, paper lanterns had been strung up and swayed in the summer breeze, booths were set with games and treats.

Hiromi, Mika, and Penny joined the dancers in the circle immediately. Clapping, then cupping their hands as if grabbing a scoop of coal. *Dig. Dig. Carry. Carry.*

They moved along in synch with the drums. After a while, Hiromi tired and left to sit in the shade of the temple with Shige.

The sun was setting, and the sky was awash in blazing oranges. Lanterns glowed, attracting moths and other creatures of the night. Another turn, and Mika's smile stretched as wide as the sky. Her eyes caught a familiar figure in the crowd. Thomas stood off to the side, lips twisted into a half-grin. He waved at her. "Your dad's here," she shouted to Penny.

Penny waved at him. "I'm going to keep going."

"I'll go say hi." Mika left the circle. The night was hot, and little pieces of hair had escaped her bun to stick to her neck.

"Hey," he said. She basked in the warmth of his smile, the way his eyes lazily settled on her, glinting with a subtle heat. Thomas had dressed plainly in a T-shirt and jeans. "This is something else." He twirled his finger around to encompass the festival. "Are your parents here?"

"In the temple." Mika tilted her head in the direction of the plain white building. She smoothed down the fabric of her kimono, navy with bright red poppies. "Penny is a natural dancer. I should have known; she's so athletic." If Mika had to choose one moment in time to live in over and over again, she'd choose this one. Right here and now. Her body light. Her heart happy.

Thomas rocked back on his heels. His hair had gotten longer these last few weeks, and he smoothed it back with a large hand. "She's in her element." They watched Penny go by, movements fluid as if she'd spent a lifetime dancing odori. "To tell you the truth, this kind of makes me feel like shit."

"Why?"

"I—We . . . *we* . . . never did anything like this for Penny."

How could they have? Mika felt for Thomas. And felt as bad as Thomas. Because some of this was her fault too. She'd given Penny to white parents, knowing something would be missing. She should have insisted on more from them during the adoption. *Buy books with Japanese characters. Find a doll with dark hair and beautiful brown eyes. Make sure she knows where she comes from. Learn Japanese, study kanji.* Mika had no doubt Caroline and Thomas loved Penny. They'd paced hallways soothing Penny while she raged with fever. They'd enrolled her in soccer and cheered her on during every game. They'd bought her groceries so she could explore (terrible) baking. Mika had the letters and pictures to prove it. Penny had been treated as flesh of their flesh. But was that enough? Was it ever enough? "You mean anything Japanese? Penny said you took her to festivals."

Thomas hung his head. "We did, but it wasn't like this. Like she belonged. We drove all the way to Cincinnati one day to go to a cherry blossom festival. Caroline and Penny wore matching sweaters. We visited the booths, and the Japanese ladies doted on Penny, then asked Caroline and me where we got her from."

"What did you say?"

"That she was adopted. But it made Caroline close off. She wanted to leave soon after that."

Mika swallowed, curbed the urge to stomp her foot. *Not fair. Not fair.* "You discussed it, right? Before you adopted her? That she was Japanese, that she wouldn't look like you?"

"We did. Caroline said it wouldn't matter. That we'd raise her our way . . ."

The confession unspooled around Mika. Anger, white-hot, speared her chest. "That is so completely wrong," Mika sputtered. She had idealized Caroline in her mind. The mother she'd wanted for Penny. The mother she wished she'd had. The mother she'd wanted to *be.*

"I know. And I'm sorry. I told you, parents make

mistakes. That's why I was okay with Penny coming here for the whole summer. She needed something I couldn't give her. Please don't be mad," Thomas said quietly. "I love Penny. I'm trying to make it right."

At Thomas's gentle plea, some of Mika's anger folded away. What made a good mother? Maybe there wasn't a perfect mother. Perhaps you just did the best you could. This new knowledge gnawed at Mika. Would Mika have been a good mother? She didn't know what to say. And she didn't know if she could absolve Thomas. If she could even absolve herself.

"Did you see me?" Penny bounded over, cheeks pink with pride. Seeing Penny happy, the tension Mika had been holding released.

"Sure did, kiddo. Got it on video." Thomas flashed his phone. "You two want to stay longer, or are you hungry?" They'd planned to go to dinner, just the three of them. "Your parents are welcome to join. My treat," Thomas said to Mika.

"That's a lovely offer, but I think they are probably tired and want to head home soon," Mika said. Shige usually fell asleep watching the NHK. She liked the idea of it being the three of them, their own delicate family ecosystem.

Penny had her phone out and was texting someone.

"Do you mind if I pass?" she said. "Olive is on her way here. I'm going to show her around and then we'll catch a ride together home."

"But what about the restaurant that cooks your food in front of you?" Thomas asked, the disappointment evident in his voice. Earlier that week, he'd made a reservation at a teppanyaki place and sent Mika and Penny the link. They have flaming onion volcano towers, he'd written, just so proud and excited.

"Oh," Penny said, looking up from her phone. "You really want me to go? I mean, I will if you really, really want me to . . ." She trailed off. Her words the opposite of what she clearly desired. To be with her friends. To be a teenager.

"No, of course not," Thomas said. "Have fun with your friends."

Let so easily off the hook, Penny beamed. "You two should totally still go."

"You sure?" Thomas's eyes jumped to Mika's. Mika peered down at her feet.

"I'm sure," Penny said, still tapping away on her phone again. "You guys go. Have a great time."

Thomas followed Mika to her car, bag slung over his shoulder. She could feel him behind her. His heat, his presence. Her heart beat fast, along with the taiko drums. The sun may have faded, but she could still feel the warmth in her bones. Near the car, Thomas caught Mika's hand and held it. She stopped short. Turned. He studied her with liquid green eyes. "Hi," he said, brows tense.

"Hi," she said back.

"Does it make me an awful person to admit I'm glad Penny ditched us?"

"If you're awful," she gently admitted, "then maybe I am too."

Chapter Twenty-Nine

The drive to Mika's house was silent. Thomas stared out the window, drumming a rhythm against his thigh. At stoplights, Mika stole glances at him. At the veins running up his arm, the curve of his cheekbones, the messy hair with a few silver strands reflecting the waning sunlight. He'd caught her looking once, and she'd glanced quickly away. But she didn't miss the sly smile that appeared on his face.

"I'll be right back out," she'd said when they'd gotten into the house, already working at the knot of the obi. "Actually, would you mind?" She scooted closer to Thomas. Her hands fell away as she felt Thomas's strong fingers work at it, untying the obi. He stilled as it unraveled from her waist. She held the kimono closed, then stooped to pick up the obi. She spun in his arms to face him. "Thanks," she said.

"Anytime." His voice sounded rough, and his hands traced down her sides.

"Be right back," she said lowly. Her hand loosened on the kimono, exposing the white undergarment.

"Okay," he said, voice even rougher.

"Okay." She placed her hands on his chest, skin burning hot under her fingers. It hurt to step away from him. But she needed a minute. Needed to take a break, a deep breath. She padded to her room and closed the door, leaning against it heavily. She undressed slowly, methodically. Folding the kimono as her mother had taught her. She could hear Thomas in the house. Walking around, opening the fridge, cracking open a beer. When she reemerged in jeans and a T-shirt, he sat on the couch, a brown paper bag on the table.

"What's that?"

"A gift, but first . . ." He held a piece of paper. "For you," he said, offering it to her.

"I'm intrigued," she said, opening the letter and reading.

Dear Mika,

Penny will turn seventeen soon, and we have had quite the year. In keeping with the tradition of children worrying their parents, Penny bought a ticket to Portland to meet you, her birth mother. Do you remember the first time I called you? I do. Actually, I don't remember everything I said. Only the fear. That I might be losing my daughter—not to you, but to the world. And I . . . I just wasn't ready yet.

Jesus. It's hard to admit, but I've been afraid for so long. Terrified of the future. I don't do well with change. Which is difficult when all your child wants to do is transform. It seems the tighter I try to hold on, the more things slip through my fingers. It is a reminder to me of how impermanent life is.

Penny's desire to become her own person is made apparent to me every day. We talk to each other less and less, especially this summer. She is out on a run or with her new boyfriend—who plans to visit her during the school year. I am pretending to be a cool parent. I have even offered to put him up on our couch. Witness my evolution. (Although, between you and me, I have stood in our living room, contemplating where I might place hidden cameras.)

She is planning to apply to several colleges— many out of state. I understand Penny has grown too big for the house I built. I know the part I must play. My job is to get her to a place where she doesn't need me anymore. My role is to put up the funds and accept I cannot keep her forever. It is another death of sorts, I think. The final goodbye of the life I had with Caroline. We were supposed to take Penny to college together. We were supposed to sit outside in our car in the driveway because we couldn't bear to go inside the house without her or the knowledge that the next time she came home, she would be a visitor. We were supposed to miss her for a week, then agree quietly while feeling a little ashamed that it was kind of nice, now that it's the two of us. How did my life go from three to two and now one? Of course, I know the answer. Death. Growing up.

It is starting to get easier, and in part, it's due to you. You have eased the pressure in my chest. For a while, all I've been able to do is look backward. And now, all of a sudden, I look forward. I am excited to see where you and I will lead. Excited to see where Penny will go, what she will discover, who she will become. I have realized, too, that while the winds of change may carry her away, I will always be her father.

I could go on. The truth is, I'm not sure how

> to end this letter. I guess I'll just finish by saying,
> I hope the days ahead are brighter than those
> behind us—for the record, I believe they will be.
>
> **Thomas**

Mika finished reading and looked at Thomas, her eyes wide. She opened her mouth to speak, but no words would form. She was too stunned by Thomas's act of brilliant generosity. He'd done what didn't come easy. And he'd done it for her, given himself freely.

"Your annual letter," he said roughly, with a hint of a smile. "Hand delivered and more than five sentences to boot. You'll have to wait on the photographs; I'm still gathering them up. Believe it or not, it's hard to get printed pictures these days. Does it make me sound old if I say, remember the time when you could go into a store and develop a roll of film? Things were so much simpler then."

"Yes," Mika replied, matching his smile. "But I won't tell anyone." She gestured at him with the letter. "You didn't have to do this," she said, but really, she wanted to wrap her arms around him. It was the best gift she'd ever received. She'd asked Thomas for more, and he'd given it to her. She curbed the urge to weep.

"I did have to." Thomas rolled his hands together.

"Now for your next gift. I am not nearly done wooing you." He grabbed the brown paper bag from the table.

Her insides buzzed, and she opened her hands, accepting the package. "For me?"

"For you," he confirmed, light gaze scraping up her body to her eyes.

"Should I open it?" She curled up on the couch next to him.

"It's nothing big. Just something I saw and thought of you." He outright grinned. "Sorry, it's not wrapped."

Her stomach somersaulted. She reached in the bag, pulling out what was inside. "Oil paints," she breathed out. The box was an introductory set. The brand high quality. Nine tubes of pure pigments—cadmium yellow, alizarin crimson, ultramarine blue, viridian green, burnt umber. She glanced out the window. Saw her reflection. *Who am I? Who am I?* Her palms grew clammy.

Thomas scooted closer. Their knees bumped. His hand landed on her thigh and squeezed. "You gave me back rowing. I wanted to give something back to you too."

She set the paints down, away from her, suddenly cold. "This is great. Thank you."

He frowned. "You don't like them?"

"It's just not something I do anymore." She turned away to hide her longing, the hurt in her heart.

"Why don't you?"

Her chest tightened. Her throat felt dry.

"Mika?" Thomas said, leaning in, his light eyes baffled. "What is it?" He pulled her into a hug. "You can tell me about it."

She buried her face in his chest. His hand ran up and down her back, easing her closer. He made soothing sounds and smelled like soap and coffee. She soaked his shirt, quietly crying. Letting out all the grief. Letting it all go.

She pulled back. "I want—" She stopped short.

"What is it you want?" His face was serious, brow pinched as if studying Mika under a microscope, peeling away the layers she hid under. His hand slid into her hair, cradling the back of her head.

She held his gaze as she thought. *I want it all back. The time I lost. I want my future back, my innocence, my bravery, my sense of security. I want to fall in love again. To be free of the cage Peter built around me.* She wanted it all. Penny. Family. Painting. Travel. The ghost life. But she'd start with Thomas . . . "You. Just you."

"Mika." He kissed her forehead. Then each of her cheeks. "Mika. You have me."

He pulled her in. Then he slowly, ever so slowly bent down until his nose grazed hers. "Okay?" he said. He was asking for permission. She clenched her hands, his shirt bunching in her fists.

"Yes," she said.

He swooped down, in. His lips caught hers softly at first. So hot and slow Mika felt as if she might explode. He shifted, clever hands sliding around her waist. Then he inched up under her shirt, right below her breasts. Mika arched into his touch, pressing herself against him. His grip tightened. His tongue slipped into her mouth. She gasped, opening her mouth to deepen the kiss.

Somehow, they moved through time and space and fell onto her bed. The window was open, paisley curtains spread wide, revealing Portland's summer sky—a wisp of clouds, a hazy border above the tree line from light pollution, a rising moon. Her heart thundered, the sound of one thousand horses' hoofbeats. Thomas reared back. He thumbed her lips. Kissed her again. She reached down, catching the hem of his shirt, and pulled it up and off him. "You too," he said. Mika complied, tossing her shirt to the side. He hooked a finger under her bra strap and pulled down, the muscle in his jaw leaping. "Wow."

"I take it that's good?" she asked, mouth quirking into a smile.

"So good." He kissed the tops of her breasts.

She hiked a leg up around his waist, pressing him

against her. Feeling how much he wanted her. They ground together. Kissed more, wet-hot and open-mouthed. He moved down her body, leaving fire in his wake. He popped the button open on her jeans and shimmied her out of them.

"Wait," she gasped—heat pulsed under her skin.

Immediately he stilled. "Did I hurt you?"

No, but he could. She slid her hands through his hair. "I want this. I want you. But I have some rules."

His face was inscrutable, and his breath tickled her belly. "Okay."

"It's okay for you to be on top, but don't put your hand over my mouth."

"I wouldn't do that." He paused. "What else?"

She shook her head. Her heart rocked like a boat caught on the edge of a swell. "I'm a little broken," she admitted.

"Me too," he said. Mika knew that. It's part of what bound them together. Two broken hearts make a whole one. "You should know, it's been a while for me," he said.

She squirmed. "How long?"

"I went on a couple dates with a woman a year ago, we slept together . . ."

"Three hundred sixty-five days. That's a lot of pressure."

"I didn't like it." Thomas locked eyes with Mika. "I can't just be with someone I'm not—that I don't care for." Mika leaned up on an elbow and ran a hand through his hair.

"Me either," she said.

"Glad we understand each other." He rested his chin on her stomach, right near her belly button. "Any other rules?"

Mika shook her head. "No."

"Alright," he said. "But you should know, I believe every woman should be touched the way she wants to be."

He said it so earnestly Mika melted and flopped backward. "Good answer. You may proceed."

Thomas laughed and kissed her belly. "How's this?"

She ground against him. "That's good."

He kissed lower, trailing down her stomach. "How about this?"

"Ah, good too."

Lower still. He pulled down her panties, then squeezed her thighs, tasting her. Her breaths came faster as the pressure mounted. "What about now?" he asked, breath hot against her core. She couldn't answer. She rolled her hips, wanting to be closer, seeking release.

Finally, she cried out. "Thomas."

He moved up her body, undoing his pants, pushing down his briefs.

"Protection. Do you have a condom?" She hooked her legs around his waist and rocked.

"Um, no. I don't." He ran a hand through his hair. "Shit."

"I might have some. In the top drawer."

Thomas was off her in a flash. He pulled the drawer out, knocking it off its tracks. "Why is there so much spandex in here?" It was from Charlie, the biking gear she'd never returned. "Got 'em." He threw the clothing on the ground and returned to the bed, little foil packet in his hand. He tore the wrapper open with his teeth and then worked the condom on. He settled back between her legs and kissed her softly and languorously, sinking deep into her. She groaned. *Gasped.* Pleasure rushed through her. Her hands spanned his back, raked against his flesh. His hand snaked down between their bodies and touched her center. On he went in a mind-blowing rhythm. He waited for her to unravel first. She came with a cry, with his name on her lips. Then he thrust, deeper, harder, burying himself into her neck with a shudder.

When it was done, Thomas collapsed beside her. The sheets in a tangled mess around them. She pulled the covers up around her limp body and stared at the ceiling.

His hand found hers under the covers. They lay there for a moment. Waiting for their hearts to stop racing. For their breaths to slow. For their minds to catch up with their bodies, to realize the bigness of this moment.

"Holy shit," he said, thumb caressing the inside of her palm.

"Yeah," Mika sighed.

He leaned up on an elbow, cupped her cheek. He thumbed her lips, and she kissed the tip of his finger. He bent down, mouth brushing hers. Her foot slid up against his calf, his hand up her side to cup her hip. Thomas flopped back. "Water. I need water." He climbed from the bed and was slipping on his boxer briefs when Mika barked out a laugh.

"Your tattoo." She rolled to her stomach and reached for the band of his underwear to pull it down. There it was, an outline of a T. rex trying to tie his shoe. "I thought you were joking."

"A man doesn't joke about humiliating tattoos," he said over-seriously. He kissed her quick on the lips. "Be right back."

By the time he returned, Mika had switched on the

nightstand light and pulled on her undies plus a large T-shirt. He had a frosty glass of water and took a long drink of it before handing it off to Mika. There was something about sharing a glass of water with him that was even more intimate than what they had just done.

The sound of a phone buzzing drew Thomas's attention. He fished it out of a pocket in his jeans. "Penny texted." His brow drew in. "Olive wasn't feeling good and went home. She wants to know where we are. She's going to catch an Uber to us."

All the warmth bled from Mika. Outside the house, a car door slammed. Time seemed to stop, then hurdle forward, moving too fast. "Did you lock the front door?" she asked, scrambling from the bed.

"What?" Thomas was behind her.

Someone knocked on the door. "Mika? Dad? You in there? I used the Find My Friends app," Penny said from outside.

Thomas and Mika rushed to the door. Not fast enough. The knob turned. Penny entered, a smile plastered on her face. "Hey, I caught you. Let's go eat." She paused, took them both in—Thomas in his underwear, Mika too, in a T-shirt. They stood stock-still, rabbits caught in a snare. Penny's smile dropped, her expression morphing to confusion. "What's going on?" she said, though it was evident enough. Penny was still in her kimono, but her hair was down. Her mouth parted. She covered her eyes and twirled away. "Oh my god. Oh. My. God. You guys are fucking?"

"Penny, language," Thomas said through his teeth.

"Are you kidding?" Penny scoffed and twisted back around to confront them. Two bright red splotches of anger appeared on her cheeks. She focused on Mika. Her chin trembled, and Mika ached to comfort her. "How could you do this to me?"

At that, Mika winced. She didn't know what to say. What *could* she say? How to make sense of this situation so Penny might understand. "We didn't mean to. It just happened—" It sounded weak even to her own ears, belied what Mika felt about the situation, about Thomas. Maybe she should amend it. *We were keeping our relationship a secret because we were doing what we thought was best for you.* Somehow, she knew Penny would take that the wrong way. What teenager liked to hear they weren't adult enough to handle something?

"Penny," Thomas interjected.

Penny turned her full displeasure on her father. "Anyone in the world and you choose *her*, my birth mother?"

Thomas shook his head. "Clearly, you're angry right now, and that's understandable. Let's talk about this."

Phone in hand, Penny tapped something out on it.

"Penny," Thomas said.

"Un-fucking-believable," she muttered to herself.

"Penny. Stop. Get off your phone for a minute," Thomas demanded. He ran an aggravated hand down his face. "Penny, look at me."

Finally, Penny turned, her eyes narrowed and pointed like the sharpest daggers. "You know what? I don't really feel like being around either of you right now." Her phone pinged. She put a hand on the door and opened it.

Outside, a car idled at the curb with its window rolled down. "Penny? You call for an Uber?" a man called out.

"Where are you going?" Thomas stepped forward. "Penny, do not walk out that door."

She looked her father up and down. "Or what? What are you going to do?"

Thomas paused, defeated.

"That's what I thought," Penny fired back as she slipped out, down the walkway, and into the car. Mika and Thomas could only watch, frozen as she zoomed off.

Chapter Thirty

Mika jumped into action. "Where are my keys?" she said, searching the living room, behind the couch cushions. Lifting up magazines. Knocking over the oil paint set. "I'm going after her. Shit." The remote control fell on her foot, and she hopped around.

"Here." Thomas lifted her keys from the coffee table. When Mika reached out to take them, he pulled back.

"Thomas, give me my keys." Mika thrust her hand out.

"Stop. Take a deep breath," Thomas said steadily. "Think about it for a moment. You're going to chase her, and then what?"

"I'm going to talk to her, I'm going to . . ." Mika

trailed off. Really, she had no idea. Her first instinct was to chase. She'd figure out what to do when she caught Penny. Shake some sense into her, maybe. Get down on her knees and beg for forgiveness, more likely.

Thomas watched her. "Give her some space. Some time to cool down. Nobody is thinking clearly right now."

Mika shook her head. It went against her natural instinct. "I don't know—"

Thomas put down the keys. "Trust me. We'll wait her out."

Mika considered his advice for a moment. Penny would come home. Kids always came home. Didn't they? "Yeah. Okay."

Thomas pulled Mika against him, wrapping her in a hug, and kissed the top of her head. They tried watching television, some sitcom, but neither of them was in the mood to laugh. Thomas left messages for Penny. At 9:00 p.m.: Hey kiddo, let me know if you're home safe. At 10:00 p.m.: I know this is probably a lot to process. Give me a call when you're ready. At 10:45 p.m.: Last time I'll call, I promise. I won't hassle you anymore. At 11:00 p.m.: Just shoot me a text and let me know you're okay.

Thomas put down his phone. "Penny turned off the

app on her phone, so I can't see where she is. But Uber dropped her off at the dorms."

"She's probably sleeping," said Mika with a wan smile, injecting all the confidence she didn't feel into her voice, trying to keep the bite of worry out of it. "She's going to wake up refreshed, and the joke will be on us because we stayed up all night."

"Come here." Thomas held an arm aloft, and Mika lay her head against his chest. They did their best to stay awake but eventually dozed on the couch, porch light and living room lights still blazing, just in case Penny came back. At 2:00 a.m., they jolted awake to Thomas's phone ringing. "Hello," he answered groggily.

"Hello, is this the parent or guardian of Penelope Calvin?" a disembodied voice said on the other end.

Thomas straightened. "This is her father."

"My name is Dr. Nguyen, and I'm a physician here at the emergency room at St. Vincent's hospital." Mika doubled over, a knife twisting in her belly. Not Penny. Her baby. No. "We have Penelope here with a suspected case of alcohol poisoning."

"Sorry? What?" Thomas said.

"Alcohol poisoning," he repeated. "We'd like permission to treat her with IV fluids, oxygen, and possibly a nasogastric tube. Do we have your consent?"

"Yes, yes, of course, you have my consent."

The doctor went on to give Thomas more information. The hospital name again. Where to find Penny. "She's okay, though?" he asked, desperation in his voice.

"Her friends did the right thing calling the paramedics."

By the time Thomas hung up, Mika had already slipped on a sweatshirt and was reaching for her keys. "I'll drive."

"Do you know where the hospital is?" Thomas buzzed around, putting on shoes, grabbing his bag.

"Yeah, you've been there before. It's where Penny was born." Mika ignored the skip in her pulse. She hadn't been back to the hospital since then.

In the car, Thomas was unnaturally quiet. His hands closed into fists, then opened again. "Penny was drinking? Who would give a sixteen-year-old girl booze?"

A lot of people, Mika thought. She'd spent a fair amount of time shoulder tapping—hanging outside of convenience stores and asking older patrons to buy beer for her and Hana—age fifteen on. Mika gripped the steering wheel. Traffic was light, and they were flying down the freeway. She didn't answer Thomas. She couldn't. She was trapped in a cyclone of prayers.

Talking to Penny again, like she had done all those years ago after Penny was born and Mika had placed her for adoption. *Please be okay. Are you there? Wake up, Penny. We still need you.*

• • •

"Penelope Calvin," Thomas said at the check-in desk, Mika behind him. Exhausted and disheveled, Thomas looked as if he'd aged twenty years in the last twenty minutes. "She was brought in an hour ago." They'd parked and come straight to the ER waiting room. To Mika's right was a man with a nasty bloody nose and a woman holding her arm and moaning.

"And what is your relationship to the patient?" the tired woman asked. The slowness of her movements agitated Mika further. *Penny could be dying right now. Penny could be sick. Penny could be asking for Mika.* After Mika had given birth, she'd thought about Hiromi constantly. Had wanted her mother to swoop in. Heal her or, at the very least, hold her.

"I'm her father," Thomas said at the same time Mika said, "I'm her mother." She'd never said it aloud before. *I am her mother.* It felt as momentous as reaching the peak of a mountain. Even more so when Thomas gave her hand a squeeze. The woman asked for identification, and Thomas pulled his wallet from his back pocket and flashed her his license. Mika did the same, fishing hers from her purse.

The woman appraised their licenses and said, "Room five." She pressed a button, and the automated double doors opened. Thomas shoved his wallet into his back pocket, and they were through the doors in seconds, counting the numbered plaques above the rooms—each little cubicle holding a life at its tipping point. Mika stopped short between rooms four and five, where a familiar figure sat hunched in a plastic chair—Devon.

"Hey, Mr. Calvin, Ms. Suzuki." Devon stood, blocking Mika and Thomas from Penny's room. His eyes were bloodshot and red-rimmed. "She's okay. The doc just came out and said she's fine. They didn't have to do that tube thingy. She's in the bathroom cleaning up." He held a baseball hat in his hands and twisted the bill between his fingers. "I'm so sorry. Penny came back to the dorms, and she was so upset. She wanted to go to this party, and I was like, cool, okay. College party, you know?" He rubbed a hand down his face. "I'm sorry," he said again. The faintest smell of alcohol clung to his breath. Her stomach lurched. She pictured Penny at a party, red Solo cup in hand. She shook the image away, struggled to remain calm. Penny's experience tonight wasn't the same as Mika's had been all those years ago at Peter's apartment. "I didn't even see how much she was drinking, then she passed out, and I couldn't get her to open her eyes." Of course Devon had been involved. Because isn't there always a boy?

"You took my sixteen-year-old daughter out drinking?" Thomas asked pointedly.

Devon paled, and Mika softened. Most of the boys she knew in high school ran at the first sight of trouble, but Devon seemed like a good kid. He'd stayed, and that was something. "I'm sorry. Penny . . . she . . . when she wants her way . . ." He hung his head.

Mika stepped forward and said gently, "You can probably go home now, Devon. It's already been a late night for you." She looked up at him. "I'm sure Penny will call you. Do you have a way back to the dorm?"

"Um yeah, okay. I can call an Uber." Devon placed his hat back on his head. "Penny knows I was here. I really . . . I really care about her."

"I can tell," Mika said. She wanted to pat his arm. Tell him he'd been dumb but that she was glad Penny had him. He'd done the right thing in the end. "Have a good night."

Devon left, and Thomas shook his head. "What was he thinking? What was she thinking?"

Mika rubbed her hands together. "I don't know." Kids

did stupid stuff all the time. *It's inevitable*, Mika thought, remembering herself as a teen, how she'd thought herself invincible. Why did some lessons have to be learned the hard way? "Come on, let's go see her."

She followed Thomas as he lightly rapped on the door to room five. "Kiddo, it's me." He slipped inside, and Mika silently followed.

Penny was in bed, a tray of uneaten food in front of her, white hospital blanket pulled up to her waist, and gown on. Jesus, it was the same pattern as the one Mika had worn years ago. Mika saw herself at nineteen in the hospital bed. Touching Penny's baby cheek, rubbing her nose against hers.

"What are you doing here?" Penny's voice came out gravelly. Dark circles hung under her eyes. Her skin was waxy and pale.

Thomas closed the door with a click. He put his hands on his hips. "What kind of question is that? We came to check on you."

"You've seen me. I'm alive," Penny said and then turned to face the wall. In the ensuing silence, Mika and Thomas looked at each other, unsure what to do. A trash can was in the corner of the room, the kimono crumpled in it like a doe shot down.

Thomas stepped forward. "That was stupid what you did, Penny."

Penny turned back to them and rolled her eyes. One time, Hiromi nearly slapped Mika for doing the same, flew at her like a Valkyrie from the sky.

Mika sighed. She placed a hand on Thomas's arm and stepped in front of him. Mika knew better than to lead with anger now. She knew teenagers. How stubborn their beautiful hearts could be.

"You scared us," Mika said quietly. "Devon was pretty freaked out too." At that, Penny winced. Mika had hit a nerve. "You could have killed yourself." Mika drew a little closer. "You're upset. And you probably feel like shit," she added, injecting some lightness into her tone. "Look, you're angry, that's clear. I'm sorry about what you saw. It wasn't ever our intention for you to find out that way. We wanted to make sure it was serious before we told you. Please, Penny." Mika sat in a chair next to the hospital bed and placed her hand on top of Penny's.

Penny eyed Mika's hand and disentangled herself. The lines of her body drew tense. "What did you think?" she asked, with a hiss, with menace. "Did you think you could sleep with my dad and become my mom? That you could replace her? News flash, I had a mother. She died," she said.

Mika blinked.

"Penny," she heard Thomas say.

Mika slowly stood. She brought her hand to her chest and rubbed where a sudden burning sensation blazed. "Oh, um . . ." She staggered back to the door, her hand reaching for the knob. A glance at Thomas showed his mouth moving, but Mika couldn't make out the words. It was as if she were underwater, everything muted, blurry. "I'm just going to . . ." she said. She tilted her chin up and found herself in the corridor outside Penny's room. Sound returned with the velocity of a scream. Machines beeped. Nurses chattered about patients. A code gray called over the intercom. The arrow of Penny's words pierced deeper. She'd called Mika an understudy. Not good enough. In one blinding moment, all of Mika's fears were realized. It only took seconds to obliterate someone, and Penny had done so with the air of a seasoned professional.

The air around her smelled like stale coffee and antiseptic. She hated the scent of hospitals. Had ever since Penny was born. Her hands clenched, the air thinned, and Mika struggled to breathe. She was dizzy, *ill*. She started walking. Hurried outside. Where she needed to be.

Footsteps thundered behind her. "Mika," Thomas called.

She broke through the double doors. Then another set, until finally, she was in the fresh air. Nights were cold during the summer in Portland. Even colder in the predawn hours. The sky was that early morning color blue, a bruise caught between night and day.

"Mika, stop," Thomas demanded. His hand wrapped around her arm, and she whirled to face him. Above them, a streetlamp swarmed with moths. He released her and rubbed his head. "Shit. That was rough. She's really angry. Angrier than I thought she'd be . . . I'm so sorry, Mika. She didn't mean that."

"I think maybe she did. All of this"—she gestured at the space between them, blood rushing to her cheeks—"You, me, Penny is a lot."

Thomas stared at his feet and nodded. "I get that, but we can figure it out."

Penny's words echoed in Mika's ears. *I had a mother. She died.* Mika may have wanted Penny, but that didn't mean Penny wanted Mika. That she was good enough for her. She'd fucked up Penny like Hiromi had fucked her up. Mika folded her arms, shielding her stomach—an act of protection. "I don't know if we can," Mika said, her voice wavering. She couldn't look at Thomas. At what she was about to lose. "She's right, you know. She *did* have a mother, one who loved her and cared for her for eleven years. I'm not . . . I can't . . . I can't replace Caroline. We can't just become some kind of insta-family. It doesn't work like that."

Mika felt small, a teenager again. A foolish girl with foolish dreams. What had she thought? That she could be Penny's mother, Thomas's lover—that together they might heal each other? She saw it clearly now. Penny and Thomas were looking for something, someone to guide them from the darkness of their grief. It could have been anyone. By a random twist of fate, it had been Mika—they'd collided at pivotal points in their lives. She didn't belong with them. They didn't belong to her. Thomas and Penny were a world unto themselves, and Mika had just been a tourist.

Thomas paced. "Penny's upset now, but she needs time to adjust to the idea," he said in a rush. "She'll get over it. She's a teenager. They change their minds all the time."

Mika's stomach plummeted. "Thomas . . . I don't think . . . I don't think this is going to work."

A shadow crossed his face. "Don't say that." His phone chimed, and he ignored it.

Mika inhaled a deep breath and exhaled slowly. *You don't deserve her,* a voice whispered in her head. *You don't deserve him. Them.* "Look at us. Where we are. We're at the hospital. Penny could have died tonight. She's not ready for any of this." His phone chimed again. "That's probably Penny," Mika said with a tilt of her chin. She swallowed past the thickness in her throat. "You should go be with her. She needs you now."

"Alright," Thomas said. A muscle ticked along his jaw. He held out his hand. "Let's go."

Mika shook her head. "No. Just you. My presence will only upset her more. And on that note." She paused, peered up at the sky, knowing there was one immutable fact. Penny was better off without Mika in her life. It was time to quietly bow out. "I think . . . I think it's best if we don't see each other anymore."

"Mika," he said hotly. "Don't do this. Not after everything we've shared. Please."

"It's already done," she said. Now she stared at her feet, afraid to face Thomas, the world. How many times did someone have to be slapped before they stayed down?

His phone chimed again. "Penny's being discharged," he said. "I need to go sign some paperwork."

Mika nodded mutely. "Of course, go," she said. "Here." She lifted her hands with her keys. "You can take my car. I don't think Penny wants to see me. I'll catch a cab or something back home. Then just let me know where to pick it up."

Thomas didn't move. Agonizing seconds passed, then, "I'll manage transportation," he said flatly.

"Okay." She brought her keys back close to her body.

He watched her for a moment. Waited. When she refused to speak, he ground out a curse word and paced away. Thomas gone, Mika stumbled back onto a nearby bench, squeezed her eyes shut, inhaled then exhaled, and opened them.

This area of the hospital was familiar.

She was outside of the maternity ward where she'd given birth, where she had waited with Hana after surrendering Penny, unable to make those final steps to the bus. When she thought she might die from grief without Penny, only to realize that there are some things worse than death. Sixteen years had passed, and she'd wound up here again. Bells chimed. The same ones she'd heard when Penny had been born. Time did move in a circle.

Every sensation in Mika's body heightened. Something cracked inside of her. Fusion failing. Icarus falling. She heard phantom voices, and memories sucked her down into a whirlpool.

Hiromi screwing up her face at Mika's drawing. *Who is that supposed to be, your friend? You made her face too full. She looks fat.*

Her art crumpling in Marcus's hand. *What's your story?*

Peter's hand over her mouth.

You're doing so good. Mrs. Pearson, as Mika signed the adoption paperwork.

Do you want to hold her one last time? Hana asking, adjusting the hat on Penny's head.

Memories surged forward, flooding the architecture of her mind. She was drowning. Gasping for air. Everything converged. Her past, her present. *Is this Mika Suzuki? Did you give a baby up for adoption?* Penny sweet, then so acidic. *I had a mother. She died.* Mika should have known better. She should have known things would end like this. *What do you know about raising a baby?* Hiromi had said.

She buckled over, sobbing into her hands, into the quiet morning, wishing the earth might absorb her. She took out her phone and looked up Pearl Jam's schedule. She wanted Hana. She wanted to be away from here. There, Pearl Jam was playing in Eugene. She stumbled back to her car, started the engine, and drove. *Fight or flight is a natural response,* Suzanne, her counselor, had said when Mika explained how she had run from Peter's apartment. What Peter had done turned Mika into her basest self, she explained. *Your mind couldn't process anything. Your body took over. It's how you stayed safe,* she had said. It's how Mika stayed alive.

Chapter Thirty-One

Halfway to Eugene, Mika pulled over at a rest stop. Guess who's coming to see you? she wrote to Hana. The lightness of the message belied the darkness creeping in.

Hana texted two hours later, just as Mika reached the outskirts of the city. WTF. You're coming to Eugene?

Mika parked under an overpass, pressed the heel of her palms to her eyes. Her car shook from the semis passing overhead. Correction, I am in Eugene. Hotel name, please.

She cupped her knees and squeezed, waiting. At last, Hana sent a map link along with a message. I'll be in the lobby.

• • •

Mika swung through the glass turnstile of the swankiest hotel in Eugene. True to her word, Hana was waiting, arms crossed, tapping her fingers against her bicep.

"Hi!" Mika smiled, but she imagined her expression appeared off. She felt off. As if she were falling from a great height and could do nothing to stop it.

"Hi," Hana said carefully. "This is a surprise."

It was morning, seven o'clock, and mostly families milled around the posh lobby. Mika inhaled. It smelled like citrus, much better than the antiseptic at the hospital. "I know. I just thought, what the hell?! I miss Hana."

"Uh-huh." Hana eyed her skeptically. "So, you dropped everything on a Sunday at five a.m. to drive here?"

"Exactly. Isn't this fun? I want a drink. Let's get a drink." Mika scanned the lobby for the bar.

"It's seven a.m., bars are closed."

"Minibar?" Mika felt very smart. She had a solution for everything.

Hana looked at the ceiling. "Alright," she said. "But mostly because I don't think you should be in public right now."

Hana's hotel room was sleek and modern, with a king-size bed, a little table, and floor-to-ceiling windows overlooking a muddy river. Mika appreciated the view for all of two seconds before finding the mini-fridge, cleverly hidden in a dresser. She grabbed the first little bottle she saw, uncapped, and drank it down. Whiskey. She wiped her mouth with the back of her hand. Her throat burned, and she liked it, the way it distracted her from the pain in her soul.

"I gotta say." Hana leaned against a wall. "You're not exactly giving me warm, stable vibes here."

"You're telling me." Mika didn't feel stable. She felt very unstable, as a matter of fact. As if she were balancing on broken branches. She went back to the fridge. Another little bottle of whiskey down the hatch. Should she eat something? No. Crazy talk. That might ruin her buzz.

Hana moved across the room and withdrew a bottle of water from the fridge. "At least sip it between shots."

"Thanks." Mika took a healthy drink of the water. Out of whiskey, she moved on to vodka. It was a good brand, even better when mixed with cranberry, but Mika shot it straight.

Hana sat on the edge of the bed. "Are you going to tell me what happened? I haven't seen you like this since freshman year in college."

Mika hit her nose. "Ding, ding, ding. You got it! What happened? I fucked up again. That's what happened. Isn't there a saying about the past repeating itself?" The booze started to take effect. Her stomach warmed. Her limbs numbed. That's what she wanted: to feel nothing, like she had the last sixteen years—it was much safer this way. Back to the mini-fridge. Another vodka? Tequila? Why not.

"Mika," Hana said calmly. "Mika!" She clapped her hands.

Mika tilted her head. "What?"

"Sit," Hana commanded as if Mika were a dog.

Mika crumpled to the floor near the minibar. Better to stay close. That tequila wasn't going to drink itself. She reached for it.

"No!" Hana's hand wrapped around Mika's wrist. How'd she moved so fast? Or was Mika just moving very slowly? "No more until you tell me what's going on."

Hana shut the mini-fridge, and Mika leaned against the dresser, pulling her legs into her chest to hug them. "I slept with Thomas, and Penny caught us." She paused for emphasis. "In our underwear."

"Yikes." Hana sank down to the floor, sitting across from Mika.

"It gets worse."

"How much worse?"

"I'd like another drink."

"No more until you tell me the whole story."

For a moment, Mika pouted but then explained how she and Thomas had kissed a while back at his hotel. How they'd agreed to keep their budding relationship a secret. How they didn't want to make Penny worry over nothing, better to wait until there was something—until *they* were something. How the next time they were alone, they'd fallen on each other like lovers reunited after war. Then Penny had walked in, face twisting in anger. "We stayed up and fell asleep on the couch." She thought of resting in Thomas's arms. Through their mutual worry, everything still felt like it would be okay then. "Penny went out drinking, I guess." It occurred to Mika she was doing the same thing Penny had. Drowning her sorrows. But she shoved the comparison away. She was thirty-five, not sixteen. She could do whatever the fuck she wanted. "She ended up in the ER for alcohol poisoning. We went to see her and . . . she was so *angry*. She said some awful things." *I had a mother. She died.* Mika's blood ran cold, remembering the venom in Penny's words.

Mika flopped her head back to stare at the ceiling. "I had Penny." Mika's hands opened and closed. "After sixteen years, I *had* her, and I did the one thing certain to drive her away. I knew it was a risk, and I did it anyway." Mika should have known. If you touched the sun, you got burned. She rubbed her eyes with the heels of her hands. "Why did I think I could have a relationship with Penny *and* Thomas? I'm so stupid."

"Wait a minute," Hana said with a frown. "What are you talking about?"

"Look at my life, Hana. Look at what a fucking mess it is. Look what a fucking mess Penny's and Thomas's lives are now. You know what the common denominator is? Me." She jammed a thumb to her chest. She'd made her mother miserable too. If Hiromi didn't have Mika, a daughter to support, would she have stayed in Japan? Lived the life she wanted? All signs pointed to yes.

"Okay, I'll give you the situation is not ideal." Hana stretched out her legs, crossing them at the ankles. "It's complex, that's for sure, and you and Thomas didn't think things through entirely. But, honey, do you really believe you somehow engineered this? That you have the strength to ruin everything?"

Mika nodded mutely.

"Please," Hana snorted. "You are far less powerful than you think."

Mika jutted out her chin. "It doesn't matter."

"It does matter," Hana stressed. "What is it you want here? You want Thomas? You want Penny?"

What is it you want? Thomas had asked her the same thing. Then she'd kissed him. Because she'd wanted to, but also to avoid the question. To avoid being honest with herself. "I want Penny. I want Thomas too. And more than that . . ." She balled her hands into fists, slammed them against her knees. "I want to be happy, and I don't want to be afraid anymore." She thought of the set of oil paints discarded on the living room floor. *What will you do with an art degree?* her mother had said. And soon after, Mika had met Marcus. At the time, Mika saw this serendipity as a reward for standing up to her mother. But when Marcus brought Peter into her life, it became a punishment instead. For disregarding her mother, for going against her wishes. How could she not have seen those two things as being linked before? Everything that had happened to her had reaffirmed what her mother had always told her. That she wasn't worthy. That if she tried to fly, she would fall. Better to stay on the ground.

"Tell me about the afraid part," Hana said gently.

A deep ache pulsated through Mika. "Don't you ever feel like life has passed you by? Don't you ever think about when we were in high school? How everything seemed so certain and then . . . I don't know. I just had the rug pulled from underneath me, Hana. And I'm so afraid it will happen again." To love was to hurt. To live was to hurt. And it had happened again. Mika curled her fingers into the carpet.

"I don't feel that way. But I see how you can."

"Sometimes I wish I could go back in time, but that means wishing away Penny, and I'd never . . . But it all just hurts so much. When I reconnected with her, it felt like a second chance. At first, I just wanted to know that I didn't fuck her up too much, but then she wanted to know me. To be with me. It all felt so good being a part of her life." As if Mika had been reincarnated. Suddenly, it felt like her life didn't have to be a train rushing by.

"You can't rely on others for your self-worth," Hana said. "That has to come from within." She moved to her knees and sat directly in front of Mika. She cupped Mika's cheeks. "Do you believe that?"

Mika looked anywhere but in Hana's eyes. Hana squeezed her cheeks a little too hard. "Ow," said Mika.

"Eyes on me, drunkie. I want you to remember this. You deserve to exist. You deserve to take up space. You deserve to have the things you want." She let go but then pressed a hand to Mika's chest. "I see you. All that hunger, to travel, to paint, it's still inside you. It's gnawing away at you, and I'm afraid of what it's going to do to you if you keep it all to yourself. You can't go back. You can never go back. But you can decide how you want to move forward."

Mika didn't allow Hana's words to sink in. The wound was still too raw, festering and open. "What happened to me?" she asked meekly.

"Life kicked the shit out of you."

Mika nodded. "Maybe I'll come on tour with you after all."

Hana sat back. "No. I'm not letting you. You've started building something in Portland." She tugged on her ear. "Plus, Josephine is coming tonight. And I mean this in the nicest way possible, but you're kind of a twat block."

Mika giggled, then hiccupped. "Twat block?"

"Beaver dam?" Hana scrunched her nose. "Any better?"

"Much better," said Mika. "Can I drink more now?"

"No." Hana crawled to her feet. She removed Mika's shoes, helped her peel the sweatshirt from her shoulders. "Now, you can sleep. I have to go to rehearsal."

Mika stood, swaying a little. Her head pounded, tears and alcohol a nasty combination. Sleep did sound good, though. "Maybe a tiny nap." Mika pinched her fingers together and stumbled to the bed. She slipped under the covers, and it was like being on a cloud.

Hana tucked her in. "You can shower and borrow some clothes when you wake up. But don't use my toothbrush. Call the front desk and ask for one."

"Poo," Mika said. "You use someone's toothbrush once . . ."

"Boundaries. Every good friendship has to have boundaries." Hana squeezed Mika's feet over the covers.

"Love your face," Mika said, snuggling in.

Hana closed the curtains, clicked off the lights. The room was cool and dark. "Love your face," she said back. The door shut, and Mika drifted off to sleep.

Chapter Thirty-Two

Mika slept for five hours. She awoke groggy and disoriented. For a while, she lay in the dark, listening to her own breathing. Counting the rises and falls of her chest. Finally, she rose, and opened the curtains. It was early afternoon. The sun shone, reflecting in the rippling water of the river. First thing, she made herself a cup of coffee, then rifled through Hana's suitcase for clean clothes. She used her finger to brush her teeth. Then ate a burger and an ice cream sundae in the hotel restaurant.

In her car, she texted Hana. Going home. Thank you. BTW I charged my food to your room. I figured you'd want to treat me.

Outside of Eugene, Hana wrote back. Glad you still have your appetite. Another text came through close on the heels of the first. Just remember, people die in the woods because they won't change direction.

Mika made the two-hour drive in an hour and forty. She pulled up outside her house and groaned, seeing a familiar car parked in the driveway. Her mother's old Honda. Hiromi was in the driver's seat. A text came through on her phone. It was Thomas. I'm taking Penny home. Back to Dayton. Our flight leaves in a couple hours. Just wanted you to know.

Mika bit her lip. Thanks. Is Penny okay?

He answered right away. She's fine. Her attitude needs some adjusting, though. Can I call you when we get in? Thomas asked. I'd like to continue our conversation.

Hiromi climbed from her car and watched Mika through the windshield. I don't think that's a good idea, said Mika.

That's it then? Thomas asked.

For now, she said, amending it to *forever* in her head.

She laid her phone down and rubbed her eyes. Despite her conversation with Hana, everything still seemed so . . . *fucked.* Finally, she opened her car door. "Mom, what are you doing here?" she said to Hiromi in English. She ducked into the back seat to retrieve the dirty clothes she'd exchanged for Hana's clean ones.

She turned, and Hiromi stared at her with her black button eyes. "Now, you don't speak Japanese anymore?"

Mika shrugged and bypassed her mother, hands fisted around her wrinkled shirt and pants. Hiromi followed her up the walkway and into the house. Mika dumped the laundry onto the couch. Hiromi's nose twitched and she wandered into the kitchen to stare out into the backyard. "I told you that tree needs to be watered." The leaves on the maple had curled in and turned brown. There was some irony in Hiromi pointing out that when you neglect something, refuse to nourish it, it dies.

Mika stopped and faced her mother, hands on her hips. She held herself rigid as if poised on the edge of a cliff. "Is there a reason you're here?"

Hiromi's brow furrowed. "I came to pick up the kimono. I called you and Penny. Nobody answering my calls," she said, her grammar slipping. She'd never allowed her jaw to soften for the English language, and it made Mika furious.

Mika scrubbed a hand down her face. "Great. I'll get it." In her room, she grabbed the kimono. Holding it a beat, she stared at the rumpled sheets. Remembering Thomas. His body. How she'd responded to him. The way Penny had spoken to her at the hospital. Her heart cracked a little more. When would it become irreparable? "I went to Eugene to visit Hana. And Penny is going back to Ohio." She handed Hiromi the kimono.

"Why?" Hiromi frowned. She took the kimono, rubbing her thumbs against the cotton. "Her program doesn't end for another week. We had plans for Wednesday. I was going to make sukiyaki."

Mika ignored her mother. "The kimono Penny was wearing got ruined. I'll pay you back for it." Mika walked to the door and opened it wide—an invitation for her mother to leave. *Please go right now.*

Hiromi didn't budge, kimono clutched to her chest. "What happened to the other kimono? Why is Penny leaving?"

The last branch that Mika had been balancing on snapped. "If you must know, Penny went to a party last night and drank too much. She wound up in the hospital and needed to be treated for alcohol poisoning."

"Why did you let her go to a party? You should be at the hospital with her." Hiromi shook her head, then her eyebrows slammed down. "What did you do?"

Of course Hiromi blamed Mika. Mika dropped her hand from the door, leaving it open. Let the whole neighborhood hear. She didn't care. She was done being silent. She'd had it. "Why is it that you think

I did something? Because it's always my fault, right? Does it even matter to you how much it hurt giving Penny up for adoption?" Mika remembered the bench, the maternity ward, the smell of antiseptic.

Hiromi shook her head. "I don't want to talk about this."

Her mother moved to go, but Mika blocked her with an arm across the door. "We never talk about anything!" she said sharply. Tears started to leak down her face. She advanced on her mother, who backed up. "And I think that's the problem. So, let's talk about it. How I gave a baby up for adoption. How I was by myself in the hospital. How I was raped." She stilled and a pang shot through Mika's abdomen. The word hung in the air between them, dropped to the ground, and ran loose. Her voice softened. "Did you know that? I was raped," she said again, and it felt good. Maybe the secrets she kept were really lies. Lies she told herself. Lies she told her mother. *Nobody has ever hurt me. You have never hurt me.*

Hiromi's eyes glittered with a sheen of liquid. She was quick to blink it away. "So what? Bad things happen all the time. You need to move on. Forget about it. I didn't want to leave Japan, but I did." Her words made Mika flinch. It was exactly how she feared her mother might react if she ever told her the truth. *Chin up. Don't be a victim.* "Why are you telling me all this?" she finished.

"I don't know," Mika sobbed, then quieted. "I don't know. I guess I wanted to tell you." Needed to lay her burdens down. "I guess I wanted you to love me through it."

Hiromi scoffed. "So, it's fine now. You have a good job. You have Penny. You always complain. Nothing is ever good enough for you."

Mika laughed. That was rich. "Nothing is ever good enough for *you*." She pointed at her mother. "And it's not fucking fine." Mika wiped at her cheeks. She stared at her mother. At the woman who gave her life. At the woman who spent years and years making Mika doubt herself. Hiromi. Mother. Creator. Destroyer. "You never believed in me." To be Hiromi's daughter, then a girl raped, felt as if moving from one prison to another. Is that what happened to girls? Was this their lives? Skipping from one cage to another?

Hiromi's walls were back in place. Mika could practically see the bricks in her eyes. Impenetrable. They'd never understand each other. "You never believed in yourself," Hiromi said.

Silence then, heavy and thick. The room dimmed

with a cloud passing over the sun. *How does this end?* Mika wondered. Not how she wanted it to. She thought of Caroline dressing Penny in clothes that matched her own. Of Hiromi forcing Mika to take dance lessons. How mothers see their daughters as echoes, as do-overs, as younger versions of themselves who might have the life they didn't or have the same life as they did, but better. *But children aren't second chances,* Mika realized with a start. It was unfair for Hiromi to believe her desires should live inside Mika. Children are made to take a parent's love and pass it along.

"I'm sorry I couldn't be the daughter you wanted," Mika said, her voice thin and weak, but inside she felt a release. A dam breaking. The last tether to her mother's approval finally snapping. She'd had an unrealistic expectation of what a mother should be, a fantasy. But no more. From now on, she'd stop asking herself what was wrong with her. "Now, if you don't mind. I have to work tomorrow." Mika stepped away, unblocking the door.

Hiromi hesitated, then, head down, she left. Mika shut the door softly behind her. She moved the curtain and watched through the window as her mother got into her car and pulled away. Then Mika shifted the curtains back, closing them completely. She locked the door and slumped against it. Her gaze focused on the couch, on the oil paints pushed underneath it. She crawled over and fished them out. Opening the package, she unscrewed a cap and put a little dab of yellow ochre on her finger, rubbing it between her thumb and pointer. She rose up. It felt as if a spell had been lifted. The truth was out. And Mika still stood.

Chapter Thirty-Three

She slept again, and it was deep and quiet—still, clear water. When she awoke, the oil paints were on the coffee table where she had left them. She stared at them for a moment, rumpled and groggy-eyed. Her stomach growled. But Mika ignored the hunger. Something else would feed her more.

It was late, near closing time, when Mika entered Art Emporium. A young guy with a goatee sat at the counter on a stool. He lifted his head from a battered copy of *I Capture the Castle* to welcome her in.

She grabbed a cart and started filling it. An easel. Palette. Varnish. Canvas. Primer. Brushes. She already had a set of oils and bypassed those. She froze in front of the solvents. *Turpentine.* Even though the bottles were capped, the smell of pine resin faintly permeated the air.

She gagged. Too soon. All she saw was Peter. All she felt was his hand over her mouth.

"Can I help you?" It was the guy from the front desk.

On the lowest shelf was a bottle of mineral spirits. She uncapped it and smelled it. A kerosene-like odor wafted up. Better, but too strong. Not right.

"Ugh, you're not supposed to open that. Don't you see the label that says use in a well-ventilated area?" the guy said. Mika put the cap back on, picked up another mineral spirits brand, uncapped it, and sniffed. The same. Should have figured. "What are you doing?" The guy inched closer, hands up. She'd seen a police officer do something similar once on the train, approaching a homeless man who'd removed all his clothes.

She regarded him, bottle in hand. "I think I've been ignoring the puzzle pieces of my past, not realizing they were the keys to my future."

The guy tongued his cheek. "*Riiight,*" he said, in a tone one used when being careful around someone. He didn't need to worry about Mika, though.

"What other solvents can I use besides turpentine and mineral spirits?" Mika shoved the mineral spirits back on the shelf.

"Lavender Spike Oil, top shelf." He pointed up. "It's more expensive than turpentine, so we only keep a couple bottles in stock."

Mika stood on her tiptoes. Her fingertips brushed the bottle, just out of reach.

The guy stepped forward. "Want some help?"

"No, thanks." Mika gave a little leap, knocking the bottle off the shelf and into her hands. "I'm helping myself." She smiled victoriously. "I think that's all I need." Her cart was full. Her heart was full. She'd forgotten how much joy she found in art supplies. The excitement was building to create something new.

The guy rang her up. When she saw the total, she had to step to the side and transfer money from her savings. "Sorry." She handed over her debit card.

He swiped it. "It's cool. We get a lot of weird artist types in here," he said, misunderstanding her apology. Behind him was a wall of quotes from famous artists. ART WASHES AWAY FROM THE SOUL THE DUST OF EVERYDAY LIFE, Pablo Picasso. ART IS NOT WHAT YOU SEE, BUT WHAT YOU MAKE OTHERS SEE, Edgar Degas. PAINTING IS SELF-DISCOVERY. EVERY GOOD ARTIST PAINTS WHAT HE IS, Jackson Pollock. YOU USE A GLASS MIRROR TO SEE YOUR FACE; YOU USE WORKS OF ART TO SEE YOUR SOUL, George Bernard Shaw.

"Thanks." She gathered her art supplies and shoved them into the back seat of her car. The day was ending, but she felt as if she was just beginning. Being reborn.

Her final stop was the grocery store. Coffee, she needed coffee. She barreled through Rare Earth, an organic grocery store that stocked wild sardines and nothing with hydrogenated oils, high fructose corn syrup, or artificial flavors. She grabbed the first bag of coffee she saw and bumped right into someone as she turned to go. "Sorry," she muttered.

"Mika?"

She stopped, looked up. A familiar blond giant stood rubbing his shoulder. "Leif."

"Thought you hated this store," he said, basket in hand. They used to shop here when they dated. Too late, Mika remembered this was the store where Leif had asked the cashier to manually type in the barcodes so lasers wouldn't touch his food. "You okay?" he asked, appraising her. "Haven't seen you since the gallery opening." When everything had gone wrong.

"Yeah." She stared at Leif, contemplating her relationship with him. What had happened to them? "Thanks again for helping me out. You didn't have to."

"Of course I had to," he said simply. "I care about you, Mika."

She stared at her feet. "I care about you too. I'm so sorry for everything." She gestured at him with the bag of coffee. "For not supporting your dreams, for messing up so much . . ." She realized now the key to staying safe had been never to take another risk again. To not fall in love. To not hope for anything beyond the next twenty-four hours. It was such a freedom to have dreams. And one she resented Leif for.

He snorted. "You think you're the fuckup here? I was high all the time, unhappy with myself, where I was in life. It wasn't just you, Mika. We were both stuck."

Mika nodded and swallowed. "I should have told you about Penny." She should have let him in. She'd never given Leif a chance. Never offered Leif what she had offered Thomas. Never been completely honest with him. She had kept a part of herself from Leif. Her pregnancy. The adoption. She had even faked her orgasms. She'd learned from her mother that for a relationship to work, you must sublimate yourself. Don't be angry. Don't be sad. Mika had been conditioned to keep the peace, to be silent. She'd never been authentic with him. She saw it clearly now. She had been too locked up in her mother's disapproval, too afraid to let him see the real her. How could you accept someone's love if you didn't believe you were worthy of it?

Someone passed them in the aisle, and they shuffled to the side to make way, leaning against a row of cereal boxes. "I loved you, Mika," Leif said quietly. "But sometimes . . ." He sighed and pressed on. "Sometimes, that's not enough. We needed to do other things, be other people. Be *with* other people."

What he said was true. Standing still together had been better than being alone. But it hadn't moved them forward. If anything, it had held them back. "We should have had this conversation way before now," Mika said. "You're a great person, Leif. I wish you nothing but the best."

"Ditto."

"Friends?" She extended her hand.

He took it and shook. "Friends."

• • •

Once home, Mika dumped the coffee grinds into the pot and set it to brew. Then she moved the couch and coffee table against the wall. With her teeth, she split open the plastic on the drop cloth and spread it on the floor. Next, she set up the easel, placing a prestretched canvas on it. She stared at it for a moment. *Is there anything more terrifying than a blank canvas?*

She slipped a piece of vine charcoal from its box and saw herself sixteen years ago in Marcus's classroom. *The story is your power.* She didn't hesitate with the first line or the second. She gave in to the want. With every stroke, she coaxed the life she wanted out of hiding. They were still there. All her dreams. They'd been stuck in a corner in the dark, afraid to step out into the light again. Afraid it might burn or hurt. But that was the point, wasn't it? To feel, to let the wound be touched, and know you'd survive. For the very first time in a very long time, Mika was alive again. *Living.* And it was a thing to behold.

Another line and another until a figure took shape. A head turned toward a stage light. A leg bent in. She'd read about an author once who described the need to write like two hearts inside her chest. One was for everyday life. The other was for her art. Mika pulled that bloody heart from her body and put it on display. Because creation demands sacrifice. She finished the underpainting in a matter of hours and fell asleep on the couch.

On Monday, she went to work as usual, and she focused on spreadsheets, coordinating Gus's calendar, inputting data. Back at home, the world receded. Mika and painting danced. *It has been too long. Too long,* they seemed to croon to each other, caught in a private waltz. The best thing she'd ever held in her hands was Penny but a very close second was a brush.

She counted down the seconds until she could go home. Emotions ballooned inside her. Her body, her mind no longer barren but full of rich soil that was at last blooming. Spring had come early. And on she went. Painting into the wee hours of the morning and working her day job. She put her whole body into it. Her hands, shoulders, legs, back—they all ached. Even though her mind had forgotten some of the techniques, her body remembered. It remembered holding a paintbrush. Remembered the right way to mix colors. Remembered how to blend and shade. *Her body remembered.*

The week passed in an intense creative blur. Thomas texted once, twice more, but Mika ignored him. She was too caught up in the frenzy. Too busy moving forward, chasing the future she'd missed. At last, Saturday midafternoon, she stumbled back, brush in her hand. It was done. The fever broken. She sat down heavily on the couch to peer at what she had made.

• • •

Hayato whistled low. "You painted this?" He held the canvas in his hands, then set it down and stepped away, appreciating Mika's work from a distance.

"Yes," Mika answered. They were in his office at Nike.

"And you're just going to give it away?" He rubbed his forehead. *Why would anyone do such a thing?*

"Right again. I want to send it to my daughter, Penny."

"How old is she again?"

"Sixteen, almost seventeen." Her birthday was a week away.

"Way too young to appreciate fine art." He drew in a breath. "This thing is going to be worth money someday. I'll give you five thousand dollars for it."

Mika let out a humorless laugh. "It's not for sale."

"Everything is for sale." Hayato couldn't stop staring at it.

"Not everything."

"Spoken like a true artist."

She peered at Hayato. "Will you help me send it?"

"You mean, ferret this through Nike mail, thereby breaking a dozen rules in my contract?" Turns out, sending a painting in the mail cost a boatload. And recently, Mika had spent most of her money on art supplies and a ticket to Paris. She'd cashed out her vacation days and would spend a week in the city. She planned to be lost and unafraid.

"You don't have to." Mika moved to pick up the painting.

Hayato's hand on her arm stopped her. "I'm kidding. I send personal shit all the time. Even to my relatives in Japan. If you're ever in Tokyo and see a bunch of old ladies wandering around wearing Ralph Lauren, they probably know me." He winked at her. "Let's wrap it up."

Mika moved to grab a roll of bubble wrap from the closet. "Wait." Hayato stopped her. "Let me look at it again." They stood shoulder to shoulder. "Is it you?" he finally asked.

It was hard to tell who it actually was. It could be Mika. It could be Hiromi. It could be Penny. The lone ballerina was on stage, en pointe, balancing on a single leg, arms open, and face turned up toward the light. A perfect Degas replica but unmistakably Japanese with brown eyes and black hair reflecting the light. A tiny dancer. Like Caroline had called Penny. Like the girl Hiromi wanted Mika to be. "I don't interpret my own work."

"Ugh." Hayato rolled his eyes up to the ceiling.

Another minute passed, and then they ever so carefully used bubble wrap, brown paper, and a giant box to package up the painting. On the outside, Mika taped an envelope containing her letter. She'd penned it the night before.

Dear Penny,

It rained the day you were born. Outside the maternity ward, the sky was the color of liquid ash, and there was a sign that read: BIRTHDAYS ARE OUR SPECIALTY. I focused on it as I labored, as the nurses and doctor clamored around me. *You're nearly there*, a nurse exclaimed . . .

Mika consoled herself that she'd done what she could. She'd offered Penny what Hiromi never did. Somewhere to come home. A soft place to land. A guarantee to always be met with open arms. She hoped it was enough. It was the only thing she had to give. The only thing she'd ever had to give. A promise of imperfect but unconditional love, and that was enough.

Mika stood back and watched the mail courier take the painting away. On to Ohio. She hoped it answered Penny's question. *Who am I?* Mika thought she knew the answer now.

You are splitting atoms, soil made rich again, silk kimonos, azaleas in the park, bento for lunch, flannels and ripped tights, oil paints, a nurse keeping vigil, college sweethearts, broken silence. A runner. A searcher. A dancer. A dream deferred. A dream come true. An embodiment of love.

Chapter Thirty-Four

The rain had started in Portland. The first few weeks of September were always wet. But Mika didn't care. She opened the windows so she could hear the pitter-patter and smell the damp earth. Her phone dinged with an email. It was from UPS. A digital copy of the receipt for the painting. It had arrived in Dayton, and Thomas had signed for it. Mika closed out of her email and set down her phone. So that was that. The next move was Penny's.

In front of her was a sandwich, and she dug into it, not realizing how hungry she was. She was eating at the counter because there wasn't anywhere to sit down anymore. The couch housed canvases. The dining table held assorted supplies. The passion, the need to paint, was a cup. Filling until, stroke by stroke of the brush, Mika emptied it. But then the cup would start filling again. The cycle endless, excruciating, exhausting, exhilarating, and undeniable. It was gravity, and Mika had no choice but to comply. The lock on the front door turned, and Mika froze, wad of bread in her cheek.

The door opened, and Hana stepped inside, duffel over her shoulder. "Honey, I'm home," she called out, letting the bag drop onto the floor, a plume of dust rising around it. Much like Mika, Hana also paused, toes inches from a drop cloth. "Wow. I love what you've done with the place. It's very late-stage Van Gogh meets *Grey Gardens*."

Mika chewed and swallowed. She supposed there was a certain madness to how the house appeared. But doesn't madness always lead to discovery? "This is awkward. You said you'd be home in a couple weeks."

"Yes, and that was almost two weeks ago," Hana enunciated slowly.

Had that much time passed? Mika wasn't sure. She still went to work, but everything sort of felt nebulous. "Huh," was all she said.

Hana flashed Mika a grin. She stepped onto the drop cloth. Mika had purchased additional easels. Wanting to work on more than one painting at a time. She'd continued with her theme. Sketching Hiromi and Shige in *American Gothic.* Recasting Josephine and Hana in Gustav Klimt's *The Kiss.* Hayato and Seth in Caillebotte's *Paris Street, Rainy Day.* Hana walked between them as one does at a high-end gallery. She stopped and examined the painting of her and Josephine. "I like this one. I feel like you really captured my essence."

Mika's chest felt warm and gooey. "Thank you."

Hana approached Mika and put her elbows on the counter. "You changed directions," she stated.

A faint smile flickered across Mika's lips. "I did. Or, I am. I think it's in progress." The world seemed bright now. Better. "Um, I'm going to be gone for a while too."

"Are you?" Hana arched one perfect eyebrow.

"Yes." Mika nodded. "Just a week. But I'm going to Paris. And . . ." A jumble of emotion clogged her throat. She thought of Thomas. *I could see us in Paris.* She blinked it away—some things you just had to do on your own. "I've been thinking about getting my own place. You know, somewhere I can fully realize my *Grey Gardens,* Van Gogh fever dreams." Mika half smiled. "But I'd need a while to save up, a few months."

"It's like that then." Hana smiled.

"It's like that."

"Good." Hana placed one finger on Mika's plate and drew it toward her, then she took a giant bite of her sandwich. She chewed, covered her lips with her fingers, swallowed, and said, "Now, I'm going to take a nap. And I expect this place to be cleaned up by the time I wake up."

Mika huffed out a laugh. "I wouldn't set your hopes too high."

"Love your face." Hana lifted herself upright.

"Love yours more," Mika said.

Hana shut herself in her room. Mika snapped a few pictures of her paintings. And opened up her Instagram account. The one she'd abandoned and Penny had found. She posted the images, with a promise of more coming soon. And because she couldn't help it, she checked her followers—all thirty-two of them. Penny's name was still listed.

Mika chewed her lip, peering at the dining room table. The tubes of oils had been squeezed, almost every drop of them used. Better to get more now if she wanted to paint all night again. She threw her purse over her shoulder and swung open the front door, keys in hand. A dark head met her vision. Hiromi was stooped down, placing a plastic bag with a yogurt container inside on the step. Mika smelled bento. Her mother straightened, her mouth a little O. They stared at each other—mother and daughter.

Hiromi was the first to speak. "You look tired." Involuntarily Mika touched under her eyes. "Have you been eating?"

Mika shook her head. Her stomach grumbled. She'd abandoned the sandwich on the counter. "No."

"Here then," Hiromi said, thrusting the bag at Mika.

Mika took it. Warmth bled through the plastic. Hiromi had cooked and brought the food over fresh. "I was just on my way out, but do you want to sit with me for a minute while I eat?"

"Sure."

"Hana is taking a nap. You mind if we stay out here?" Their porch was just big enough for a couple of metal red chairs, a little bistro table between them.

"That's fine."

"Okay, let me just get some hashi." Mika dashed inside and grabbed the utensils and was back just as Hiromi settled in a chair.

Hiromi opened the plastic bag and set out the container, peeling the lid off it. Steam rose from the bento. "It's cold out today." Hiromi placed the container in front of Mika. And Mika observed her mother's hands, dry skin stretched tight over her bones like a canvas to a frame. Mika's hands were similar now, rough and chapped.

Mika nodded noncommittally. Using her hashi, she

brought a bite of sticky rice to her mouth. "At least it's not raining." The sky was overcast, but there was a break in the showers.

A few minutes passed. "You talk to Penny?" Hiromi finally asked, staring out at the street. The skin under her eyes was purple and puffy. A car drove by, kicking rocks onto the sidewalk.

"No. She's not speaking to me."

Hiromi pursed her lips. "Now you know how I feel."

Indeed, Mika did. Having a daughter made you vulnerable. "I guess so."

Hiromi crossed her legs at the ankles. She hiked up her chin. "I did the best I could," she said, as if standing in front of a tribunal. Mika thought of her relationship with Penny. Thought of Penny's relationship with Caroline. It was inevitable. All daughters felt disappointed with their mothers. No woman could ever get it right. The expectations were impossible.

Mika put down her hashi and regarded her mother. Seeing her mortality, all five feet two inches of it. "I believe that." Her mother loved her. It was in the sacrifices she made for Mika. In the early mornings, in the oil burns on her hands from the wok, in the late-night washing laundry by hand. It was Hiromi's approval that eluded Mika. What she had craved most but could never seem to win or court because to do so would be a betrayal of herself. What Hiromi wanted was at direct odds with what Mika wanted, with *who* Mika was. And now, Mika reveled in herself. In all her parts—painter, mother, dreamer, daughter.

Hiromi sucked in through her teeth, expression turning thoughtful, then said, "Shouganai." Roughly translated to "It cannot be helped." Salarymen muttered it when stuck in traffic. A mother might say it to her daughter after her heart had been broken. Or a policeman to a woman when she is groped on a train. It was a reminder that environments were fickle, uncontrollable, sometimes cruel. Better to move on without regrets. Mika didn't reply. Didn't want to fight anymore. She just picked up her hashi and started eating again.

"You've been painting again?" Hiromi eyed Mika's clothes, her hands splattered with paint.

"Yes." She paused. "Do you want to come in and see?"

She shook her head once. "I better not. I have to get home to your father." Hiromi stood.

"Okay. Thanks for the food," Mika said, surprised to find that she meant it. To find the electric zap of Hiromi's dismissal was absent.

Hiromi stepped away and stopped. "Make sure you keep the container," she said over her shoulder. "Bring it back to me the next time you come home."

"I will." Mika knew she'd see her mother again. She'd go to church with her parents and to dinner at their house. Like it or not, she might never be able to cut the tie. But she could move on, discard the fear that without her mother, she might be nothing. She knew where she must look for love now. And where she must give up looking for it.

Once in the car, Hiromi waved to her daughter. Mika waved back. Two old enemies, tired of their feud. Mika stayed on the porch a little longer. She leaned back, watched the rain start again.

She might not ever be able to get over it. The assault. The adoption. But she could make sense of it. Find meaning. She could reach into the darkness and come out with hands full. She'd seen Peter and the adoption as punishment. Because she'd been a bad daughter. Been disobedient. She'd blamed herself. Thinking something was wrong with her. That she didn't deserve to be loved, that she didn't deserve to be happy. But that was the real lie. She wouldn't suffer her mother's discontent any longer. Didn't have to siphon Hiromi's unhappy life.

Thomas had been a lovely distraction. Penny too. She still wanted them both, with an intensity that stole her breath. She ached with the bigness of the love she had to share. But there was something else she needed right now. Hiromi couldn't let go of her ghost life, but maybe Mika could. She stood, gathered her purse again, and drove to the art store. *Dive deep*, she'd wished for Penny, but she should have wished it for herself. No more swimming in shallow water. No more constantly drifting to shore. No more gasping for breath, confused at what tides had pushed her there. No more disorienting illusions of before, of what she wanted or who she was at eighteen, trying to capture what could have been. Time to make a new memory. Time to travel farther out into the ocean.

Chapter Thirty-Five

Mika set down her canvases, leaning them against her car. Across the gravel lot, she saw Leif and waved to him. He jogged toward her. "Alright, let's see." Leif reached for the paintings.

Mika scooted to block him. "Before you look, I want to say thank you for helping me."

Leif flicked a hand. "It's no problem. Stanley decided to move to Mount Hood. The space has been empty for a couple weeks now. I'm happy to let you use it. Plus, I'm going to advertise that it's available. You'll draw in the crowd, and maybe I'll get a new tenant. Win-win. Now you going to let me see?"

Mika drew in a deep breath and stepped to the side. She'd finished nine paintings. Ten would have been ideal, but First Thursday would be shutting down in

November. If she wanted to exhibit, it was now or wait until the spring.

"I'm still a little rusty," she said as Leif turned over a painting. It was the second one she had made. Hana and Josephine in Klimt's *The Kiss*. Mika wrung her hands. There was a natural fear in putting her work on display. A gallery was where people came to judge you. "I'm thinking of enrolling in some night classes at U of P."

Leif stuck up a hand and quieted Mika. He put the painting down, then turned to the next. A painting of Shige and Hiromi recast in *American Gothic*. He turned to another, then another. The last one, a self-portrait. Mika as the Virgin Mary—she'd just finished it a few days ago after she'd returned from Paris.

The trip had been all her dreams fulfilled and more. She had stayed in a small room with a saggy mattress in the heart of the city. She'd walked everywhere and seen the *Mona Lisa*, *The Coronation of Napoleon*, Van Gogh's self-portrait . . . but it was a sculpture that made her finally weep—the *Winged Victory of Samothrace*. A headless woman with feathery wings spread wide, standing against the wind. Undaunted.

"These are amazing," Leif said.

Mika beamed. "Thanks."

It didn't take long to hang the art. All nine pieces

positioned at eye level. Mika set up a table with refreshments, then walked the area, watching artists
prep their booths outside. She came to the place she
and Thomas had had their first moment, nearly touching, laughter between them. She felt it then, the weight
of the solitary, lonely nights pressing against her. But
it wasn't suffocating. Maybe someday she'd find some-
body to spend time with. She was ready now. More
willing. Her heart open. Mika had surrendered Penny
but what she really needed to do was surrender herself
to life. The inevitability of pain and suffering, of happiness and joy.

Penny hadn't responded to her painting or letter.
But Mika held out hope. Penny could take decades to
come around, and Mika would be there. She had meant
what she'd said. *I will wait for you.*

"Hey! I've been looking for you. What are you
doing out here?" Hana strode to Mika, pulling her coat
around her. "People are arriving."

Mika let out a long breath, pushing Thomas and
Penny from her mind. "Let's go."

• • •

The gallery seemed to fill up in a matter of seconds.
Everyone came to celebrate Mika and eat the sweaty
cheese she'd put out. Tuan and Charlie loved their

likeness in Homer's *Summer Night*. Mika was deep in conversation with the artist next door, chatting about how she'd developed her concepts. "It's like you're re-inventing the European canon," he said. "You really should meet my agent . . ."

Mika blushed. She opened her mouth to reply when a hand tapped her shoulder. "Excuse me," she said, turning away from the artist. Her mouth parted in surprise. Dark hair. Dark eyes. A face that mirrored hers. "Penny! What . . . what are you doing here?"

"Surprise," Penny said meekly, opening her hands.

Mika moved quickly and steered them to a quiet corner. "What are you doing here?!" she asked again. "Wait. Does your dad know you're here?" Mika pictured Penny boarding a plane on her own. Thomas returning home from work to find an empty house. She wanted so badly to touch Penny. Stroke her hair. Hold her hands. But she held back. She didn't want to scare Penny off. Didn't want to disrespect her boundaries. Even though she wondered if Penny still held a space in her heart for her. Even though all she wanted to chant was: *Let me love you.*

Penny rolled her eyes. "Of course he does. He's here, actually. Well, at the hotel. He thought we might want to chat first." Thomas was *here*? In Portland? "Anyway, I saw your post on Instagram about your first show tonight." Penny chewed her lip. "I wanted to come, and I thought you might want that." She gestured at the door, where Mika's dancer painting lay carefully wrapped and leaning, ready for display. Mika's throat squeezed tight. Her eyes fell heavily on Penny. "It's cool that I'm here, right? I read your letter, and I thought it was kind of an open invitation . . ."

"Yes." Mika's voice sounded flimsy and weak, happy and relieved too. "Of course it is. I am so happy to see you." *You returned to me.*

"Well, good." Penny rocked back on her heels. They stood gazing at each other for a moment. Their smiles seeming to draw all the light in the room toward them.

"Should we hang it up?" Mika asked after a moment.

They found an empty space on the wall and placed the dancer painting there. That made ten. The collection was finished. *Complete.*

Penny tilted her head. "It's a beautiful painting. It's been hanging in my room. Every time I see it, it's like the first time. I discover something new in it."

Mika's mouth gently curved upward.

"It reminds me of my mom. Both of you, actually. My moms." Penny glanced unsurely at Mika.

Mika chewed her cheek. "That was the purpose, I think. Sometimes, you don't know what the art is until you create it. The meaning, you know? But it kind of crystallized for me just now. I think you've been focusing on the finding and not the loss." It had been the opposite for Mika. She'd been focusing on the loss, what she'd had, the baby she'd let go of. She could never get that time with Penny back. The time she'd missed not painting. *The past is set, but the future is fluid.*

"Explain," Penny said seriously.

Mika regarded Penny. "You dove headlong into this relationship with Portland and me, finding something, I think, to fill you up. When all along, I think you should have been focused on what you've lost—the grieving. Your adoptive mother died. I couldn't keep you. It's okay to be sad."

Penny considered Mika's words for a long while. She inhaled. "I miss my mom a lot. Growing up, I missed you a lot, even though I never knew you. Does that make sense?" Penny hurried to say.

"Perfect sense."

"I don't know . . ." A tear slid down Penny's cheek. "I don't even know why I'm crying. It's not because I'm sad. Or maybe I am. But I'm mad too."

Mika dragged in a breath. "At me?"

"At you, at myself, at my mother, my dad. The whole world."

"Fair enough." Mika nodded. "Does it help at all to know I'm mad at my mother too?"

"What are you mad at her for?"

Mika gazed over Penny's shoulder and caught Hana's and Charlie's eyes. They were watching, smiles asking if she was okay. Mika smiled back and returned to Penny. "What am I mad at my mother for?" Mika repeated. She wasn't sure what circuitous path Penny was leading her on, but Mika would follow her down. All roads led to Penny. She'd always been the destination. "For not believing in me." For being angry. For being unhappy. For being unable to bear what happened to her daughter. But just as Mika was angry, she also understood. Hiromi couldn't carry that weight, the knowledge that her daughter had been hurt. Hiromi had done the best she could. Mika had done the best she could too. Too often, mothers were villains or saints. It started with fairy tales. A wicked stepmother so jealous of her daughter, she makes her sleep near the fireplace and forbids her from going to a ball. Or a fairy godmother who makes all the heroine's dreams come true. Why was there no in between? "What are you mad at yours for?"

"For dying. For writing me a stupid letter that I can never respond to. For never taking me to an Asian grocery store." The tears had slowed. Penny took a steadying breath.

"Penny," Mika whispered, feeling an acute ache.

Caroline's death had shoved Penny onto the same path as Mika. Both disconnected from their mothers. The loss was incalculable. Left them in the woods to figure out life for themselves. No mother to learn from. They had to discover themselves alone. That was the reason Penny sought Mika out. And Mika had accepted it because she'd wanted something from Penny too. A way to make everything okay. She saw in Penny salvation. Redemption. But that was unfair. "Tell me more. Why are you mad at your dad?" She could guess, but Mika didn't want her relationship with Penny to be like her relationship with Hiromi—stilted with silence, letting things fester like an open wound.

"You two slept together," Penny said flatly.

"I won't deny it, but what exactly bothers you about it? Is it me? Would it be different if it was another woman? A stranger?" The crowd had thinned—the hour growing late.

"This is really uncomfortable to talk about," Penny pointed out.

Mika thought about silence again. About breaking it. "We don't have to, but I think we should."

Penny was quiet for a moment. "You were supposed to be only for me. Not for him. But then again, I don't know if it would have been better if it was a stranger. I'd probably still be upset. My dad is the consistent one.

I can count on him, you know? I think of my parents as having this great love story, and seeing him with someone else doesn't feel right."

"So, you want to change, but you want everyone else to stay the same?"

"Pretty much," Penny answered, jutting her chin up.

Mika smiled but didn't let it show in her voice. "Seems a touch unfair."

"Life is unfair."

"True."

"What's up with you two anyway? Was it like . . . serious?"

Mika sucked in her cheeks. If she wanted Penny to be an open book, Mika would have to reciprocate. Even if she didn't want to admit the truth to herself. "It was, on my end, at least. I can't speak for your father." *I can't be with someone I don't care about,* Thomas had said. Mika's throat felt like it was going to collapse. "I liked him. He's fun and funny. At first, I think we were lonely without your company. You leave quite the gap. But then it grew into something else. You should talk to him about it," Mika encouraged.

"I did," Penny said. "He said you made him happy."

"He made me happy too," Mika said. Wasn't there an adage out there about finding a partner based on who you become with them?

"Well, I'm emotionally spent." Penny wiped the last of her tears away, done crying.

"Me too. But I'm so glad you're here. What about school?" Mika lifted a lock of Penny's hair and stared at her bemusedly.

"Psh," said Penny. "I'm playing hooky for a long weekend. Senior year doesn't matter much anyway."

"I feel like that's not true," Mika said.

Penny grinned and hooked an arm through Mika's. "Come on and give me a tour. I want to hear all about the paintings. Mostly how I inspired them, and I am your muse for life now."

Mika steered Penny around the gallery, introducing her to Hayato, who'd stopped by with Seth. Soon enough, the wine ran dry, and all the sweaty cheese had been consumed. Friends kissed Mika's cheeks goodbye; Leif left to handle a delivery at his store. The crowd dwindled to Hana, Penny, Charlie, Tuan, and Mika.

Hana held up a glass. "To Mika!" she said. "For a while, I was afraid I would have to recover your body from the forest, but now I feel like my little bird has finally flown the nest. My baby turtle is taking its first tentative steps into the ocean . . ."

Mika clicked her glass against Hana's. "That's enough metaphors, I think."

They drank. Penny sipped a soda. All at once, Hana's happy expression morphed to surprise. Mika turned to follow her friend's gaze to the door. Thomas had just arrived.

• • •

Thomas stood there. He wore a navy blue sweater and his hands were jammed into his jean pockets. He nodded to Hana, to Tuan, to Charlie, to Penny, and stopped on Mika. "Hey, Mika," he said, looking right at her.

Mika blinked, outrageously unable to speak for a moment. "Hi," she said back.

He wandered closer. "It's good to see you."

Mika could feel everyone watching her and Thomas. "You too," she managed.

"These portraits . . ." Thomas surveyed the gallery and palmed the back of his head. "You're an amazing painter. I had no idea you were so talented. I was blown away when I saw the painting you sent Penny and now . . . I'm kind of awestruck."

Mika swallowed. "I've been working on some new stuff. Experimenting with the palette knife, using different trowel shapes to create textural strokes, focusing more on color . . ." She trailed off. Silence then. Mika sought to fill it. "Thanks for bringing Penny out," she said, and at the same time Thomas said, "Do you want to go somewhere?"

They stopped. Smiled at each other. Thomas was the first to speak. "Can I take you out for a cup of celebratory coffee?"

Mika stole a glance at Penny. Her daughter blinked, smiled slightly, and dipped her chin. Mika turned back to Thomas. "I'd like that."

"Alright," he said. Then he crossed the room and held the door open. Mika found her coat and shrugged it on. But she stopped short of the exit. She should probably stay and clean up. She hadn't said goodbye to her friends either.

"You ready?" Thomas asked.

"Ready," she said on an inhale, and the word tasted good in her mouth, like fresh air. Then she walked through the door, Thomas behind her.

Dear Penny,

Today you are sixteen, and I will not be there to see it. The first time I held you, I rubbed your cheek against mine, then traced the shell of your ear while whispering promises. *I will be strong for you. I will love you unconditionally. I will always be here.* I'm sorry we won't have more time together.

On the flight home from the hospital sixteen years ago today, I refused to put you down. You were so tiny. I was afraid of all the things that could go wrong, all the things that might hurt you. Over the years, I watched you grow. Crawling at seven months, then walking just two months later. We childproofed the house: covering outlet plugs, taping up sharp corners, fencing off the stairs. But you were curious and tenacious. You pulled the fence down. You removed the outlet covers. You chewed the sharp corners. Maybe more puppy than baby. I wondered how I was supposed to keep you alive. On it went, your thirst for the unknown. No obstacle was too big. I imagined you conquering anything, climbing a mountain, and beating your chest—always victorious.

At one and a half years old, you ran down sidewalks. At two, you rode a scooter for the first time. I chased you down the pavement, catching you before you crashed or crying when I wasn't fast enough and you did. On it went—time passing in a happy blur. I stood under the monkey bars while you hung from them. Followed on the balance beam while you carefully traversed it. Always there, teeth gritted, waiting to save you. *Be careful*, I'd say. *Don't go too fast*. It was all my misguided attempt to slow time, keep you, my little girl, longer. But we can't stop from moving forward, from getting old, from dying.

When you were four, you started to ask why. Why do I have to brush my teeth? Why do I have to stop playing? Why do I look different from Mommy and Daddy? A lightning bolt struck me then, piercing the heart of my insecurities. I feared I wasn't enough for you. That you had questions I would never be able to answer. That someone else might take you from me. That although you were mine, you were someone else's first. When you feel something slipping from your fingers, it is a natural instinct to clench your fist. I told you it didn't matter that we looked different. What mattered was the love we shared. I saw the dissatisfaction in your eyes. Over the years, you asked more questions. I answered, but not in the way I should have. I knew you felt it, the sharp edges of my discomfort. I'm sorry too now, for all the things I never said.

In our bedroom closet, on the top shelf (behind the awful hat your father bought for our vacation to Mexico), is a box. Inside is your original birth certificate, adoption paperwork, and copies of packages I sent to your birth mother. Her name is Mika Suzuki. You should know, we agreed to a closed adoption. I am unsure if she will welcome you. But it is my hope she will.

I hope she will help quench your thirst for the world. I hope she will answer all the questions I never could. I don't want to hold you back anymore. Don't let me hold you back. You have my permission to run. To go. Not that you need it. But there it is. My blessing to find your birth mother. To ask what I could never answer. I get it now. I'm sorry, honey, I didn't see it before. I think that's what being a parent is all about—loving something and letting it go.

I love you,
Mom

Acknowledgments

I wrote this book in a craze. Between publishing one book and writing another, I penned *Mika in Real Life*. I pushed myself mentally and physically past my limits to finish this book.

I also pushed my family to their limits—zoning out at the dinner table, rushing to my phone to write book notes, dropping what I was doing because I just figured out the perfect piece of dialogue. This book allowed me to explore what I haven't been able to in writing before, the bond between a parent and child. Since giving birth to my twins four years ago, I have marveled at the intensity of my love for them. Motherhood is so very terrifying in many ways. As Caroline writes at the end of the novel, it truly is the art of loving something and letting it go. I am grateful to my kiddos and partner, Craig, for being patient with me as I unraveled this story. And for how patient they've been with me since I've started writing another book (it turns out this wasn't a singular experience). Craig, you have always been my biggest supporter. You've shown me through words, actions, and unconditional love that I am enough just as I am—thank you. I am also deeply appreciative to my parents and family, who have always been pillars of support.

To Erin and Joelle, agents and friends, thank you for coming with me on this wild ride of a book. Also, thank you for loving this book just as much as I do. And even more, thanks for tolerating my "Have you read it yet?" emails. Your edits elevated this novel to a realm I didn't think possible. Erin, you helped me find the story I wanted to tell. Joelle, I can't quite find the right words, so I'll just say: to second chances! Also, thanks to the folks over at Alloy and Folio, who have championed this book from the beginning.

To my editor, Lucia, thank you for reading this book and seeing its soul. My gratitude also to the whole William Morrow team: Liate Stehlik, Asanté Simons, Kelly Rudolph, Jennifer Hart, Jes Lyons, Amelia Wood, Ploy Siripant (when I saw the cover, I gasped), and Jessica Rozler.

To Tami, thank you for becoming a lawyer instead of

a doctor. Thank you for working so hard on my behalf. Thank you (and Randy) for the late-night, after-hours phone calls. You gave me much more than you'll ever know.

And finally, my heartfelt thanks to readers, book groups, and booksellers—I get to do what I love because of you.

HARPER LARGE PRINT

We hope you enjoyed reading
our new, comfortable print size and found it
an experience you would like to repeat.

Well – you're in luck!

Harper Large Print offers the finest in
fiction and nonfiction books in this same larger
print size and paperback format. Light and easy to read,
Harper Large Print paperbacks are for the book lovers
who want to see what they are reading without strain.

For a full listing of titles and
new releases to come, please visit our website:
www.hc.com

HARPER LARGE PRINT

SEEING IS BELIEVING!